DE

Rudi and Hanna have escaped from their village into the dark and dangerous wilds. Desperate to uncover the truth behind his father's involvement in a Chaos cult, they head to the city port of Marienburg. But their road is not without danger and they are soon tracked down by a witch hunter, who is convinced that they are members of the same diabolical cult. Fate is rarely kind in the Warhammer world and their lives hang in the balance...

More Sandy Mitchell from the Black Library

· BLOOD ON THE REIK ·
DEATH'S MESSENGER

· CIAPHAS CAIN ·
*Outrageous adventures in the far future with
Commissar Ciaphas Cain*

FOR THE EMPEROR
CAVES OF ICE
THE TRAITOR'S HAND

A WARHAMMER NOVEL

DEATH'S CITY

SANDY MITCHELL

To Caroline, for all the research material.

A BLACK LIBRARY PUBLICATION

First published in Great Britain in 2005 by
BL Publishing,
Games Workshop Ltd.,
Willow Road, Nottingham,
NG7 2WS, UK

10 9 8 7 6 5 4 3 2 1

Cover illustration by Alex Boyd.
Map by Nuala Kinrade.

A CIP record for this book is available from the British Library.

ISBN 13: 978 1 84416 240 6
ISBN 10: 1 84416 240 0

Distributed in the US by Simon & Schuster
1230 Avenue of the Americas, New York, NY 10020.

Printed and bound in Great Britain by
Bookmarque, Surrey, UK.

See the Black Library on the Internet at
www.blacklibrary.com

Find out more about Games Workshop
and the world of Warhammer at
www.games-workshop.com

THIS IS A DARK age, a bloody age, an age of daemons and of sorcery. It is an age of battle and death, and of the world's ending. Amidst all of the fire, flame and fury it is a time, too, of mighty heroes, of bold deeds and great courage.

AT THE HEART of the Old World sprawls the Empire, the largest and most powerful of the human realms. Known for its engineers, sorcerers, traders and soldiers, it is a land of great mountains, mighty rivers, dark forests and vast cities. And from his throne in Altdorf reigns the Emperor Karl-Franz, sacred descendant of the founder of these lands, Sigmar, and wielder of his magical warhammer.

BUT THESE ARE far from civilised times. Across the length and breadth of the Old World, from the knightly palaces of Bretonnia to ice-bound Kislev in the far north, come rumblings of war. In the towering World's Edge Mountains, the orc tribes are gathering for another assault. Bandits and renegades harry the wild southern lands of the Border Princes. There are rumours of rat-things, the skaven, emerging from the sewers and swamps across the land. And from the northern wildernesses there is the ever-present threat of Chaos, of daemons and beastmen corrupted by the foul powers of the Dark Gods. As the time of battle draws ever nearer, the Empire needs heroes like never before.

CHAPTER ONE

Escape was clearly impossible. Surrounded by horse-men, the trio of fugitives had nowhere to go. Rudi felt the bitter bile of defeat rising up in him as he caught a glimpse of the woodland beyond the shifting barrier of horseflesh and cursed the impulse which had taken them away from its shelter out onto the open moor. Beneath the trees they would have been safe from pursuit, but since he'd discovered the unmistakable tracks of beastmen in one of the clearings the risk of remaining there had seemed far too great. Had he known the witch hunter was so close, with a troop of mounted soldiers to back him up, he would have taken his chances with the mutants.

'You killed my mother!' Fritz bellowed, thrusting his spear at the man in black. Gerhard leaned easily back in his saddle, seizing the shaft behind the metal point, which gleamed like silver as it reflected the moonlight and twisted it. Somehow, the simple motion broke the muscular youth's grip on the wood. Gerhard snatched the weapon out of his hands completely and swatted him on the side of the head with the blunt end. Fritz fell to his knees, stunned, and before he realised what he was doing, Rudi found himself taking a step forward to stand between the witch hunter and his old enemy from Kohlstadt.

'You were harbouring a mutant,' Gerhard pointed out, his tone as mild and conversational as ever. 'She could have been tainted by your actions.'

'He was protecting his brother,' Rudi said. Hans Katzenjammer had been warped by the blood of a beastman, which had entered his body through the minor scratches left by a tainted thorn bush. Despite the enmity he'd always displayed towards Rudi, he had saved the young forester's life twice since his transformation, something which had only added to the welter of questions which buzzed around the inside of his head like tormenting flies.

Magnus knew the answers to some of them at least, his adoptive father's dying words had told him that much, but the merchant had been missing since the fateful night in the forest which had forced him and Hanna to flee for their lives. Rudi had hoped to find him in Marienburg, but right now his chances of reaching the city seemed remote to say the least. 'You can't blame him for that.'

'Of course I can,' Gerhard said, an edge of asperity entering his voice. 'Harbouring a mutant is an act of heresy. If he really wanted to help his brother he should have reported him at once, so at least his soul could have been saved.'

'Is that why you burned my mother?' Hanna asked, her voice slurred by loathing and hatred. 'You thought you were saving her soul?' She glared at the witch hunter, an expression of barely contained fury on her face. Rudi shuddered. He'd only seen her like this once before, when the powers she barely understood and could hardly control had erupted from her body under the impetus of fear and manifested in a ball of blazing death which had incinerated the skaven attacking her.

'It was far too late for that,' Gerhard said, shaking his head regretfully. 'It was claimed by the dark powers long ago.'

'So you say.' Hanna glared up at him, the silver light of Mannslieb transforming her blonde hair into a nimbus of rippling light. Morrslieb, the ill-favoured moon, was close to the horizon now. Its pale, greenish glow was all but extinguished, yet somehow it managed to cast deep shadows across her face, transforming it into something almost bestial. 'Why don't you go and find out?'

Rudi flinched, seeing the flicker of reddish flames flare into existence in the air in front of her. Another heartbeat and they would burst forth in ravening fury, consuming everything in their path. Fritz, who so far had only seen the girl lighting campfires and conjuring up phantom candle flames, and been abjectly terrified on every occasion, whimpered and hunkered down on the ground reciting the blessing of Sigmar. The soldiers surrounding them seemed scarcely less afraid, clinging grimly to their mounts as they pawed the ground, bucking and rearing in panic. Only Gerhard seemed sanguine, he and his sable steed remaining still.

'More powerful witches than you have tried,' he replied evenly. 'And I'm still here. Sigmar protects His faithful servants.' He raised his hand, in which something caught the moonlight, flashing too brightly for Rudi to make out what it was. Hanna staggered as though she'd been struck, the ball of flame winking out of existence. Rudi put out an arm to support her and she clung to him, trembling violently.

'Hanna, are you all right?' He raised his voice, addressing Gerhard directly. 'What did you do to her?'

'Nothing.' The witch hunter shrugged and looked impatiently at the soldiers, who were beginning to get their mounts under control. 'I just let her do it to herself.'

'Push magic too hard and it pushes you back,' Hanna said, rubbing her temples and looking slightly dazed. 'Isn't that what Alwyn said?' Rudi wasn't so sure it was as simple as that, but Gerhard nodded.

'Magic can't prevail against righteous faith,' he said, returning the tiny object to the recesses of his cloak. He gestured to the soldiers. 'She's harmless, you idiots. At least for now. Bring them in.'

The armed men were evidently more afraid of the witch hunter than anything the fledgling sorceress might do. Most of them dismounted at once, only a few remaining in the saddle to point heavy pistols at the fugitives. Before he could react, Rudi found himself seized by rough hands, the sword and knife at his belt torn away and Hanna wrenched from his grasp.

'If any of them resist, kill the girl and the simpleton,' Gerhard added. Rudi felt a chill strike deep in his heart. There could be only one reason the witch hunter wanted him kept alive and he quailed inwardly at the prospect.

'Why not me too?' he asked, masking his feelings with a display of anger more convincing than he would have believed possible under the circumstances. To his surprise the witch hunter looked uneasy for a moment.

'There are things I need to know.' The conversational tone was back in his voice now, his habitual composure settling around him like a cloak. 'But this is hardly the time or the place.' To Rudi's surprise he held out a hand, leaning down from the saddle of his horse. 'Get up behind me.'

His head reeling, Rudi complied. He'd never been on horseback before, but Gerhard's grip was firm and he found himself being hoisted aboard with little difficulty. The back of the saddle was distinctly uncomfortable to sit on, but he wasn't going to give the witch hunter any satisfaction by complaining about it. He put his arms round the man's torso, feeling strangely uneasy at the sensation of close physical contact with so mortal an enemy.

'I'm surprised you trust me so close,' he said.

'I don't. But I trust your concern for your friends.' Gerhard's companions were obviously less sanguine about their captives' good behaviour. Hanna and Fritz were swiftly manacled and thrown across a pair of horses in front of their riders like sacks of grain. Fritz still seemed groggy from the blow to the head, but Hanna kept up a tirade of abuse for most of the journey, which seemed to shock and amuse the troopers in roughly equal measure.

Shortly after she fell silent, having finally run out of synonyms for illegitimate birth and deviant sexual practices to attribute to the soldier escorting her, Rudi noticed a faint orange glow in the sky ahead of them. It was far too early for sunrise, and that would surely have appeared more to the east in any case. A flicker of apprehension shot through him.

'Something's burning,' he said. Vivid memories of Greta Reifenstahl's cottage rose in his mind, flames leaping from the thatch, while Hanna tried frantically to get inside and rescue her mother. His jaw tightened.

'Not yet,' the soldier guarding Fritz said, snorting with amusement at his own wit.

As the horses crested the next rise in the moorland, Rudi could see where the light was coming from. A chain of watch fires crowned a hill slightly larger than those surrounding it, spaced along a ditch and an embankment of earth, which seemed to run right around the crest. Inside it were tents, more than he could accurately count, and even at this hour of the night there seemed to be a lot of activity.

The hooves beneath him began to clatter on a plank bridge and he realised they were crossing the ditch. The ridge of earth beyond it was roughly the height of a man and looked raw and new in the light from a brazier standing next to a gap in the earthworks just wide enough for two horses to pass abreast. Firelight gleamed on levelled halberds.

'Halt.' The voice was firm and resolute. 'Who goes there?'

Gerhard reined in and Rudi became aware of a group of men standing on top of the embankment. They were all dressed in identical livery and were levelling gently smoking matchlocks at the party on the bridge.

A strange scent, like burning pepper, drifted towards him from the smouldering tapers.

'Luther Gerhard and Hochmeyer's troop,' the witch hunter replied. The leader of the halberdiers stepped forward, a torch flaring in his hand, bringing the light further out.

'Advance and be recognised.' At the invitation, Gerhard spurred the horse into gentle motion, moving fully into the circle of illumination. The sergeant looked up at him, taking in Rudi's presence. 'Who's this?'

'A good question,' Gerhard said, clearly not inclined to answer it. The sergeant nodded once and stepped aside.

'Clear the way,' he said. The halberdiers stood aside hastily and the hand gunners on the earthworks melted away with equal alacrity.

Rudi turned as the horse began to walk into the compound, trying to keep the entrance in sight. There was no gate to bar it, but a wagon stood nearby, clearly intended to plug the gap in the event of an attack. He kept twisting his head as the group of horsemen penetrated deeper into the encampment, trying to memorise the route back to the entrance. Despite his best efforts, it was futile. The place was a maze, marked out by tents, parked wagons, piles of baggage and equipment he could barely begin to fathom the purpose of. And it was crowded, even at this hour of the night, with purposeful figures scurrying to and fro, many of them armed.

The troop of horsemen came to a sudden halt in a cleared area he estimated must be almost at the centre of the canvas village. It occurred to him that there must have been almost as many people camped there as there had been living in Kohlstadt. A banner stood, flaring in the wind, in front of a tent larger than most of the others he'd seen, and a pair of soldiers stood guard before the entrance. The coat of arms on the flag meant nothing to him, although the implication was obvious; these were the quarters of someone important, perhaps the captain Alwyn had mentioned speaking to when she'd arrived back at the mercenaries' camp earlier that evening.

Gerhard reined in his own horse, swung himself easily from the saddle, and disappeared inside the pavilion without a word or a backward glance. Rudi dropped to the ground too and stretched gratefully, trying to seem relaxed. Making a run for it would be impossible, he thought. Too many watchful eyes followed his every move. He would be brought down within a handful of steps. Even if he wasn't, he couldn't leave Hanna and Fritz. He knew Gerhard too well to believe that his threat had been an idle one and attempting to escape would simply mean the deaths of his companions.

'How about letting us down too?' Hanna asked, squirming round to glare at the soldier behind her.

He grinned. 'I wouldn't be so impatient to get started with that gentleman if I were you.' The grin widened. 'Besides, I like the view as it is.' He slapped her lightly on the rump to emphasise the point, eliciting an outraged squeal from the girl and a bellow of raucous laughter from his comrades.

'Verber.' Gerhard's quiet voice somehow managed to cut through the noise as though it were wrapped in silence. 'I thought I made my views on the mistreatment of prisoners quite clear.'

'Sorry, sir.' The soldier's face and voice both seemed drained of colour. 'It was just a bit of fun. No harm meant.'

'I doubt that the young lady would agree.' Gerhard strolled over to the horse, slipped an arm around Hanna's waist and lifted her off. She fell hard on her back, only partially cushioned by the witch hunter's support, the breath driven from her body by the impact. Before she could recover, Gerhard knelt, a knee on either shoulder pinning her down, her head immobilised between his thighs.

'Leave her alone!' Rudi started forward, his fists balling, then stumbled and fell as a halberd shaft crashed into the back of his knees. Before he could rise, a couple of soldiers had seized his arms, pinning him to the ground. He twisted his head, frantically trying to see what the witch hunter was doing to the girl.

'This won't take a moment,' Gerhard said, as though they were merely passing the time of day. A soldier standing next to him passed down a flickering candle and a small stick of something Rudi couldn't identify. 'But I'm afraid you might find it a little uncomfortable.' His hands moved, apparently over her face, and Hanna screamed, more in shock and surprise than from pain, Rudi thought. 'There. That's better.' He stood and glanced across at Rudi. 'It's all right. Let him up.'

The soldiers restraining him slackened their grip a little and Rudi got to his feet, shaking with anger.

'What did you do to her?'

Hanna was struggling awkwardly to her feet, finding it hard to balance on the mud with her hands still shackled behind her. She looked unharmed, apart from the thin coating of grime she'd acquired from the ground. As she turned her head to look at him, an expression of cold fury on her face, his breath caught. A wax seal, like the ones he used to see on the letters he'd once delivered around Kohlstadt, had been pressed into the centre of her forehead. As he looked closer at it, he could make out the familiar twin-tailed comet symbol of Sigmar embossed into the surface.

'A simple precaution,' Gerhard said. His meaning was obvious. Somehow the seal would prevent her from using her powers.

'What about this one?' A new voice said. The speaker was more opulently dressed than the common soldiers, but his livery was the same and he carried a sword at his belt. Rudi assumed he was the captain in charge of the camp. He strolled over to Fritz, still hanging limply over the neck of the horse he'd been brought in on.

'I've no further need of that one,' Gerhard said. 'Execute him at dawn.'

'What?' Fritz positively howled in bewildered outrage. 'No, you can't...' His voice choked off as he was dragged unceremoniously to the ground, the breath driven out of him by the impact.

'Be careful!' Hanna said. 'He has an injured arm.'

'Not for much longer.' The captain gestured to a couple of nearby soldiers. 'Take him away.' Each man took hold of an arm, hoisted the heavyset youth between them and strode off between the tents, leaving a faint double rut in the ground where Fritz's feet dragged. He must have recovered his breath after a moment, as his progress was marked by a gradually diminishing wail, which was finally lost among the other noises of the camp.

'I thought you wanted to interrogate him?' the captain asked.

'I did.' Gerhard nodded. 'I hoped he might lead me to these two. But now I have them, he's of no further use.'

'I see.' The captain eyed Rudi and Hanna sceptically. 'I'm sure you have your reasons. But it seems like a lot of trouble to go to just for a couple of peasant brats.'

'Believe me, captain, I sincerely hope your cynicism is justified. But if I'm right, at least one of these peasant brats is potentially more dangerous than the entire beastman warband you're hunting.'

'Well, you're the expert.' The captain shrugged. 'Anything else I can do for you?'

'I'd appreciate the loan of your tent,' Gerhard said mildly. 'If that wouldn't be too much trouble.'

The captain nodded. 'Fine by me. I won't be needing it now, I've a hanging to organise.'

'Hanging?' Gerhard shook his head in mild reproof. 'I think not. The boy's a proven heretic. He should be burned.'

'Not a problem. I'm sure the cooks have enough kindling for a good bonfire.' The captain shrugged again and melted away into the shadows. Rudi and Hanna's eyes locked, each mirroring the horror the other felt. Gerhard cleared his throat and gestured towards the tent.

'If you would,' he said. 'I think it's time we talked.'

CHAPTER TWO

INSIDE, THE TENT was surprisingly well-appointed. Rudi found himself tracking muddy footprints across a canvas groundsheet, evidently intended to insulate the occupant from the dampness of the earth beneath it, and the walls, though billowing a little, kept enough of the breeze out to raise the temperature within by an appreciable degree. A camp bed stood in one corner, the first such he'd ever seen, and a couple of folding chairs stood next to a lightweight table on which the remains of a meal were still scattered. Despite himself, he couldn't resist taking an interest in the bread and cheese on the platter. It had been a long night and the hastily snatched food he'd eaten before leaving the drugged mercenaries back at their camp had long since worn off.

'Help yourself if you're hungry,' Gerhard said, noticing the direction of his glance. He followed Rudi and

Hanna through the flap and secured it, after a perfunctory nod to the two soldiers on guard outside.

'That might be a bit difficult,' Hanna said acidly.

Gerhard nodded and produced the key to her manacles. 'I take your point,' he said mildly, releasing her wrists. Hanna rubbed them for a moment, glaring defiantly at the witch hunter, and reached up to the crimson seal disfiguring her forehead, but before she could touch it she winced and her hand fell away again.

'Don't think for a moment that this civilised act of yours is fooling anyone,' she said, with as much dignity as she could muster. Gerhard shrugged.

'If you'd rather go hungry to prove a point, feel free,' he replied, seating himself comfortably in the nearest chair. As he turned away, Hanna's hand crept towards her bodice and the knife she'd concealed there when the mercenaries had divided up the spoils from the dead skaven, clearly wondering whether she'd be able to draw it and stab the witch hunter before he had time to react.

Rudi caught her eye and shook his head almost imperceptibly, acutely conscious of the spare blade he'd tucked into his boot at the same time she'd acquired her own dagger. He blessed the foresight which had led him to follow Conrad's advice and carry a second one where the soldiers' perfunctory search of the captives had failed to find it. The hidden weapons were the only chance they had of turning the tables, but attacking Gerhard here would gain them nothing. Even if they could beat him, and he honestly doubted that, the commotion would attract the attention of the soldiers outside long before they could escape.

Biding their time was the only sensible option if they were to have any hope of getting away. He tried to ignore the little voice which told him they had precious little time to do that if they were going to rescue Fritz. Besides, the desperate hunger for answers which had consumed him ever since Gunther Walder's final words was back, driving all other thoughts from his head.

'What do you want to know?' he asked, helping himself to a chunk of bread and cheese. After a moment, Hanna joined him, her eyes still directing a stream of venom at the witch hunter. She began bolting the food as though she hadn't eaten for days. After a moment, catching his look, she slowed down, looking faintly embarrassed.

'That failed spell really took it out of me,' she said.

Gerhard nodded. 'I gather that's fairly common,' he said. 'Especially with one as powerful as that.' His tone was no more than mildly curious. 'Where did you learn it?'

'I didn't,' Hanna said. 'I just know how it's done.'

'Really?' The witch hunter sounded politely sceptical. 'Most of the witches I've encountered have had a mentor. A few have learned petty magicks purely from books, although the ability to do that without guidance or losing their souls in the process is extremely unusual. None of them have been able to cast powerful spells spontaneously.'

'Perhaps you don't know as much as you think,' Hanna snapped. To her visible annoyance, Gerhard laughed, with every appearance of genuine good humour. Remembering how the witch hunter's affable demeanour had suddenly changed to cold murderousness after he'd refused to let him read the letter he'd been carrying when they first met, Rudi wasn't fooled for a moment.

'My dear young lady, the only thing I'm absolutely sure of in my pursuit of the minions of Chaos is how little I truly know of their nature and intentions.'

'So we're agents of Chaos now, are we?' Hanna chewed and swallowed, her words becoming a little more distinct as her mouth cleared. 'Is that better or worse than heretics?'

'That depends on how willing your service to the dark gods is.' Gerhard folded his hands. 'Some of their agents are unwitting dupes. Others are well aware of their true masters. Which are you, I wonder?'

'We're neither,' Rudi snapped, feeling his face flush with anger. 'Our lives were perfectly peaceful until you accused us of heresy for no reason at all.'

'No reason?' Gerhard shook his head. 'The son of a Chaos worshipper and the daughter of a sorceress, who just happens to be a witch herself. What exactly do you feel is unfair about my accusation under the circumstances?'

'My father was a forester,' Rudi snapped. 'A Taalist! He never had anything to do with Chaos in his life!'

'I beg to differ.' The witch hunter's voice took on a harder tone. 'His body was found among a coven of cultists attempting some damnable sorcery, in pursuit of which they'd all but sucked the life out of an entire village.'

'That can't be true,' Rudi insisted, fighting to remain impassive. Memories of that fateful night in the forest rose unbidden in his mind and he dreaded the reflection of them appearing on his face. The gathering he'd stumbled into, guided by some instinct he couldn't name, had seemed more like a celebration than anything to do with dark sorcery. His father had been there, true, and so had Magnus, the richest merchant in Kohlstadt and a good friend to both, but before either of them could explain the reason for their presence the party had been attacked by beastmen. His father had been cut down before his eyes and only the intervention of the inhuman thing which had once been Hans Katzenjammer, who seemed to have found refuge with the mutants' warband, had saved his life.

'It most certainly is.' Gerhard inclined his head. 'There were no survivors in a fit state to talk, but enough of their families and associates were forthcoming for me to be able to piece together something of what had been going on.'

'So how many more innocent people did you burn after we left?' Hanna snapped.

Gerhard looked surprised at the question. 'None at all. I've never burned an innocent in my life. Most of your fellow villagers were guilty of nothing more than an inability to comprehend the true meaning of what had been going on around them for so many years. If that were a capital crime we'd soon run out of stakes.' He shrugged again. 'There were only a couple of willing accomplices and they paid the full price of their bargain with the Lord of Decay, you can be sure of that.'

'Who?' Rudi asked, his head spinning.

Gerhard gave him a level stare, searching his face for Sigmar knew what. 'Would you say you were blessed by the grandfather?' he asked. Despite himself, Rudi felt a jolt of recognition at the question. Magnus had mentioned his grandfather's blessing that night in the woods, just before the beastmen attacked. Hoping his confusion hadn't shown on his face, he shook his head.

'I've no idea who my grandparents were,' he said. 'I was a foundling. Surely everyone in Kohlstadt told you that.' And no doubt nodded wisely as they did so, relishing the confirmation of all the gossip about him that had accumulated over the years.

'They did.' Gerhard nodded too. 'But you must have come from somewhere.'

'My father – I mean Gunther Walder – found me in the forest when I was little more than a year old. I've no memories of any other life.'

'I see.' The witch hunter nodded, turning to Hanna. 'And who was your father?'

'I've no idea.' Hanna glared at him, affronted at the question, clearly stung by its implication about her mother's morals. 'He died before I was born. Mother never spoke about him.'

'But she taught you to use magic, didn't she?' Despite his interrogative tone it sounded like a statement rather than a question.

Hanna sighed, realising there was no point in denying it. 'Just a few simple spells. To help us help people, that's all. There's nothing evil in being able to light a kitchen fire or see in a darkened room.'

'Or incinerate anyone you think of as an enemy?' Gerhard asked mildly.

'I don't make a habit of that,' Hanna said, with heavy irony. 'You're an exception, believe me.'

'I suppose I ought to be flattered,' Gerhard said. 'But it is hard not to take these things personally.'

'How do you expect me to take it?' Hanna shouted, before bringing her voice back under control with a visible effort. 'You killed my mother.'

'In all fairness, she was trying to kill me at the time.' The witch hunter nodded reprovingly. 'I'd gone to her cottage to consult her about the progress of the fever in the village, which by that point I was convinced was far from natural. No doubt if she'd been expecting me she would have removed certain items from the room, or concealed them more carefully. As it was, I noticed them the moment I walked in.'

'What items?' Hanna asked.

By way of an answer Gerhard picked up a quill and a scrap of paper from the chest beside the bed and sketched for a moment.

'Do you recognise this?' he asked.

Rudi felt an inexplicable sense of loathing rise up in him as he stared at the hastily inked lines. They were the same as the ones tattooed on the beastman he'd found dying in Altman's field, and that Hans had daubed on himself before going into battle against the people in the forest.

Hanna nodded. 'It's a picture frame,' she said impatiently. 'We had one like it in the cottage, round the icon of Shallya.' Comprehension suddenly dawned in her eyes. 'Is that it? You thought it was some Chaos thing?'

'It is.' Gerhard consigned the scrap of paper carefully to the flame of a nearby candle, holding it gingerly between finger and thumb until every trace of the sketch had been reduced to ashes. 'It's the sigil of one of the dark gods.' He smiled, without mirth. 'Clever, in its own twisted way. She could pray to her patron openly, while appearing to invoke the goddess of healing. And any fellow cultist passing by would recognise a kindred soul.'

'You killed her for that?' Outrage made Hanna's voice rise in pitch. 'Because you thought a picture frame was an icon of Chaos?' She made a sound of disgust deep in her throat. 'You're the twisted one, not her!'

'As soon as she realised I'd recognised it, she attacked me,' Gerhard went on, as though the interruption had never come. 'Using sorceries more potent than you can even imagine. If Sigmar hadn't blessed me with His protection I would have died on the spot.' He made the sign of the hammer as he invoked the holy name. 'Even so, I barely made it back outside to rejoin the militia detachment I'd co-opted. I expected her to follow and warned my companions to be on their guard, but instead she barred the door.'

'So you set fire to the cottage and burned her to death.' Hanna glared hotly at him, tears of anger welling in her eyes. A familiar expression of concentration flickered across her face and Rudi flinched, anticipating another globe of incandescent death flaring into existence in the air in front of her. But instead the girl staggered, clasping her hands to her head with a cry of pain. Rudi stepped in to support her, finding her surprisingly light in his arms, and led her to the vacant chair. His guess about the purpose of the seal on her forehead seemed correct.

'She would have burned anyway,' Gerhard pointed out, his tone as conversational as ever. 'It made no difference in the long run. She was a witch, after all.' The implication was clear, and Hanna paled as his eyes turned towards her.

'If that's what you've got in mind for me, then why not get on with it?' Her tone was defiant, but Rudi knew her well enough to detect the undercurrent of fear in her voice.

Gerhard nodded thoughtfully. 'I'm afraid your execution is a foregone conclusion. Your practice of witchcraft makes that inevitable. But there are far less painful and protracted ways of carrying out the sentence than burning.'

'What are you saying, exactly?' Rudi asked, conscious that once again events were moving in an unexpected direction. Gerhard filled a goblet from a pitcher of water on the table and handed it to the girl. Rudi half expected her to throw it in his face, but she seized it in trembling hands and drank deeply.

'I want information. A good deal of it, from both of you. If I get it, her death will be swift and painless.' The witch hunter shrugged. 'Otherwise she burns. Clear enough?'

'If I'm going to die anyway, why should I help you at all?' Hanna asked. Though her voice was still defiant, her face was white, and she slumped in the chair as though her bones had liquified.

'That's your choice, of course. Perhaps after you've seen your friend burn you'll be in a better position to make up your mind.' He turned to the tent flap and lifted it, glancing quizzically at the small patch of sky thus revealed. It was the thin, translucent grey which precedes the dawn. 'That'll be in about half an hour's time if I'm any judge.' He stepped through the flap, glancing back at the prisoners within. 'Perhaps you'd like to talk it over while I check on the arrangements?'

* * *

'WE HAVE TO get out of here,' Hanna said grimly, sliding the dagger out of her bodice as soon as the witch hunter had gone.

Rudi nodded. 'You'll get no argument from me.' He glanced around the tent, looking for anything which could help them. The wooden chest next to the bed caught his eye and he opened it hastily. Clearly the captain had forgotten to lock it in the confusion of their abrupt arrival. It contained clothing, for the most part of a quality and cut far superior to the garments he was used to, and he briefly considered stealing some as a makeshift disguise. A moment's more rational thought dissuaded him: he had no idea of the significance of the various items of heraldry embroidered on practically everything he could see, and the risk of discovery from acting inappropriately for his assumed station was far too great. They'd just have to try to blend in with the bustle of the camp as they were. That shouldn't be too hard, he'd seen plenty of apparent civilians on their way in. Even a few women, so with any luck Hanna wouldn't stand out too much either.

His eye fell on the seal in the centre of her forehead, and he touched his own in the same spot as he met her gaze.

'That'll have to go,' he said.

'Too right.' Hanna reached up towards it and winced as her hand approached the thing. For a moment she persisted, her expression growing ever more pained the closer she came to touching it, then gave up with a stifled cry of anguish. 'I can't. It won't let me.'

'What do you mean it won't let you?' Rudi moved next to her, apprehension coursing through his body. Time was flooding away and they had to get moving.

'I can't touch it. It feels like needles in my head.' She sighed with frustration. 'I can't take it off.'

'Let me try.' Rudi reached out a cautious hand, but before he could reach it, she twisted her head away.

'Stop it! It hurts!' She pushed him in the chest, opening up the space between them.

'We'll just have to deal with it later.' Rudi rummaged through the pile of clothes again, not sure quite what he was looking for. At the bottom of the chest was a travelling cloak, plain and unadorned and showing the marks of hard use. Evidently the captain was practical enough not to bother with his finery in the field. 'Try this on.'

Hanna took it. It was a little too large for her, but that was no bad thing. With the hood pulled forwards enough of her face was hidden to conceal the waxen blemish.

'It'll do,' she said after a moment. She hefted the dagger in her hand, a little uncertainly. 'How do we take out the guards?'

'Maybe we won't have to,' Rudi said. The prospect wasn't one he relished. Despite the lessons he'd learned from Theo Krieger and the inexplicable sharpening of his reflexes he'd noticed in his fight with Fritz, he was by no means sure he'd be able to hold his own against a pair of trained soldiers. Even if he could, the noise would be bound to attract attention and he shied away from the prospect of what victory would probably mean. He'd come close to killing Fritz in the heat of combat, but he'd never actually taken a human life, and the thought of doing so in cold blood disturbed him.

He drew his own blade from its hiding place and stepped to the side of the tent. Faint torchlight stained the canvas of the back a dull flickering orange and the occasional shadow danced across it, indicating that there was a thoroughfare of some kind behind them. Breaking out there would draw as much attention as trying to get past the guards. But the sides were dark, which seemed more promising.

'What are you doing?' Hanna asked.

Rudi shrugged. 'I've no idea. I'm making this up as I go along.' He poked the tip of his dagger through the weave of the fabric and cut down. As he'd hoped, the faint tearing sound was lost in the general bustle of the camp. He poked his head out and looked around cautiously.

To his great relief, there was no one about. Another tent stood a yard or so away, forming a narrow alleyway between them. Dim torchlight leaked down the narrow passage from both ends, but the middle was reassuringly dark. He enlarged the slit carefully, stepped through, then turned to proffer a helping hand to Hanna. To his vague surprise she took it.

'Which way?' she whispered, returning her dagger to its sheath. Rudi did the same, not wanting to draw any more attention to themselves than they could help.

'Over there.' He gestured towards the rear of the tent, then glanced towards the front, momentarily afraid that they'd made enough noise to attract the attention of the guards. Something about the pattern of shadows by the side of the tent seemed odd and he studied it for a moment before realisation dawned. 'Stay here for a moment.'

'What?' Hanna began, but subsided as he started to move away. Every instinct for stealthy movement he'd learned in the woods came into play as he wove carefully around guy ropes and tent pegs as easily as if they were the forest undergrowth among which he'd grown up among. 'Right, fine, I'll just sit here and wait to get caught then, shall I?'

Rudi ignored her muttered imprecations, conscious only of the necessity of moving quietly enough to avoid attracting the attention of the guards. As he got closer to the pool of torchlight leaking in from the avenue beyond the line of tents, his heart skipped. He'd been right. Their packs and weapons had been dumped on the ground next to the captain's tent, no doubt for Gerhard to examine in detail at his leisure. Dropping to the ground, he wormed his way forward, hoping the guards would be keeping their gaze at head height.

To his profound relief, he turned out to be correct. Muttered snatches of conversation drifted to his ears as he reached out for the bundles ahead of him.

'Gone a bit quiet in there, hasn't it?' The voice sounded young and a little eager. Rudi tensed. If the speaker went inside to investigate they would be caught for sure.

'That's the idea.' The second voice was older, reminding Rudi somehow of Sergeant Littman of the Kohlstadt militia. 'He's leaving 'em to sweat for a bit. Think about their options.'

'Shouldn't have thought they've got any.'

'Well, no. That's the whole point, isn't it?' The speaker made a sound of disgust. 'Bloody heretics. Dunno why he doesn't just burn the lot of 'em now and have done with it. I would.'

Rudi reached out carefully, grabbing the shoulder strap of his pack. Absorbed in the new topic of Fritz's impending execution, neither guard appeared to notice. He pulled it cautiously towards him, sighing with relief as it passed into the shadows. Hanna's satchel followed just as easily, then the pack Fritz had taken from Theo. Their weapons were more of a problem and he moved as slowly as he dared, fearful of revealing himself by a careless *clink* of metal against metal, but after a moment he'd retrieved his sword belt and the knife which normally hung from it. Fritz's spear he left where it was. It was too unwieldy to risk taking.

'Here.' He handed Hanna her satchel, shrugging his own pack into place. The girl shouldered it and held out her hand for Fritz's belongings too. 'I'll take that. You might need your hands free.' A quick glance down at the sword made her meaning quite clear.

'I hope not.' He led the way to the far end of the canvas crosswalk and looked out cautiously. A double line of tents lined up on either side, like a temporary village street, and the tempo of activity along it seemed to be increasing. Men, and a few women, were busying themselves hauling pails of water and blowing fresh life into smouldering cooking fires. A steady stream of armed soldiers were trotting past on incomprehensible errands. Rudi took a deep breath. 'Come on.'

Without waiting to see if she followed, he stepped out from between the tents as though he had every right to be there. His shoulder blades tensed for a moment as he anticipated a shouted challenge, but none of the passers-by took any notice of him at all. A moment later Hanna joined him.

'What do we do now?' she asked.

'We keep moving.' So long as they looked as if they knew where they were going no one was likely to notice them. He hoped. 'And try to find Fritz.'

Hanna nodded. 'We'd better be quick,' she said, gesturing to the east. Rudi turned to look, his breath freezing in his throat. The first faint flush of sunrise was beginning to stain the sky. He swallowed hard. There could only be moments left before the execution and he had no idea how he was going to find their companion.

'We'll try this way,' he decided, turning left at the end of the row of tents. Fritz had been dragged off in roughly that direction and if the ground hadn't been trampled too much there just might be some tracks left he could read. Even as the thought came to him, he realised just how slim a chance that was.

'What's that?' Hanna asked. A horn blared in the distance, harsh and urgent, and over it rose the sound of raised voices and the clash of steel. Sharp reports, like the sound of twigs snapping in a bonfire, echoed among the tents. All around them, people started running, the soldiers carrying their weapons with an air of grim determination.

'Run!' An overweight man in a cook's apron barged past them, moving against the tide of soldiers. 'The beastmen are attacking the camp!'

CHAPTER THREE

'WHAT?' RUDI TRIED to grab the man's arm, hoping to detain him for long enough to get a little more information, but by the time he recovered his wits the fellow had already gone, vanishing into the milling crowd which squawked and flapped its panic like a flock of startled chickens.

'Clear the way!' A troop of soldiers ran past, almost trampling him in their hurry. Hanna pulled him to the side of the thoroughfare just in time. The sound of combat was louder in that direction, the roars and squeals he remembered from the night in the forest rising above the clash of arms and the hoarser shouts of the human commanders.

'What do we do now?' Hanna asked, glancing around as though she expected to see a shaggy mis-shapen giant bearing down on them at any moment.

'We find Fritz and get out of here,' Rudi replied. The sudden raid seemed almost like a miracle, and for a moment he wondered if Hanna had prayed at the tainted shrine in her cottage too, unwittingly invoking the deity the beastmen seemed to follow. He dismissed the thought angrily. Greta Reifenstahl had been the innocent victim of Gerhard's paranoia, nothing more and Hanna's soul had been no more corrupted by Chaos than his own. He'd heard enough of Sergeant Littman's campaign stories back in Kohlstadt to know that dawn was a particularly good time to attack an enemy. The beastmen's arrival was a fortuitous coincidence, that was all.

'And where do you suggest we look?' Hanna asked, the habitual edge of asperity creeping back into her voice. Once Rudi would have resented it, but since getting to know her better he was beginning to realise it was just a mask for her own insecurities. And Sigmar knew she had enough to be worried about at the moment. She gestured to the scene of confusion surrounding them.

'This way.' He began jogging in the wake of the soldiers, moving against the stream of non-combatants trying to get as far away from the fighting as they could. As the faint grey light of daybreak began to pierce the shadows around him, he started to feel more certain of the layout of the camp. They'd come in on the western side, and the slope of the ground had almost levelled off in the direction they were moving in. The reddish stain of sunrise was to his right, which meant they were moving north, and assuming the hill-top was roughly circular the centre of the camp must be right about here.

'Fritz!' Hanna sprinted past him, heedless of the danger of attracting unwanted attention, although under the circumstances Rudi supposed the risk was minimal. His guess had been right. A large clear space had been left between the tents, for all the world like a glade in a canvas forest, presumably for the troops to drill in. A thick wooden stake had been driven into the ground in the centre of it, surrounded by brushwood. Fritz stood against it, his posture slumped, held upright only by the thick ropes wound about his body. 'Shallya's mercy, what have they done to him?'

'Kicked the dreck out of me,' Fritz said, his voice slurred. His face was bruised and bloody, and each breath clearly hurt. He raised his head, an expression of puzzlement crossing his features. 'What are you doing here?'

'Saving your skin,' Rudi said, drawing the knife from his belt and beginning to hack at the ropes. A small part of him was as confused as the simpleton he was rescuing. He didn't like Fritz, he never had, and it would certainly have been a lot easier to get away if they hadn't wasted time looking for him. On the other hand, he'd made the youth a promise, and that still meant something. 'Where are the guards?'

'Ran off when the fighting started,' Fritz said indistinctly, trying to raise his head. 'Lucky that.'

'Chew this.' Hanna rummaged in her satchel, producing a couple of dried leaves, which she slipped between Fritz's swollen lips. 'Not as good as a proper preparation, but it'll have to do for now.'

'What is it?' Fritz mumbled, but complied anyway.

'Manbane.' She clamped a hand across his face just in time to prevent him spitting them out.

'That's poison!' Rudi said in horror. 'You'll kill him!'

'Only when it's refined,' Hanna said impatiently. 'Or in a much larger dose than this. All it'll kill is the pain. Unless you want to carry him.'

'Not particularly,' Rudi said, as the ropes finally parted. Fritz staggered a pace or two forwards, kicking the brushwood aside and pulling free of Hanna's grip. An expression of surprise worked its way slowly across his face.

'She's right. I do feel better.' A grin began to form beneath the mask of blood and bruising. 'I feel great.'

'Enjoy it while it lasts,' Hanna said. 'You'll feel twice as bad when it wears off.'

'How do we get out of here?' Rudi asked, seizing the hulking youth by the arm. Fritz shrugged, and Rudi tightened his grip. 'You were camped here before you deserted, right? You must have some idea of the layout.'

'That way.' Fritz gestured towards the rising sun. 'There's another gate, where the supply wagons come in.'

'Then we can get out the same way,' Rudi said. 'Come on.' He turned to lead the way and his blood froze. A familiar black garbed figure was standing on the edge of the open space, backed up by a troop of soldiers. Not everyone in the camp, it seemed, had hurried off to engage the invaders.

'I think this illustrates my earlier point quite nicely,' Gerhard said mildly. 'How did you get past the guards?'

'Work it out for yourself.' Rudi edged out in front of his companions, drawing his sword. The gesture would be futile, he knew, the tricks Theo had taught him of no avail against so many trained opponents, but he might just buy the others a little time to get away. The mercenary captain's advice echoed in his ears. *Never go into a fight you don't know from the outset you're going to win.* Well, it was a little too late for that.

'Kill the simpleton. Take the other two alive.' Gerhard gestured the soldiers forward and Rudi tensed. The rising sun glittered from his outstretched blade, turning it the colour of blood, like some baleful prophecy.

With a roar which seemed to tremble in his bones, something huge and covered with matted hair charged out of the tents behind him, sending canvas crashing to the ground as powerful limbs snagged and snapped the guy lines. A beastman, like the one he'd found dying in a cornfield outside Kohlstadt a few weeks before, sprinted into the open space, a bloodstained cleaver grasped purposefully in its hand. This one, however, was strong and uninjured, radiating malevolence and the desire to kill.

'Shallya protect us!' Hanna gasped, and Rudi remembered that she'd never actually seen one of the mutants before. He turned to face it, prepared to defend her to the best of his ability, but to his relieved astonishment it ignored the little knot of fugitives entirely, charging home against the group of soldiers.

'Bring it down, you idiots!' Gerhard had his sword drawn and lunged at the creature, striking home against its chest. The beastman bellowed, retaliating with a swing of its own weapon, which would surely have taken the witch hunter's head from his shoulders if he hadn't ducked with an instant to spare. 'The prisoners are escaping!'

The soldiers scattered, trying to get past it, making what strikes and sallies they could with their polearms, but the creature was enraged, flailing wildly with inhuman strength and resilience. A couple of the men went down, blood spraying bright against their gaudy uniforms, but the majority were getting through, running towards Rudi, Hanna and Fritz with grim and unmistakable purpose.

'Come on!' Rudi got his companions moving at last, heading towards the gap in the tents Fritz had indicated, but the stocky youth was moving far too slowly. Weakened by the beating he'd taken, his legs were still too stiff to run properly. The soldiers were going to cut them off for sure.

Abruptly, the knot of men in front of him went down, shrieking, wreathed in flames of a vivid blue colour unlike anything he'd ever seen before. The hairs on the back of Rudi's neck prickled. Surely Hanna couldn't have... No, a quick glance behind him was enough to confirm that whatever talisman Gerhard had fused to her flesh was still working. Her expression was one of undisguised shock. But if not her, then who?

'Run, you idiots.' The voice was familiar, a harsh croaking timbre as though the throat producing the words was no longer properly adapted to human speech, and Rudi felt a premonitory tingle down his spine even before the speaker came into view. Hans Katzenjammer? Here? How was that possible?

A moment later, his confusion was swept aside as his old enemy appeared at the head of a swarm of beastmen, who fell on the surviving soldiers with all the bestial ferocity of their kind. A desperate battle began to rage about the fugitives, as reinforcements started to pour into the open space from both factions. Rudi saw men struck down by talon, blade and cudgel, while shaggy beastmen were hacked apart in their turn, or bloody craters erupted through their flesh as firearms barked, blanketing the scene in thick, choking smoke.

Hans flung the body of a soldier aside and turned back to regard Rudi with an expression of amused disdain. His three eyes blinked in unison.

'Getting to be a bit of a habit, isn't it? Saving your life.' He blocked a cut from Gerhard's sword with the bony ridge along the edge of his forearm. Since Rudi had seen him last, in the forest near Kohlstadt the fateful night he'd run for his life, the bone had thickened and extended, developing a sharp cutting edge. He swiped back with it, tearing the witch hunter's cloak and provoking a parry in return. 'Don't make it a wasted effort.'

'Hans?' Fritz goggled at the creature which used to be his brother. 'Is that really you?'

'More or less.' The mutant laughed, revelling in the combat, moving easily to keep his body between the witch hunter and the fugitives. 'I see you haven't changed at all.'

'Come on!' Hanna urged the simpleton into motion. 'While we still can!'

'Good advice.' Hans punched Gerhard in the stomach and snapped a knee up into the witch hunter's descending face. Gerhard went limp and the mutant clamped a hand around his throat, lifting him to eye level. It was only then that Rudi realised he'd grown a couple of feet as well and now towered over him.

'Kill him! Kill him!' Hanna shouted suddenly. 'He murdered your mother too!' The expression of malevolent loathing was back on her face and Rudi shuddered at the intensity of it.

Hans shook his head regretfully. 'I wish I could,' he said. 'But she won't let me. Not yet.' Then he shrugged and threw the barely conscious witch hunter to the ground.

'Who won't?' Rudi asked. Hans looked up towards the edge of the open space, where a caped, cowled figure stood impassively. For a moment, he wondered how Hanna had got all the way over there so quickly, then realised she was still standing by his shoulder. Besides, the figure's cape was a different colour, and although he couldn't quite distinguish the hue, it seemed to shift and change as he looked at it. Whoever it was, her face was in shadow, and the memory came back to him of the horned woman he'd seen with Hans and the leader of the beastman herd. Could this be her? Had she cast the spell which had killed the soldiers standing between them and safety? A moment later, there was no more time to think about it. The mysterious woman shimmered into the shadows and was gone. 'Who is she?'

'Look after my brother. He doesn't understand much about the world.' Hans whirled and was gone, loping after the horned woman, if it had even been her, with a swiftness and grace which belied his monstrous appearance.

'Move!' Rudi said, forcing his confusion to the back of his mind. The skirmish was beginning to peter out, fresh troops appearing from all directions to engage the beastmen. If they stayed where they were they were liable to be cut to pieces by either side. He began running in the direction Fritz had indicated, trying not to look at the charred corpses of the soldiers Gerhard had ordered to arrest them. No one else seemed to have heard his orders, and while he remained unconscious the news of their escape wouldn't travel far.

Rudi glanced back. Fritz was jogging doggedly in his wake, but Hanna had paused beside the slumped body of the witch hunter. With a thrill of horror, he saw her hand move to the hilt of her concealed dagger. If she killed the man now the soldiers surrounding them would notice, he was certain. He drew in his breath to call out something, anything to stay her hand, but to his intense relief she checked the gesture and ran over to join them.

'I thought for a moment you were going to kill him,' he said.

Hanna looked at him with guileless blue eyes. 'I was,' she said matter-of-factly. 'But now's not the time. Not while he's unconscious.' An edge of venom entered her voice which struck Rudi like a winter chill. 'When the time comes, I want him to know it was me.'

CHAPTER FOUR

FRITZ HAD BEEN right about the other gate. As the fugitives ran through the camp, the sounds of combat diminishing behind them, Rudi began to see boxes and bundles stacked all around, until the tents had been almost entirely displaced by heaps of items he didn't have the time to stop and identify. Many had been covered with sheets of canvas, leaving only the vague outlines of whatever they concealed, while in other spots barrels and sacks had been carefully stacked. There were hardly any people about, the handful he spotted all civilian camp followers huddled behind whatever concealment they could find, no doubt fearful that the tide of battle would sweep in this direction without warning.

'Over there.' Fritz pointed. A wagon had been drawn across the gap in the embankment, like the one Rudi remembered being poised to block the other gate. It had evidently been done in haste, because the horse drawing it was still between the shafts, whickering nervously at the distant howls of the beastmen. Presumably, the wagon had only just arrived and been pressed into service as a barricade simply because it was the nearest. He said as much and Hanna looked at him quizzically.

'How can you tell?' she asked.

'It hasn't been unloaded yet.' The back was still full, the load it contained concealed by one of the ubiquitous canvas coverings.

'You're right.' The horse whinnied and pawed the ground. The girl's expression softened for the first time since she'd almost killed Gerhard. 'The poor thing. It's terrified.'

'It's not the only one,' Fritz mumbled. His steps were faltering. 'Let's just get out of here while the going's good.'

'Wait,' Rudi cautioned. He couldn't believe the gate wouldn't be guarded at least as diligently as the one they'd come in by. 'Something's not right.'

'Nothing's been right since you found those beastman tracks,' Fritz said. His eyes were glazing and he swayed on his feet. Hanna looked at him appraisingly, an expression of mild alarm crossing her face.

Rudi caught her eye. 'What's the matter with him?' he asked.

'Apart from being beaten almost to death and dosed with a powerful toxin you mean?' she asked acidly.

'Can you give him some more? We have to keep going.'

'If I give him anything else he's not going anywhere,' Hanna said flatly. Rudi glanced around, half expecting to find armed men already hurrying to arrest them, but seeing no signs of life apart from the horse. His scalp prickled. Something was undeniably wrong.

'Wait here. Do what you can for him.' He darted forward, keeping to the cover of the stacks of supplies and parked wagons as best he could. Though he moved swiftly, as rapidly as he had through the forest he'd grown up in, his progress seemed to be agonisingly slow. Every moment stretched with the anticipation of a shouted challenge, or the report of a discharged firearm.

At length he reached the wagon, becoming conscious as he did so of a disturbingly familiar smell; the stench of charred flesh. No wonder the horse was spooked. Crouching low, he scurried between the wheels and pushed aside a couple of the barrels, which had been lined up beyond the cart with the obvious intention of preventing intruders from gaining entry the same way. The smell intensified and his gorge rose in his throat.

The reason for the absence of any guards was obvious. They were all dead, most of them seared by magical fire just like the luckless troopers who had tried to bar their way a few moments before. Most were charred practically beyond recognition as anything remotely human, but a few of the corpses were relatively intact. Some had been slaughtered in a more brutally straightforward fashion than their fellows, ripped apart by talons which had reduced flesh and bone to bloody strips.

One body lay apart from the others, a score of paces away, a smouldering crater in its back. Clearly the man had tried to run from whatever had attacked his comrades and had failed to escape. Something about the corpse sparked a nagging sense of familiarity in the back of Rudi's mind, and after a moment the image of the dead goblin he and Hanna had found shortly after fleeing from Kohlstadt floated to the surface of his memory. It too had been cut down by pyromancy attempting to escape the herd of beastmen slaughtering its fellows. Had they fallen victim to the same warband and the sorceries of the mysterious horned woman who seemed to travel with them?

His blood ran cold at the thought. If that was true, all the time he and Hanna had thought they were relatively safe they could have stumbled across the path of the mutant marauders at almost any moment.

Sickened at the sight of the slaughter, he began to turn away, then hesitated as he noticed something about one of the bodies. The man was one of those who'd been killed in close combat rather than by magic and his right hand still grasped the hilt of his sword, which was half out of its scabbard, as though he'd died in the act of drawing it. Half hidden beneath his body was the unmistakable shape of a quiver, the arrows within fletched with grey goose feathers, and a strung bow lay on the ground next to him. Rudi could picture the scene all too vividly. The man had only had time for a single shot before dropping the weapon as his opponent closed, reaching desperately for the falchion at his belt in a vain attempt to defend himself.

Swallowing hard, and trying to keep his rising nausea in check, Rudi walked over to the body. The bow was intact, the expert eye for such things his father had taught him, serving him well, and to his even greater relief, the arrows were equally undamaged. Stilling a slight trembling in his hands, Rudi rolled the corpse over a little to reach the buckle securing the quiver to the man's shoulder.

'What on earth are you doing?' Hanna's voice was shrill with horror. Startled, Rudi looked up. The girl was standing next to the horse, trying to calm it, while Fritz clambered awkwardly up onto the horizontal plank which served the wagon as a seat. He slumped there, gasping for breath, gazing at Rudi with his usual expression of bovine idiocy.

'He can't use this any more. We can.' Vaguely surprised at his own callousness, Rudi retrieved the weapon. As an afterthought he picked up a discarded spear too. Fritz knew how to use it, after his militia training in Kohlstadt, and the burly youth would be a lot more use to them armed. He certainly wasn't about to give the simpleton a sword – he'd probably cut his own thumb off.

'Are you going to go through their purses too, while you're at it?' Hanna asked, an edge of disgust entering her voice.

Rudi hesitated. The men certainly didn't need their money any more, but every moment he spent scavenging was a moment gained by their pursuers. Gerhard would be on their trail the second he recovered from the mauling Hans had given him, he was sure about that.

'There's no time,' he said. He shrugged into the quiver and slung the bow across his back, as he had so many times back home in the forest. The familiar weight of the weapon felt good, comforting. It wasn't quite the same as the one he'd lost when the captain of the *Reikmaiden* revealed his treachery, but it would certainly do well enough. He beckoned to his companions. 'Come on.'

'I can't.' Fritz shook his head. 'I'm all in.'

'You're all dead if you stay here!' Rudi snapped, amazed at his stupidity.

Hanna shook her head. 'It's the leaves. They're wearing off faster than I thought and I daren't give him any more. If he didn't have the constitution of an ox as well as the brains of one he'd be unconscious by now.'

'Then we'll have to carry him,' Rudi said, appalled. Fritz was no lightweight, and encumbered with him they stood little chance of getting far enough away to elude the inevitable pursuit before the battle ended. Once again, the thought of simply abandoning the youth forced its way to the surface of his mind, and once again, he angrily dismissed it. If they left him to an agonising death simply to save their own skins they were no better than Gerhard.

'Don't be stupid,' Fritz said, gazing at Rudi in slack-witted astonishment. 'Get on the cart.'

'Brilliant idea,' Rudi said, sarcasm dripping from every syllable. 'Except I've never driven one before in my life.' He turned to Hanna. 'Have you?' She shook her head.

'I have. Helped my uncle Otto bring the harvest in every year since I was eight.' Fritz picked up the reins with the easy dexterity which only comes with experience and practise and stared impatiently at Rudi. 'So are you coming or what?'

'Fine.' Masking his surprise with a display of indifference, Rudi clambered up beside him and leant down to proffer a helping hand to Hanna. She took it, hitching up her skirts and dropping to the plank beside him. Acutely conscious of the faint pressure of her body against his, and the fleeting sight of her slender calves which had evoked memories of a great deal more, Rudi let go of her hand hastily.

'Walk on.' Fritz flicked the reins and to Rudi's astonishment the horse responded, wheeling to avoid the remaining barrels and walking out through the gap in the earthen wall. The sudden lurch took him by surprise, throwing him against the girl and she pushed him away with a faint sigh of irritation. The wheels rumbled against planking, a wooden causeway bridging the ditch just as it had on the western gate and after a few moments of astonishingly rapid progress the encampment disappeared behind them.

IN DAYLIGHT, THE landscape was almost familiar, evoking memories of the barren moorland Rudi and Hanna had fled across after leaving Kohlstadt. This time, however, there was a definite trail to follow, marked by the wheel ruts of innumerable wagons, the hoof prints of horses and the thin coating of trampled mud left by the infantry columns and the ragged cluster of camp followers which trailed in their wake. Even Fritz was able to keep to its course, despite the fatigue which left him slumped on the seat, barely able to keep his eyes open. It seemed to make little difference to the horse, however, which plodded on regardless of its driver's inattention.

'Where do you think we're going?' Hanna asked after a while. As the sun rose, the day began to grow warm and she shifted restively in the travelling cloak. Eventually she discarded it and rummaged in her satchel for a piece of cloth which she tied around her head to hide the seal on her forehead. It was bright blue, matching the colour of her eyes, and even without asking Rudi knew it had to have been another present from Bruno. Once it had been knotted into place she relaxed visibly, even smiling a little. Rudi was suddenly struck by the resemblance she bore to her mother. Greta had always worn a headscarf, from which a wisp or two of blonde hair invariably escaped, just as her daughter's did now.

'Towards the river, I guess,' Rudi said. Remembering what Shenk, the treacherous riverboat captain, had told him, he assumed that the supplies for the camp had been landed at a local wharf somewhere and been carted the rest of the way. Either that, or the baggage train was a permanent feature of the regiment, following it about wherever it went. 'I suppose we'll find out soon enough.' He hoped it would be soon. The narrow trail across the moorland felt like a trap to him. Aboard the wagon they were unable to leave it and lose themselves in the rugged terrain surrounding them as they had before. Moreover, given the depth and number of wheel ruts he could see, it was obviously heavily travelled. Sooner or later they were bound to run into some traffic coming in the opposite direction.

'I suppose so,' Hanna said, clearly thinking the same thing. She delved into Fritz's pack, producing some of the cold pork they'd taken from the mercenaries the evening before, and leaned across Rudi to nudge the older boy. 'Here. You'd better eat something.'

'Thanks.' Fritz took it mechanically, chewing and swallowing like an automaton. His posture remained slumped, however, and he swayed gently with the motion of the cart. Rudi dipped into his own pack, pulling out the bottle of rough spirit he'd given to Alwyn when she'd appeared suddenly the evening before, suffering the effects of too much magic in too short a time. It had seemed to revive her, and the sorceress had left a fair amount in the bottom of the bottle. He passed it over.

'Maybe this'll help too.' He glanced at Hanna as he said it, wondering belatedly if it would only make things worse, but she simply shrugged.

'Can't hurt,' she said. Fritz drank deeply, coughed and slipped the bottle into a convenient gap in the woodwork where he could get to it easily. Rudi didn't challenge him about it, as he was certainly not going to risk drinking the stuff himself.

'Can't stay awake.' Fritz nudged Rudi in the ribs and yawned widely. 'Take the reins.'

'What do I do?' Rudi was nonplussed.

'Nothing. Hold them like this.' He threaded the thin leather strap through Rudi's fingers with surprising dexterity. 'Keep the head straight and the horse'll do it for you. Pull this one to turn left and this one to turn right, got it?'

'Got it,' Rudi said, with more confidence than he felt. It seemed easy enough. He gave the reins a faint experimental tug and the horse veered to the left with alarming alacrity, heading for the edge of the track. His heart leaping within him, Rudi pulled gently on the other rein and the wagon straightened out again. 'Nothing to it.'

'Right.' Fritz didn't sound very convinced. 'Try not to turn us over or put us in a ditch.' He slumped even more, wedging himself into the corner of the seat, and closed his eyes. A moment later he started snoring faintly. Rudi raised a quizzical eyebrow and Hanna shrugged.

'Best thing for him.'

'Good.' He tried to think of something else to say, but nothing came to mind, so he concentrated on steering the horse. It seemed easy enough, but he hadn't had to make any critical manoeuvres yet, just letting the creature follow its nose. A sudden thought occurred to him and he turned to Hanna, trying to keep an edge of alarm from his voice. 'Do you have any idea how we get it to stop?'

'None whatsoever,' she said.

IN THE EVENT, Fritz woke up before the issue became an urgent one, beginning to stretch before cutting the motion short with an inarticulate strangled sound of acute discomfort.

'Sigmar's blood, I'm stiff.'

'I'm not surprised,' Hanna said. 'The battering you've taken I can't believe you can move at all. I'll take a look at you when we stop.'

'And do what?' Fritz looked at her with every sign of apprehension.

Hanna sighed. 'It depends what I find. Probably a poultice to reduce the bruising.'

Fritz still looked wary. 'That's all, right? None of the... other stuff.'

'If you mean magic, say it,' Hanna snapped. 'The words can't hurt you.'

'So you say.' Fritz considered what he'd said for a moment, Hanna's reputation back in their home village no doubt percolating slowly through his mind.

Wincing with the discomfort it clearly caused, he forced his swollen face into what he no doubt thought was a conciliatory smile. 'It's just that, you know, seeing you do stuff is a bit... You know.'

'Well you won't have to worry about that any more,' Hanna said bitterly. Fritz's face resumed its habitual expression of vague bafflement.

'Gerhard did something to her,' Rudi explained. 'She can't cast spells any more.'

'Oh. Oh, well that's good, isn't it?' Fritz tried to sound encouraging. 'If you're normal now he won't be after you any more, will he?'

'It's not as simple as that,' Hanna said, swallowing her temper with a visible effort, much to Rudi's surprise. Presumably she felt that Fritz's lack of tact was only to be expected in someone of his limited intellect. 'The power's still in me, I can feel it. I just can't focus or direct it any more.'

'I see.' The hulking youth clearly didn't.

Rudi nodded sympathetically. 'That must be very frustrating.'

'You don't know the half of it.' The girl acknowledged his attempt at sympathy with a wan smile. 'It's like, I don't know, trying to talk with your mouth full of bread. You know what to do, but you just can't get the words out.' The smile faded. 'And the worst thing is, it's still getting stronger. I can feel it trying to escape, burst out of me. What happens if it just keeps growing, until I can't keep it in any more?'

'We'll think of something long before that happens,' Rudi said, with all the assurance he could muster. He squeezed her hand in a momentary gesture of sympathy, withdrawing again before she might object.

'I think we're coming to a road.' Fritz reached across to retrieve the reins and swung the horse's head with easy precision. The cart bumped a little over a raised lip of soil and came to rest on a broad highway of closely packed earth. He pulled gently on the reins, bringing the beast to a halt, and glanced across at his companions. 'Which way do we go?'

CHAPTER FIVE

THE ROAD LOOKED identical to the one Rudi and Hanna had stumbled across before, wide, hard-packed and baked firm in the summer heat. Rudi glanced up and down it, hoping to find some clue as to where they were, but it wound its way across the moorland in both directions with few signs of life apart from some scattered rabbit droppings. He hoped there might be a milestone nearby, like the one Hanna had read before, but the trail to the camp was evidently a temporary one and had no need of such things.

'Looks like the coach road again,' Hanna said, confirming his guess. Fritz looked blank. 'Rudi and I found it before. It's the main highway from Altdorf to Marienburg.'

'Oh.' Fritz shrugged indifferently. 'You'll be wanting to go north then.' Rudi had told him of their intention of heading for Marienburg when they escaped from the bounty hunters the evening before. Rudi felt a shiver of apprehension.

'I'm not sure,' he began. The last time he'd suggested that, Hanna had pointed out that Kohlstadt had also lain in that direction. It was only a fortuitous milestone and her gift of literacy which had prevented them from marching straight back into the arms of their enemies. Realising the direction of his thoughts, the girl nodded.

'It should be all right. We're much further north than we were last time. The junction for Kohlstadt should be back that way.'

'Marienburg it is, then,' Rudi said, feeling a sudden surge of optimism. Fritz started the horse moving again.

Wary of pursuit, they kept going for the rest of the morning. As the sun climbed higher in the sky, across which clouds were scudding in a surprisingly chill wind, Rudi kept glancing behind them, but the troop of armed men he expected to see never materialised. Despite the faint tingle of apprehension which never quite faded, he began to feel a little more relaxed with every mile that passed. The soldiers, he supposed, would have enough to worry about finishing off the beastmen, and without Gerhard to divert their attention would undoubtedly concentrate their efforts in that direction.

As they'd found the last time they'd been on the highway, traffic was sparse, most of it evidently local. They passed a couple of carts almost identical to their own heading in the opposite direction, laden with vegetables, and once the overland coach they'd seen before hurtled by, raising a cloud of choking dust in its wake.

This time, Rudi was able to get a better view of it and marvelled anew at the opulence of its furnishing and the evident wealth of its passengers, who turned their gaze away, evidently affronted at being gawped at by a peasant lad. Once they overtook a small group of travellers on foot, all armed with swords or bows; he tensed, half expecting them to be Krieger's mercenary band, but there were no dwarfs among them and he relaxed again as soon as he realised they were strangers. A couple of them glanced up as the cart passed, and glanced away again with palpable indifference, resuming a good-natured argument with one of their number who seemed scarcely taller than a child.

'All I'm saying is, if I have to listen to one more chorus of *The Road Goes On Forever* I'm not going to be responsible for my actions, all right...?'

'That's good,' Hanna said, once they were out of earshot.

'It is?' Rudi asked, trying not to sound too confused.

The girl nodded. 'They didn't take any notice of us at all. If news of Gerhard's arrest warrants has got this far no one's likely to recognise us.'

'Course not,' Fritz said. 'They'll expect us to be on foot.'

'Why would they have cared anyway?' Rudi asked.

Hanna clicked her tongue impatiently. 'You saw their weapons, the way they were dressed. They're adventurers, like Theo and the others. If they'd known we were fugitives they'd have tried to grab us for the reward.'

'Tried is right,' Rudi said, with more assurance than he felt.

Fritz nodded in agreement. 'They'd know they'd been in a scrap, right enough.'

'Course they would,' Hanna said, the familiar sarcastic tone seeping into her voice. 'Rudi could bruise their knuckles, you could bleed on them and I could show them what a really bad headache looks like.'

'Is it getting worse?'

Hanna sighed and massaged her temples. 'No, not really. It's just like when you've got a really bad cold and your head feels heavy and swollen, you know?' Rudi, who had never had a day's illness in his life that he could recall, nodded sympathetically.

'Sounds bad,' he said. He was spared the necessity of trying to say more by a sudden lurch of the cart as Fritz pulled off the road onto a patch of greensward. 'Why are we stopping?'

'The horse needs a rest,' the stocky youth said. He stretched, wincing. 'And so do I.'

'We all do,' Hanna said, jumping from the cart and heading for a convenient clump of bushes. Rudi climbed down a little more slowly, surprised at how stiff he felt, and held out a hand to help Fritz disembark. The stocky youth hesitated a moment, then took it, pride overcome by the stiffness of his limbs.

'Thanks.' He half jumped, half fell to the ground, and limped round to the horse, releasing it from the shafts with the ease of long practice. He unfastened the reins, removing the bit from its mouth, and ruffled its mane with surprising gentleness. 'Good boy. Bet you're hungry too, aren't you?' Rudi watched him lead it over to a small pool, where it bent its head to drink, trying to hide his astonishment. He'd always thought of the older boy as nothing more than a feeble minded thug, and this sudden revelation of another side to his character was hard to assimilate.

'People are always more complicated than you think,' Hanna said, returning from the bushes rather more sedately than she'd gone, and clearly reading the thoughts on his face.

Rudi nodded. 'I'm beginning to find that out,' he said. The horse whickered, butting Fritz gently with its forehead, and the stocky youth patted it.

'Sorry,' he said. 'I'm out of apples. You'll just have to make do.' The horse turned and began to crop the grass.

'Looks like you've made a friend,' Hanna said.

Fritz shrugged, trying to hide his embarrassment at the implied compliment. 'I've always got on well with animals.' Rudi bit down on the instinctive retort which almost escaped his lips. They'd have to work together, at least until they reached Marienburg, and antagonising the lad with a smart remark wouldn't help anybody. Instead he nodded.

'I'm impressed,' he said, trying not to make the praise sound grudging. He'd never had anything to do with horses himself and hadn't realised that Fritz had either. Uncle Otto, whoever he was, had clearly taught his nephew well.

'It's just something I can do.' For some reason his attempt to be friendly seemed to make Fritz more uncomfortable than their usual state of simmering hostility. The hulking youth coughed and glanced at their packs. 'What have we got to eat?'

'I'm not sure,' Rudi said, grateful for the change of subject. 'We just grabbed what we could before we left the bounty hunters.'

'Cold pork.' Hanna was ferreting through her satchel. 'Some bread, cheese, that's about it.' She glanced at Rudi. 'How about you?'

'Some dried fruit.' He rummaged in his own pack. 'A flask of water. And that bottle of ale Theo had.'

'You took the ale?' Hanna stared at him in horror. 'You know what that means, don't you?'

'What?' Apprehension flared as he took in her alarmed expression.

'Bodun will track you to the ends of the earth.' Then her serious mein dissolved into laughter, which, after a moment, Fritz joined in with.

'That's not funny,' Rudi said, which only seemed to make his companions laugh all the more, and after a moment he found himself cackling just as hysterically as the others. All the tension and horror of the last few days seemed to fade with it, and once he recovered his breath he found he felt more relaxed than he could recall feeling since the whole thing had started in the woods outside Kohlstadt all those weeks before.

'I get it,' Fritz said, mumbling around a plug of bread and cheese. 'Dwarfs are very keen on their ale, right?'

'That's right,' Hanna said, taking a swig from the bottle. 'So we'd better get rid of it before he smells it on the wind.'

'Good idea,' Fritz agreed, gulping a couple of mouthfuls in turn and passing the bottle to Rudi. The drink was welcome, washing down the makeshift meal. He found himself savouring the late summer sunshine and the scent of the grass almost as though they were just on a sociable picnic instead of fleeing for their lives.

'Better get moving,' he said after a moment.

Hanna sighed reluctantly. 'I suppose so,' she agreed. While Fritz led the horse back to the shafts, she and Rudi collected their packs and returned to the cart. It was only as she slung her bundle up under the seat that something seemed to occur to her and she veered off towards the back.

'What are you doing?' Rudi asked.

'Don't you want to know what we've stolen?' she asked, tugging at the cords holding the sheet of canvas down.

'We haven't exactly stolen…' Rudi began, then trailed off as the realisation took root that this was precisely what they had done. The cart wasn't theirs and neither was whatever it contained. In the panic and confusion of their escape from the soldiers' camp he'd thought of it purely as a means of transport and hadn't spared a moment to consider the rightful owner or what it might be carrying.

Conscience fought briefly against pragmatism and lost. What was done was done, and any other course of action would have led to their deaths. Conscious that some vital but vaguely defined line had been crossed, he sighed and followed Hanna, curious to see what she'd found.

'Boots,' she said after a moment. 'It's full of boots.'

'Boots?' Rudi pulled the shroud back further, to find that the cart was indeed stuffed with boots identical to the ones on Fritz's feet.

The youth joined them and nodded. 'Standard issue,' he said. 'They gave me a pair when I joined up. Good ones too.'

'Maybe we could sell them,' Rudi suggested. 'They must be worth a few shillings at least. Maybe even a couple of crowns.'

'Maybe we could,' Hanna agreed, rummaging through the pile. 'If we had any left ones.'

In the end, they dumped them in a convenient hollow behind a clump of gorse in case any searchers spotted them from the road, and moved on. Conscious of a sense of disappointment among his companions, Rudi did his best to raise their spirits.

'Maybe it's a good thing,' he said after a while, as the road unwound itself beneath the wheels. 'We can rig the canvas over the back and sleep in there now. It should keep the rain off nicely.'

'I suppose so,' Hanna said.

Fritz glanced at him, then returned his attention to the highway ahead. 'Does it look like rain to you?'

Rudi nodded. 'It's clouding up,' he said. 'You can't see much now, but you will by nightfall.' The sun was still bright, but thin ribbons of dull grey cloud were visible to the north, hanging like smoke against the bright blue dome of the sky.

'Well, you're the nature boy,' he said.

To RUDI'S QUIET relief, his presentiment of rain was borne out just enough to impress the others with his knowledge of fieldcraft, a faint but persistent drizzle beginning shortly before dusk.

'Best start looking for somewhere to camp,' he said after a while.

'Good idea. I don't fancy trying to get set up when we can't see what we're doing.' Only a faint edge of bitterness to her voice betrayed her frustration at the loss of her ability to conjure a light from nothingness.

'We could try one of these side roads,' Fritz volunteered. They passed one every few miles, mostly leading off towards the river, where presumably small waterside hamlets nestled next to the wharves which sustained them. Rudi and Hanna exchanged uneasy glances. There was no telling where the *Reikmaiden* had put in after they'd parted company with her so abruptly, and the thought of running into Shenk and his crew again was a sobering one. 'There might be a tavern or something we could stay in.'

'Best save our money,' Rudi said, skirting the real reason for his reluctance. 'We've only got about seven shillings between us.' A thought occurred to him. 'Unless you've got something too?'

'Sorry.' Fritz shrugged resentfully. 'Even if I'd had some cash when I made a run for it, you'd have it yourself by now.' He glanced pointedly at Rudi's pack. According to the rules of the band of bounty hunters Rudi and Hanna had fallen in with, blithely unaware that the quarry they'd been tracking was another fugitive from Kohlstadt, their captive's possessions had belonged to whoever had brought him down.

'Seven shillings won't last long between the three of us,' Rudi said, sidestepping the issue with more tact than he was aware that he possessed. 'Especially in Marienburg.' He had only the sketchiest idea of what urban living entailed, but he suspected that it would be expensive. 'Best save as much as we can.'

'Fair enough.' Fritz shrugged again, although Rudi couldn't tell how much he was mollified, and returned his attention to the horse's rump ahead of him. 'Let me know when you see a spot you like.'

That was easier said than done. Both dusk and the rain were beginning to fall in earnest before Rudi pointed to a small copse off to one side of the road.

'Over there,' he said. 'If you think you can make it.'

'No problem.' The cart lurched as Fritz urged the horse away from the road, the wheels bumping awkwardly over the pitted moorland.

'Why there?' Hanna asked, peering from beneath the hood of the travelling cloak she'd donned as the weather got worse. 'Why not one of the others we've passed?'

'It's further back from the road,' Rudi said. 'Less chance of somebody seeing us if they pass. And the leaf canopy looks thicker. There should still be some dry wood there to get a fire going.'

'Sounds good to me,' Fritz said, with something approaching enthusiasm. As they neared the stand of trees and the going underfoot became more treacherous, he jumped down and began leading the horse. 'Will this do?'

'I think so.' Rudi clambered down as the wagon came to a halt in the lee of the copse. Out of the wind, the temperature seemed appreciably warmer and the rain less intense. 'Better find some kindling before the light goes.'

'Do it yourself.' Fritz began tending to the horse, releasing it from the shafts again. 'I'm busy.' He looked as though he'd be some time at the task, and Rudi fought down a surge of resentment. The older boy had a point, he supposed, the welfare of the animal was vital to them all, but he couldn't help feeling he'd lost the initiative.

'I'll do it.' Hanna swung herself down to stand at his side. 'If you're going to set some snares you haven't got much time before it gets dark.'

'Good point,' Rudi said, grateful for her support. Her suggestion was a sound one, a couple of rabbits would stretch their supplies long enough to keep them comfortably fed for another few days, and he wouldn't lose face by appearing to follow Fritz's lead. He began to move off in search of the rabbit runs he was sure would be there, but Hanna called him back.

'Aren't you forgetting something?' she asked, with a glance at his pack.

'What?' For a moment Rudi couldn't think what she meant, then realisation struck. He rummaged through it for his tinderbox and handed it over. Hanna took it quickly, then turned away, trying to hide her expression. She wasn't quite quick enough, and Rudi felt a pang of sympathy. The simple tool was a tangible reminder of the abilities that the witch hunter had so cruelly ripped away from her, and handling it must have gnawed at her like acid in her soul.

'Thank you.' Her voice was tight and sufficient warning for him not to say any more. Instead he shrugged and walked off in search of somewhere to lay his snares.

When he returned she'd managed to coax a small, smoky fire into life in the shelter of the largest tree she could find, which he regarded with a smile of approval, trying not to compare it with the brighter blazes she'd kindled by magic earlier in their travels. Fritz was hunkered down next to it, warming his hands at the flames.

'Shame we haven't got a stew pot,' he said.

'Shame we haven't got first class coach tickets as well,' Hanna said flatly.

'We've got better than that,' Rudi said, indicating the wagon. 'We've got transport and a dry place to sleep.' In his absence, one of his companions, Fritz, he

assumed, had rigged the sheet of canvas over the body
of the cart to make a comfortable shelter.

'I suppose so,' Hanna said, shrugging, and handing
him a chunk of bread and cheese and a mug of one of
her herbal infusions. Fritz sniffed suspiciously at the
steaming drink before sipping at it cautiously. A smile
began to spread across his face.

'That's good,' he said in tones of mild surprise.

'You're welcome.' A reciprocal smile flickered briefly
on Hanna's face and Rudi forced down a brief stab of
jealously. He'd grown used to the two of them depending on each other and Fritz's presence was already
changing the way they interacted. 'It should help relax
you and ease the stiffness in your muscles.'

'Help us sleep too, I should think,' Rudi said.

Hanna nodded. 'Not that I'll need any help with that
tonight.' By way of an answer, Rudi yawned widely.
None of them had slept since the night before last, and
in the interim they'd escaped the mercenaries, been
captured by Gerhard, eluded him and the beastmen
and travelled further than he'd ever thought possible
in a single day. He echoed her gesture.

'Best get turned in,' he said.

'I'm for that.' Fritz stretched and ambled across to
the wagon. Hanna had placed the bedrolls in it
already, her own to the left and Rudi's in the middle,
leaving Fritz to settle over to the right. He clambered
in, kicked his boots off and was snoring within
moments.

'Maybe I should stay on watch,' Rudi suggested. 'At
least for a while.'

'I don't see the point. You're too tired to stay awake
even if you tried.' As if to underline her words, another

yawn forced its way past his jaws. Rudi nodded, conceding the point.

'You're the healer,' he said.

'Yes. Yes, I am.' A new note of decisiveness entered her voice, a trace of the animation he was used to hearing there. 'And I don't need magic for that.'

'You're a good one, too,' Rudi went on, fanning the spark of renewed self-esteem he seemed to have kindled in her.

A faint smile appeared, twitching the corner of her mouth. 'I'm a competent apprentice really. But I can still learn.' Abruptly, the darkness was back in her eyes. 'That's something he can't take from me.'

'We still don't know that whatever he did is permanent,' Rudi ventured cautiously. 'That thing must come off somehow.'

'It'll need magic,' Hanna said flatly. 'There's a powerful ward embedded in it, I know that much. Every time I try to touch it, it's agonising.'

'It's mainly wax,' Rudi said, leaning closer to examine the thing as best he could by the flickering firelight. 'Perhaps if we soften it with an ember from the fire I can prise it off.'

'No!' A note of panic entered her voice. 'When you tried to touch it before it felt just as bad. If you start tampering with it you'll kill me, I just know it!'

'Then we'll just have to wait,' Rudi said, shocked at the terror in her voice. Moved by an instinct he barely understood, he put his arms around her, holding her close, half expecting her to pull away. To his surprise, however, she hugged him in return, moving deeper into the embrace. Unsure what to do next, he just waited, acutely aware of the warmth of her body and the pliant softness of it against his chest. Hanna laid her head on his shoulder, her hair tickling his neck. 'There must be a mage in Marienburg who can help.'

'Thank you.' Hanna pulled away from him after a moment, her voice trembling slightly. 'I really needed that.' A moment later, to his delighted astonishment, Rudi felt her lips brush against his cheek. 'I've never said it before, but I'm lucky to have a friend like you.'

'Me too,' Rudi said. 'Like you, I mean.' He hovered irresolute, wondering if he dared return the kiss, but before he could make up his mind, Hanna was turning away, heading for the shelter of the cart.

'Hurry up,' she said. 'You'll catch cold if you stay out here much longer.'

Rudi followed, barely aware that the rain was growing harder. He settled on the bedroll, nudging Fritz out of the way, and pillowed his head on his pack.

'Goodnight,' he said, listening to the pattering of the rain on the fabric overhead and blessing whichever deity it was who had provided the shelter just as the weather broke. Shallya he supposed, she was Hanna's patron, although he couldn't quite see why the goddess of healing and mercy would have killed so many soldiers just to help them. Maybe Magnus had been right when he said the gods help those who help themselves?

'Goodnight.' Hanna sighed, wriggled against him in a manner he found most distracting, and was asleep in moments. Conscious of the closeness of her body, which evoked distracting memories of the night they'd been forced to shed their clothes in order not to freeze to death after swimming to the bank of the Reik, and still feeling the ghost of her lips on his cheek, Rudi took a long time to fall asleep despite his exhaustion.

CHAPTER SIX

IT WAS LIGHT when Rudi finally woke and a grey, cheerless illumination filtered through low, leaden clouds. He turned over, finding himself alone in the wagon, and sat up abruptly, reaching for the hilt of his sword. A moment later, attracted by the noise, Hanna's face appeared around the edge of the tarpaulin.

'Morning,' she said.

'Morning.' Rudi yawned widely and swung his legs over the tailgate. His head felt fuzzy from having slept so long and so deeply, and he inhaled the familiar smell of damp earth and leaf mould gratefully. It reminded him of the woods he'd grown up in and a brief, unexpected pang of homesickness reared up in him. He forced it away. 'You should have woken me.'

'You needed the sleep.' Hanna grinned briefly, her own mood clearly improved by a few hours of rest. 'Healer's orders.'

'Then I wouldn't dream of arguing.' Rudi flushed, suddenly reminded of some dreams in which she'd featured prominently, and turned to the remains of the fire. It was smoking faintly and Fritz was crouching over it, blowing it back into life. 'Anything I can do?'

'You could see if we've got rabbit for breakfast,' Hanna suggested, tugging her headscarf a little further down on her forehead. She didn't wince as her hand neared the faint bulge near the centre, so Rudi assumed the talisman could somehow tell whether she intended touching it or not. A few wisps of blonde hair had escaped the scarf and she tucked them back with a gesture identical to the one her mother had constantly made. As she did so, Rudi was struck anew with the closeness of the resemblance between them.

'Right.' He walked off to check the snares he'd set, finding to his relief that Taal had evidently been listening to his request to fill them the evening before. When he returned to the camp he had three dead coneys swinging at his belt, and his head felt much clearer from the fresh air and exercise.

'You've done well,' Fritz said, in tones of grudging approval which reminded Rudi of his attempt to complement the older lad on his skill with the horse the previous evening. He nodded, appreciating the effort his erstwhile enemy was making to be cordial.

'I was lucky.' He approached the fire, which was now crackling cheerfully, and began cleaning the rabbits with the knife from his belt.

'He's just being modest,' Hanna said, taking the first skinned and gutted corpse to spit on a stick. 'He kept us well fed when we were crossing the wasteland together.' That was a bit of an exaggeration, but Rudi appreciated the compliment, feeling a smile spread across his face.

'You did your part too,' he pointed out, before remembering too late that much of what she'd accomplished had been by the covert use of her magical gifts. Seeing her face harden, he hurried on. 'All those edible plants you found.'

'Sounds like you had quite a good time of it,' Fritz said, 'all things considered.'

'It was an interesting experience,' Hanna said, but the conversational tone had left her voice, and Rudi cursed himself silently for reminding her once again of the harm Gerhard had done. Their talk for the rest of the meal remained desultory, concerned mainly with the prospects for the day's weather, which Rudi felt were less than encouraging, how much further Marienburg was, which nobody knew, and what they were likely to find when they got there. On this topic, at least, they all had opinions, although most of what they thought they knew had been gleaned at second or third hand from gossip and the few travellers who'd passed through Kohlstadt on their way to Dribruken and the scattering of hamlets beyond.

'They've got elves living there,' Fritz said. 'Imagine that. Real elves.' He seemed quite taken with the idea. 'It's the only place in the old world where they still live.'

'Apart from some of the forests,' Rudi replied. 'So people say.'

'You spent all your life in a forest,' Fritz pointed out. 'Did you ever see one?'

'Wrong forest,' Rudi said. 'They only live in the really big ones.'

'Maybe.' Fritz shrugged. 'But they're definitely in Marienburg.'

'I just hope Magnus is,' Rudi said. He'd told his companions he was hoping the merchant had survived the massacre in the forest and had fled to his home in the city to escape Gerhard, but had kept his real reasons for doing so to himself. Magnus knew who his parents had been, his adoptive father's dying words had told him so, but why the merchant had kept something like that a secret for so long continued to elude him.

'How will you find him?' Fritz asked. 'It's a big place.'

'I don't know.' Rudi shrugged. 'He's an important man, wealthy and influential. Someone must know where he lives.'

'He's important and wealthy in Kohlstadt,' Hanna said. 'That might not mean much in the city.'

'Well, we'll find out soon enough,' Rudi said, not wanting to pursue the subject any further.

'Maybe. At least we'll be safer from Gerhard there.'

'Will we?' Fritz looked doubtful. 'He doesn't seem like the kind to give up easily.'

'Marienburg's independent,' Hanna reminded him. 'They seceded from the Empire ages ago, remember? Imperial officials don't have any jurisdiction there, not even witch hunters.'

'He might not let that stop him,' Rudi said.

Hanna nodded. 'Probably not. But it ought to slow him down a bit. At least we'll see him coming next time.'

Rudi nodded too and hoped she was right.

BY THE TIME they were ready to move and Fritz had harnessed the horse, the weather had closed in again.

A light, pervasive drizzle enveloped everything, seeping through their clothing and shrinking the world around them as the horizon softened and blurred through the watery haze. After some discussion Fritz claimed the travelling cloak, which Hanna relinquished with clear misgivings, and sat bundled up in it on the driver's seat of the cart. Rudi and Hanna rode in the back, listening to the rain patter on the oiled canvas above them, their view of the road restricted to an oblong of receding carriageway. Today nothing passed them, the hard packed earth remaining unrutted by any wheels other than their own.

'Well, it could be worse,' Rudi ventured after a while. Hanna turned to look at him, but didn't bother to respond. Since they'd set off she'd just sat, propped up against one side of the cart, her chin on her knees, staring pensively into space. Encouraged, Rudi went on. 'We're dry and we're moving.'

'You're dry,' Fritz commented from the seat up front, his voice testy. 'I should have shown you both how to do this before the weather broke.'

'I managed all right before,' Rudi offered. He'd lived all his life outdoors and the rain was just a mild inconvenience to him. No doubt Fritz, the only urbanite among them, used to sheltering streets and indoor living, found it a great deal more onerous. 'I'll take a turn if you like.'

'Better not.' The acknowledgement was grudging, Fritz clearly tempted to take him up on his offer. 'The road's getting slippery. If we're to keep up the pace we need an experienced driver.'

'Later then,' Rudi said. 'When it clears.'

'Count on it,' Fritz said. Silence descended again, broken only by the creaking of the cart, the squeaking of its wheels, the pattering of the rain and the rhythmic plodding of the horse, which for some reason Fritz had christened Willem.

'We can't just keep calling him "horse", ' he said, when Hanna asked him why. 'And he looks like a Willem.' Rudi and Hanna had looked at each other, and from then on Willem it was.

Though the lowering clouds made it hard to estimate the time, Rudi was fairly sure it was only mid-morning when the cart began to slow. Taken by surprise, he poked his head out, balancing precariously on the lip of the tailboard to peer over the canvas at Fritz's back, narrowing his eyes against the persistent drizzle.

'Are we stopping already?' he asked.

'There's someone up ahead.' Fritz gestured with his free hand. Rudi hoisted himself a little higher, almost losing his balance as the cart lurched through a pothole. A solitary human figure was plodding along the road ahead of them, swathed in a cloak so spattered with mud it was hard to tell where the garment ended and the carriageway began. As the cart drew level, it started visibly and gestured with the staff it carried.

'Oh! Goodness me.' Watery blue eyes blinked behind spectacles, the first Rudi had ever seen, regarding the travellers with mild curiosity. 'I had no idea you were there. Quite lost in thought, I'm afraid.'

The voice was mild and conversational, although after his experiences with Gerhard, Rudi wasn't about to take that at face value.

The cloaked figure fell into step beside the wagon, still talking. 'Rather a foolhardy state of mind on the open road, you might think, and you'd be right. Bandits, orcs, goblins and beastmen, no telling what you might come across on a day like this. But then they say Shallya takes care of the foolish, and I suppose they must be right, because here I still am after all the wandering I've done.' The strange little man glanced up at Fritz as though expecting a response, then redirected his gaze to Rudi. 'But I'm forgetting my manners. Artemus van Loenhoek at your service.'

'I'm Rudi. That's Fritz.' If the stranger noticed his omission of their surnames he gave no sign of it.

'Delighted to meet you. Safety in numbers, they say, and in my experience they'd be right.'

'So what are you doing out here on your own?' Fritz asked bluntly.

The little man smiled ruefully. 'Alas, I fell out with my travelling companions. A trivial matter, about which I'd rather not speak, beyond mentioning that some people have inordinately suspicious natures where games of chance are concerned, particularly when rash wagers are made in the heat of the moment.'

'They thought you were cheating?' Fritz asked.

Artemus looked hurt. 'Most certainly not, although I'd wager a crown or two that somebody was. The run of cards was quite against me, and despite my word of honour, no one seemed inclined to trust my note of credit, so we parted company. Somewhat acrimoniously, I might add. Harsh words were spoken, which I hope on sober reflection might be regretted.'

'Herr von Leyenhook…' Rudi began, trying to stem the apparently endless torrent of words, but the effort was futile. The muddy traveller raised his hand reprovingly.

'Van Loenhoek, young man. I have the inestimable honour to be a citizen of the free city of Marienburg rather than your admirable Empire, through which I have been a most fascinated wanderer for many years past, and never have been nor ever will be von anything. But your manners, it must be said, do you credit.'

'Oh,' Rudi said, whatever he'd been about to say fleeing from his brain.

'We're heading for Marienburg ourselves,' Fritz volunteered, with the open candour of the feeble minded.

'Then we are well met indeed.' Artemus swung himself aboard the cart without seeming to break stride, seating himself firmly beside the heavyset youth. 'For my part I seem to have acquired a pair of most fascinating travelling companions, not to mention relief for my aching feet, while you, I feel sure, have many questions about the great city I have the privilege to call home.'

'How do you know we haven't been there before?' Rudi asked, trying to regain some of the initiative.

Artemus laughed good-naturedly. 'Had you done so, you would hardly have mispronounced my name so egregiously. If I read you right, and I seldom read anybody wrong if I may say so without sounding both presumptuous and egotistical, you are a pair of young men for whom the drudgery of rural living has begun to pall. And why not? You're young, the world is there for the taking and the path to your destiny must surely begin in Marienburg. For there the whole world comes. Am I right?'

'Up to a point,' Rudi said. 'For one thing, I have a friend there I need to see. And for another, there's three of us.' He urged Hanna up beside him, which, after a moment of glaring, she consented to do. 'This is Hanna.'

'Charmed.' Artemus nodded courteously to the girl. 'Artemus van...'

'I heard your name.' Hanna ducked back under the tarpaulin.

'Then I feel honoured to have it known by such a strong minded young woman. You say what you think, plain and simple, which is an admirable trait indeed. Far too many folk these days simply prattle on without thought, or a moment's consideration as to whether their conversation is actually welcome. Garrulousness, they say, is the sign of a feeble mind, although there are some philosophers of a contrary view. Most of them, however, are so tedious to read they all but undermine their own case.'

Rudi followed Hanna back beneath the tarpaulin, bracing himself for a furious diatribe. She was back in her original place, braced against the side of the cart, hugging her knees. She seemed to be trembling violently and Rudi quailed, anticipating the eruption of her temper. Then she raised her face, stuffing her fist into her mouth, and he breathed a sigh of relief. She was shaking with silent laughter.

DESPITE RUDI'S INITIAL misgivings, their unexpected companion turned out to be a considerable help to them. For one thing, he could drive a cart at least as well as Fritz, which meant they made far better time than he'd dared to hope, and for another he was a fascinating raconteur. Artemus had been away from the city of his birth for many years and had tales of places the trio of fugitives from Kohlstadt had barely heard of. He'd trodden the ramparts of Middenheim, seen the legendary Detlef Sierk performing his own plays in Altdorf and discussed philosophy with the learned men of Nuln. But nothing he'd seen, he swore, could hold a penny candle to the splendours of Marienburg.

'But how do you make a living?' Rudi asked when they camped together for the night.

Artemus spread his hands. 'However I can,' he said with a smile. 'I've turned my hand to a lot over the years. But mainly as a scribe. There's always someone needing a document read, or a letter written, or a book copied.'

'I thought they used some kind of machine for that,' Hanna said. 'So they can print dozens at a time.'

'Hundreds,' Artemus said. 'But not all books are for wide dissemination.' Hanna nodded, almost imperceptibly, but if the scribe noticed he made no sign of the fact that Rudi could see.

'So tell us about Marienburg,' he said.

'Now there's a subject I never get tired of.' He paused, to wipe a smear of grease from his chin. 'Excellent rabbit, by the way.'

'You're welcome,' Rudi said. 'Now about Marienburg...'

'How to describe the greatest city in the world?' Artemus looked at a loss for a moment. 'What do you want to know?'

'I want to know how to find my friend when I get there,' Rudi said. 'If it's as big as you say that might be a problem.'

'There are no problems in Marienburg which can't be solved,' Artemus assured him. He dipped his head and made a curious sign with his hand not unlike the grasping of a coin. 'Hendryk willing, of course.'

'Of course.' Rudi nodded, recognising the name of the god of commerce and merchants after a moment's thought. Magnus had mentioned that he was the patron deity of Marienburg, so he supposed it wasn't too surprising that the natives of that city would swear by him.

'How?' Hanna asked.

Artemus smiled. 'Ah. Now that's something you really need to know. First of all, information is a commodity, like anything else. Whatever you want to know, somebody already does, you can count on that. It's simply a matter of finding out who and coming to a suitable arrangement.'

'You mean pay for it,' Rudi said.

Artemus nodded. 'You can do, that's usually the simplest way. Certainly the least complicated.'

'What if you can't afford to?' Hanna asked. 'Or you don't want to attract attention?'

'There are ways,' Artemus assured her. A note of warning entered his voice. 'But be very careful about starting down that canal, if you catch my meaning.'

'I think I do,' Hanna said.

Rudi nodded too. 'We can take care of ourselves,' he said.

'I'm sure you can.' Artemus ladled another portion of stew from the cooking pot, which he'd produced from

his pack to Fritz's unconcealed delight, but sounded
unconvinced. Rudi began to wonder if perhaps the city
was not such a good idea after all, but forced the
thought away. He'd fought beastmen and a witch
hunter, and he doubted there was anything in Marienburg quite as dangerous as either.

'Is it true there are elves there?' Fritz asked. Artemus
nodded, apparently relieved to be back on safer
ground.

'Indeed there are, my young friend. Hundreds of
them, walking the streets and sailing the canals as
openly as you or I. Most of them stick to their own
quarter, but then so do the other folk by and large, so
you can hardly fault them for that. My goodness, the
splendour of the architecture there must be seen to be
believed, and you really must take a stroll in the gardens of the Grand Circle canal at the earliest
opportunity.' He paused to smile at Rudi and Hanna.
'It's a favourite spot for the young and romantic. I
spent many happy hours there in my younger days you
can be sure.' Rudi felt himself flushing, and felt sure
that somehow Hanna had seen and was amused by it.

Nevertheless, despite Artemus's habit of digressing
into half-completed anecdotes about his youth and
the people he'd known in it, by the end of the evening
Rudi felt he had a much better idea of the size and
complexity of the city than he'd ever had before. The
names of districts and wards, places and notables,
swirled around his head in a confused jumble, but he
was sure he'd be able to make sense of them once they
arrived.

'I had no idea it was so big,' Fritz said, awestruck.
'Imagine, over a hundred and thirty thousand people.'

The figure was so huge as to be incomprehensible, almost a thousand times the population of the village he'd grown up in, and he kept repeating it as though it would somehow make sense this time.

'You won't have to imagine it for long,' Artemus assured him. 'Only another few days and we'll be there.'

CHAPTER SEVEN

THE NEXT DAY dawned just as overcast as before. Mindful of his promise the previous morning, Rudi offered to take a turn behind the reins and let Fritz ride in comfort in the back of the wagon, but to his surprise the youth demurred.

'We'll make better time if Artemus and I take turns,' he said, climbing up onto the driving seat with far less visible effort than he had before. Clearly Hanna's poultices and herbal infusions were having the effect on him she'd hoped; the bruising across his face had faded almost to invisibility, and his injured arm moved as freely as the other one now.

'That certainly seems the most pragmatic course of action,' the scribe agreed, clambering up beside him with remarkable agility. Under the hood of his travelling cloak his hair had proved to be flecked with white, and Rudi had been surprised to discover how old he was. Fritz nodded and picked up the reins, no doubt eager to hear more of the man's wanderings and the remarkable city he called home.

Well, so far as Rudi was concerned, he was welcome to them. Artemus was an amiable companion, he couldn't deny that, but his exuberance and volubility could be wearing. Besides, while Artemus was blathering about elves, he could talk to Hanna without risk of their new friend overhearing.

'It sounds as though we'll be able to find someone to help you when we get to the city,' he said quietly. Hanna nodded. Among the torrent of information Artemus had poured out the previous night was the revelation that sorcerers were less rigidly controlled in Marienburg than in the Empire. Mages could be found, in the right places and for the right price, to carry out any kind of enchantment desired.

'Let's hope so,' she said. Her face seemed drawn in the deep shadows under the makeshift canopy, and she massaged her temples in a gesture that was becoming habitual. 'I don't know how long I can go on like this.'

'Is it getting worse?' Rudi asked, moving closer to her.

'A little, I think. And I keep having these dreams...' She looked up, fixing him with a gaze so intent it was almost a physical blow. 'Rudi, I'm afraid something terrible's going to happen.'

'It's not,' Rudi said decisively. 'We won't let it.' He ventured a tentative hug, which she didn't respond to in any way, and after a moment he let go with a feeling of vague disappointment. Any reply she might have made was forestalled by a sudden lurch as the cart slowed abruptly.

'What's going on?' he asked.

'Stay quiet,' Fritz said. 'There are people on the road. Spreading out across it. They look armed.'

'Gerhard?' Hanna breathed. 'How could he have got ahead of us?'

'I don't think so.' Rudi shook his head. 'Fritz would have recognised him.'

'I'll do the talking, if you'll permit the liberty,' Artemus said, apparently unaware of the brief, whispered exchange behind him. 'I've had experience of ruffians of this sort. They're none too bright and we may well escape unmolested, albeit a little lighter in the purse if I fail to convince them.'

'Go right ahead,' Rudi murmured, loosening the sword in his scabbard.

Hanna looked at him in horror. 'You can't be intending to fight them?' she whispered.

'I'd rather not. But I'm going to be ready if I have to.' Rudi picked up the bow and nocked an arrow, tensing the string ready to draw and loose the instant he had a target. For a moment he worried that the new found expertise with the weapon he'd discovered shortly before losing the one he'd left home with would desert him again, then forced the thought away irritably.

'Me too.' Hanna drew the knife from her belt and held it ready with a confidence which surprised him for a moment before he remembered Bruno offering to teach her some knife fighting techniques while they'd been travelling with the bounty hunters. She'd obviously been a fast learner.

'Good morning,' Artemus said, a little too loudly, evidently intending his voice to carry. A couple of throaty chuckles answered him, as the cart came to a halt. 'Although the weather is somewhat inclement, I'm forced to admit. Hardly a day to be abroad, I would have thought, if you could avoid it.'

'Honest men have to work whatever the weather,' a gruff voice replied, amid a ground swell of further laughter. Rudi thought it sounded as though there were three or four men out there at least. 'What's in the back?'

'What's it to you?' Fritz snapped, provoking further laughter, which Artemus overrode with more good-humoured banter.

'You'll have to excuse my young friend. It's been a long damp journey, and he's impatient to find a fire and a mug of ale.'

'Aren't we all?' a new voice cut in, before being hushed by the first voice to have spoken. Their leader, Rudi supposed. 'Then we'll make it quick. Pay the toll and you'll be on your way before you know it.'

'I see.' Artemus was plainly unsurprised. 'And that would be how much?'

'That depends.' All trace of pretended good humour left the man's voice. 'How much have you got?'

'Very little, alas.' Artemus sighed audibly. 'You know what they say, lucky at cards, unlucky in love? Unfortunately I appear equally ill-starred in both spheres. What little worldly wealth I once possessed is now several leagues distant, in the purse of a soldier of fortune named Ruffio Manzinni. Unless he's squandered it already on ale and whores, which I most certainly would have done in his position.'

'I see.' The leader was clearly unconvinced. His voice hardened. 'Get down, both of you.'

'If you insist.' Artemus sighed loudly. 'Your arm, young man, if you'd be so kind. I'm not as young as I was and my bones are stiff.' He broke off abruptly, with the sound of a loud impact against the road and a bellow of raucous laughter. When he spoke again he sounded winded. 'Much obliged.'

'Karl, Hubert, see what's in the back.' The leader's voice was businesslike again. 'We can get thirty guilders for the nag at least.'

'You leave Willem alone!' Fritz shouted, before the sound of a blow silenced him. Rudi and Hanna exchanged glances. There seemed no alternative but to fight. Rudi drew back the bow, hissing in frustration as Hanna moved in front of him, blocking the shot.

'It's a girl, Chief!' A head appeared beyond her, a grimy face surrounded by lank, greasy hair. 'Looks like our lucky day.' The expression of gleeful malice changed abruptly as Hanna dropped, revealing Rudi and the fully drawn bow behind her. 'It's...'

He never completed the sentence, as the arrow took him clean in the chest. He went down screaming, blood beginning to seep from his mouth. His companion, Karl or Hubert, Rudi never found out which, tried to vault into the cart and tackle the young forester before he could reload. Realising he wouldn't make it in time, Rudi let the bow drop and reached for his sword, but before he could clear the scabbard the bandit fell back, gurgling, the hilt of Hanna's knife protruding from his throat. She'd clearly been an apt pupil of Bruno's knife-throwing tricks.

'Come on!' Her face suffused with the same vindictive expression he'd last seen when she contemplated stabbing Gerhard, she dived past him and out of the cart, plucking her blade from the neck of the fallen bandit as she went. Rudi followed, drawing the sword.

Outside was a scene of complete confusion. Fritz was grappling with a fellow of similar build to himself, intent on preventing him from unharnessing the horse. As Rudi watched, he sent the bandit reeling with a head-butt and piled in with a flurry of blows to the torso as the fellow tried to disengage. Artemus was leaning casually against the front wheel of the cart, an expression of mild interest on his countenance. Three armed men were running towards Rudi and Hanna, swords in their hands and murder on their faces. The one in the centre was probably their leader, as his clothing was a little more ornate, and the other two hung back a pace behind him.

'Oh dear. Pardon me, how clumsy.' Artemus tripped the man nearest him with an outstretched foot, reached out a hand as if to steady him, and swung him into the solid wood of the side of the wagon with a loud crack. The man staggered and folded. Remembering the lessons Theo had taught him, Rudi stepped into the gap left in the line before either of the other two could react and aimed a cut at the leader's suddenly exposed flank. The bandit parried hastily, deflecting Rudi's blade down and away, and Rudi kicked out at the back of his knee, bringing him down. For a second, he considered stabbing down with the point of his sword, finishing the ruffian with a blade through the chest, but the remaining bandit forestalled him by aiming a vicious cut at his head.

Rudi ducked, made a counterstrike at the man's torso and watched with satisfaction as the tip of the blade sliced through cloth to leave a red mark along the exposed skin. If his opponent hadn't jumped back at the last possible minute he would have killed him for sure. The same sense of vindictive satisfaction he'd felt before when he fought Fritz in the forest rose up in him, time seeming to slow as his reactions grew sharper than he'd ever thought possible. The man he'd downed cut at his ankle and he leaped over the sweeping blade, driving the heel of his boot into the bandit captain's groin. The man howled and curled into a foetal position, dropping his sword.

'Nice move.' Fritz punched his opponent hard in the face and turned to seize the man Artemus had tripped by the scruff of the neck, hoisting him upright. The ruffian swayed on his feet, glassy eyed, making no attempt to defend himself, and Fritz slammed the two men's heads together. They dropped to the ground.

'Get out of here!' Hanna's voice was charged with the power building inside her. She might not be able to channel it now, but under the impetus of fear and anger it was welling up uncontrollably. A sudden burst of wind ruffled her hair, and a trickle of blood began to run from her nose. 'While you still can!' Then she clasped her temples, screamed in agony and slumped to the roadway.

'Hanna!' Enraged beyond measure, Rudi drove hard at the bandit he was engaging, parrying every attack the man made with a speed and efficiency which astonished him. Blind panic was evident on the fellow's face now, which turned to one of pain and surprise as Rudi finally found an opening and thrust his blade deep into his chest. The man screamed and fell, almost wrenching the sword out of Rudi's hand as he did so. The steel came free of the wound with a moist sucking sound.

'Run for it!' The bandit's captain was back on his feet now and began to stagger down the road as fast as he could. The two Fritz had downed crawled after him, regaining their feet after several attempts.

'They're getting away!' Fritz shouted, clearly on the verge of following. Artemus forestalled him with a hand to the shoulder.

'Let them. They'll think twice about resorting to banditry again, I shouldn't wonder. And unless I miss my guess, your friends need our help.'

He was right about that. Rudi came back to himself slowly, the magnitude of what he'd done just beginning to sink in. The man he'd stabbed twitched at his feet for a moment, gurgled and went limp, his fate now clearly in the hands of Morr.

'Rudi?' Fritz sounded uncharacteristically hesitant. 'Are you all right?'

'Yeah. Course I am.' Rudi wiped the sword blade clean of blood, his breath coming in short, sharp gasps. His hands were trembling and it took him several tries to restore it to the scabbard. 'Why wouldn't I be?'

'You just killed three men.' The note of awe was clear in the simpleton's voice. 'And you're not even scratched.' He gestured towards the rear of the wagon, where two more bodies lay inert in the roadway.

'Two.' Rudi turned, slowly coming to terms with the fact that he'd taken human lives. It ought to change things in some way, deeply and fundamentally, but he didn't feel any different. He was still Rudi Walder and he'd done what he'd had to do to defend himself and his friends, that was all. Somehow he couldn't see the bandits being conscience stricken if he'd been the one left lying in the mud. 'Hanna got one of them.'

The mention of her name was enough to start his mind working again and he turned, looking for the girl. She was stretched out on the roadway, her face white, barely breathing.

'She fainted,' Artemus said, kneeling next to her. 'The excitement must have been too much.' The blue eyes behind the spectacles blinked mildly, clearly not believing his own explanation, but offering it nevertheless.

Rudi nodded gratefully. 'Must have been,' he agreed.

'We'd better get her under cover,' Fritz said, bending down to lift the unconscious girl as if she were no heavier than a child. Rudi felt a pang of mingled jealousy and alarm, but let the youth carry her to the wagon and stretch her out on her bedroll. He couldn't do everything, after all.

'Shall we take the bodies?' Artemus asked. 'Chances are there's a bounty out on these fellows and we might be able to claim it somewhere around here.'

Rudi shook his head. 'I don't want to be paid for killing,' he said.

Artemus nodded wisely. 'I take your point,' he said. 'Besides, all that bureaucracy, the form filling and what have you, probably far more trouble than it's worth.' He bent to examine the nearest body. 'Still, they might keep us fed for another day or two.'

'They might,' Rudi said, pulling the man's purse from his belt. None of the men had much of value apart from their money, but he collected their weapons too, and one of them had a pair of boots which seemed about his size so he stripped them off before dumping the corpse at the side of the road. They'd clearly been stolen from some other traveller, as they were of far higher quality than the rest of the man's garments and an intricate decorative pattern had been worked into the leather.

'Better get moving,' Fritz called from the driver's seat. Shaking himself free of the morbid thoughts which were beginning to gather around him Rudi hurried back to the cart.

'How ARE YOU feeling?' Rudi asked. Hanna stirred, pulled herself upright, and sat supported by the side of the wagon. By unspoken consent Fritz and Artemus had resumed their places on the driving seat, leaving Rudi to tend to her as best he could in the back, although that had amounted to little more than letting her sleep and hoping for the best. As her eyes flickered open he proffered a little water from the bottle in his pack and she swallowed it gratefully.

'I've had better days,' she admitted. She raised a hand to her head and winced. 'Ouch.' She wiped the back of the other hand across her face and stared bemusedly at the smear of blood left on it. 'Oh.'

'It's not as bad as it looks,' Rudi assured her hastily, dampening a scrap of rag and passing it across. Hanna cleaned her face with it, then lay back with the strip of cloth across her eyes.

'It feels a lot worse. Trust me.'

'What happened?' Rudi asked. 'Artemus thinks you fainted. At least that's what he says he thinks…'

'Then we'll stick to that.' Hanna sighed. 'I could feel the power welling up inside me, the way it did when the skaven attacked us. But I couldn't control it, or direct it, and there was nowhere for it to go. So it just…' Words failed her. After a moment she went on. 'It felt like it was eating me alive, from the inside out.' A note of panic entered her voice. 'We have to get this thing off me. It'll kill me if we don't.'

'We will,' Rudi said, as reassuringly as he could. 'There must be someone in Marienburg who can help.'

'So you said.' She sounded unconvinced. After a moment she hauled herself upright, removed the bandage from her eyes, and began rummaging in her satchel.

'What are you looking for?' Rudi asked.

'Anything that'll help.' After a moment she found something that looked suspiciously like the manbane she'd given to Fritz and chewed it vigorously. Despite Rudi's concern, it seemed to help and she sat back looking a great deal more relaxed, the lines of pain and tension fading from her face. 'That's better.'

'Good.' Rudi passed her the water again and the girl drank deeply. 'Something to eat?'

'No. Not yet.' She tried to smile, but the effort was too much. 'The way I feel now it would just come straight back up again anyway.'

'Perhaps when we stop for the night,' Rudi said.

'Perhaps.' Something seemed to occur to her for the first time. 'What happened to the bandits, anyway?'

'Ran away.' Rudi shrugged, uncomfortable about the direction the conversation was taking. 'Some of them at least.'

'What about the rest?' Hanna asked, foreknowledge of the answer already in the tone of her voice.

'We killed them,' Rudi said, feeling a cold space in the middle of his stomach as he articulated the words. Everything he'd tried not to think about, or rationalise away, rose up in his memory, vivid as if he was experiencing it for the first time. Even more so if that were possible, as details he hadn't noticed at the time replayed themselves in his head: the expression of astonishment on the face of the man he'd shot and the way the blood had spread across the front of his tunic as he fell backwards. The way the light had faded from the eyes of the bandit he'd stabbed.

'When you say "we",' Hanna said slowly, 'you mean...'

'The two of us,' Rudi said hollowly. 'I killed two. You stabbed another one in the throat.'

'I remember that.' Hanna nodded, as though it was of little consequence. 'I didn't know I could throw that well.'

'Is that all you can say?' Rudi asked and the girl looked surprised.

'You know what they were going to do to me. Serve the bastard right, and the one you got too. I hope they're screaming in hell now.' She shrugged. 'They were no better than the skaven. Worse, if you ask me. At least the rat things weren't preying on their own kind.'

'I suppose not,' Rudi said. Hanna grinned, and pointed to the small bundle of possessions in the corner of the cart.

'Picking up habits from Theo I see.'

'They don't need it any more,' Rudi said, determined to match her apparent detachment. 'Or their purses.'

'Exactly.' Hanna leaned forwards, an incongruous expression of eager expectation on her face. 'So, how much did we get?'

CHAPTER EIGHT

THEY DIVIDED THE spoils evenly when they made camp for the night, following the example Rudi and Hanna had learned from Krieger's company. It seemed the fairest way, since all of them had taken part in the fight with the bandits, even though Rudi felt Artemus had been more of a bystander for most of it. The scribe seemed pleasantly surprised by his generosity.

'Most kind,' he said, nodding and smiling. 'Equal shares all round is by far the soundest principle, I've found, but you could well have argued that I wasn't a real part of your company. After all, we've known each other little more than a day, and though that has been more than sufficient for me to form a good opinion of your characters you might well continue to harbour reservations about mine.'

'I don't know about that,' Rudi said. 'But you fought beside us and that's what counts.' He divided the contents of the bandits' purses as evenly as he could, astonished to find several gold coins, the first he'd ever seen, among them. 'Which means you get two crowns, eight shillings and four pence ha'penny, the same as the rest of us.'

'Eight crowns,' Hanna said, awestruck. 'We're rich.'

'Hardly rich,' Artemus said. 'But we have enough for passable lodging, for a while at least.'

'I hate to break it to you,' Fritz said gloomily, 'but we've only got three crowns. These others are forgeries.' He held up one of the coins from his own share, pointing out the mermaid embossed on the front where the emperor's head should have been. 'Unless Karl Franz has suddenly sprouted a tail and a pair of...'

'They're Marienburg guilders,' Artemus said. 'Worth exactly the same as an Imperial crown.' A wide grin stretched across Fritz's face. 'Which won't prevent a lot of helpful people offering to change your Imperial currency to guilders as soon as you reach the city, for a modest commission. I suggest if they do that you politely decline.'

'I'll do that all right,' Fritz said.

THE REST OF the journey was surprisingly uneventful, despite Rudi's constant apprehension about running into more bandits, or Gerhard suddenly appearing in pursuit. The only traffic they saw was as harmless and nondescript as the other travellers they'd encountered before, although it seemed to be increasing in volume and frequency as the city grew closer. Several times they passed or were passed by merchants and traders, their wagonloads of goods guarded by armed men, and riders on horseback becoming increasingly common.

At length, the road met another, which looked almost identical to Rudi, who was sitting on the driver's seat between Artemus and Fritz. Since their encounter with the bandits, he'd taken to riding up front more frequently, his bow close at hand, leaving Hanna to rest undisturbed in the back. Artemus sighed happily and pointed to a milestone set back from the carriageway.

'The Gisoreux road, highway to Bretonnia.' He gestured to the right. 'And Marienburg lies that way. Tomorrow we reach our destination.'

'Good.' Rudi nodded and gestured to the westering sun. The weather had improved again over the last couple of days and the afternoon had been bright, but chilly in the wind. 'We'll need to find somewhere to camp soon.'

'Camp? Nonsense.' Artemus seemed in fine spirits, no doubt at the prospect of seeing his home again the next day. 'I have gold in my purse, and if I remember correctly there's a charming rural tavern not far from here. I insist on repaying your generosity with a little of my own. A warm bed, a hot meal and far from least, hot water to wash in!'

'I don't know...' Rudi began, mindful of their unfortunate experience at the Jolly Friar the night they'd met Krieger and his band. Inns seemed like trouble to him, especially if they wanted to avoid attracting attention. 'Perhaps we should save our money for later...'

'Later we might be dead,' Fritz said, sparking a good-natured laugh from Artemus. Hanna poked her head out from under the tarpaulin and caught Rudi's eye. She'd recovered slowly from the effects of the seizure she'd had, but seemed almost her old self again now.

'Hot water,' she said wistfully.

Rudi sighed. 'All right,' he said at last. 'I know when I'm outvoted.'

'Good lad.' Artemus flicked the reins, getting Willem moving again, and the horse began plodding in the direction of Marienburg. As the evening wore, on the unvarying desolation Rudi had grown used to on either side of the road began to change, isolated pockets of habitation beginning to appear around them. For the most part these were unimpressive enough, being little more than patches of tilled earth walled off from the highway, but now and again a shack or a more substantial cottage would appear, smoke rising from the chimney.

'Have we reached the outskirts already?' he asked, and the scribe laughed.

'Goodness me no, we've another day's travelling yet. But there are a few hamlets and villages scattered around the wasteland, and if memory serves we pass through one before long.' Rudi nodded, reminded of the occasional clusters of habitation, too small to be considered villages in their own right, along the road to Dreibrucken. He'd passed through a couple running his messages for Magnus, back when the narrow valley containing Kohlstadt and its surroundings had been his entire world, and he knew what to expect: a handful of houses, three or four perhaps and possibly a farm nearby where the inhabitants worked.

His guess proved accurate. As dusk fell the unmistakable outline of a small group of buildings began to appear through the murk, so familiar in appearance that had it not been for the wide road skirting them he might almost have fancied himself home again. Only one thing stood out as unfamiliar, a long, low building, which might have been a barn had it not been for the number of windows along its length and the large, fenced-off yard surrounding the place. Artemus beamed.

'Just as I remembered,' he said.

'That's an inn?' Fritz asked, disbelief colouring his voice. Rudi had described the Jolly Friar to him and he was clearly expecting something a little more elaborate.

The scribe nodded. 'Most assuredly so. Not up to the standard of a coaching inn, I'll grant you, but welcome enough.' Rudi nodded. Clearly whoever lived here had realised they could make more from the travellers passing their door than from scrabbling in the fields and had converted one of the outbuildings for the purpose. 'The beds will be soft enough and the food good, I can vouch for that.'

'You've stayed here before?' Rudi asked, and the scribe nodded.

'Some years ago, it's true, but it doesn't seem to have changed much.' He steered the horse off the road, through a wooden gate which seemed to be propped permanently open judging by the way it sagged on its hinges, and drew up outside the building. A stable stood off to one side and a lad of about Rudi's age hurried across to them.

'Take care of your horse, sir?'

Fritz scowled at him. 'You'd better,' he said.

Rudi shook his head. The last thing they needed was Fritz reverting to type and antagonising everybody. He dug a couple of pennies out of his purse, reflecting wryly that once he would have considered that a small fortune, and handed them to the lad.

'My friend's rather fond of it,' he explained.

'Don't you worry, sir.' The stable boy grinned widely, as though they were the best customers he'd had all year, and began unfastening the traces with skill and care enough to mollify the muscular simpleton. 'He'll get the best care in the wasteland.'

'I'm sure he will.' Artemus jumped down from the seat with surprising athleticism for a man of his years and raised a hand to help Hanna down from the bed of the cart. Rudi and Fritz retrieved their packs, the bedrolls and the small bundle of possessions they'd taken from the dead bandits. Fighting a strange sense of déjà vu, Rudi followed his companions into the inn.

His first impression had been right. The building had clearly once been a barn, the roof timbers arching overhead so far above him that he had to tilt his head back to look at them properly. The wide space had been broken up with tables and benches, not unlike the ones he'd seen in the Jolly Friar, but all much older and showing signs of hard wear. A rickety staircase at one end of the cavernous hall gave way onto a mezzanine floor, probably once the hayloft, which had been partitioned off into a number of rooms, no doubt where the customers slept.

The biggest surprise was that the place was almost deserted. A handful of folk at a couple of the tables glanced up as they entered, then returned to their conversations, clearly uninterested. By their clothes, Rudi gathered that they were local farm workers rather than travellers like themselves.

'It's a bit quiet,' he said. The thought disturbed him; he'd been counting on the anonymity they would have had as part of a crowd.

'It'll liven up later, young sir, no doubt about that.' A middle-aged woman looked up from behind a bar counter made from a plank of timber balanced on a couple of upended barrels and smiled a professional welcome at him. 'Once the sun goes down, no one with any sense passes the Drayman's Rest.'

'I don't doubt it,' Artemus said, dropping a gold coin and a scattering of silver on the counter. The woman's smile became wider and more genuine. 'I have very pleasant memories of a previous night's lodging in your establishment and I'm sure I'll leave tomorrow with them freshly burnished. We'd like two rooms, one for the young lady and one for the rest of us.' He paused and glanced at the others. 'Unless of course you'd like some privacy too?'

'No, that would be fine,' Rudi said, conscious that Artemus had already spent more than half the money he'd handed to him that afternoon. He could afford a room of his own, of course, but a small voice of caution urged him to keep his purse untouched for as long as possible.

Fritz nodded too. 'Fine by me,' he said. Artemus looked faintly relieved. 'We'd like to clean up a little too,' he said, and the woman nodded.

'That won't be a problem. I'll get the kitchen heating the water now. Would you care for something to eat while you're waiting?'

'We certainly would,' Fritz said, with an enthusiasm which amused everybody.

'There's enough here to take care of that too,' the landlady assured them, scooping up the coins and plucking a quartet of tankards from a shelf behind her. 'And no doubt you'll be wanting something to wash it down?' She drew four mugs of ale from the barrel next to them and placed them on the counter. 'Any table you like.'

Rudi picked one in the corner, which looked as though it might be relatively quiet when the tavern got fuller, and sat where he could keep an eye on the door. A part of him was mildly surprised that he was beginning to take such precautions instinctively now, but he supposed it was no bad thing. The world, he was discovering, was a far more dangerous place than it had first appeared and it only made sense to be cautious.

The food, when it arrived, was simple but well prepared and everyone dived into it with enthusiasm. Fritz and Artemus called for more ale, but Rudi and Hanna drank a little more cautiously, each recalling the aftermath of their night of overindulgence with Krieger and his friends. Nevertheless they were both beginning to relax, feeling warm, full and comfortable, when the door banged open to admit a trio of men whose dress marked them out as carters. In the last few days Rudi had begun to be able to distinguish the different types of people they'd been passing, with a little help from Artemus. Their clothes were too well made for them to be peasants and protected by linen aprons, while one was carrying a cart driver's whip. He didn't take much notice of them at first, as, true to the landlady's promise, the tavern had filled steadily with passing travellers as the evening wore on.

'Evening, Beatrice.' The man with the whip greeted the landlady in the relaxed manner of a regular customer and picked up the ale she'd drawn for him without being asked. 'Got a room for us tonight?'

'I can always find you a bed, Norbert.' The joke was evidently an old one, because everyone laughed and began chatting as though they were picking up a conversation they'd abandoned shortly before.

Norbert looked round the taproom, frowning in bemusement. 'Where's Bardold?'

'Haven't seen him in two, three weeks now. Been hauling supplies for the Imperial army up by Gutter's Wharf.' She shrugged. 'Seemed a long way to go to me, but the pay was good and he's got family there, so he jumped at it.'

Norbert's expression of puzzlement increased. 'His horse is in the stable and his cart's outside. Are you sure he hasn't been in?'

The landlady shook her head. 'The only folks with a horse and cart are the ones over there.' She gestured to Rudi and his companions, and Rudi felt a chill run down his spine. 'You must have been mistaken.'

'I sold him that horse myself,' Norbert said. 'I'd know it like my own. And it's his cart all right, you can see where that plank was replaced last autumn.' He began to pick his way through the crowd towards them.

Rudi nudged Fritz under the table. 'I think we're in trouble,' he murmured.

Fritz nodded and balled his fists. 'Not for long,' he said. Artemus and Hanna exchanged worried glances.

'Is that your horse and cart outside?' Norbert asked, leaning over the table. His arms were heavily muscled and he held the whip in a casual manner which didn't fool Rudi for a moment. His companions were a pace or two behind him, hanging back for the moment with elaborately feigned disinterest. As the other customers noticed the incipient entertainment, the murmur of background conversation died away and attention became focussed on the table in the corner.

So much for keeping a low profile, Rudi thought ruefully, trying desperately to come up with an answer which would pacify the man.

'Not as such, no.' Artemus moved along the bench, making room for Norbert to sit down, and gestured for him to join them. Taken aback, the man hesitated. Whatever response he'd been anticipating, this clearly wasn't it. 'It's a fascinating story and one well worth hearing over an ale or two if you have the time.' He gestured to the landlady for refills. 'A few days ago we had an encounter with some ruffians on the road, intent on depriving us of our worldly goods and this poor innocent lass of far worse. Suffice to say that they found us rather more difficult to subdue than they expected, and when the dust settled we found ourselves in possession of a horse and cart.'

'That's right,' Rudi said, hiding his astonishment as best he could. Nothing Artemus had said was actually untrue, but he'd contrived to give the impression that the bandits had stolen the cart from its rightful owner before they'd even laid eyes on it. 'There were six of them, so they obviously thought we wouldn't give them any trouble.'

'You fought off six bandits?' Norbert sounded sceptical, but the arrival of a tankard of ale in front of him seemed to incline him to listen, and he sat on the bench.

Fritz nodded eagerly. 'Rudi killed two of them himself.' He looked a bit crestfallen. 'I tackled a couple as well, but they ran away.'

'Staggered away,' Hanna corrected. 'Just barely. Following their leader, who ran off snivelling like a mummy's boy as soon as he got a good kick where it really hurts.' Appreciative laughter rippled around the carters and some of the nearby tables.

'You killed two of them?' Norbert sounded sceptical.

Rudi nodded. 'Dropped one with the bow before he got too close and took the other one with the sword.' He took a deep draught of his own drink, uncomfortable with the memories and not sure quite what to say to make the account sound convincing. Somehow, though, his reticence seemed to carry more weight than any amount of boasting could have done.

'He was magnificent,' Artemus put in. 'I've never seen swordplay like it. Countering every strike and against two opponents into the bargain.'

'Two?' Norbert began to look sceptical again. 'What happened to the other one?'

'He was the leader,' Hanna explained. 'Kick, ran off, remember?' She sipped at her ale, apparently enjoying the renewed laughter around the room. 'Rudi must have got lucky, it seemed like a small enough target.'

'That only accounts for five of them,' one of the carters put in, moving closer to listen to the story. 'What happened to the sixth?'

'Hanna got him,' Fritz explained happily, unaware that the girl's expression had suddenly become uneasy. True to form, the simpleton had dropped their real names into the conversation, and in a context anyone in earshot would be sure to remember. 'Knife to the throat. He went down like a sack of turnips.'

'That's hard to believe,' the carter said.

Hanna glared at him, nettled. 'I can take care of myself. Want to make something of it?' Something of her old fire was visible below the surface now and the man quailed.

'I wouldn't dare,' he said, saving as much face as he could by pretending he was joking.

'It's a fine story,' Norbert said, waving for more ale. 'But can you prove any of it?'

'I told you we should have kept the bodies,' Artemus said archly, keeping the mood light.

'They'd have got a bit ripe by now, don't you think?' Rudi was rewarded with another ripple of laughter, which gratified him more than he would have thought possible.

'We kept anything that looked worth having though,' Fritz put in, hoisting the bundle of loot onto the table. 'Anyone want to buy a sword?' The room fell suddenly silent as everyone stared at the pathetic collection of odds and ends.

'Simeon Oestlinger's boots.' One of the customers pointed at the footwear Rudi had removed from the dead bandit and made the sign of Hendrik. 'I'd know them anywhere, he had that pattern made specially. Bandits stole them right off his feet about three months back. Remember him limping in here in his stockings, yelling for the road wardens?'

'Then I'm sure he'll be pleased to see them again,' Rudi said impatiently, throwing them across to the man who'd spoken. Taken by surprise, the man barely caught them in time. Norbert and his friends exchanged looks of incomprehension.

'An honest man's his own worst enemy,' Artemus said, apparently a local proverb, as his Marienburg accent thickened noticeably as he spoke and knowing nods were mixed in with the laughter that followed. 'And this one's fresh out of the Empire.'

'Well, it's the only way I know how to be,' Rudi snapped.

Norbert laughed and handed him another mug of ale. 'That's good. A man should be true to his nature. But when you get to the city, you might try being a little less Empire and a little more Marienburg. They do things differently there.'

'I'm not sure I understand,' Rudi said, finding the ale fumes clouding his mind a little more than he expected.

Artemus explained. 'If this Simeon is as fond of his boots as all that, you might have got a reward for returning them. Now this fellow will get it instead of you.'

'I see,' Rudi said. 'You expect me to take advantage of the misfortunes of others?'

'Not exactly,' Artemus said, deflecting any offence the remark might have caused. 'More like consider the opportunities they present.' He shrugged. 'It's the Marienburg way.'

Rudi wasn't sure he liked the sound of that, but there didn't seem to be anything he could do about it and he didn't want to lose the goodwill of the crowd, so he nodded.

'I'll bear that in mind,' he said.

'Good lad,' Artemus said. 'Stick with me when we get there and I'll steer you round the deepest canals.'

'So what would a Marienburger do about the horse and cart?' Hanna asked speculatively. 'We can hardly take it all the way back to Gutter's Wharf, even if there is a reward for it.' Rudi caught a fleeting grin, hastily suppressed, as Norbert rose to the bait.

'I might be able to help you there,' he said.

'That would be most kind,' Artemus agreed, nodding sagely. 'I'm sure some satisfactory arrangement could be made, beneficial to all parties.'

'Exactly.' A cunning grin appeared on the carter's face. 'Like, for instance, I'm sure Bardold would pay, oh, ten guilders or so to get his horse and cart back in one piece. Suppose I give you five, on his behalf, and put up the stabling and storage costs out of the rest until he turns up or I can get a message to Gutter's Wharf?'

'That sounds fair...' Fritz began, then broke off with a puzzled frown as Rudi kicked him under the table.

'Or we could assume our friend Bardold would be so delighted he'd pay twenty,' Artemus suggested. 'Which would mean you'd scarcely be out of pocket giving us fifteen on his behalf.'

'I don't know.' Norbert frowned thoughtfully. 'He's not a rich man by any means. He might go as high as fifteen, which means I could let you have ten...' After a few more moments of apparently light banter and another mug of ale, he suddenly dug into his purse and produced twelve of the gold coins Artemus had called guilders. 'That's it. All I can afford. Take it or leave it.'

Rudi glanced at Artemus, who nodded almost imperceptibly.

'That's very kind,' he said, taking the money and dropping it into his purse. 'Bardold's lucky to have a friend as considerate and generous as you.' The thought suddenly surfaced that Bardold might well be dead and Norbert the proud new possessor of a horse and cart for a tenth of their actual value, but that wasn't his problem. Luck or fate had contrived to hand them enough money to survive in the city for some time to come, and he silently blessed whichever gods were responsible.

THE NEXT MORNING dawned bright and clear and Rudi made a hearty breakfast with his companions. After the privations of life on the road, he'd slept more soundly than he could have believed possible on the softest bed he'd ever felt in his life, and the hot water he'd washed in the previous evening had left him feeling relaxed and invigorated. Everyone else seemed in high spirits, particularly Hanna, and he smiled at her over the wooden table.

'Feeling better this morning?' he asked.

'Much. Even...' she broke off. 'You know.' Rudi nodded and she went on. 'It's eased off a bit. I seem to have found something which helps relieve the pressure.'

'That's good.' Rudi changed the subject hastily as Artemus and Fritz appeared and began helping themselves to smoked sausage. 'I didn't realise how grubby I was feeling.'

'You and me both.' Hanna stretched. 'I didn't realise how much I was missing clean clothes.' Another shilling had been sufficient to get their laundry done, and her blue dress seemed a different shade. She tucked a stray lock of hair behind her headscarf.

'Did I exaggerate?' Artemus asked, his mouth full. Rudi shook his head. 'Was the accommodation here not more than adequate?'

'You were right,' Rudi conceded. The brief interlude of rest had been good for them all and he tried not to think about the impression they would have made. If Gerhard met one of the travellers who'd been in the taproom last night he'd know precisely where they were.

'I invariably am,' Artemus said. He indicated the bundles of possessions they'd brought in from the cart the previous night. 'Are we ready to go? Even on foot we should be there before nightfall.'

'I'm ready,' Rudi said. A small flutter of excitement tickled the base of his stomach as he shouldered his pack and quiver. After all this time he was almost at Marienburg and the chance to discover the answers to the questions which continued to torment him.

'Me too.' Hanna took up her satchel, her purse a few shillings heavier after managing to dispose of the weapons they'd taken from the dead bandits. Many of their listeners the night before seemed to think it had been worth buying something simply for the pleasure of hearing the story and Rudi hadn't been inclined to argue about that.

'So am I.' Artemus stood too, leaning on his staff and collecting his bundle of belongings. He turned to Fritz, who was finishing the last of his breakfast with a thoughtful expression. 'How about you?'

'In a moment,' Fritz said, standing slowly. 'I just want to stop by the stables first.'

'The stables?' Rudi shrugged, not understanding. 'What on earth for?'

Fritz turned reproachful eyes on him. 'To say good-bye to Willem, of course,' he said.

CHAPTER NINE

AFTER SEVERAL DAYS of riding on the cart it felt odd to be walking again, but Rudi found he was enjoying the experience. The day was fresh, with the first hint of the coming autumn chill on the breeze just sufficient to offset the heat generated by the exercise. He inhaled the scent of growing things from the fields around them with pleasure sharpened by the reflection that it could be some time before he was able to savour such things again. The thin straggle of farmsteads had developed into larger, more prosperous ones and the late summer sun fell on waving fields of yellowing grain as far as the eye could see. Hanna walked beside him, apparently feeling better than she had in some time.

'I never knew there could be so many people about,' she said. By this time the steady trickle of traffic on the road had swollen to a constant stream in both directions, wagons, carts, riders and travellers on foot mingling with one another as they passed or overtook. Many of them were dressed in fashions Rudi had never seen before and several times he heard snatches of conversation in a language he didn't know. Bretonn-ian, he assumed, as that was where the road went, but for all he knew he could be hearing others too.

Artemus laughed. 'If you think this is crowded, wait till you see the streets in Marienburg,' he said. He stood aside to let a young woman on a pony trot by, with a smile and a nod of acknowledgement. She was dressed in mail, with a dark travelling cloak thrown over it and a sword at her belt. A shield, embossed with the twin comet symbol of Sigmar, hung over her shoulder and out of the corner of his eye Rudi saw Hanna flinch at the sight. She didn't seem to be the only one, though. As the young woman rode on into the distance many of the passers-by glared at her with barely-concealed hostility.

'Who was that?' Fritz asked.

Artemus was watching her go with a puzzled expres-sion. 'One of the sisters of Sigmar. A warrior order, dedicated to the service of your Empire god. Unusual for one of her kind to have business in Marienburg.'

'Why so?' Rudi asked, feeling a chill of apprehension in his stomach. Gerhard was a templar of the church of Sigmar, he'd said as much the first time they met, and it was possible the woman was an agent of his.

'The worship of Sigmar is...' Artemus paused, choos-ing his words carefully. 'Not encouraged in Marienburg. After all, he's the patron deity of the Empire we seceded from. The state religion is the cult of Manann, although the common folk swear mostly by Hendryk.' As he pronounced the name he made the coin-counting gesture Rudi was beginning to associate with the deity.

'The gods of commerce and the sea,' he said. 'That makes sense, I suppose.'

'We are, after all, a maritime trading nation,' Artemus said. He paused for a moment and inhaled deeply through his nose. A beatific smile spread across his face. 'The sea! Can't you smell it?'

Rudi tried, but all he thought he could smell was the dust of the road.

'So any agent of the church of Sigmar would find it difficult to get cooperation from the authorities?' Hanna asked casually.

'Extremely difficult, I would have said. It would depend on their business, of course, but they'd need a deep purse and a lot of patience to get anything done if you ask me. Even witch hunters have a hard time of it and they're the most likely to find someone to listen to them.'

'So there are no witch hunters at all in Marienburg?' Fritz asked, disbelief palpable in his tone.

Artemus laughed and shook his head. 'I said no such thing,' he corrected gently. 'The templars of Morr are as welcome in Marienburg as they are any-where in the old world and the Solkanites aren't too worried about what people think of them anyway. There are usually one or two of each wandering around the city looking for signs of Chaos; probably a few more these days, after all that unpleasantness in the north last year. But it's mostly the temple of Manann that deals with such matters, and quite effi-ciently too if rumour is to be believed.' He made another sign with his hand, like the movement of a fish, as he spoke. 'But it's best not to dwell on topics like that.'

'Quite,' Rudi said, with a glance at Hanna. The girl nodded her agreement, but he knew her well enough to tell that she was quietly relieved at the news. It seemed that even if Gerhard was able to track them to Marienburg he would be hindered in his attempts to find them. Hanna smiled, and to his delighted astonishment slipped her hand through the crook of his arm.

Around noon they stopped for something to eat, patronising one of the wooden stalls which had begun to grow up alongside the road to cater for travellers. They still had some supplies left in their packs, but the aroma of hot food was almost irresistible and a penny apiece bought them bowls of vegetable stew which filled their stomachs and left them feeling warm and invigorated.

'That beats bread and cheese again,' Fritz said, with a satisfied sigh. The booth was doing good business and several other customers were standing on the grassy verge spooning down the pottage with every sign of satisfaction. He scraped his spoon around the wooden bowl a final time and looked around vaguely for somewhere to put it.

'Here, let me.' Rudi collected the receptacles together and took them back to the booth.

'Much obliged, squire,' the owner said, barely glancing up as Rudi balanced the stack precariously on the rim of the counter and turned to go.

'Pardon me.' Another customer stepped back hastily as Rudi turned, almost colliding with him, and glanced at the wares on display. 'How much are those pasties?'

'However much they are you can pay for them yourself,' Fritz said, looming up behind the fellow, the familiar truculent expression on his face. Rudi shook his head warningly, fearful of attracting attention again, and put out a restraining hand to take the simpleton by the arm. Fritz shrugged it off.

'I intend to. If it's any of your business,' the man said. He was a thin-faced, sallow individual, who somehow reminded Rudi of a ferret.

'Good. Then you won't need my friend's purse, will you?' Fritz tightened his grip around the man's wrist. Ferret-face tried to pull away, but Fritz was by far the stronger and lifted his hand clear of the concealing folds of his cloak. Sure enough, a familiar leather pouch was gripped tightly in his fingers.

'Hey!' Rudi said, understanding at last. 'That's mine!' His hand darted to his belt, finding the pouch of money gone.

'No it's not!' Ferret-face raised his voice. 'I was just taking my purse out and this ruffian assaulted me! Someone fetch a road warden!'

'How inconvenient,' Artemus said, materialising at Fritz's shoulder. 'There never seems to be one around when you want one, does there?' He smiled at the stallholder. 'I'm sure we can sort this out amicably enough, aren't you?'

'Nothing to do with me,' the man said. 'I just serve the food.' He turned away to stir a pot of the stew.

'It's mine, I tell you.' Ferret-face raised his voice again. 'Help! Thieves!' Out of the corner of his eye Rudi caught a glimpse of a couple of bystanders edging closer, hands beneath their cloaks. He rested a hand on the hilt of his sword and they backed off a little.

'You're the thief, you pathetic little piece of refuse.' Hanna glared at the man, daring him to contradict her. 'That's his purse and you know it.'

'So you say.' Ferret-face was apparently emboldened by the appearance of his confederates. 'It's just my word against his, though, isn't it?'

'This should be an easy matter to resolve,' Artemus said. He pulled a scrap of parchment from his pack, and a stick of charcoal, which he held out to Rudi. 'My young friend here will write down how much was in the purse.'

Rudi felt his face flush. 'I can't write,' he said. The thief looked at him scornfully. 'You've got some nerve,' he said, 'an ignorant bumpkin accusing honest people of thievery.'

Rudi's hand tightened on the hilt of his sword. 'I don't need to be able to read to know a knave when I see one,' he said.

'I'll write it down,' Hanna said. 'I know how much he's got.' She took the implements from Artemus, scribbled a moment and folded the parchment before handing it out to Ferret-face. 'Your turn.'

'I... can't write either,' the man said hastily.

'No matter,' Artemus said cheerfully. 'Now my young friend has written it down all you have to do is name a figure. Surely you know how much is in your own purse.'

'Three guilders,' the man said hastily, 'mostly in copper.'

'Not even close,' Rudi said, holding his hand out. He appealed to the stallholder. 'Could we ask you to look inside and tell us how much you think is there?'

'All right.' The thief shrugged. 'Let's get this farce over with.' He opened his hand, letting the purse fall to the grass. As Fritz made an instinctive grab for it his grip on the thief's wrist loosened and the man twisted free, running into the crowd surrounding them. Fritz picked the purse up and handed it to Rudi with a nod. Somewhat to his surprise the older lad didn't seem inclined to pursue the thief, which was probably just as well as his confederates were quietly slipping away too.

'Thanks.' Rudi took the pouch and made sure it was securely fastened somewhere rather less accessible. 'I owe you one.'

'Three of those guilders are mine,' Fritz pointed out reasonably.

DESPITE RUDI'S MISGIVINGS, the incident at the food stall didn't seem to have attracted much attention and he began to feel a little more secure among so much traffic. Even if Gerhard was in hot pursuit, he would hardly be able to pick them out from so large a throng, and Rudi was able to enjoy the walk almost as much as he had in the morning.

'The nerve of that man,' Hanna said, still seething over the encounter with the thief.

'A very minor thief,' Artemus said, 'to be working so far outside the walls. No doubt his masters have a low opinion of his abilities to give him a patch where so many potential victims will be unaware of the danger.'

'His masters?' Rudi asked. 'You mean he was part of a gang?' He remembered the confederates who'd seemed ready to back the man up. They didn't look as though they'd been all that formidable either.

'Oh, undoubtedly,' Artemus said. 'But I meant his superiors in the guild.'

'Thieves have a guild?' Fitz asked, astonished.

'Of course they do. Every occupation in Marienburg does, even if they're not always visible. Even the beggars.' Rudi looked for some sign that the scribe was joking, but he appeared completely earnest. 'I really do advise you not to contemplate practising whatever occupation you habitually go about without going through proper channels first. That's the best way to avoid any misunderstandings and concomitant unpleasantness.'

'What sort of unpleasantness?' Hanna asked.

'That would depend on the guild in question and how much they felt slighted. I'm sure you'll find gainful employment before long, but it's best to be sure you're not treading on any toes while you look, if you get my drift.'

'I think I'm beginning to,' Rudi said. Any further comment he might have been going to make was driven from his head as the road crested a small rise and he stopped moving, stunned into immobility by sheer astonishment.

'There she is!' Artemus proclaimed. 'Marienburg, the greatest city in the known world, and for all I know the realms beyond.' He gestured proudly at the vista laid out before them.

'It's very big,' Hanna said, an uncharacteristic edge of uncertainty creeping into her voice. Rudi nodded, dumbstruck.

Contrary to what he'd expected, it wasn't the city itself which first caught his eye, but the sea beyond. It glittered like silver, stretching further than he would ever have dreamed possible, until it seemed to merge seamlessly with the blue dome of the sky. The Reik had been impressive enough, but this was something else, something beyond huge, and he felt the breath still in his chest with the sheer magnitude of it.

The city lay between them and the sea, a dark mass of buildings still too distant to distinguish, so that it seemed to spread like a bruise across the landscape. Reflections struck back from a scattering of domes and towers large enough to stand out in their own right, and Rudi felt his head begin to reel as he took in the scale of it. Thin veins of sparkling water threaded their way through the acres of densely packed masonry, making the whole vista shimmer against the back of his eye. Kohlstadt had seemed bustling and crowded enough, but the entire village could have been put down in the valley ahead of them and seem no more substantial than a cluster of chicken coops.

'Look at the ships!' Fritz pointed excitedly out to sea, where dozens of sails dotted the ocean, coming and going from the harbour as ceaselessly as ants from their hills. 'Are any of them elves?'

'That one there, unless I miss my guess.' Artemus pointed to one sleeker and more elegant than the others, just rounding the outer wall of the harbour. Rudi squinted, unable to make out any detail at all at this distance, but he was prepared to take the scribe's word for it. Fritz seemed happy enough at any event.

'Come on,' he said at last, conscious of the curious and amused glances the little group was beginning to draw. 'We'll never get there at this rate.'

CHAPTER TEN

THEY ENTERED THE city by the Westenpoort gate, the walls rising above them to a height Rudi had never before conceived that stone could reach. The long grey bulk, like a lowering thunderhead, had loomed steadily larger as they approached it along a causeway constructed across a dreary expanse of marsh, which seemed to recede to the horizon on both sides of the raised road, as if the boundary between land and sea was blurring into a viscid soup of almost liquid mud. Mindful of their experiences in the bogs bordering the Reik, Rudi kept well away from the edge of the carriageway. To his jaundiced eye it seemed that a single incautious step would mean a messy and unpleasant death, sucked down irretrievably into the heart of the marsh.

'It's not quite as bad as that,' Artemus assured him. 'Some people actually make a living out there. But I wouldn't venture off the road without a guide, I must admit, and even then not without some pressing reason.' By this point the wall seemed even larger than Rudi had first imagined, its very bulk making it seem to recede as they approached, forcing him to reassess the perspective.

'The Vloedmuur,' Artemus said proudly, noticing his expression. 'A miracle of engineering, sufficient to keep even the mighty ocean at bay in times of need.' He pointed to thin plumes of smoke, rising at intervals along the ramparts. 'Great pumping engines, the finest ever created by dwarven artisans, are kept ready to begin their work at a moment's notice.'

'Are they needed often?' Hanna asked.

'Often enough, Marienburg lives by the sea and we've learned to respect it. Manann sends us the odd flood from time to time, just to make sure we're not getting complacent.'

'But the city stays dry?' Fritz asked, with an air of vague apprehension.

'Most of it,' Artemus assured him. 'They have a hard time of it on the flats and a couple of the other low-lying districts, but they're mostly fishermen down there so at least they have boats.'

'No doubt a great comfort to them,' Hanna said dryly. By now the road was disappearing into a gateway higher and more impressive than Rudi had ever seen, fully five times the height of a man and wide enough for four wagons to pass one another without hindrance. Even so it was choked with traffic and armed men were bustling about trying to keep order. Their weapons and clothing varied, but all wore distinctive hats, black and voluminous.

'The Honourable Company of Lamplighters and Watchmen,' Artemus said, when Rudi pointed them out. 'Better known as the Black Caps. They're supposed to keep order and apprehend criminals.'

'Supposed to?' Rudi asked.

'Some are more zealous than others,' Artemus said. 'And those are the ones best avoided, if you see what I mean.'

'I think so.' Fritz nodded thoughtfully. 'Like throwing their weight about, do they?'

'That's one way of putting it,' Artemus said.

Rudi shivered as the shadow of the gate fell across him and the babble of sound around them suddenly rose in volume, echoing and folding back on itself in the confined space. The air felt damp and chill, with a faint odour of decay, and he hurried his pace a little, eager to regain the comparative warmth of the evening sun.

In this he was to be disappointed however, as the lowering walls above him cast their shadow across the rest of the narrow strip of shoreline that they enclosed. Desolate salt marsh spread out on either side of the cobbled road, thin tidal pools and patches of slick mud interspersed with tenacious grasses and other plants which clung grimly to life on the margins of the sea. Great masses of seabirds wheeled and screeched overhead, like malevolent clouds, and flocks of them darted about on the mud flats, scrabbling Taal knew what from the treacherous surface with eager stabs of their beaks.

And they weren't the only ones; to his astonishment he could make out the unmistakable shapes of crude hovels dotted around the desolate landscape and a few flat-bottomed boats grounded on the mud from which the smoke of cooking fires rose lazily against the sky.

'People actually live out here?' he asked in astonishment.

'People live anywhere they can,' Artemus said. 'The whole city's built on a chain of islands, don't forget.'

'I know, you told us,' Rudi replied, but only now did the full implications of the scribe's stories begin to sink in. The road was rising by this time, towards a bridge across a wide channel, along which a number of boats were moving. Some were under sail, but most were being rowed or poled along and all were packed with goods, people, or both. Beyond the span the city itself began, a jumble of buildings higher and narrower than any he'd ever seen, jostling for space like the people swarming around them, without a single patch of open land to be seen. Some seemed to be tottering on the brink of the waterway and a few were even built out over it on pilings, as though their owners had roofed over a wharf.

'That's incredible,' Fritz said, his jaw dropping. 'I've never seen so many people in my life!'

'We're entering the Winkelmarkt,' Artemus told him. 'It's one of the more salubrious wards on the southern side, though not what it was.' He paused in the middle of the bridge, in a narrow space between two tiny houses which had been built partly on the roadway and partly hanging over the edge. There were several similar structures choking the thoroughfare, a mixture of shops, homes and some makeshift wooden stalls between them. Rudi began to appreciate just how much of a premium space of any kind must be at in a place like this. He crowded in closer to the scribe, already feeling nervous from the constant press of bodies around them, and noted with relief that Hanna and Fritz were still in sight. If they ever got separated in this maelstrom of people they'd never find one another again.

'Stick close together,' he said and Hanna nodded, her face drawn, evidently coming to the same conclusion that he had.

'Everyone here? Good.' Artemus nodded and gestured over the parapet to the flotilla of watercraft passing to and fro below. 'See those skiffs?' He pointed out a small boat, in which a couple of passengers sat, being rowed along by a taciturn oarsman. 'They're for hire. If anyone gets lost, head for the water and hail one. Tell the boatman you want to get to the Dancing Pirate tavern in Winkelmarkt and they'll take you to the nearest wharf. Up the steps, turn left, third alley on the right, about halfway down. Try to remember that.'

'We will,' Hanna assured him fervently.

'Good. I'm probably being a little over-cautious, but none of you are used to large crowds and it's best to be sure of these things.'

'Quite.' Rudi nodded, suddenly aware that a city this size could swallow you whole and never leave a trace of your passing. As he watched, one of the skiffs Artemus had indicated turned suddenly, vanishing up a side channel so narrow the boat barely made it through, and he became aware that the far bank was riddled with narrow inlets and canals. He pointed it out and Artemus nodded.

'There are thousands of them,' he said. 'Most only go a little way inland, but some are back channels between the main canals.'

'Is that one of the main ones?' Fritz asked, glancing down at the wide expanse of water beneath them.

'Yes and no,' he said slowly. 'There's a lot of traffic at this end, but it doesn't go much further upstream.' He pointed into the distance, where a wider tributary marked the break between this island and the next. The buildings beyond it were shabbier, showing unmistakable signs of dereliction, and a couple of wharves sagged visibly on their pilings, on the verge of sliding into the canal. 'That's Doodkanal, and it's well named, let me tell you. No one goes there if they can avoid it. Even the watch give it a wide berth if they can.'

'That's hard to believe,' Rudi said. 'If space is so valuable, why would it just be left to rot?'

'Because clearing it out would be more trouble than it's worth,' Artemus replied, in a tone which clearly implied that the subject was closed.

'Well it's a big enough city,' Hanna said. 'I'm sure we won't need to go there.'

'Quite,' Artemus said, changing the subject with evident relief. 'Now if we should pass a hot sausage stall, you really must try one. The Winkelmarkt sausages are widely renowned as the finest in Marienburg, which makes them the finest in the world, and there's nothing like eating one in a bun with a smear of Bretonnian mustard. In all my wanderings, that's the thing I've missed the most.'

IN TRUTH THE sausages Artemus persuaded them to try, purchased from a street trader in a small courtyard surrounded by ramshackle buildings, were little different from any others Rudi could recall having eaten. Nevertheless, not wanting to disappoint his host, whose expression as he bit into the snack was almost ecstatic, he nodded his head appreciatively as he chewed. Perhaps his palate was simply less sophisticated than a city dweller's would have been, he thought. At least the food was welcome after the day's long walk and their circuitous progress through the narrow streets, which seemed to have been going on for an awfully long time. By now he could have walked through Kohlstadt from end to end three or four times, and they were still only part of the way through a single ward of the vast metropolis.

'Is it much further?' Hanna asked, swallowing her last mouthful.

'Just a couple of streets away,' Artemus assured her. Fritz looked hopefully back at the sausage stall, then shrugged, seeing that no one else intended repeating the experiment.

'Then let's go,' he suggested, striding out in the scribe's wake with every sign of outward confidence. Rudi had just begun to resign himself to another long walk when, almost without warning, Artemus turned at the mouth of a narrow passageway he had taken for nothing more than the back entrance to a house and gestured along it.

'Just down here,' he said.

The alleyway Artemus had indicated was dark, even at this hour, hemmed in with the tall, narrow buildings Rudi was beginning to realise were characteristic of the local architecture. Torches flared at intervals and enough light leaked from the windows lining the passageway for him to make out their surroundings in rather more detail than he felt entirely comfortable with. A steady stream of people were passing up and down it, chattering and laughing, and several times he had to step hastily out of the way, avoiding as much of the detritus underfoot as possible. A surprising number of them appeared to be remarkably plump children, just as they had been in the last few streets they'd passed through, and he mentioned the fact to Artemus, who laughed.

'Those aren't children. We're near the Kleinmoot,' he said, as though that explained everything. Rudi frowned. 'The halfling quarter. Most of them live down that way, on the eastern fringe of the ward.' He gestured in the direction of the slums he'd pointed at from the bridge. 'Next to the Doodkanal, but it doesn't seem to bother them too much. I suppose compared to the neighbours they've got at home, even that's an improvement.'

That meant nothing to Rudi, but Fritz nodded in agreement.

'You mean the Sylvanians. I've read about them.'

'Far better read about than encountered in person, let me assure you,' Artemus said.

Rudi felt a flush of embarrassment. Even Fritz could read, it seemed, and he had all the intellect of a squirrel. It couldn't be as hard as he'd assumed after all, then. Perhaps if he asked Hanna nicely she might show him the basics - he'd cut his own throat rather than ask Fritz.

'Here we are,' Artemus said at last, pointing to a narrow doorway. 'The Dancing Pirate. Hasn't changed a bit!' Rudi wondered if that was quite such a cause for celebration as the scribe appeared to believe, but was prepared to take his word for it. After all, he knew the city well and he hadn't let them down yet.

'Oh, I get it,' Fritz said, snickering. 'Dancing Pirate, very good.' Rudi wondered what he meant at first, until the smudges on a slab of timber fastened insecurely to the wall above the door resolved themselves into a crude image of a sailor with an eye patch twisting at the end of a hangman's rope. Artemus pushed the door open, stepped through, and beckoned them inside.

To Rudi's surprise the taproom beyond was warm, comfortable and relatively clean. It was larger than he'd expected too, the narrow frontage of the building stretching some way back, with a scattering of tables and chairs between the door and the bar. A couple of the customers were eating and the appetising smells emanating from a door at the back of the room, presumably leading to the kitchen, made him regret the sausage he'd already eaten.

Several of the tables were occupied, although to his relief no one seemed to notice their arrival, and Hanna nudged him surreptitiously in the ribs.

'Look over there,' she murmured. 'The table in the corner.' Rudi glanced across in the direction she indicated, unsure of what she'd spotted, involuntarily tensing in anticipation of seeing Gerhard. But the table was occupied by two people he'd never seen before; a halfling with watchful eyes, who glanced up and seemed to take in every detail of his appearance as he looked in that direction, and a slightly overweight young man, swathed in robes. Embarrassed at being caught staring at them, Rudi averted his gaze hastily.

'What about them?' he asked.

'A mage,' Hanna said, too quietly for either of their companions to overhear. 'He might know something about... you know.' She lifted a hand to adjust her headscarf.

'How can you tell?' Rudi asked dubiously.

Hanna looked at him scornfully. 'Oh for Shallya's sake, look how he's dressed.' Then she shrugged. 'Besides, I just know. Like that night we met Alwyn and the others, I had this feeling about her, even before we spoke. And she could tell...' She broke off uncomfortably.

'So maybe this fellow can tell too,' Rudi said, a stab of unease running through him at the thought. If that were the case there was no telling how he might react.

'It's possible,' Hanna said. Before either of them could pursue the topic, Artemus waved to them from the bar.

'Hurry up, you two. Can't let good ale go to waste.' Rudi and Hanna resumed their progress to the polished wooden counter, where their companions were waiting for them, tankards already in their hands. Fritz tilted his and swallowed gratefully.

'Gods, I needed that,' he said with an appreciative sigh.

'Artemus says you need rooms,' the man behind the counter said. He was short and stout, though still tall enough to tower over the small knot of halfling customers reaching up to take their drinks from the counter top, and Rudi glanced down onto a shining pate surrounded by thinning brown hair.

The scribe nodded. 'Two, I think.' He glanced at Hanna. 'Assuming you'd prefer the same arrangement as last time?'

'I would, thank you.' The girl nodded.

The landlord echoed the gesture. 'That shouldn't be a problem.' He glanced at their packs and gestured to a passing potboy. 'Koos, take these people's baggage upstairs, there's a good lad.'

'Don't trouble yourself,' Rudi said hastily. Having lost all he had once before he wasn't about to let his possessions out of his sight.

The landlord nodded. 'As you wish. He's got plenty of other work to do, isn't that right lad?'

'Yes, Dad.' Koos sloped off, clearly wishing he was somewhere else, and collected a couple of empty tankards from the table in the corner. The sorcerer and the halfling glanced up, looked at Rudi and Hanna again, and resumed their conversation.

'They want the same again,' Koos reported, slamming the mugs down on the counter.

'Who does?' Rudi asked, slipping a penny from his purse and handing it to the lad. 'You look as though you could do with a drink yourself, working so hard.'

'You don't know?' Koos looked vaguely surprised as he rounded the corner of the bar and drew another couple of drinks from the barrel. 'I thought everyone knew Sam.'

'We've just arrived in town,' Rudi said.

'I'd never have guessed.' He picked up the drinks. 'Sam gets around, if you know what I mean. Knows things, hears things. Good friend if you need one and can afford it, but he's not someone you want to cross. The one with the beer gut is Kris. He's all right for a spellslinger, graduated from Baron Henryk's a couple of years back. Does enchantments, basic wizardry, he's cheap but reliable. Usually.' He shrugged, with the trace of a smile. 'But then I would say that, he's my cousin. Manann alone knows what he's doing with Sam, but I've got more sense than to ask.' He disappeared in the direction of the back table, leaving Rudi feeling foolish and a little uneasy. No doubt Koos would tell his cousin of his interest in him at once, and sure enough the mage looked up again almost as the thought came to him. Seeing Rudi's eyes on him he smiled, nodded a polite greeting and resumed his conversation with the halfling. Sam, whoever he was, made no obvious attempt to look, but somehow Rudi knew he was being studied with an intensity all the more disturbing for being so discreet.

Oh well, no point fretting about it. What was done was done.

'What's Baron Henryk's?' Hanna asked, sipping her ale and trying to sound casual. Rudi knew her well enough to pick up on her barely concealed excitement, though. Her guess had been confirmed, the man in the corner was a mage, and he just hoped she wouldn't do anything foolish until they had a chance to discuss the situation.

'Baron Henryk's College of Navigation and Sea Magics,' Artemus said, breaking off from his conversation with the landlord. 'The finest university in the known world, although there are hidebound scholars in Altdorf and Nuln who would dispute that claim. They also train and licence mages, in the same way as the colleges of Altdorf. Why do you ask?' Rudi's stomach clenched at the question, but before either of them could find a convincing answer everyone's attention was mercifully diverted.

'Two fish pies and an eel stew.' A cheerful, slightly harassed woman darted through the door from the kitchen, a tray in her hands laden with steaming dishes. She dumped it on the counter, began to turn and caught sight of Artemus. 'Oh, it's you. I thought you were dead. What do you want?'

'Nikolaas was just telling us you had a couple of rooms free,' Artemus said.

'Was he?' The woman stared hard at her husband, who shuffled his feet uncomfortably. 'Two guilders a week, per room. Up front.' She looked challengingly at Artemus.

Rudi coughed. 'That sounds very reasonable, thank you. We'll take them.' He drew four of the gold coins from his purse and dropped them into the woman's palm. She closed her hand over them reflexively, an almost comical expression of astonishment crossing her face.

'Food and other services are extra,' she added, and Rudi nodded.

Hanna smiled. 'Perhaps you could let us have an itemised bill at the end of the week?' she suggested.

'We could.' The woman's expression softened a little. 'I'm sure you're tired after such a long journey.'

'We are,' Hanna said.

Artemus nodded. 'Long and eventful,' he began. 'Beset by bandits, who my young friends here drove off in a manner well worth the heari–'

'And even if it's not you'll tell us anyway,' the woman interrupted. She smiled at Hanna again. 'I'll show you to your room.'

'Thank you.' Hanna darted another glance towards the table in the corner, but it was empty now, save for two discarded beer steins. Rudi turned his head, catching movement out of the corner of his eye, just in time to see the door closing behind the young wizard and his halfling companion. Hanna shrugged, looking vaguely disappointed. 'I am rather tired.'

'And I'm hungry,' Fritz said, as the two women retreated through the door at the back of the bar. 'What have you got to eat?'

'I'd recommend the fish stew,' Artemus said, indicating the food on the counter which Koos was picking up to distribute. 'Marta's a real artist in the kitchen.'

'She doesn't seem to like you very much,' Fritz said, with his usual tact.

Artemus shook his head. 'A small misunderstanding, many years ago. But you know how women can be about these things.' Rudi, who didn't, nodded politely. 'But that's all in the past. Tonight we have good food and comfortable beds. What else matters?'

'Not a lot,' Fritz agreed.

RUDI WOKE SLOWLY the following morning, a shaft of sunshine shouldering its way through a chink in the shutters to bathe his face in warmth and light. He yawned and stretched, pleasant memories of the evening before seeping slowly into his mind.

The sausage he'd eaten earlier didn't seem to have blunted his appetite nearly as much as he'd expected. When the food arrived he'd eaten far more than he'd expected and washed it down with more ale than he would normally have drunk as well. He'd seldom eaten fish before and the flavours and textures of the stew had been a fascinating novelty.

While they'd eaten, Artemus had kept Nikolaas, Koos and a handful of their customers entertained with stories of his travels around the Empire, although

to Rudi's quiet relief the scribe had passed over the circumstances of their meeting in favour of some of the
tales he'd regaled them with on the road. Even Marta
listened, although she'd been pretending to ignore the
conversation, betraying her interest with occasional
wordless sounds of disbelief. By the time Koos had
shown the three of them upstairs to a small but comfortably appointed room he had been so ready for
sleep he could barely walk straight. Even the discovery
that there were only two beds had seemed a minor
inconvenience and he had barely made more than a
token protest at Artemus's offer to sleep on the floor
before collapsing onto the nearest mattress.

Rudi sat up, stretched again, and swung his feet off
the bed. Used as he was to a simple pallet, or a bedroll
out in the open air, it still felt strange to be lying on
something so soft. A pang of conscience struck him; he
should have been the one to sleep on the floor. He
glanced across at Artemus, prepared to apologise for
his thoughtlessness, but the scribe had gone, no doubt
downstairs for some breakfast. Appetising cooking
smells were rising from the kitchen below and the
young forester felt an unexpected pang of hunger. No
doubt his body was taking full advantage of the opportunity to make up for the privations of the long
journey and the hardships they'd endured along the
way.

He got dressed quickly and glanced at the shrouded
bulk of Fritz, still snoring away in the next bed. After a
moment of internal debate he decided to leave the
older lad to sleep. Perhaps Hanna was awake too by
now and they could discuss some of the business
which had brought them to Marienburg. If not, he had

no doubt that Artemus would provide some interesting conversation. Perhaps if he was discreet enough he could learn about some method of finding Magnus without having to explain his reasons for asking.

Picking up his feet carefully, he walked around the bed, not wanting to trample on Artemus's bedroll, but it had gone too, along with his pack. A tingle of worry began to work its way up Rudi's spine. His own belongings and Fritz's were still where he'd left them, of course.

Trying to ignore the sudden flare of suspicion, he picked up his quiver, removed the arrows and plunged his hand inside. His fingers closed on nothing but empty air.

His purse was gone from its hiding place, and with it the money they needed to survive here.

CHAPTER ELEVEN

'HANNA!' LEAVING FRITZ to gather what wits he had after being shaken awake, Rudi hurried down the corridor to the door of the adjacent room. So profound was his sense of agitation he tripped the latch and barged straight in without knocking, or a second's thought as to whether she might even be awake. Well, she'd be awake, obviously, or the door would still have been barred, but it only occurred to him belatedly that she might not be dressed yet.

'What do you want?' To his mingled relief and disappointment the girl was fully clothed, but she looked up sharply as he entered. 'Shut that damn door for Shallya's sake!' She was seated on the edge of the bed and as he'd come in it had looked as though her head had been bowed. Now, as she raised it to glare at him, the seal on her forehead was clearly visible. The sight shocked him. He'd grown so used to seeing her with a headscarf on, the talisman concealed, that he'd almost managed to ignore its existence. As he closed the door the ugliness and cruelty of the thing struck him anew, and he flinched at his thoughtlessness.

'ARTEMUS HAS GONE. So has our money,' Rudi said, unable to think of any way of softening the blow. He flinched, anticipating her usual forthright reaction to adversity, but to his surprise she simply nodded calmly.

'I suppose we should have expected something like this,' she said. She had something in the palm of her hand, which she returned to a small leather pouch on a thong around her neck and tucked into the top of her bodice. After a moment, Rudi recognised it as the chip of shiny stone she'd taken from the dead skaven out in the wilderness. Seeing the direction of his gaze, she shrugged. 'It takes some of the pressure away from inside my head. I don't know how, but if I just hold it and sit quietly it seems to help.'

'Good.' Rudi nodded, pleased that she seemed to be coping so well. 'That mage we saw last night seems to be a regular here. Perhaps if we get a chance to talk to him–' He broke off as a loud rapping resounded from the door.

'It's me,' Fritz called.

Hanna sighed. 'Come in, it's open.' She began to tie her headscarf as the simpleton entered the room, his face purple with anger.

'I'll kill him. I'll break his bloody neck. Thieving, two-faced son of a–'

'That's not helping,' Hanna said mildly.

Fritz blinked at her in astonishment. 'It'll make me feel better.'

'Me too,' Rudi said, still reeling from the scribe's treachery. First Shenk, now Artemus; it seemed that everyone who seemed well disposed towards them had a hidden agenda. He resolved not to trust anyone from now on, however plausible they might seem. Apart from Hanna, of course, and Fritz if he had to.

'The main thing is not to panic,' Hanna said reasonably. 'We've paid for the rooms a week in advance, so Marta's not going to throw us out before then.'

'We've still got to pay for our meals, though,' Rudi pointed out.

Hanna nodded. 'But not until the week's up. Unless we give her some reason to doubt that we've got the money, and we could have found Artemus by then. Or got jobs or something.'

'Maybe,' Rudi said slowly. Her words sounded reasonable. Perhaps the situation wasn't as bad as it first appeared. 'But we'll need money for other things in the meantime.'

'Fritz and I still have a couple of guilders apiece,' Hanna pointed out. She looked at the older youth. 'Unless he got your purse too.'

'No chance,' Fritz said, drawing it out. 'I slept with it inside my shirt.'

'Well at least one of you seems to have some common sense,' Hanna said.

Rudi sighed, ignoring the slur. 'So what do you suggest we do now?'

'What do you think?' Hanna said. 'Go down to breakfast.'

* * *

'SEEN ARTEMUS THIS morning?' Rudi asked, as casually as he could contrive. Nikolaas shook his head and placed a newly baked loaf on the table along with some boiled eggs and some hot smoked meats. The smell was so appetising that Rudi almost forgot the reason for his question.

'Isn't he back yet?' The innkeeper shrugged. 'I thought he went out again last night. Wasn't that right?' He turned, appealing to Marta, who nodded as she poured out drinks for the three companions.

'That's right. And I don't suppose he will be, either. ' She didn't seem too distressed at the prospect. 'He had all his luggage with him.'

'Do you know where he's likely to be?' Hanna asked. 'He was going to show us around the city a bit, help us get our bearings.'

'The only bearings you'd get from that one you're better off not having,' Marta said flatly. 'Knowing him he won't have got any further than Tilman's up the street.'

'What's at Tilman's?' Rudi asked.

'Nothing a respectable young gentleman like yourself need be concerned with,' Marta said, returning to the kitchen.

'It's a gambling den,' Nikolaas said, once he was sure his wife was well out of earshot. 'Artemus used to be in there all the time, before he left town. Quite a few other places too, truth be told.'

'I'm a pretty fair hand with the dice,' Fritz said speculatively. 'I don't suppose they'd let me have a go, do you?'

'They'd welcome you with open arms,' Nikolaas said. He glanced around furtively and dropped his voice.

'It's in the back room of the cobbler's shop on the corner. Tell them I sent you and you shouldn't have any trouble. And if you ever mention this conversation to my wife you can find somewhere else to sleep, all right?'

'Understood,' Rudi said, feeling a good deal happier than he had since waking up.

IN BROAD DAYLIGHT the narrow thoroughfare outside seemed less claustrophobic and threatening than it had in the half-light of the evening before. Rudi hesitated on the threshold of the tavern door, his nostrils suddenly assaulted by the smell of the city. Yesterday it had built up gradually, so he'd barely noticed it, but today it hit him in the face all at once, a strange mixture of rotting mud, human waste, decaying vegetables and a sharp, clean odour he didn't recognise but somehow instinctively understood must be the sea. He glanced up and down the alleyway, trying to get his bearings and keep his balance as passers-by shouldered their way past.

'This way,' Hanna said confidently, turning left. Rudi and Fritz fell in behind her.

'How do you know?' Rudi asked and the girl sighed.

'Nikolaas said it was behind the cobbler's shop on the corner. We didn't pass one on the way in last night, so he must have meant the other end of the street.'

'Right,' Rudi said, trying to sound as though the fact had simply slipped his mind for a moment. A sign caught his eye over the heads of the endless crowd, a boot large enough for an ogre hanging from the front of a building, and he pointed. 'Do you think that's it?'

'It's the only one on the corner,' Hanna said.

The shop was small and cramped, as Rudi was beginning to expect by now, but laid out with a good eye to maximise the use of space. A counter at one end projected almost the width of the room, blocking off a door leading to the rear of the building, and a workbench with a cobbler's last was ranged along one side. A man was working there, hammering nails into the sole of a half-completed boot. He looked up as the three of them entered.

'Can I help you?' he asked, removing a couple of nails from the corner of his mouth.

'I hope so.' Hanna smiled at him, adopting the simple girlish persona she'd used to try to distract Gerhard's horsemen on the moors. It didn't seem to be working any better here than it had then. Rudi wondered briefly if the strength of her character was too great to conceal, or whether city people were just naturally suspicious. 'Would you be Herr Tilman, by any chance?'

'And you'd want to know because?' the cobbler answered, shifting his grip subtly on the hammer he still held. Rudi stepped forward, bumping his head against a pair of shoes hanging from the rafters, like much of the stock. He stood next to Hanna, hoping to back her up by his presence and impede Fritz from charging in too hastily if he'd also noticed the implied threat.

'We thought we might find a friend here,' he said. 'Artemus van Loenhoek. They told us at the Dancing Pirate that he often came in shopping for shoes.'

'I know him.' The cobbler put his hammer down and jerked his head towards the door at the back of the shop. 'He's through there. Haven't seen him in a good few years, but he doesn't seem to have changed much.'

'Thank you.' Hanna smiled again and led the way towards the door behind the counter. The cobbler shrugged and resumed his work.

The back room was far larger than the shop, and for a moment Rudi thought they'd stumbled through the rear entrance of a tavern by mistake. There were the same tables and chairs scattered about the place and the same reek of bodies and sour ale, but the atmosphere was subtly different. Instead of the babble of raised voices, punctuated by loud laughter, that he'd grown used to in places like that, the hum of conversation was subdued. Men and a few women were clustered around the tables, cards in their hands or rolling dice and exchanging coins with a rapidity and intensity that bordered on grimness. Even the ones who appeared to be winning didn't look too happy about it, continuing to concentrate on their games with a single-mindedness which seemed to be squeezing any vestige of joy from what ought to have been a pleasant recreation.

Glancing around the room for some sign of the scribe, Rudi hesitated a moment, thinking he recognised a couple of the figures slouched at a bar in the corner as the mage and halfling he'd asked Koos about the night before, but the place was so crowded it was hard to be sure. A small knot of gamblers passed between them and by the time he had a clear line of sight to the bar again, Sam and Kris had disappeared, if they'd ever been there in the first place. He had no time to worry about it though, as his attention was deflected by a nudge in the ribs, delivered none too gently.

'Over there,' Fritz said, pointing. Sure enough, Artemus was sitting at a table near the back, his eyes fixed on the cards in his hand. He didn't seem to have noticed them come in, although someone evidently had: as Rudi and Hanna began to follow Fritz through the maze of tables, surprisingly many of them still in use even at this hour of the morning, a young man stepped forward, his hand hovering close to the dagger in his belt. He was dressed in what Rudi assumed to be a fashionable manner, since the garments didn't seem terribly practical, although the cloth was clearly cheap and thin.

'Can I help you at all?' he asked.

'I don't think so,' Rudi replied, ignoring the implicit challenge. 'We just want a word with our friend over there.'

'Really.' Cheap-suit nodded, his eyes taking in the sword at Rudi's belt and the knives visible on Fritz's and Hanna's. 'Make sure that's all you have. Unless you fancy trying your luck.' It was clear he wasn't inviting them to play cards.

'It's tempting,' Fritz said, never one to let a challenge go by. 'But I'm used to better odds.' He nudged the fellow out of the way with his shoulder, confident that his greater size and musculature would give him the edge if things got physical. Rudi wasn't so sure about that. It looked to him as though at least two other men were keeping a close eye on the exchange, but Cheap-suit let them pass without any further attempt to impede them.

'Hello, Artemus,' Rudi said, moving up to the table and standing just behind the scribe. He wasn't sure quite what sort of reaction he ought to expect, but in the event he was surprised. Artemus barely glanced up from the table, taking in Rudi and Hanna and Fritz who flanked him, effectively pinning the scribe into his chair. Several of the seats around the table were vacant, empty mugs in front of them mute testament to other players who had evidently had enough of the game or run out of money.

'Hello,' he said, with a faint air of abstraction. Five guilders and a handful of silver lay on the table in front of him. 'Be with you in a moment.'

'Where's our money?' Rudi asked, horrified by how little of it seemed left. Less than half the contents of his purse were visible. 'What have you done with the rest of it?'

'Invested it,' Artemus said. 'On everyone's behalf.' He discarded one of the cards in his hand. 'Draw one.'

'One.' The dealer handed him a fresh card. Like everyone else around the table he seemed to be ignoring the conversation.

'I stick,' the man on Artemus' left, a prosperous-looking merchant with a faint Bretonnian accent, said, smiling. He threw two more guilders into the pile of coins in the middle of the table. Hanna's eyes widened as she took it in. There must have been fifty of the gold coins there at least, and twice as many pieces of silver.

'Draw two,' the man next to him said. He was thin and shabbily dressed, his hair plastered to his scalp with a sheen of sweat. His mouth tightened almost imperceptibly as he received his replacement cards and his shoulders slumped dejectedly for a moment before he squared them with a brave show of confidence. 'That'll do nicely.'

'I'm out,' a hard-eyed woman with a sword at her belt said, throwing her cards on the table face down. The man next to her grinned. His clothes were finer than any Rudi had ever seen before, intricate designs embroidered in gold thread on a rich blue background, and he made a show of studying his cards carefully.

'I can't be paying you enough, obviously.' He nodded thoughtfully. 'I'll stick with these. If anyone wants to know why, it'll cost you another five guilders.' He threw the money into the pot as he spoke and Rudi felt an air of tension settle across the table, like the crackle of an approaching thunderstorm. He had only the vaguest idea of what was going on, but things were obviously building to a head.

'Too rich for me,' the Bretonnian said, throwing in his hand. The dealer nodded. He wasn't actually playing, Rudi realised, just distributing the cards to those who were; presumably he was employed by Tilman, or whoever really owned the place.

'Anyone else?'

Artemus reached forward to pick up the remaining gold coins in front of him, but Fritz was faster, pinning the scribe's hand to the table before he could reach them.

'Hang on a minute,' he said. 'That's all we have.'

'That's all we have at the moment,' Artemus said. He nodded to the pile of gold coins in the middle of the table. 'All that's ripe for the taking. But I need to make this bet.'

'And lose the lot? I don't think so,' Hanna said. By way of an answer Artemus tilted his hand so she could see the cards in it. Rudi leaned across for a better view.

The hand was a good one, he knew. Although he and his father had never played for anything but acorns, they'd whiled away the evenings with card games for as long as he could remember, and there were only a couple of combinations that could possibly beat it. The chances were that Artemus really did have the winning hand, and if that was true they'd walk out of here rich. But if he was wrong… He hovered in an agony of indecision.

'How about you?' The dealer addressed the shabbily-dressed man between the woman and the Bretonnian. The fellow shrugged.

'I'm in.' He pushed a handful of silver across the table. 'You'll take my marker for the rest?'

'You know the rules. Cash only.' The dealer's eyes moved back to Artemus. 'Are you in or out?'

'That decision seems to have been taken out of my hands,' the scribe said mildly. He glanced back at Rudi. 'Well?'

'In,' Rudi said, feeling a knot of excitement in the pit of his stomach. Hanna and Fritz stared at him in astonishment for a moment. Then Fritz withdrew his hand, allowing Artemus to pick up the money and add it to the pot.

'Well played,' the richly-dressed fellow said drily. 'But if you think I'm about to be bluffed into folding by a piece of amateur theatrics you're very much mistaken.' He began to turn over his cards.

'Wait!' The shabby man cried desperately. He scrabbled inside his shirt. 'I've got this. It's worth twenty guilders at least!' Despite himself Rudi couldn't help turning his head to look. It was a painting of a woman on a horse, who seemed to be waving some kind of

cup in the air, in a plain wooden frame. The Bretonnian glanced at it with an air of carefully concealed
interest.

'A grail icon,' he said at last. 'Common enough, but
quite well done. I'll give you three guilders for it.'

'Three?' The little man was outraged. 'It's worth five
times that at least.'

'I doubt that.' The merchant shrugged. 'But you can't
bet with it, can you? The man said cash only.'

'All right!' The little man said fiercely. 'Four guilders
eight shillings. That's all I need!'

'No skin off my nose,' the Bretonnian said at last.
'I'm out of the game anyway. But if you win you buy it
back for ten, agreed?'

'Agreed!' The little man thrust the painting into his
hands and after a moment the merchant pulled a stack
of coins out of his purse. 'Thank you.'

'Are we quite finished?' the richly dressed man said
dryly. 'No more last minute soliloquies from Tar-
radasch, no more recitations from Sierck?' He
flipped his cards over with an air of smug satisfaction.

'A good hand,' Artemus conceded, 'but not quite
good enough, I fear.' He laid his own cards on the table
and the rich man shrugged.

'Congratulations,' he said.

'Just a minute.' The shabbily dressed man spread his
own cards out and a jolt of pure horror punched Rudi
in the stomach. The fellow grabbed a handful of coins
from the pot and handed them to the Bretonnian with
a theatrical flourish. 'Ten guilders you said? Cheap at
half the price.' The icon disappeared inside his shirt
again.

'That was… extraordinarily lucky,' Artemus said heavily, slumping back into his chair. The little man had the rarest hand of all. 'With the cards falling as they did, the chances of that combination turning up were–'

'Pretty much inevitable,' Hanna said acidly. 'Since the cards are quite clearly marked.'

'Marked?' The dealer rose to his feet, incensed. 'Tilman's has always played straight! We're known for it!' He beckoned with his hand and Cheap-suit and a couple of other men started moving towards the table.

'Three of cups. Five of cups, two of coins, hanged man, ace of wands.' Hanna gestured to the hand of cards the woman had discarded, still face down.

'That was my hand,' she agreed levelly. She stood, drawing her sword and stepping protectively in front of the richly dressed man. 'Looks like you've just been fleeced, boss.'

'Not just him,' Rudi said, reaching towards the pile of coins. Before he could reach them, the Bretonnian stood abruptly, kicking the table over and scattering the contents.

'Don't just stand there, run for it!' he cried, all trace of his accent suddenly vanishing and grabbing the shabby fellow by the elbow. The little man moved, drawing a blade from a concealed scabbard.

'Right behind you,' he said.

'I don't think so.' Rudi moved in to challenge him, but before he could get close he was buffeted off his feet by someone charging into the back of his knees. As he went down hard, he realised the floor was now seething with people scrabbling after the rolling coins.

By the time he scrambled to his feet, the little man and the fake Bretonnian were nowhere to be seen.

'We have to get out of here,' Artemus said. The room was turning into a free-for-all, as brawls broke out over the scattered money and the house enforcers moved to break them up. 'Things are about to turn very ugly if I'm any judge.'

'What about our money?' Fritz asked grimly, but Rudi nodded in agreement with the scribe.

'Not worth dying for,' he said, taking in the turmoil in the room. Cheap-suit and the heavies with him started trying to break up the nearest brawl, forgetting about them for the moment. Rudi began to draw his sword, but Hanna laid a hand on his arm, forestalling him.

'You'll just make yourself a target,' she said.

'Good point.' Rudi turned to Fritz. 'Fists and feet. We punch our way through and clear a path for Hanna.' For a moment he expected the girl to argue, but she simply nodded grimly.

'Suits me,' Fritz said, turning and lashing out at the nearest face. Now he had something straightforward to do he seemed almost happy. His fist met flesh and the man fell backwards, opening up a tiny space in the maelstrom of bodies surrounding them. Rudi stepped in, kicking out at a sallow faced man who was trying to draw a knife, knocking the feet out from under him.

'Coming?' Hanna asked Artemus as she started to follow them.

'My goodness yes, most certainly.' The scribe picked up his pack and followed them.

'Not so fast.' The dealer grabbed her by the arm. 'You were in with them, weren't you? Caused all this so they could escape!'

'Without the money?' Hanna retorted. 'You're stupider than you look.'

'Let her go!' Rudi punched the man in the stomach, surprised by the surge of anger he felt. The dealer folded and rolled under the table for whatever degree of protection the item of furniture might afford.

'Thanks,' Hanna said, hurrying to stay in the small patch of clear space which followed Rudi and Fritz like the wake of a boat.

'Pardon me, coming through, mind out, oops, sorry about that...' Artemus said, sweeping around them with his walking staff, which somehow seemed to deflect a large number of retaliatory punches.

'Follow them, stick close.' The woman from the card table shoved her charge bodily ahead of her to join Hanna and Artemus, then moved in to stand behind them, facing outwards, walking backwards, her sword at the ready. She flashed a grin at Hanna. 'I'm Mathilde, by the way, that's the Graf von Eckstein.' She parried a sudden thrust from a dagger and retaliated. Someone outside Rudi's field of vision screamed and when he saw the woman's blade again the tip of it was red. It wasn't the only one, either. Many of the weapons drawn had been used. 'Your friend was right, this is going to get ugly.'

'You have no idea,' Hanna said, her face paling, and with a thrill of horror Rudi realised that the power dammed up in her by Gerhard's talisman was beginning to stir again. He punched out savagely at the nearest milling figure, clearing a few inches of space, and put his arm around her waist as she began to sag at the knees.

'Help me!' Rudi snapped at von Eckstein, barely conscious that he was addressing a nobleman in a tone so peremptory that it would have seemed rude to a servant. The man didn't seem to mind though, stepping in to take Hanna's arm across his shoulders.

'With pleasure,' he said. 'Never let it be said that a von Eckstein ever left a damsel in distress.' He picked her up with surprising strength, cradling her in his arms like a child, and nodded affably to Rudi. 'After you.'

'Thanks,' Rudi said, returning to the fray with renewed vigour. Someone swung what looked like a chair leg at his head and he ducked, blocking the blow with his arm and snapping out a counter-punch which caught the fellow full in the face. Something cracked under his knuckles and the man fell, leaving a smear of red across his fist.

'Keep going,' Mathilde said calmly, her sword flickering to and fro, warding off any blows aimed at von Eckstein and keeping most of the crowd at bay by the threat of its presence. Bright metal showed through a couple of slashes in her shirt, revealing the presence of a coat of concealed mail.

'We're trying,' Rudi called back, exerting all his strength against the press of bodies, but they were becoming hemmed in. Even Fritz was making little headway, his muscles more than outmatched by the sheer amount of flesh facing them. Over the heads of the crowd he caught sight of Cheap-suit and his friends making their way towards them as fast as they could. He tried to draw his sword, but couldn't get a hand near the hilt.

Suddenly, without warning, he was blinded by a bright flash of lightning and deafened by a peal of thunder, which echoed through the confined space loud enough to hurt his ears. As he blinked his eyes clear, the babble of voices around him grew even louder, tinged now with panic.

'Sorcery!' Von Eckstein said, sounding intrigued rather than frightened. A gust of wind erupted from nowhere, howling through the room, and Rudi tensed against it, keeping his feet with an instinct honed by a lifetime in the open air. Fritz remained standing too, more by sheer strength than skill, and the rest of the group seemed sheltered behind them, doing little more than swaying on their feet. Most of the other patrons were less lucky, though, being blown to the floor if they hadn't been down there already.

'There must be a wizard or two in here,' Artemus agreed. 'Not that surprising, I suppose. They enjoy a game of chance as much as the next man, although they inevitably get accused of cheating by thaumaturgical means if they hit a winning streak.'

'Who cares?' Mathilde said. Somehow the gust of wind had left a relatively clear path to the door and she pushed von Eckstein into motion. 'Just use it.'

As the graf rushed past him, Rudi glanced at Hanna, wondering if somehow the power within her was manifesting in spite of Gerhard's seal, but she seemed unconscious, slumped in von Eckstein's arms. Her face was pale and her nose was bleeding again and Rudi's jaw tightened with anger. Somehow, he swore, he'd see to it that the witch hunter's curse was lifted and vengeance taken for the atrocity.

'Coming?' Mathilde asked, glancing back as she fled. Galvanised into motion, Rudi followed her, Fritz and Artemus a mere pace or two ahead of him.

CHAPTER TWELVE

'COME ON, BOSS.' Mathilde glanced up and down the street outside the cobbler's shop. 'Not a good idea to be found here.' She'd re-sheathed her sword, after wiping it clean, but her eyes remained watchful. They were an unusual colour, with a faint greenish tinge where the daylight caught them, and the hair under her floppy hat was a rich, dark red. Behind them, more dazed gamblers were escaping into the street and disappearing into the ever-present crowd. Passers-by were beginning to slow down and look. There had been no sign of Tilman in the narrow workshop as they'd rushed through it. Whether he'd run off to fetch help or simply waded into the brawl in the back room, Rudi had no idea.

'I know.' The nobleman hesitated nevertheless, glancing down at Hanna, who was still cradled in his arms. 'Will she be all right?'

'I'm sure she will,' Rudi said, reaching out for her. Von Eckstein handed the girl across and she stirred fitfully as Rudi took her weight, on the verge of regaining consciousness. 'We're staying right down that alley over there.'

'At the Dancing Pirate,' Fritz put in helpfully, ignoring the hard look Rudi gave him.

Von Eckstein nodded. 'Good,' he said, turning abruptly and vanishing into the throng, his bodyguard at his shoulder. 'Look after her.'

Mathilde turned to smile at Fritz as they went. 'Nice right hook,' she said.

'Are you still here?' Fritz turned menacingly towards Artemus, his fists clenching. 'You're stupider than you look.'

'This isn't the time,' Rudi said. As if to underline the point, the girl in his arms moaned gently. 'We have to take care of Hanna.'

'Of course we do,' Artemus said.

'I think you've done enough,' Rudi replied flatly.

The scribe looked crestfallen. 'I hope this unfortunate incident isn't going to cast a shadow on our admittedly fresh, but until now undeniably pleasant, association,' he said. 'If I'd had the remotest idea that the game was rigged I'd never have gone within a league of the place, you can be sure of that.' He shrugged, looking disappointed. 'Tilman's was always known for its honesty too. How times change.'

'You owe us twelve guilders,' Fritz said. He still looked ready to make his displeasure felt physically, but for now seemed content to take his lead from Rudi.

The scribe nodded sadly. 'I'll make full restitution, have no fear on that score.' He turned to go, then glanced back. 'When cooler heads prevail you can find me at the guildhall of the Company of Scriveners, Illuminators and Copyists in the Tempelweik.'

'Don't hold your breath,' Fritz muttered.

'HENDRICK'S PURSE, WHAT happened to her?' Marta cried, bustling forwards the moment Rudi entered the taproom of the Dancing Pirate. Hanna was regaining consciousness and stirred feebly in his arms as they crossed the threshold.

'She fainted,' he said, the same half-truth they'd used on the road slipping easily past his lips. 'I think she found the crowds a little too much to take.'

'I should think she did, the poor lamb. Don't just stand there like a bottle of wine in the Arabiastad, sit her down.' Marta pulled a chair out from under the nearest table and rounded on Koos. 'Go and get her some broth.'

'I'll be fine.' Hanna slithered out of Rudi's embrace, tried to stand for a moment and slumped in the chair, her head pillowed on her arms.

Marta tutted impatiently. 'Yes, you look it.' She glanced up as Nickolaas approached the table with a bowl of water. 'What have you got there?'

'Koos said the young lady wasn't feeling well.' The innkeeper shrugged. 'I thought maybe a cold compress?'

'Two good ideas in one lifetime, Nickolaas? Who would have thought it?' Marta wrung out a cloth in the cool water and began to clean the blood off Hanna's face. 'Oh my goodness, what on earth have you been doing?'

'I bumped my nose when I fell,' Hanna said shortly.

'What was the other good idea?' Fritz asked, looking confused.

'Marrying me.' Marta wrung the cloth out again and folded it into a pad. 'Here.' She held it out. 'Take that nice scarf off and hold this to your head.'

'I'll be fine, thank you,' Hanna said hastily, and Rudi hesitated, trying desperately to think of something to say or do which might deflect the woman's well-meaning attention.

'Nonsense.' Marta didn't seem deflectable by anything short of a cavalry charge. 'It's by far the best thing.' She reached out a hand towards the knot securing the scarf, batting Hanna's hand aside as she tried to fend her off.

'Don't fuss so much, auntie.' A new voice joined the conversation and Rudi turned, startled; he hadn't heard an approaching footstep. Kris the mage stood there, smiling in an apparently open and friendly manner. Given his physique it seemed even more astonishing that he'd been able to approach unheard and Rudi felt a tingle of unease. Alwyn had been able to conceal her movements with sorcery and maybe this affable young man could too. 'I'm sure the young lady knows what's best for her.'

'She does,' Rudi assured them, grabbing the chance the sorcerer's intervention had given him to take control of the situation again. 'She's a healer.' He glanced at Hanna. 'Is there anything in your satchel I can get that might help?'

'No, thank you.' Hanna shook her head, wincing at the sharp movement, and smiled gratefully at Koos as the boy approached with a steaming bowl of broth. 'That's the best possible medicine, I think.'

'Nothing beats good home cooking,' Marta agreed, mollified by the implied compliment, and turned to go. 'If you need anything else, just ask.'

'I will.' Hanna sipped a spoonful of the soup and glanced up at the mage. 'Won't you join us?'

'Thank you.' The portly young man pulled up a chair next to her and smiled again. 'I'm Kris, but of course you already know that.' He glanced briefly at Rudi, with barely concealed amusement, then back to the girl. 'How should I call you?'

'Hanna will do,' Hanna said. Rudi felt baffled. That was her name, so why should she want to be called something else, or imply that she might be? Alwyn had asked her the same question the night they met at the Jolly Friar, he recalled, so perhaps it was a sorcerer's thing. Kris glanced questioningly at Rudi and Fritz. 'They know,' she said.

'I thought so.' Kris nodded. 'But it's always safest never to assume.' Then he smiled widely. 'It was pretty obvious when I saw you in here last night, though.'

'How?' Fritz asked, slipping into another chair.

'Some of us can see the imprint of sorcery where normal eyes can't. I take it from the way you were looking at me that you have the sight as well?'

'Yes,' Hanna said heavily. 'I have the sight. I also have a problem…'

'FASCINATING,' KRIS SAID, gazing at the seal on Hanna's forehead. They'd returned to the girl's room, where they'd be sure of some privacy, and Rudi stood beside the door where he could intercept any further attempts at well-meaning interference from the landlady. That didn't seem terribly likely, as Hanna had made the excuse of needing some sleep before he and the mage had helped her up the stairs, but he remained all too aware of the danger the girl was in and there was no point in taking any chances. Fritz had remained downstairs, ostensibly to prevent anyone else from intruding, but Rudi suspected he was actually more interested in grabbing some food while he had the chance. Come to think of it, the brawl in the gambling den had been pretty strenuous exercise, and now the adrenaline was wearing off he was beginning to feel hungry himself.

'That's not how I'd describe it,' Hanna said, and the mage nodded sympathetically.

'I'm sure.' Kris raised a hand towards the thing. Hanna flinched and he pulled it back hastily. 'I'm sorry, I hadn't realised it was that sensitive.'

'Do you know how to take it off?' Rudi asked.

Kris shook his head. 'To be honest, I've never seen anything like it before. I'd heard stories about some witch hunters using things like this, but I'd always assumed they were just rumours.'

'Evidently not,' Hanna said dryly.

'Quite,' Kris agreed, bending his head for a closer look, then nodding in quiet satisfaction. 'One good thing, anyway, judging by the comet tails embossed in the wax, it's obviously been blessed in the name of Sigmar.'

'How does that help us?' Hanna asked.

Kris smiled grimly. 'He's not a popular god around here. Any enchantments done in His name are going to be weaker in Marienburg than anywhere in the

Empire. That gives us a much better chance of getting rid of it.'

'You'd really do that for her?' Rudi asked.

'Most mages would, unless she's obviously been corrupted by Chaos.' He grinned at Hanna for a moment. 'And I can't see any horns or tentacles.' His expression changed again and he pointed at the talisman with every sign of loathing. 'That could have been me, or any one of my colleagues, if the witch hunters had found us before we recognised our gifts and found somewhere to get properly trained. Something like that touches us all.'

'Do you think I could do that?' Hanna asked, an edge of carefully restrained hope creeping into her voice. 'Get one of the colleges to take me on as an apprentice?'

'It's possible,' Kris said, 'if you made it to Altdorf. We don't have them here.'

'But Koos said you were trained by a college,' Rudi interrupted.

The young mage nodded. 'Baron Henryk's. It's the only institution in Marienburg which can. They provide tuition and issue licences to practise magic which are recognised throughout the known world. Just like the Imperial colleges really, only a bit less hidebound by tradition.'

'Could I enrol there?' Hanna asked eagerly.

'Undoubtedly, if you can find the fees.' Her expression was the only answer he needed and he forced a smile. 'But this is Marienburg, don't forget. You can always cut some kind of a deal.'

'If I can't get this thing off me it's all academic anyway,' Hanna said.

'Quite.' Kris's tone became businesslike again. 'So first things first. We need to find someone who can get rid of it for you.'

'So how do we do that?' Rudi asked.

Kris glanced at him and shook his head. 'You don't. I've got some contacts at the university and among the local mages. I'll ask around.' He grinned suddenly. 'And there are a couple of things I can mention that should incline them to help.'

'Which are?' Hanna asked suspiciously.

'Well for one thing,' Kris said, 'helping you would be a poke in the eye for an Imperial witch hunter. That certainly won't hurt.'

'And for another?' Hanna asked.

'You're a very pretty girl,' the mage said. 'And wizards are just as susceptible to that as the next man.'

Hanna blushed furiously, her mouth working like a landed fish, apparently lost for words for the first time Rudi could ever recall.

'Do you TRUST him?' Fritz asked. He'd still been sitting at the same table when Rudi and Kris had come back after leaving Hanna to sleep off the effects of the seizure as best she could, and watched the mage's departing back with a scowl.

'I don't know,' Rudi replied, still trying to ignore the pang of jealously the young man's words had kindled in him. He had no idea why he should have felt so strongly. After all, he hardly had a claim on Hanna and it was true that she was quite attractive if you liked bossy blondes with a bad temper. 'But I don't think we've got a choice in the matter.'

'I suppose not,' Fritz conceded, dismissing the matter from his mind with an ease Rudi found quite annoying. Kris had promised to bring what news he could the following day and there was nothing more to be done before then. With a sigh, he turned his attention to the matter of lunch. 'Marta's done this thing with eels. You should try it.'

'Might as well,' Rudi agreed.

To HIS VAGUE surprise Rudi felt much better after eating something, and trying not to think too much about how the size of the food bill was escalating, he pushed his chair back from the table at last with a sigh of satisfaction. It was shortly after noon, by his reckoning, although precious little sunshine made its way down the narrow alleyway to the windows of the inn. Now there was nothing for him to do, he felt restless and confined. He stood up to pace the floor of the tavern.

'Do you have to do that?' Fritz asked irritably. 'You're making the place look untidy.'

'Sorry.' Rudi stopped pacing, but remained standing. Used to life in the open air, he felt stifled by the close press of buildings all around them and the teeming crowds which thronged the streets all day and seemingly on into the night. 'I think I need some air.'

'If that's what you call it,' Fritz said sourly. Clearly the ever-present reek was as unwelcome to him as Rudi found it.

'Do you want to come?'

'No thanks,' Fritz said, to Rudi's unspoken relief. 'If you're going out I'd better stay here.' His eyes flickered upwards for a moment, in the general direction of Hanna's room. 'Just in case.'

'Good idea,' Rudi said, trying not to notice the older lad ordering another ale even before he'd reached the door.

The narrow alleyway was as crowded as ever, although the smell seemed to have diminished a little, but Rudi assumed it was just that he was beginning to get used to it. Picking a direction at random, he merged with the hurrying throng, content for a while just to be moving again and taking in the sights and sounds of the city around him.

The first surprise was that there seemed to be water everywhere, narrow channels between the buildings he'd taken for alleyways from a distance, frequently turning out to be thin canals, barely wide enough for a single boat, over which the roadways were carried by bridges. Occasionally, as he glanced down one, he caught a glimpse of more open water, where they opened out into lagoons wide enough for a small dock, where a house or place of business had an entrance opening directly onto the waterways. Almost as often, the narrow passageways turned out to be paved after all, offering an alternative route to his wandering feet.

A couple of times, he crossed more substantial bodies of water, where the canals were wide enough to carry almost as much traffic as the streets; possibly even more so, as the vast majority of land routes were too narrow to accommodate carts or horses and nearly all the commercial traffic appeared to be conveyed by boat. Some of these bridges were almost indistinguishable from the rest of the street, as they were encrusted with shops and houses like the one they'd entered the city by.

Once he turned into a square full of shops and market stalls, his senses battered by the brightly-coloured wares on display and the raucous cries of their owners. He'd been to the market in Kohlstadt a few times, but this was bigger, louder and more crowded than that by an entire order of magnitude. Everywhere he looked were goods of finer quality and in greater profusion than he could have imagined in his wildest dreams: clothes, food, tools, pots, everything he'd ever heard of and a good few things he hadn't. He paused in front of a stall full of books and shook his head in wonder. There seemed to be hundreds, of all shapes, sizes and colours, and behind them pictures, printed on paper and hung from the awning, depicting scenes of battle, pastoral landscapes and images he couldn't identify. A few of the books had been left open and he stared at the black squiggles, wondering what secrets they held.

'Were you looking for something in particular, young sir?' The stallholder smiled at him and Rudi shook his head.

'No, not really,' he said, a faint flush of embarrassment at his inability to comprehend the words in front of him colouring his cheeks.

'Perhaps some artistic engravings?' the stallholder suggested, lowering his voice a little. 'Newly arrived from Bretonnia, quite exceptional, if you know what I mean.'

'No thank you,' Rudi said. The man clearly thought he was some kind of art connoisseur as well as a reader. 'I was just looking.'

'As you like,' the stallholder agreed. 'We're here every day if you change your mind.' He turned to another customer. 'We have that in the original Tilean too, if you're fluent in that tongue.'

Rudi moved on, his mouth watering as the breeze wafted the scent from a hot sausage stall in his direction. It was only then that he realised he was becoming hungry again and that he must have been walking for several hours. His hand moved to his purse, as he intended to spend one of his few remaining coppers on some food, then he hesitated. It would be better to return to the inn and eat there than squander even more of the limited funds at his disposal.

With that in mind he turned, intending to retrace his steps. He felt a faint chill, like an internal echo of the twilight already beginning to gather in the shadows of the square. All the streets leading into it looked the same and were still bustling with crowds.

He didn't have the faintest idea where he was, or how to get back.

CHAPTER THIRTEEN

PANICKING WON'T DO any good, Rudi told himself firmly. The first thing to do was consider his options. He doubted that he had enough in his purse to hire a boatman to take him back to the Dancing Pirate, despite Artemus's advice on the bridge the previous day, so that option was out. He'd just have to rely on his tracking skills. Despite the buildings hemming him in on all sides ever since he'd set off, he was pretty sure from the angles of the shadows he'd seen that he'd spent most of the afternoon heading roughly north-westward. The thing to do was set out towards the south-east and hope he found a landmark he recognised.

First things first, though. He couldn't afford to have his wits dulled by hunger, so he sacrificed a penny from his dwindling store of cash and ate one of the sausages from the stall which had first attracted his attention. Feeling somewhat restored, he took a bearing from the setting sun, which by now was gilding the tiles of the buildings above his head, and set off in what he felt was roughly the right direction.

At first the going was easy, his route lying along a relatively broad thoroughfare, but gradually the streets he was traversing narrowed. As the sun disappeared entirely, the shadows in the doorways and alley mouths darkened, becoming impenetrable, and he tried to keep as close to the centre of the street as he could. To begin with this wasn't too easy, as the passageways between the buildings were as crowded as ever, but as the evening wore on the press of bodies around him began to thin out. The gaps between torches and lighted windows grew ever greater too and what Rudi could see of the buildings in the fitful illumination they gave seemed crumbling and dilapidated. Uncomfortable memories of the conversation on the bridge the day before began to surface, Artemus pointing out the area of dereliction he'd called the Doodkanal.

Rudi loosened his sword in its scabbard and hurried on. The few passers-by were now gaunt and haggard, their clothing ragged, mirroring the decayed state of the buildings they evidently lived in. None seemed inclined to approach him, presumably wary of someone so well-muscled and visibly armed. The main thing, Rudi told himself, was to seem confident. If this really was the quarter he'd been warned about, the only people rash enough to enter it would be the ones with nothing to fear, which by definition would be the ones more dangerous than the denizens Artemus had hinted at. In a way, his very presence there was his best protection.

He kept moving as though he had a destination in mind, and the more he did so the more the conviction grew in him that this was indeed the case. It was like the night in the forest outside Kohlstadt, when he'd been drawn to the gathering in the clearing where he'd met his father and Magnus, just before the beastmen had attacked. A peculiar sense of well-being settled over him at the thought and he increased his pace.

Gradually, the few remaining passersby disappeared altogether, although he could still hear stealthy movement and muffled voices in some of the buildings that surrounded him. There were no more fires or torches to be seen either, just a faint glimmer of necrotic light from Moorsleib as it raised a sliver of itself over the surrounding rooftops. The feeble illumination was enough to allow him to see, despite a thin, freezing mist which began to flow through the streets, bringing with it the odour of water and rotting mud. Inhaling it, Rudi smiled. At least he knew the direction of the waterfront now.

Ahead of him a large building loomed, blotting out the light of the Chaos moon like a block of solid darkness against the sky. As he moved closer, still guided by the unerring instinct which had drawn him this far, Rudi was able to make out gaps in the planking of the walls, through which faint yellow light flickered and danced. There were sounds too, voices raised in what sounded like a chant or a song of some kind, and he smiled again, remembering the revellers he'd encountered in the woods that night. Perhaps it was another celebration, like the one the beastmen had so brutally interrupted.

'Barhum yu! Barhum yu!' The words were nonsense, but resonant somehow and curiously reassuring. Rudi picked up his pace and moved towards their source. Deep down in the recesses of his mind a faint voice urged caution and his pace slowed involuntarily. As it did so a surge of anger and frustration washed over him. Baffled by the storm of unprovoked emotions, Rudi checked his pace and took stock of the situation. Some nameless instinct spurred him on, just as it had that night in the woods, but now his conscious mind was back in control. When he resumed his progress it was slower, more cautious, using all the skill and stealth he'd learned growing up in the forest.

The deep patches of shadow were helping him now and he flitted between them as carefully as if he were stalking game in the woods. Up close, the warehouse was clearly derelict, timbers rotted and sagging, planks missing from the walls. Whether they'd been scavenged by the denizens of this blighted quarter for reasons of their own or simply fallen out as the wood around the nails which held them had crumbled away he couldn't tell, but one of the larger ones served him as an entrance. Guided by the flickering yellow radiance of the fire within, he slipped through the gap and into the building.

His first impression was one of space, despite the sense of enclosure which came from being indoors. The warehouse was cavernous, larger than any building he'd ever seen, except for the ancient elven ruins where he and Hanna had fought the skaven. He advanced cautiously, the mould-softened planks beneath his feet giving faintly under him like springy turf, but they held his weight well enough. The fire-light was brighter here, seeming to rise up from a pit in the floor ahead of him and he inched his way towards it. The voices were louder too, some still chanting the gibberish he'd heard before, while others provided a counterpoint in Reikspiel.

'Hail the vessel! Hail the vessel!' Rudi felt his heart beating a little faster, recognising the phrase Magnus had used in the forest clearing. Perhaps these people knew the merchant and could tell him where to find his friend.

Encouraged, Rudi moved a little more quickly, his confidence growing as his eyes adjusted to the greater level of light. Irregularities in the walls and floor hinted at long-gone walls and upper storeys, tumbled heaps of timber here and there giving clues as to their fates. What he'd taken for a pit in the floor was more than just a hole. As he drew closer to it, he could make out the straight edge marking its boundary and the top of a flight of steps leading down. Impelled by curios-ity, and buoyed by the growing conviction that he was among friends, he made his way to the top of the stair-way.

About to descend, he glanced downwards and stood still for a moment, paralysed by shock and delighted surprise.

The steps led down to a wharf, over which the ground level floor projected; in the days of this build-ing's prosperity, boats could be unloaded here and the cargoes they brought stored directly above them. Thick, oily water lapped at the pilings, pulsating like some vast living organism, red and yellow highlights reflecting the fire which had been kindled in a large brazier. Men and women were ranged about it in a rough semi-circle, their faces for the most part obscured by hooded robes of green and yellow, and many held offerings of offal and other waste which they cast into the flames whenever the chanting reached a particularly resonant phrase. In the centre of the group, his face bare and clearly recognisable, was Magnus.

Relief and delight robbed Rudi of his breath for a moment and he hesitated, reluctant to interrupt the ritual. The merchant was holding a book. Its leather cover was spotted with mould and several pages were loose. As Rudi watched, Magnus stepped forwards and began to read from it in a firm, resonant voice.

'Grandfather, we ask of you a boon. As our bodies reap the bounty of your gifts, so our hearts burn to spread the glory of your word. Guide your vessel to us, so your herald may be free to do your work. Hail the vessel!'

'Hail the vessel!' Magnus's companions echoed his words in a great shout, which echoed around the cavernous building. A deep sense of peace and contentment settled across Rudi and he reached out a foot to descend the stairs. Somehow, he felt, he belonged with these people. All he had to do was get to Magnus and the answers to the questions which had tormented him ever since he'd heard the dying words of his adoptive father in the forest clearing outside Kohlstadt would be made clear.

Magnus and his friends hesitated, the echoes of their cry fading slowly into the foetid air around them. The air of expectation in the ruined wharf was palpable, and Rudi half expected the boat they were evidently waiting for to be putting into the dock beside them even as he moved.

'You really don't want to go down there.' A hand, inhumanly strong, clamped itself around Rudi's bicep, yanking him back into the shadows. Unable to draw his sword he turned, pulling the knife from his belt with the other hand, and prepared to defend himself. Three eyes gazed down at him, taking in the blade he held with sardonic amusement. 'Nice to see you again too.'

The thing which had once been Hans Katzenjammer let him go, batting the blade from his hand with a careless flick of the wrist. It fell point first, sticking into the rotten planks like a steel reed.

'I'll go where I like!' Rudi snarled, all rational thought swept aside by a torrent of rage which roared up from nowhere to leave him shaking with the strength of it. He drew his sword and struck at the mutant with a speed and strength which would have gutted any mortal man. Hans simply parried the blow with the bony ridge along his forearm and shook his head reprovingly.

'Temper, temper,' he said, the familiar malicious grin beginning to spread across his face. He deflected another couple of sallies and retaliated, backhanding Rudi on the side of the head. The young forester fell, pain flaring through his skull, his sword skittering off into the darkness. 'I'm supposed to keep you alive, but she didn't say anything about undamaged.'

'Who didn't?' Rudi spat, clambering awkwardly to his feet. By way of an answer, Hans jerked a talon-tipped thumb in the direction of the bonfire.

Rudi turned his head and gazed down at the derelict wharf. The people there were turning to look at something as well, becoming aware of it one by one, and he craned his neck to see what it might be.

'This is an unexpected pleasure,' Magnus said, in tones which made it clear that it was anything but. 'I heard you were dead.'

'You know how these stories get exaggerated,' a feminine voice responded. There was something familiar about it, and after a moment a lithe figure stepped out of the shadows into the circle of firelight. Her back was to Rudi, but there was no mistaking her identity – the hood of her travelling cloak was drawn back and highlights gleamed from the tips of the horns protruding through the blonde hair covering her head. 'I'd hoped the same about you.'

'A mistake I'm sure we can correct,' Magnus said, tilting his head almost imperceptibly towards her. As the sorceress walked unhurriedly forwards, a couple of the people at the ends of the line began closing in behind her, their hands reaching under their robes. When they emerged, bright steel reflected the firelight as though they were holding blades of gold.

'I doubt it.' The sorceress gestured idly with her left hand and the nimbus of blue fire which had consumed the soldiers back at the camp on the moors erupted around her would-be attackers. They screamed and writhed for a moment as the flames consumed them, then slumped to the decking of the wharf as charred, hissing corpses. The familiar stink of burned flesh filled Rudi's nostrils and with it the realisation that Magnus was in danger. Without thought, he hurled himself at the stairway, filled only with the compulsion to defend his friend. If Magnus died, he might never discover the secret of his origins.

'You're persistent, I'll give you that.' Hans intercepted him, blocking his path. Rudi swung a punch, which jarred his hand and wrist painfully, but the mutant seemed not even to feel it. He seized Rudi by the upper arm and jerked him back. Rudi kicked out at his groin, but even this failed to loosen Hans's grip. 'Just watch.'

Unable to do anything else, Rudi watched.

'You've learned some new tricks, I see.' Magnus was trying to sound calm, but his body betrayed him, his muscles tensing even as he spoke. His companions didn't even try to pretend, falling back from the sorceress with every sign of acute fear. Rudi couldn't blame them for that.

'Not really.' The horned woman sounded amused. 'I just didn't reveal all I could do.'

'You revealed enough for the witch hunter to find you out,' Magnus said.

The sorceress laughed. 'I revealed enough for him to react the way he was supposed to,' she replied. 'No doubt the Changer will reward him for his assistance in due course.' She shook her head in a parody of sympathy. 'Your plans, on the other hand, he disrupted quite thoroughly.'

'Not everything's lost,' Magnus said venomously. 'We can still recover the vessel.'

'And do what?' An edge of contempt entered the woman's voice. 'The time has come and gone. All you can do is release what it holds, and what purpose will that serve?'

'What it always would,' Magnus said angrily. 'Spreading the Grandfather's gifts throughout the known world.'

'In a random and undirected fashion,' the sorceress said. 'Far less than you'd hoped to achieve.' She shrugged. 'But I'm afraid we can't allow you even that minor victory.' She turned suddenly, unleashing another hail of blue fire, which struck a knot of the hovering bystanders. As they burned, the others turned and fled, their cries of panic all but drowning out the shrieks of the dying. Rudi gasped in horror.

'Why's she doing this? She didn't have to kill them!' He made another futile attempt to break free of Hans's grip and the mutant's throaty, inhuman chuckle resounded in his ear.

'She's making sure there aren't enough of them left to repeat the ritual,' he explained, the words rasping though his altered throat. Rudi glanced back at the tableau below. Left alone now, Magnus tried to stare the sorceress down.

'This won't stop us,' the merchant said. 'Sooner or later everything comes to the Grandfather. It's simply a matter of time.'

'Time you no longer have,' the sorceress said, raising her hand again. Rudi drew in his breath to shout a warning, but there was no need; Magnus had turned and run for the edge of the dock. He jumped, his form suspended in the air for a long, slow moment, the first faint azure nimbus beginning to flicker around him, but before the magical fire could coalesce he disappeared into the water with a loud splash. Steam rose for a moment and the sorceress shrugged. How disappointed she was at failing to kill the merchant Rudi could only guess.

Despite the danger he was in, a sudden surge of elation buoyed Rudi up. Magnus was alive and in Marienburg and all he had to do was find him again. If he got out of here in one piece.

DOWN BELOW, THE sorceress stepped back into the shadows and was gone. As soon as she disappeared, Hans released his grip and Rudi backed away, looking around for the weapons he'd dropped, or something else he could use to defend himself. But to his surprise, the mutant remained standing where he was.

'You want to go back up the street you came down,' he said. 'Turn right just past the second bridge. Keep going until you get to the statue, take the left-hand exit from the square facing you as you enter it, third left, second right and if you can't find your own way from there you're even stupider than I've always taken you for.' Before Rudi could react he turned and loped away.

Dazed, Rudi retrieved his fallen weapons and followed his old enemy out into the pale, diseased light of the Chaos moon. The mist was thicker now and he could see no sign of the mutant, the horned sorceress, or any of the people who'd been down on the wharf.

One thing was clear though – he now knew for certain that Magnus was here in the city, and that he was getting closer to the answers he sought. It was with a lighter heart that he set out to retrace his steps along the street which had led him here and to such a bizarre encounter with the people from his past.

CHAPTER FOURTEEN

To Rudi's vague surprise Hans's directions proved accurate. Even despite the steadily thickening mist, he had no trouble following them, and shortly after leaving the square with the statue he found himself back on a street he recognised. At the sight of the first familiar landmark he breathed a faint sigh of relief. He had no reason to trust the mutant, even though for reasons he still couldn't fathom his old enemy had intervened to keep him from harm on several occasions, and he wouldn't have put it past Hans to have steered him into even greater trouble for no better reason than the sheer joy of malice. Certainly the old Hans Katzenjammer he remembered from Kohlstadt, before the beastman's blood had wrought its terrible transformation, would have done so with alacrity.

That led to another disturbing idea. It was clear that Hans was acting as an agent for the horned sorceress, although perhaps not entirely willingly, and now it appeared that she and Magnus were bitter enemies. A sudden, terrible thought struck him, with all the power of a blow to the stomach, and he stumbled as it hit home with almost physical force. He'd seen her with the beastmen in the woods before they killed all the villagers at the gathering in the clearing. Could she have sent them there, out of the enmity she held for the merchant? If so, she was responsible for his father's death, at least indirectly.

Still reeling from the notion, Rudi shook his head, trying to make sense of the conversation he'd overheard. Magnus clearly knew the woman well, but he couldn't imagine how their paths had initially crossed. It must have been in Marienburg, he assumed, because he'd known everyone in and around Kohlstadt at least by sight. At that thought a faint sense of familiarity tried to force its way to the surface of his mind, but it refused to come into focus and he dismissed it angrily. Speculation was futile, he knew, the thing to do was find Magnus. Once he did that and asked the questions consuming him, everything was bound to make sense.

His mind occupied by a maelstrom of speculation, he was barely aware of his surroundings, until the sudden scrape of shoe leather against cobbles warned him he wasn't alone.

Shocked back to the present, Rudi glanced around, trying to orientate himself. The mist had closed in with a vengeance, reducing visibility to a handful of yards, the guttering of torches outside businesses and homes further along the narrow street doing little more than imparting an eerie yellow glow to the fog. Perhaps because of it, the constant bustle of people he'd grown used to since his arrival in the city was now absent, the thoroughfares strangely deserted.

Almost. A shadow in the mist thickened and solidified, taking on the form of one of the largest men Rudi had ever seen. Bare-chested in spite of the chill, he had long, greasy blond hair and a bushy, unkempt beard. A large hammer swung at his side, held easily in a ham-like fist.

'Is this the one?' he asked, elongating his vowels in a curious sing-song manner.

'One of them.' The new voice belonged to Tilman, although tonight the cobbler was dressed in well-cut clothing far more expensive than an artisan would normally be expected to wear. He had a knife in his hand and an ugly expression on his face. 'You cost me a lot of money, boy.'

'I could say the same,' Rudi riposted, drawing his sword. The pair of them clearly meant business. 'But I didn't cheat you out of yours.'

'You see, that's the problem.' Tilman's eyes flickered past Rudi's shoulder. 'All my games are honest. My reputation's my fortune, you might say and you and your friends have damaged it. Nothing personal, but I need to be seen to do something about an accusation like that, or people might start believing it.'

Forewarned by the cobbler's involuntary glance behind him, Rudi turned, bringing up the sword just in time to deflect a vicious blow to the back of his head with what looked like a short club studded with iron nails. The man wielding it seemed vaguely familiar, and after a moment he recognised Cheap-suit from the gambling den. Rudi pivoted on the balls of his feet, keeping the weapons locked together and continuing the downward momentum of his assailant's strike. Cheap-suit kept going with it, until his face met Rudi's rising knee with a resonant *crack*. Flailing his arms, he fell backwards, blood streaming from his nose, just in time to get caught up in the legs of another thug rushing to the attack a pace or two behind him. They both went down in a tangle of limbs and profanity and Rudi turned to face the blond giant, who was bearing down on him with a yell which echoed from every surface in the street.

It was almost too easy, Rudi thought, stepping aside and ramming the pommel of his sword into the fellow's stomach. He had no wish to kill anyone if he could avoid it, although having done so once in self-defence he was under no illusions that he couldn't if he had to. To his surprise and consternation, though, instead of folding as he'd expected, the giant shrugged off the blow, which had felt to Rudi like he was hitting stone, and laughed.

'Is that the best you can do, little boy?' The hammer swung down, striking sparks and chips of stone from the cobbles as Rudi jumped out of the way. Rudi shook his head. 'The best I can do is kill you. Don't make me.'

'Big words.' The hammer swung again and Rudi leapt backwards, deflecting it with the flat of his sword. The impact jarred his arm and he almost dropped the weapon. 'But it takes more than words to kill a Norscan.'

'You broke my nose, you little snotling-fondler!' Cheap-suit staggered to his feet, glanced down at his blood-drenched jerkin, and returned to the attack with a howl of outrage. 'And look what you did to my shirt!'

'I'll do a lot more if you don't back off!' Rudi cut at him as he raised the club again, opening a gash along his arm. Cheap-suit shrieked and dropped the weapon, just in time to stumble into the path of the Norscan. The blond giant batted him out of the way with his free hand and Cheap-suit fell over again. His friend smiled and drew a sword of his own.

'Let's see how good you really are with that.'

'My pleasure.' Rudi spun out of the way of another hammer blow, time seeming to slow as it had before when he was fighting for his life. Once again a detached portion of his mind wondered at the power and skill he was displaying, far more than his limited experience should have made possible. On the verge of kicking out at the back of the Norscan's knee, he hesitated for an instant, unsure if the trick would work against someone so strong, then tried it anyway. To his relief the blond giant fell after all, looking surprised and Rudi struck as hard as he could at the base of the man's skull with the sword hilt. The hit was a solid one and the Norscan just had time to look surprised before his eyes rolled up in their sockets and he pitched forwards onto his face. 'Oh, shut up.' He kicked out again at Cheap-suit, who was still screaming, and the fellow finally lapsed into unconsciousness too.

'Well that's a relief,' the swordsman said, smiling sardonically. 'I was beginning to find all that noise quite off-putting.' He cut suddenly at Rudi's stomach and Rudi parried the blow instinctively. 'Well done. They generally don't see that one coming.'

'Make a habit of picking on blind men?' Rudi asked, stepping in to counter.

His opponent grinned. 'Only if I'm paid to.' He made an attack in earnest and Rudi began to realise that despite his opponent's flippant attitude, he was facing an adversary whose skill far exceeded his own. His only chance was to finish things quickly, before the swordsman found an opening in his defences.

'Then consider this a bonus,' Rudi said, flinging his purse at his adversary's face. It opened as it flew forwards, showering the swordsman with stinging copper coins. Despite himself, the man flinched and Rudi rushed in past his arm, slamming the hilt of his sword into his face. The swordsman yelled in anger and pain, all pretence at relaxation gone. He tried to turn, but Rudi was too quick, looping his arm around the fellow's throat and pulling back, closing off the artery in his neck. The swordsman struggled for a few moments, then went limp.

Rudi released him, letting him fall, and turned towards Tilman, who was still rooted to the spot, an expression of terrified astonishment on his face. Rudi raised his sword and the cobbler took a step backwards.

'Look, there's no need to be hasty. I'm sure we can work something out...'

'Twelve guilders,' Rudi said, astonished to hear the words falling out of his mouth. 'That's how much we lost.'

'Twelve you say?' Tilman scrabbled for his purse. 'That sounds very reasonable. As I said, my reputation's my livelihood and I wouldn't want it said that any customer had left my establishment dissatisfied.' He counted out a dozen of the gold coins, then added another. 'And that should more than make up for the change you spilled a moment ago.'

'I imagine it will,' Rudi said, stooping to pick up his purse. When he straightened up Tilman was gone, although the echoes of his footsteps were still audible. It wasn't until after he'd stowed the coins and tucked the leather bag away that Rudi realised the footsteps were getting closer, not further off, and they were being made by more than one pair of feet.

'Drop the sword!' a voice shouted and a quartet of armed men loomed up out of the mist. Rudi began to bring the weapon up into a defensive posture, then hesitated. Two of them carried polearms, their leader had a drawn sword in one hand and a pistol in the other, and the fourth had a loaded crossbow pointed firmly at the centre of his chest. As they came fully into focus, illuminated by the diffuse yellow glow leaking through the vapour around them, Rudi breathed a sigh of relief. All four were wearing the black, floppy hats Artemus had pointed out at the gateway to the city. Watchmen. He opened his hand and the weapon clattered on the cobbles.

'Good call.' The group's leader kept him covered with the pistol in any case and stared hard at his face. 'I don't know you, do I?'

'I don't think so,' Rudi said, returning his gaze levelly. The man had dark hair and a thin, hard visage. A faint scar ran across one brow, making him look vaguely sardonic. After a moment he nodded.

'I know most of the troublemakers around here. Been in town long?'

'Since yesterday,' Rudi said. 'And I didn't make any trouble.'

'Really?' The Black Cap glanced at the trio of feebly-stirring bodies behind him. 'That looks like trouble to me.' Then he turned and gestured to his subordinates. 'Take them in too. Charge them with brawling in public.' The other watchmen approached Rudi's erstwhile assailants, producing manacles from their belt pouches as they did so, and he turned back to Rudi. 'That'll do for a start, until we can get to the bottom of this.'

'Hendryk's Purse!' One of the watchmen rolled the big Norscan over and stepped back in astonishment. 'It's Wulf Hammerhand!' He glanced across at Rudi with wary respect. 'He took out Big Wulf!'

'And Dandy Douwe!' One of his colleagues looked up from manacling Cheap-suit. Their leader looked at Rudi appraisingly, his scarred eyebrow rising a little.

'All by yourself?'

Rudi nodded. 'They didn't seem so tough.'

'Really.' The man nodded and pointed to the third assailant. 'And he would be...?'

'I haven't a clue,' Rudi said. 'He just came at me with a sword.'

'Watse van Os,' the nearest watchman volunteered, hauling the man to his feet.

'Watse van Os,' the senior Black Cap repeated. 'One of the best duellists in the ward. And you beat him.' Rudi nodded. 'And the others.' Rudi nodded again. 'By yourself.' He was clearly disbelieving.

'I've fought bandits and beastmen,' Rudi retorted, nettled by the man's scepticism. 'I killed a skaven with my bare hands. Why should a handful of cutpurses be that much of a challenge?'

'Because they're a lot more than that,' the Black Cap said. After another appraising stare he tilted his head towards Rudi's fallen sword. 'Better put that away

before it rusts.' He waited until the young forester had
picked up and sheathed his weapon, then nodded
thoughtfully. 'And I think we should have a long talk
about things back at the watch house.'

'You're arresting me?' Rudi asked, in outraged astonishment.

The Black Cap smiled sardonically. 'I'm inviting you
to accompany us. For the moment.'

'I see,' Rudi said, feeling that once again events were
getting out of control.

IN SPITE OF his apprehension, however, the Black Cap
officer continued to treat him as a witness rather than a
suspect. The watch house turned out to be surprisingly
comfortable, though solidly built with an obvious eye
to defence, backing directly on to one of the larger
canals. The front faced the street and narrow alleyways
ran down either side to meet the small landing stage
built out over the waterway to the rear. The main door
led directly into a large common room, where several
watchmen sat around a fireplace, drinking ale and playing cards, their weapons lying easily to hand. Most
looked up with expressions of surprise as the trio of
prisoners was escorted through and Rudi noticed satisfied grins on a number of faces; presumably his
erstwhile assailants had few friends among the watch.

'Gerrit, get them booked in.' The leader nodded to
one of the watchmen who'd helped him make the
arrest. 'And send a runner to the barracks. I want Captain Roland in on this.'

'Right you are, Sarge.' The watchman, an eager young
man not much older than Rudi, nodded and herded
the prisoners away. The sergeant sighed.

'Waste of time processing them really, they'll be out by morning. But the law's the law and while we've got them we'll stick to due process.'

'Won't they be tried or something?' Rudi asked.

The sergeant shook his head and ushered him to a nearby bench. 'Not those three. Their lawyer will be in here within the hour with enough in his purse to pay their fines and we'll have to let 'em go. Unless there's something you want to tell me.'

'Like what?' Rudi asked.

'Like how you've managed to upset the league so badly in less than two days. Assuming that's really how long you've been in town, of course.'

'What league?' Rudi asked, his obvious confusion being all the confirmation the sergeant needed. He sighed.

'The League of Gentlemen Entrepreneurs. It's got other names, but to all intents and purposes it's a guild like any of the others in the city. The difference is that the business it regulates is generally illegal.'

'I see.' Rudi nodded. 'I'd heard the guilds ran pretty much everything here, but I never thought that extended to crime.'

'Only in Marienburg,' the sergeant said, with heavy irony. 'Which brings me back to my original question. What have you done to upset them?'

'Let me guess,' a new voice cut in. Rudi glanced up and the sergeant stood, nodding a respectful greeting to a middle-aged man with a well trimmed beard in which traces of grey were beginning to show. Despite this and the beginnings of a stomach, he looked very capable of defending himself if he had to. 'Might you have been in the back room of a cobbler's shop this morning, at about the time an altercation broke out?'

'I might,' Rudi said, feeling there was no point in denying it.

The newcomer smiled and extended a hand. 'I'm Gil Roland, captain of the Winkelmarkt watch. Sergeant Rijgen you've already met.'

'AT TILMAN'S?' RIJGEN looked sceptical. 'His games are always fair. You must have made some mistake.'

'It certainly looks that way,' Rudi said. 'Those men seemed pretty insistent on the point.'

'And they're likely to remain so,' Roland said. 'Unless you can get some powerful protection. Which guild do you belong to?'

'None,' Rudi said, feeling bewildered again. 'We've only been in the city since yesterday. There hasn't been time to look for work.'

'Then you'd better be quick,' Rijgen put in. 'With the right guild behind you they'd think twice before trying again. What do you normally do?'

'I'm a forester,' Rudi said. 'I hunt game, mostly.' The two watchmen looked at one another.

'Not a lot of call for that in Marienburg,' the sergeant said.

The captain grinned. 'I think we can do a lot better than that,' he said. 'You really took all three of them out single-handed?'

'Yes.' Rudi nodded. 'I'm sorry if it was against the law, but I tried not to hurt anyone too badly.'

'Did you indeed?' Roland looked dubious for a moment, as if Rudi might simply have been bragging after all, but the sergeant nodded.

'He says he's killed men before in self-defence and I believe him. If he hadn't he wouldn't have been so careful with those three. Besides, he knows about the rodent problem.'

'Does he?' The captain nodded, as though he'd made up his mind about something, and turned to smile at Rudi. 'Then I think we can help each other.'

'We can? How?' Rudi asked, confused.

Captain Roland's smile grew wider. 'We can do with someone of your calibre in the watch,' he said. 'And if you join us you can be sure the league will back off. If they mess with one watchman they mess with us all, and however hacked off they are with you it's not worth that amount of trouble to them.'

'The money's lousy and the hours are worse,' Rijgen added, grinning. 'But at least you get a new hat. What do you say?'

CHAPTER FIFTEEN

'WHAT HAPPENED TO you?' Fritz asked, glancing up as Rudi entered the taproom of the Dancing Pirate. He was still sitting at the same table he'd occupied when Rudi left, although the tavern was now much busier than it had been. Several of the patrons started visibly as Rudi stepped through the door, then took great pains to avoid eye contact. For a moment he wondered why, until he remembered that his new hat did a lot more than keep his head warm.

'I got a job,' he said, removing it, to the barely concealed relief of several of the patrons. Only one of them caught his eye, Sam the halfling, who was occupying the same back table he'd been at last night. He just smiled, as if at some private joke and returned his attention to the platter of food in front of him. He seemed completely at ease, although he sat alone. Rudi assumed he was there to meet Kris and paid him no further attention.

'Me too,' Fritz said, with a wide grin, hitching his chair over to make room for Rudi.

'Doing what?' Rudi asked suspiciously, dropping into the seat next to him. Nikolaas seemed far too sensible to have taken Fritz on as a potboy and he couldn't imagine any other employment his companion could have found without leaving the premises. He glanced around – the room was crowded with patrons and on the whole he thought it best not to mention that he'd recovered their money from Tilman until they were alone. By way of an answer, Fritz nodded affably to someone approaching the table with a couple of mugs of ale.

'You remember Mathilde?' he asked. Taken aback, Rudi simply nodded. For a moment he'd mistaken the woman for a serving girl, although she was hardly dressed like one. She smiled and sat opposite the two youths, handing one of the mugs to Fritz.

'How could I forget?' Rudi replied, covering up his momentary confusion as best he could. The bodyguard grinned at him.

'You made quite an impression yourselves. That's why I'm here.' She signalled for another drink and passed the second mug to Rudi. He took it and drank gratefully. The sausage in the marketplace had been a long time ago and an awful lot had happened since then.

'I'm not sure I follow,' Rudi said. Koos wandered over with Mathilde's fresh ale and he took the opportunity to order some food.

The woman nodded. 'Good idea. Three of those and some of that Bretonnian bread with the garlic in it.' She grinned at Rudi's horrified expression. 'Don't knock it till you've tried it. The boss had some business in Couronne a couple of years back and I got a taste for the stuff while we were there.' She handed the potboy a guilder. 'And get yourself a drink while you're at it.'

'Thanks. I will.' Koos wandered off, looking slightly dazed, and Mathilde chuckled.

'You know the best thing about working for nobility? The expenses. He's got no idea what things cost in the real world, just keeps handing over more cash whenever I tell him it's gone. You're going to love it.'

'Love what?' Rudi asked, feeling as dazed as Koos had just looked.

Mathilde smiled again and started piling into the food as soon as it arrived. 'Didn't Fritz tell you?'

'I was trying,' the simpleton said, clearly as overwhelmed by the torrent of words as Rudi was. He turned to the young watchman. 'The graf was impressed with the way we handled ourselves this morning. He wants us to go and work for him.'

'Doing what?' Rudi asked. In spite of his confusion, the odour of food was too strong to ignore and he began spooning up mouthfuls of fish stew.

'Helping me,' Mathilde said cheerfully. 'After this morning he feels one bodyguard might not be enough while he's here. I suppose I should feel insulted, but it's his money and I always feel happier with some expendable muscle standing between me and the crossbows, anyway.' She frowned at Rudi's expression and grinned again. 'Hey, I'm kidding about the expendable part. Mainly. But when push comes to shove and the job's about protecting the boss whatever it takes.'

'Your job,' Rudi said. 'I've already found one.' He indicated the hat which he'd folded and tucked into his belt.

Mathilde stared at it and laughed again. 'As a Black Cap? You're joking, right?' Rudi shook his head.

'I signed on this evening.' In actual fact he'd simply scrawled a ragged X, next to which, for reasons he couldn't quite fathom, Captain Roland had insisted he dab his thumb after dipping it in the ink.

'Tell them you've changed your mind.'

'I can't,' Rudi said. 'I swore an oath.' He'd recited a promise to uphold the law which Rijgen had prompted him through line by line, with the air of a man for whom the fine sounding words had long since ceased to have any meaning. They'd sounded resonant enough to Rudi and he still felt the power of them and the sober weight of the responsibility they'd conferred.

'You've got principles. Good for you. Not that they'll do you much good in a place like this.' She turned to Fritz and grinned again. 'Looks like it's just you and me then.'

'I'm sure that'll be enough to keep him safe,' Rudi said sourly. 'Assuming he hasn't been assassinated while you're off on your dinner break.'

'Don't worry about that,' Mathilde said cheerfully, taking a bite out of the bread she'd ordered and chewing with every sign of appreciation. 'He's tucked up safe and sound in the Imperial embassy. No one's going to croak him there, too many guards.' The grin was back on her face. 'So tonight I'm footloose and fancy free. And one thing you can say for the boss, he does have a knack of finding interesting places to spend your leisure time.' She wiped the remains of the bread around the bottom of her bowl, chewed it, and swallowed with a sigh of satisfaction. 'Care to check a few out?'

'Sounds like fun,' Fritz said, turning to Rudi. 'What do you think?'

'I think someone should check in on Hanna,' Rudi said.

'She's been sleeping all day. She'll be fine by the morning.'

'I hope so,' Rudi said, feeling rather less certain. The last time the dammed-up magic inside her had induced a seizure it had taken her several days to recover fully. 'But I'd feel a lot more comfortable if I hung around here and kept an eye on her.'

'Suit yourself,' Mathilde said and turned to Fritz. 'Looks like two's company then.' Fritz hesitated a moment, grinned sheepishly at Rudi, and trotted out after her. Feeling vaguely deflated, Rudi watched them go and ordered another ale.

FRITZ STILL HADN'T returned by the following morning. When Rudi woke from a surprisingly restful slumber the other bed in the room had clearly not been slept in. Shrugging, he descended the stairs in search of breakfast and was pleasantly surprised to find Hanna already seated at a table in the taproom, the remains of a hearty meal scattered in front of her.

'You look good,' he said without thinking, and the girl looked up, smiling in response.

'I feel good,' she said. 'The stone thing seems to be helping still and Kris is taking me to the university this morning. There are some people there he wants me to meet.'

'That's great. Really.' He sat down next to her and started spooning down the large bowl of porridge

Marta placed on the table in front of him. 'I'm sure at least one of them will be able to help you.'

'Provided I can pay for it,' Hanna said. 'That seems to be the way things work around here.'

'I think I can help you with that,' Rudi said. He produced his purse and handed her seven of the gold coins he'd so unexpectedly acquired the previous night. 'Three of these are yours anyway and you can have four of mine too. And three are Fritz's, so I'd better hang on to those until he surfaces again.'

'Where did you get these?' Hanna asked, surprise and suspicion mingling in her voice. She looked at him appraisingly. 'You haven't done something stupid, have you?'

'I had an unexpected conversation with Herr Tilman last night. He insisted on paying us back the money we lost.'

'Did he?' Hanna didn't sound terribly convinced. 'That sounds a bit out of character for the owner of a gambling den.'

'He said something about needing to maintain a reputation for honesty,' Rudi said, half-truthfully. 'I was quite surprised myself.'

'Then he shouldn't allow people to play with marked cards,' Hanna said acidly. After a moment she slipped the coins into her purse, and to Rudi's delighted surprise leaned across to kiss him lightly on the cheek. 'Thank you. I'm sure it'll help, and I'll pay you back somehow, I promise.'

'Don't worry about it,' Rudi said. 'I found a job. I'll be getting paid next week.'

'Really?' Hanna stared at him in astonishment. 'Doing what?'

'He's joined the Black Caps,' Kris said, wandering over to the table with a plate of steaming sausage in his hand. He dropped into a chair opposite. 'It's all over the ward. He took out three of the dirtiest fighters in Winkelmarkt all by himself last night, so it's no wonder they wanted him.'

'I see.' Hanna looked at Rudi in an appraising manner the young watchman found vaguely disturbing. 'I assume you were going to mention that at some point?'

'Of course.' Rudi flushed guiltily and applied himself to the food with exaggerated diligence.

'Do try to be careful. I'd hate to lose you too.'

'Not much fear of that,' Kris put in cheerfully. 'After what he did last night, no one's going to mess with him unless they're crazy.' He smiled at Rudi. 'So what are you going to do this morning?'

'I'm not sure,' Rudi said. 'I'm not due back at the watch house until noon, so I thought I'd just wander around the neighbourhood for a bit, try and get my bearings.'

'You'll get enough of that once you're on duty,' Kris said, finishing the last of his sausage. He smiled in an amiable fashion which reminded Rudi of Artemus. 'If you've got nothing better to do, why not tag along with us? At least that way you'll get to see a bit more of the city than just the Winkelmarkt.'

'That sounds like a good idea,' Rudi said, glancing at Hanna for approval, and deciding not to mention his impromptu foray into the Doodkanal.

'Fine with me,' she said.

* * *

THE MIST RUDI remembered from the night before had evaporated by the time they set out from the Dancing Pirate, although the breeze through the streets still had a chill edge to it. Kris smiled when Hanna remarked on the fact.

'It'll be a lot colder before long,' he said. 'Summer's almost gone, don't forget. And we're on the coast here, which doesn't help.'

'How?' Rudi asked. By his reckoning they should still have almost a month of relatively warm weather before the autumn chill descended. Hanna and he had left Kohlstadt in high summer, and even the astonishing number of events they'd lived through in the meantime hadn't been enough to blunt his instinctive affinity for the cycle of the seasons.

'The whole city's built on a swamp. It's humid in summer, freezing in winter, and clammy in between. Before you know it the fogs will be rolling in every night.' He shot a tight grin at Rudi. 'You'll be earning your pay then all right, believe me.'

'I've seen fog before,' Rudi said.

'Not like these. You can hardly see a hand in front of your face. You'll see.'

'Apparently not,' Rudi said and the wizard laughed.

Despite the chill the air was crisp, shafts of pure sunlight striking down through the gaps between the buildings, and Rudi found he was enjoying the walk. He was getting more used to the ever-present crowds too, he discovered, moving through them more easily, and was able to spare some of his attention to take in the sights Kris pointed out as they progressed through the streets in a relatively leisurely fashion. The Marienburger was evidently proud of his home and clearly relished the chance to show it off to his new friends.

Rudi wasn't altogether sure he could blame him for that. Marienburg was even more vast than he'd imagined and the different districts they passed through all had their own character. Not, perhaps, as distinct as the dereliction of the Doodkanal, but noticeable nevertheless.

'This is the Suiddock,' Kris said, as they passed through an area which seemed to consist largely of warehouses and taverns. There were more wharves and canals here too, which Rudi mainly glimpsed through gaps between the larger structures, most of the berths occupied by ocean-going vessels whose masts towered over the buildings surrounding them like trees in the forest. Other docks played host to riverboats, none of which, to his quiet relief, was the *Reikmaiden*. Sweating stevedores swarmed over ship and boat alike removing and loading cargoes, or transferring them between the two. The vast majority of bundles and barrels seemed to be destined for the warehouses surrounding them and several times Rudi had to stand aside to let a laden handcart trundle past. 'It's a bit out of our way to be honest, but I thought you'd like to see it. You can't really get a sense of what Marienburg is all about until you've seen the docks.'

'It's amazing,' Hanna said, gazing around at the bustle of activity, and Kris smiled delightedly.

'If you can't find it in Marienburg it doesn't exist. Everything in the world passes through here sooner or later.'

'I can believe it,' Rudi said, following Kris onto the cobbles of a nearby bridge.

'There. I bet you've never seen anything like that in the Empire.'

'You'd win,' Hanna said, awestruck and Rudi could do little more than nod in agreement. In the far distance, yet still able to dwarf the warehouses and other buildings in between, a vast viaduct rose, higher than any structure he would have believed possible.

'The Hoogbrug bridge. Longest and highest in the known world. The arches are large enough for an ocean-going ship to pass through under full sail and the ramps around the outside of the towers are wide enough for two coaches to pass one another.'

'That's amazing,' Rudi said, drinking in the sight. 'What's on the other side?'

'The northern half of the city,' Kris said. 'And unless you've got a boat or you fancy a swim, there's no other way to get there.'

'Are we going to cross it?' Hanna asked, an edge of apprehension entering her voice.

'Not today. Baron Hendryk's is this side of the Reik. But there are some pretty good restaurants in the elf quarter you ought to try if you get the chance. And some halfling place Sam recommends.' He pulled a face. 'Only trouble is, if you eat there you'll end up with your knees under your chin and your head in the rafters. He swears the food's worth it, but I have my doubts.'

'He's a pretty good friend of yours then?' Rudi asked casually.

'I wouldn't say that, exactly. We've done a bit of business from time to time.'

'I see,' Rudi said, although he wasn't sure that he did.

The buildings on the other side of the bridge were bigger and more elaborate than those in the Winkelmarkt and marked by time and decay. Plaster was crumbling, paint flaking, and many of the once grand mansions they passed had clearly been subdivided into dwellings and offices. A faint air of decay seemed to hang over them all, and Kris nodded when Hanna remarked on the fact.

'The Oudgeldwijk,' he said. 'A few hundred years ago the wealthiest merchants in the city lived here. But after the bridge was built the real money moved over the river, where there was room for bigger houses. Some of the families stayed, but the ones that did are struggling.' He shrugged. 'Now half the houses are let and the rest are being circled by the speculators.' Rudi nodded thoughtfully. It seemed as though this was the sort of area Magnus might live in. Now he'd seen a little more of the wider world, Rudi was beginning to realise that what had seemed a vast fortune in Kohlstadt wasn't necessarily so in a place like this. He was about to ask if Kris knew whether one of the mansions might belong to a von Blackenburg, but before he could they crossed another of the myriad bridges stitching the city together and the character of the buildings around them changed again.

'This is it,' Kris said. 'The Templewijk.' He waved an expansive hand at the bustle surrounding them. The streets here seemed busier than the languid pace of the Oudgeldwijk, almost as much as the Suiddock had been, but instead of carters, stevedores and artisans, most of the passers-by seemed to be mages or priests, hurrying along with the hems of their robes lifted slightly to keep them clear of the patina of mud which

coated the cobbles as thickly as it seemed to everywhere else Rudi had been. Here, despite the shortage
of building land which afflicted the whole city, broad
squares wider than any he'd seen since his arrival in
Marienburg opened out, fronted by buildings of a size
and magnificence he could scarcely have imagined.

'What's that?' Hanna asked, awestruck, craning her
neck back to look up at the vast structure dominating
the skyline ahead of them. It was the largest building
Rudi had seen since arriving in Marienburg, reducing
the endless stream of people hurrying in and out of
the titanic doors to the scale of mice. A frieze of owls
and the kind of balancing scales Rudi had seen merchants use to weigh out their wares was carved into the
marble portico, and the same images seemed to be
repeated wherever he looked.

'The cathedral of Verena,' Kris said, and Rudi belatedly recognised the symbols of the goddess of justice.
He shot a grin at the young watchman. 'Perhaps you
should go in for a blessing, given your new profession.'

'Maybe I should,' Rudi said, not quite sure whether
the mage was joking or not. He pointed to a side wing
almost as large as the church itself. 'Is that part of the
cathedral too?'

'The great library,' Kris said, a tone of near wistful-
ness entering his voice. 'The greatest repository of
wisdom in Old World.'

'Can anyone use it?' Hanna asked, and Kris nodded
slowly.

'Anyone presenting evidence of real scholarly intent.
In theory at least. Usually a letter of introduction from
the college is enough. But they're badly understaffed,
so even if they approve your request you can be in for

a long wait. And their records aren't all they might be, so even when you get in you might not be able to find what you're looking for.' His mood brightened as they passed down a narrow street lined with taverns and boarding houses. 'Scholar's Row. Nearly there.'

'Good,' Hanna said, and Rudi looked at her with sudden concern. Lost in the wonders the young mage was pointing out to them, he'd almost forgotten how weak she still was. Catching his eye she smiled wanly. 'I'm all right, really.'

'Glad to hear it,' Kris said, failing to understand. They came out into another square and he gestured to the palace facing them. It was almost as large as the cathedral had been, but constructed of brick and timber rather than stone. Statues and gargoyles encrusted every surface, for the most part spattered with the droppings of the gulls which roosted there, their raucous squawks all but drowned out by the bustling of the humans below. Sunlight shone golden from hundreds of windows and Rudi gasped at the realisation that they were all glazed, a display of wealth more dazzling in its own way than the light they were reflecting. 'Here we are.' Kris led them to a small gate set in the wall and Rudi caught a glimpse of a courtyard beyond. Clearly the college rambled for some distance behind this monumental facade, newer, more utilitarian buildings having been added to the original palace, donated to the city by Baron Henryk when he endowed the institution in the first place.

'It's… Impressive,' Hanna said, for once almost lost for words. Kris grinned happily, as though he'd just performed some amusing party trick. A man seated just inside the archway stood as they approached.

'Kris Goudriaan,' the young mage said. 'Professor Aaldbrugh is expecting us.'

'Of course it is.' The porter smiled with what looked like genuine warmth. 'You had rooms in the Contessa Esmeralda wing. I never forget one of my young gentlemen.' He glanced across at Hanna and the smile became slightly less certain. 'Or ladies.'

'She's with me,' Kris assured the man, and he nodded slowly.

'Of course.' The man's eyes took in Rudi and the folded hat tucked into his belt, clearly recognising its significance. 'Is this gentleman with you as well?'

'No,' Rudi said, before either of his friends could respond. It was obvious that he would stand out here as a conspicuous outsider, not to mention an off-duty watchman, and it would hardly help Hanna to draw any more attention to her than was absolutely unavoidable. 'I'm on my way to the cathedral of Verena. I just walked this far with my friends for the exercise.'

'I see,' the porter said, with a faint air of relief, and stood aside to let Hanna and Kris enter. As she passed under the archway the girl looked back at him with a faint, nervous smile and he hoped she understood why he was letting her go in alone. Conscious of the porter's eyes, Rudi turned and sauntered away in the direction of the cathedral, resisting the urge to turn back for a last glimpse of her.

Now that the idea had been planted, he found the notion of seeking a blessing was becoming more attractive. He'd never been particularly devout, beyond leaving the occasional offering to Taal in the forest glades whenever the hunting had gone particularly well or badly and fidgeting uneasily through Father Antrobus's interminable sermons in Kohlstadt's tiny chapel of Sigmar on the handful of feast days when the pressures of social convention had dragged the Walders out of their woodland home to participate along with everyone else. But somehow the notion seemed appropriate. Not only was he beginning a new life as an upholder of the law, he and Hanna were innocent victims of the witch hunter's vindictiveness; an appeal to the goddess of justice might just help them both.

As he approached the vast building, angling towards the main door which stood open, dwarfing the steady stream of figures entering and leaving, his footsteps began to falter. Sick apprehension churned in his gut and the palms of his hands began to sweat. As he got closer to the looming pile of masonry his heart began to beat faster, a sense of fear rising up from nowhere to practically overwhelm him, as powerful and unexpected as the other inexplicable surges of emotion he'd experienced from time to time since that fateful night in the forest. His vision blurred, the uncountable tons of stone seeming poised to crush him where he stood.

'Rudi!' A cheerful voice hailed him, snapping him back to himself, and he turned to find Artemus smiling uncertainly at him from a handful of paces away. 'This is a most unforeseen pleasure. I have to admit I hadn't expected to see you for some time, if indeed at all.'

'I could say the same,' Rudi said. He still wasn't sure if he trusted the scribe or not, but right now the sight of a familiar face was undeniably welcome.

'And I could hardly blame you for that.' He looked at the young watchman a little more closely, an expression of solicitude touching his face. 'Are you all right? You look a little pale.'

'I'll be fine,' Rudi said, turning away from the finely-carved oak doors. As he did so he began to feel a little better. 'The walk from the Winkelmarkt was further than I expected, that's all.'

'I've noticed the same thing myself on many occasions,' Artemus assured him. 'A league across a city can seem like ten on the open road.' Rudi nodded an assent, unable to argue with those sentiments. The scribe hesitated a moment before continuing. 'My chambers aren't far from here if you'd care to rest for a while before returning.'

'I think I would. Thank you.'

'I REALLY HAD every intention of returning, you know,' Artemus said earnestly. He was sitting on the narrow bed in the larger of the two rooms he occupied in the Scriveners' guildhall, a surprisingly modest edifice by the standards of some of its more ostentatious neighbours. The other room was almost filled by a desk, angled to make the most of the light from the narrow window, on which a half-completed manuscript stood along with the book from which it was being copied and a bookshelf containing almost a dozen volumes. Rudi occupied the single chair. 'I was sure I could repay your kindness by doubling our funds at the very least.'

'Maybe you would have done if the game hadn't been rigged,' Rudi said, trying to give him the benefit of the doubt.

'At Tilman's, of all places. I would never have believed it. But Hanna knew that woman's hand all right, so there must have been some chicanery involved.' His voice took on an expression of puzzlement. 'What I don't understand is how she was able to spot the tampering. I've seen plenty of marked decks in my time and it looked perfectly all right to me.'

'I suppose we were just lucky she did,' Rudi said, not wanting to discuss the topic any more than he had to.

'Small recompense for you, though. I hope you haven't been left in too dire a situation by my folly.'

'Not so bad,' Rudi admitted. 'Tilman and a couple of his thugs came after me, but I saw them off and got most of our money back.' He hesitated, feeling a little uncomfortable for the first time. 'I'm afraid I wasn't too concerned about recovering your share, though.'

'Easy come, easy go.' To Rudi's relief he didn't seem too upset about it. 'I'm simply pleased that things are a little easier between us than they might otherwise have been.' An expression of concern crossed his face. 'But you might find some rather unpleasant people holding grudges as a result of your actions. You should all take care to be vigilant.'

'If you mean the league,' Rudi said, the scribe starting slightly at the sound of the name, 'I think we'll be all right. Hanna's going to be spending some time at the college with Kris, Fritz is working for that Imperial nobleman we got out of Tilman's in one piece, and I've just joined the Black Caps.' He indicated the hat tucked into his belt.

'My goodness, how very enterprising of you all,' Artemus said. He stared at Rudi with growing respect. 'And you're quite right, those are all positions which should protect you from any overt reprisals.' He shrugged again. 'But I still feel I should make some sort of restitution, even though the money's been repaid. If there's anything I can possibly do for you?'

'There is,' Rudi said impulsively.

Artemus raised an eyebrow in polite enquiry.

'Teach me to read.'

CHAPTER SIXTEEN

'I LIKE IT,' Hanna said, glancing around the narrow room. 'It's very homely.'

'Thanks,' Rudi said, not quite sure how to respond. It was the first time he'd ever lived in a space that was exclusively his, and the first time he'd ever had a guest in it, unless you counted the other residents of the watch barracks he'd made friends with since moving in here a month or so ago. The accommodation was a little more spartan than it had been at the Dancing Pirate, and the food in the mess hall considerably more basic, but he couldn't have afforded to carry on living there on a watchman's wages anyway. 'Not bad for a shilling a week.'

'Is that all?' The girl sounded impressed. 'I'm paying nearly twice that.' She shrugged, trying to sound cosmopolitan, like the lifelong city dwellers they were slowly becoming used to living among. 'But that's Templewijk prices for you.' Kris had found her lodgings near the college, in a boarding house occupied entirely by female students and guarded by a landlady Rudi strongly suspected had been a pit fighter or a templar marine in her younger days. The only occasion on which he'd attempted to visit he'd been stopped at the door by a muscular arm casually carrying a meat cleaver and asked his business in no uncertain terms. Only his watchman's hat, he suspected, had prevented him from being ejected bodily from the premises.

Hanna had laughed when he told her, having been grudgingly admitted as far as the front parlour, where a couple of equally uncomfortable-looking young men in scholar's robes had been waiting for their own friends.

'Don't let her fool you,' she'd said. 'Clara's bark's a lot worse than her bite.' But Rudi had been more than happy to leave when she'd suggested eating at a tavern she liked nearby.

'Are you all right for money?' he asked awkwardly. Hanna nodded, resting her elbows on the small table which occupied most of the space left free by the bed and the chest of drawers, which now contained all of Rudi's worldly possessions with considerable room to spare. Except for the bow and his sword, which were propped up in one corner.

'I'm getting by. The college is letting me help out in the faculty of Herbalism and Alchemy.' She laughed at his awestruck expression. 'It's not as exciting as it sounds, just boiling things and distilling things mostly, so the students don't have to prepare their ingredients from scratch. It doesn't pay much, but it covers the rent.'

'Any progress on the other thing?' Rudi asked cautiously, noticing the faint bulge in her headscarf was still present.

'Not much, no,' she said, a more sombre expression crossing her face for a moment. 'The good news is Professor Aaldbrugh has seen things like it before. He even prepared a few for the temple of Manann a couple of years back, when their witch hunters broke up a major Chaos cult.'

'So he must know how to get it off,' Rudi said, with a sudden flare of optimism.

'That's the problem,' she said. 'This one isn't supposed to be removed. Gerhard thought he was going to kill me in a couple of days at the most, remember?' Rudi nodded sombrely, clenching his fists involuntarily at the thought. Hanna was silent for a moment, then sighed. 'I might as well tell you the rest.'

'Tell me what?' Rudi asked, a shiver of apprehension running through him. Hanna rose to her feet and began pacing the yard or so of clear floor. Whatever she was going to say was going to be bad, he could feel it. The girl hesitated again, then hurried on.

'If we can't find a way to remove it, it'll kill me. Not for a while yet, but probably by the end of the year. The seizures will keep on getting worse, until eventually my body won't be able to take the strain.' Her voice was unnaturally level, fighting for calm. Abruptly she lost the battle, her blue eyes flooding with tears. 'Oh Rudi, I'm so scared!'

'It'll be all right.' Instinctively he moved towards her, enfolding her in his arms. She responded instantly, clinging tightly to his torso, while her body shook against his. After a while she pulled away, with a loud sniff, and wiped her eyes with the back of her hand.

'Thank you.' She swallowed, a trace of her old decisiveness beginning to come back. 'I needed that. It was just… putting it into words made it more real, somehow.'

'If there's anything I can do to help…'

'I wish there was. But sometimes I think it's completely hopeless.'

'It's never hopeless,' Rudi said. 'Your professor will come up with something.'

'That's exactly what Kris says.' Hanna's expression softened and Rudi felt an irrational surge of resentment. 'I don't know what I'd do without him. He's been a tower of strength.' Something of his feelings must have shown on his face, because she smiled at him with greater fondness than she'd ever shown before. 'And so have you. All the way from Kohlstadt. I'd never have made it here without you.'

'I wouldn't have made it without you either,' Rudi said, and her smile broadened.

'Flatterer. But with Kris I feel like I can really be myself for the first time in my life. Apart from mother, I've never been able to talk about the magic to someone who completely understands and accepts me for what I am. You've no idea how much that means to me.'

'You spent a lot of time with Alwyn,' Rudi pointed out. 'She was a mage too.'

'Not like Kris,' Hanna said. 'He's more subtle. Much better grounded in the theory of it all.' She glanced up again, her eyes shining with excitement. 'Oh, and I nearly forgot the most important thing! They're letting me take some classes while I'm there! Just the theoretical side of it, obviously, as I can't cast spells at the moment, but they're treating me like a real student!' She shrugged, with an attempt at appearing casual which was as transparent as it was futile. 'I suppose it's the least they can do for presenting them with such an interesting challenge.'

'That's wonderful,' Rudi said, feeling a little out of his depth. Fate had thrown them together as reluctant travelling companions and now it seemed their paths were diverging again. He knew Hanna's gift would always make her part of a world he could never hope to understand, but he felt a twinge of regret anyway. As if sensing his mood, the girl smiled at him.

'And talking of being a student, how are your studies progressing?' She indicated the thin bundle of bound paper Artemus had given him a few days before, lying on the table where he'd left it. It had clearly been printed cheaply and in bulk. The type was uneven, and the pictures crude and poorly executed, but it was the first book Rudi had ever owned and he pored over it religiously every chance he got.

'Quite well, I think. I've got all the letters now, and I'm starting to get a feel for how they go together.' With a sudden surge of bravado he flicked the primer open and began to trace the line of type with a hesitant forefinger. 'Karl is a rabbit. See Karl hop.' He glanced up shyly, half-expecting a scornful remark, but Hanna was looking at him with a faint expression of surprise.

'You can really read that? After just a few weeks?'

'Yes.' Then his innate honesty made him add, 'it was a bit harder the first time though.'

'I see.' To his relief there was still no trace of mockery in her tone. 'That's really quite remarkable. Artemus must be very proud of you.'

'Haven't you seen him at all?' Rudi asked, grateful for the chance of changing the subject. Unused to praise, he found it vaguely embarrassing.

'No,' she said, her tone a trifle defensive. 'Templewijk's a big place and I spend most of my time at the college. It's not all that surprising we haven't run into one other yet.'

'Oh.' Rudi had told her how to find the Scriveners' guildhall as soon as she'd returned to the Dancing Pirate, the day he'd met the scribe again. Since then he'd visited Artemus regularly once a week, initially for reading lessons, but on the last occasion the scribe had handed him a quill and encouraged him to try forming the letters for himself. The experience had been an intoxicating one. With rising excitement he had laboriously spelt out 'Karl is a rabbit,' and found that the words were just as easy to read as the ones in the printed book. Artemus had smiled broadly and promised to show him how to link the letters together, making whole words easier to write.

'I'm sure I'll see him around sooner or later,' Hanna said.

'I'm sure,' Rudi agreed tactfully. Clearly she hadn't forgiven Artemus for the incident in the gambling den. Looking for another subject to discuss, he asked the first related question which came into his head. 'Seen anything of Fritz lately?' To his surprise Hanna nodded.

'Not for a couple of weeks, though. That nobleman, von Eckstein, came to the college and Fritz was with him. Mathilde whatshername as well.' A mischievous grin flitted across her face. 'I think he's a bit smitten with her.'

'Well she's been working for him for a good few years,' Rudi said. 'I suppose they see quite a lot of each other.'

Hanna snorted in the way he remembered so vividly from their old life in Kohlstadt, and looked at him scornfully.

'I meant Fritz, you numbskull. If you ask me von Eckstein's not really interested in feminine company.' Rudi, who didn't have a clue what she meant, nodded vaguely, and Hanna grinned. 'Just as well Fritz isn't too quick on the uptake sometimes. It's probably saved the both of them no end of embarrassment.'

'Fritz and Mathilde?' Rudi shook his head in disbelief. 'But she's so old. She must be twenty-five at least.'

'Some men like the mature type,' Hanna said dryly. 'And you know Fritz. Easily impressed by anyone who can take him in a fight.'

'That's true,' Rudi said, ignoring the implied slur. 'So how was he?' He hadn't seen the older boy for almost a month now, on the last day of the week at the Dancing Pirate they'd paid for in advance, when Fritz had returned to collect the few possessions he'd left behind in their shared room. Fritz had moved out to new quarters at the Imperial embassy the day after commencing his new job, and Rudi had barely had time to give him the three guilders he'd recovered from Tilman before he went.

The last time they met they'd shared a meal together, with a peculiar sense of finality, before carrying their packs away from the Pirate in different directions; Rudi towards the watch barracks and Fritz northward to the Hoogbrug and the opulence of the Paleisbuurt ward, where the foreign embassies jostled for position with one another and with the residences of the wealthiest merchants in the city. Who, it seemed, formed the government of the place, or at least the richest ten did. Competition to join or force the weaker members out of that exclusive group was fierce and sometimes bloody, and Rudi didn't envy his colleagues in that part of the city at all.

'Same old Fritz,' Hanna said. 'Just smarter clothes.' Rudi nodded. It had been the first thing he noticed the last time they'd met. The simpleton had acquired a whole new wardrobe, which carried the unmistakable aura of high quality tailoring, and an ornately-worked cudgel of some hard, dark wood, which hung at his belt. Rudi had been quietly amused by that. Von Eckstein was evidently too shrewd to have trusted his new employee with a sword. 'He bought us lunch.'

'Really?' Rudi said, in some surprise. 'That was very generous of him.'

'I'm sure von Eckstein paid in the end,' Hanna said, and remembering Mathilde's remarks about expenses Rudi nodded in agreement. 'But it was nice of him all the same. He was at a bit of a loose end anyway. Von Eckstein was talking to someone in the Faculty of Navigation and they said he could only take one servant in. Not surprisingly he chose Mathilde.'

'So you came across Fritz just hanging about the place,' Rudi said, trying to picture the hulking youth in the quiet cloisters of the college without smiling. He would have been as obviously out of place as an ox in a bakery. Hanna nodded.

'More or less,' she said. 'We were just passing, on our way to the Quill, so we asked him to join us when we saw him. We weren't expecting him to pick up the bill, though.'

'We?' Rudi asked, quietly dreading the answer, and Hanna nodded.

'Kris.' She flushed a little. 'We've been spending quite a lot of time together actually.' She shot him an appraising look. 'You don't mind, do you?'

'Of course not,' Rudi said, a little too hastily. 'Why should I?'

'Good.' For some reason the faint blush of red in her cheeks deepened a little. 'I'm glad you like him.'

'Why wouldn't I?' Rudi asked, baffled.

'No reason.' Hanna glanced around the little room, searching for another topic of conversation. Unable to find one, her fingers began toying idly with the thong supporting the leather pouch around her neck. An awkward silence began settling over them like dust.

'Is that still helping?' Rudi asked, more for something to say than because he expected an answer.

Hanna nodded gratefully. 'Yes. Although no one seems to know why.' She smiled at some amusing memory. 'When I showed it to them, and told them where it had come from, they practically wet themselves. They thought it was something really dangerous. Apparently it falls from the sky sometimes, if you can believe that, and it's so charged with Chaos just holding a piece can turn you into a mutant.'

'Should you be carrying it then?' Rudi asked, alarmed at the thought.

'Luckily it turned out not to be whatever they thought it was, or Shallya alone knows what they might have done.'

'Do they know what it really is?' Rudi asked.

'It's just a bit of rock. It doesn't even look magical if you've got the sight. But it seems to drain off the energy that damn talisman's blocking, somehow. If it wasn't the only thing stopping my head from exploding they'd have it locked up in a workroom with a team of experts working on it day and night.'

'Perhaps you can sell it to them,' Rudi suggested. 'Once you don't need it any more. If it's as unusual as that it must be worth a fortune.'

'Maybe I will,' Hanna said, although the tone of her voice said otherwise. 'Or trade it for a scholarship, so I can complete my training and get a licence.' Her voice became a shade wistful. 'Imagine that. I could go anywhere I liked and do anything I wanted and never have to worry about looking over my shoulder for someone like Gerhard.' Her voice hardened. 'I could walk right up to him and spit in his eye and there wouldn't be a damn thing he could do about it.'

'He might not see it quite like that,' Rudi said cautiously. There was a brooding intensity around the girl now, which he found disturbing, and he suspected she was contemplating revenge again. He smiled in an attempt to lighten her mood. 'Besides, he's probably leagues away. With any luck we'll never see or hear of him again.'

'I suppose you're right,' Hanna said, although for once her expression was unreadable.

CHAPTER SEVENTEEN

RUDI'S SANGUINE MOOD lasted the rest of the afternoon, which he passed pleasantly enough walking
Hanna back to her boarding house and sharing an
early supper with her and Kris at the Quill and Ink,
the tavern round the corner they generally frequented,
only to evaporate at the conclusion of Sergeant Rijgen's briefing at the evening shift change. This week
he was on the night watch, which unlike most of his
colleagues he preferred. The streets were emptier, and
although the chances of trouble were higher after dark
so were the corresponding chances that anyone in the
vicinity would turn out to be responsible for it. On a
couple of occasions when they hadn't been, he'd been
able to lead his patrol to the perpetrators by following
footprints and other signs which had apparently been
invisible to his urbanite colleagues. He still wasn't
sure who'd been the most surprised, the felons, the

watchmen, or himself to discover that his tracking skills could still be applied in this utterly unnatural environment.

'One last thing,' Rijgen said, after running through a brief list of the day's earlier incidents and any interesting gossip the watchmen might find useful in finding or avoiding any trouble, depending on their temperaments. 'The Suiddock watch has passed on the news that an Imperial witch hunter arrived on a barge there this morning. Not really our problem at the moment, but word gets around, and if he starts making trouble this side of the river something might get shaken loose on our patch too. So keep an eye out, and if anything weird happens don't take any chances, back off, contain it if you can, and send a runner back here to report it. That's what the Special Wizardry and Tactical teams are for, so let them deal with it.'

He paused for the chorus of agreement to die away. None of the watchmen felt they were being paid enough to tackle wizards at the best of times, except the occasional licensed one getting drunk and disorderly and therefore by definition in no fit state to cast spells, and most of them said so. Rudi listened with a chill of apprehension, certain he knew the identity of the new arrival, but afraid to draw attention to himself by asking the sergeant for more details. Rijgen concluded as he always did. 'Any questions?'

'What if this witch hunter turns up on our patch?' Gerrit asked. He and Rudi often worked together; being younger than most of the other watchmen and both living in the barracks they spent a lot of their leisure time together too. They'd soon developed a rapport which made them a good team, and Rijgen had been astute enough to take advantage of the fact. Rudi glanced across at the other youth, wondering if his concern had somehow been visible, but Gerrit was watching the sergeant with his usual expression of eager inquiry.

'A good question.' Rijgen nodded. 'And a good answer is to use your own judgement. He'll probably make all kinds of demands and expect you to take orders from him. Don't. Unless he can actually point to a daemon swimming down the Doodkanal, just refer him to a higher authority. Which would be me, until I can palm him off on the captain.' He paused for the laughter to die down. 'We work for the city of Marienburg, not the Empire, and especially not for the church of Sigmar.' He paused again. 'Remember, while he's here he's subject to our laws. If he breaks one, bring him in like you would any other lowlife.'

Despite himself, Rudi felt a grin stretch across his face at the prospect, and entertained a brief fantasy of actually arresting Gerhard. Not that that would be easy, he knew. He'd seen the man fight, but the image was distinctly appealing nonetheless.

'Something amusing you, Walder?' Rijgen waited for Rudi to recompose his features. 'Any other questions? Good. Then get out there and try to be careful.' He waited until most of the watchmen had filed out of the room before raising a hand and beckoning to Rudi. 'Walder. Wait a moment.'

'Sergeant?' Rudi approached the man, trying to hide the sudden flare of apprehension he felt. Did Rijgen know something about the connection between him and Gerhard? He forced his features into an expression of guarded neutrality. 'Something wrong?'

'Why don't you tell me?' Rijgen glanced up at Gerrit, who was hovering by the door, waiting for his partner. 'Go and do something.' He waited until the other watchman had vanished before turning back to Rudi. 'Well?'

'I'm not sure what you mean,' Rudi said, wondering how he'd betrayed himself.

'Then let me refresh your memory. The city is divided into twenty wards, at least for administrative purposes. Correct?'

Rudi nodded. In addition to the officially recognised districts there were a bewildering number of so-called boroughs, areas with their own distinct identities and remarkably fluid boundaries, the largest of which in the Winkelmarkt was the halfling quarter known colloquially as the Kleinmoot.

'And each of those has its own watch barracks, its own watch houses and its own watch captain, am I right?'

Rudi nodded again, unsure of where this was heading. In practice the Elfsgemeente, where the elves lived, was outside the watch's jurisdiction, and the Doodkanal was a no-go area they left strictly alone except for occasional incursions in force, but that was technically true.

Rijgen fixed him with a glare which seemed to penetrate like a sword thrust. 'So why are you spending so much of your off time wandering around the Oudgeldwijk asking questions? The local Caps don't like it, they think you're treading on their toes and technically you are. Which means the captain doesn't like it, which means I don't like it. Are we clear?'

'Perfectly clear, sergeant,' Rudi said, trying to hide his relief. 'I'm just trying to find an old friend. I know he lives in Marienburg somewhere and I think he's most likely to be there.'

'I see.' Rijgen gazed at him levelly for a moment. 'Well in future leave your hat behind if your inquiries take you into a different ward, all right?'

'Right.' Rudi nodded eagerly and the sergeant jerked a thumb at the door.

'Good. Then go and make some trouble for someone who's making trouble. I'm off home before the wife forgets what I look like.'

'WHAT DID THE old man want?' Gerrit asked, lifting his lantern a little higher to illuminate a pile of old rags propped up against the back door of a baker's shop.

'Just a bit of advice about protocol,' Rudi said. He dug a copper coin out of his purse and flicked it at a beggar, whose age and sex were indeterminate. He was pretty sure it was human, though, as he'd become familiar enough with halflings and dwarfs, whose borough bordered the Kleinmoot. He'd even seen a few elves since his arrival in the city, although most of those remained closeted in their own quarter and few of the exceptions had business taking them south of the river. He wasn't sure quite what to make of them. They looked more human than the other races, although they tended to be taller and slimmer, but they moved with a fluid grace no human could possibly have matched and they had an air about them which raised his hackles without him ever being able to pin down precisely why. 'Here, get something to keep the cold out. Preferably solid.'

'Shallya bless you,' the beggar said, stretching out a slim, delicate hand to pick up the coin. Rudi shrugged, surprised by the glimpse of a lace cuff on his sleeve, but not enough to show it. It seemed even the high born of Marienburg could slip on the social ladder badly enough to join the guild of the Unfortunate Brethren.

'I keep telling you, it's a mug's game giving them handouts,' Gerrit said. 'You'll just end up getting a reputation as a soft touch.'

'You think?' Rudi said. 'After I took out Tilman's thugs most of them seem to reckon I'm the toughest thing on two legs since Konrad.'

'Who?' Gerrit asked.

'In the ballads.' His friend still looked blank. 'Never mind. I guess it's an Empire thing.'

'You're the one seeking the merchant, is that not right?' the indigent aristocrat asked suddenly. 'Rudi the woodsman?'

Startled, Rudi turned back to him. Absorbed in his conversation with Gerrit, he had already forgotten the beggar's existence.

'That's right.' Surprise and suspicion mingled in his voice. 'You really know Magnus von Blackenburg?'

'Not socially.' The man's laughter was still redolent of the drawing room, in spite of the bitterness and melancholy which infused it. 'But the Brethren hear a great deal, since we're so little noticed. You won't find him in the Oudgeldwijk, I can assure you of that.'

'You can?' In spite of his instinctive cynicism, Rudi felt his heart begin to beat a little faster. 'Where should I be looking?'

'In the dark, dead shadows.' The barely seen head nodded slowly. 'Where rot and decay hold sway.'

'This is all dreck,' Gerrit said. 'You've had your hand-out, now bugger off and get ratted with it.'

'Shut it, Ger.' Rudi spoke a little more sharply than he'd intended and turned back to the beggar, leaving his partner looking almost comically confused. The clearing in the forest outside Kohlstadt, where he'd met his father and Magnus, had been blighted with disease, he remembered. Perhaps the indigent did know something. 'You mean the Doodkanal?'

'Schwartzwasserstraat,' the man said. 'There's a house there owned by von Blackenburg.' The hand extended again. 'And that knowledge, you must agree, is worth a shilling at least.'

'It might be, if it's true.' Rudi hesitated. After a moment he dug a silver piece out of his purse and handed it over. 'If it's not, I know where to find you.'

'I think you'll find that cuts both ways.' The beggar took the coin with a courtly bow and vanished into the shadows.

'What the hell was all that about?' Gerrit asked.

'I've been looking for someone. Personal business. I guess I've made a few ripples in the process,' said Rudi.

'That might not be such a good thing,' Gerrit said slowly. 'Ripples have a habit of travelling further than you expect.' He nudged Rudi in the arm. 'So what's this personal business then? Does she have a name?'

'It's personal,' Rudi said, in a tone which left no doubt that he didn't want to discuss the subject any further. Noticing his friend's disappointed expression he grinned. 'But it's nothing to do with a girl, I can tell you that.' A flash of movement caught the corner of his eye, his hunter's instincts picking it out from the rest of his surroundings. Someone was standing in the shadows, close enough to have seen and heard his conversation with the beggar. He turned his head casually, angling it so that he seemed to be concentrating completely on the exchange with Gerrit, and studied the hidden figure covertly. Too short for an adult, too slim for a dwarf, too muscular for a child. A halfling.

Gerrit chuckled. 'I can believe that. I saw your girlfriend this afternoon, Anna was it? You'd have to be out of your mind to be two-timing a looker like her.'

'She's not my girlfriend,' Rudi said, trying to ignore the sense of acute discomfort the words stirred up in him. 'And if you're thinking of trying your luck there, forget it. She's involved with someone else.' He strained his eyes, trying to make out the lurking figure through the thickening mist. Kris's prediction about the fogs had turned out to be true, although somewhat exaggerated; as the nights had grown colder, tendrils of mist had begun to rise from the network of waterways with increasing regularity, but he had only experienced a real Marienburg fog once so far. That had lasted for nearly three days before an onshore breeze had dispersed it, and watch houses throughout the city had been stretched to the limits trying to keep a lid on the felons and opportunists making the most of the chance to move around unobserved. According to Sergeant Rijgen things only got that bad two or three times a year, and he wasn't looking forward to the next occasion.

'Oh, I get it,' Gerrit said. 'She fancies this other bloke and you want to warn him off.' He shrugged. 'Not a good idea if you want my opinion...'

'I don't,' Rudi said. He tapped Gerrit on the arm and lowered his voice. 'That alley over there. Someone's watching us.'

'Where?' Gerrit turned his head. The mist in the mouth of the alley swirled briefly for a moment and when Rudi looked again the halfling had vanished.

'Never mind,' Rudi said.

THE REST OF the night passed relatively uneventfully, which meant they rousted a few drunks, collected fines for disorderly behaviour from the usual quota of revellers, ran in a couple more either too bellicose to cooperate or too lacking in funds to pay on the spot, and chased a fleeing burglar who had been unfortunate enough to rouse the owner of the house and even more unfortunate enough to have done so within earshot of the young Black Caps. By that time the night was so well advanced that even the most die-hard of pleasure seekers had retired to their beds or moved on to establishments so discreet that they might just as well have done. Rudi and Gerrit had been getting bored. Their last arrest had been over an hour ago and the steadily-thickening mist had wrapped itself around them so insidiously that they were beginning to feel cut off from the world.

'It can't be long now,' Gerrit said, for the umpteenth time, and shivered. Their shift ended at dawn and he'd been looking forward to returning to the watch house and a warm fire for some time.

'If it gets any thicker we'll never notice,' Rudi said, unable to resist teasing his friend. 'Sunrise could have come and gone for all we know.'

Gerrit shook his head mournfully. 'Wouldn't surprise me,' he agreed. He blew on his hands. 'What I wouldn't give for a mulled ale about now.' He appeared to be on the verge of elaborating, when a piercing scream echoed through the streets. 'Hendryk's purse, what was that?'

'Our job,' Rudi said, breaking into a run. The jumble of buildings around them was distorting the sound with overlapping echoes, but his hunter's instincts gave him a bearing and he sprinted down a nearby alleyway without a moment's hesitation. After a second of stunned surprise Gerrit followed, drawing his sword as he did so and raising the lantern to illuminate the way as far ahead as possible.

'Help! Thief!' A middle-aged woman in a voluminous nightgown was leaning out of an upper-storey window about halfway along the street. Glancing down she caught sight of the two watchmen and pointed dramatically. 'He went that way! A huge ruffian! Hurry!'

Rudi came to a halt below the window. A shadow was visible at the far end of the alleyway, almost two hundred yards away and moving fast. By the time they reached the intersection the thief would have been long gone, vanishing into the maze of side streets beyond any hope of detection. Rudi began to unsling his bow from across his shoulders and nocked an arrow. The housewife continued to shriek.

'Don't just stand there! Get after him!'

'That won't be necessary, ma'am,' Gerrit assured her. The first few times Rudi had taken the bow out on patrol his colleagues had teased him mercilessly; most watchmen who carried missile weapons preferred crossbows or firearms, which were easier to use. That had changed the first time he'd used it, picking off a drunken sailor who'd been holding a knife to the throat of a tavern girl who'd rejected his advances. The arrow had taken the man clean through the shoulder, making him drop the weapon without endangering the girl, and his reputation had risen even further. Quite why everyone had been so impressed, Rudi couldn't understand. The shot had been an easy one, smooth and instinctive; it had never occurred to him that he wouldn't hit the mark. The same feeling was with him now as he drew back the string and loosed.

'Holy Ranald!' The fleeing thief tumbled to the cobbles, thrashing like a landed fish. He looked up as Rudi slung the bow again and strolled the length of the street, taking his time to close the distance between them. 'You've crippled me, you bastard!'

'It'll heal.' Rudi was already certain of that. Despite the distance and the absence of a clear target, he knew the arrow had gone through the right calf muscle, missing the bone and the major blood vessels, just as he'd intended it to. Quite how he could be so certain was a question his mind skated around, simply accepting it as a fact. A single glance was enough to confirm it. 'Keep some pressure on it, like this. It'll stem the bleeding.' He picked up the pack the thief had dropped and turned back. 'Don't go away.' He walked back down the alley and raised his hat to the housewife, who by now was staring at him in stunned disbelief. 'Yours, I believe, madam.'

BY THE TIME Rudi and Gerrit had finished booking the limping thief into the holding cells, sunlight was beginning to leak around the shutters of the watch house. Gerrit stared at it gratefully and yawned.

'That's it then. I'm ready for bed.' He shook his head and stared at Rudi for a moment. 'To be honest I thought that sailor had been a fluke. But now...' His voice trailed away, awestruck. 'I've never seen shooting like it.'

'If you think I'm a good shot, you should have seen my dad. He really was a marksman.' Rudi walked across to a large urn, containing some dark, bitter drink imported from Lustria. He'd never heard of kaffee in the Empire, but it was popular in Marienburg and he was beginning to develop a taste for it. He poured a steaming mug and offered it to Gerrit. 'Something to warm you up before you go?'

'No thanks.' The young watchman shook his head. 'Can't stand the stuff.' He yawned again and began walking towards the door. 'I'll see you back at the barracks.'

'All right.' Rudi sipped at the drink until he was sure his friend was gone, then went out into the street himself. He still wasn't sure how much he could trust the mysterious beggar, but the encounter had stirred up all the questions which continued to plague him. Consumed with the thought that at last he might be getting closer to the answers he wanted so desperately to know, he hurried south, towards the Doodkanal and the address the man had given him.

CHAPTER EIGHTEEN

IN THE HARSH light of day the dereliction of the Dood-kanal looked even worse than it had done the night Rudi had blundered into it shortly after his arrival in Marienburg. The transition from the bustle of the Winkelmarkt had been abrupt. All he'd needed to do was turn down an alleyway almost indistinguishable from a thousand others and within a score of paces a palpable air of blight and decay had settled across the buildings. Plaster cracked, paint peeled, and patches of mould infested their crevices.

The people in the streets seemed much the same, blighted by the same miasma which seemed to poison the district in which they lived. Grey sullen faces stared at him with open hostility as hunched figures clad in rags scuttled along the gutters, or peered from within the shelter of the squalid dwellings surrounding him. Packs of feral children, seeming more animal than human, lurked in dark corners, or scattered, squealing, from his path.

Rudi ignored them all, confident after his last foray into the area that none of these debased specimens of humanity would have the courage to attack him openly. The weapons he bore and his muscular physique marking him out as too dangerous an intruder to challenge.

Only once did he prove to be mistaken in this assumption, as he crossed a narrow bridge over a waterway so choked with sewage that its surface looked almost solid – the stench rising from it was overpowering, making his breath catch in his throat, but in some curious fashion he found the reek invigorating too. It meant he was getting closer to his goal.

'What have we here?' A small man with a large mole on his cheek, whose voice held a strange, nasal timbre which reminded Rudi of a peevish duck, stepped out of the shadows on the far side of the bridge, barring his way. A trio of other ragged figures followed him, fanning out to block the pathway completely, and the scuffing sound of feet against cobbles told Rudi that any potential retreat had been closed off with equal efficiency. They all carried knives or clubs. 'You look a bit lost, mate.'

'I don't think so.' Rudi continued to stride forward, his hand falling to the hilt of his sword, and the first hint of uncertainty began to appear in the leader's eyes. 'This is the way to Schwartzwasserstraat, isn't it?'

'It might be.' The man rallied, clearly taking courage from the proximity of his confederates. Not that he had much choice; in this blighted quarter of the city any sign of weakness would undoubtedly cost him the leadership of his shabby little band and probably his life into the bargain. 'But it's across our bridge, innit?' His confederates sniggered and Rudi nodded in satisfaction. There were only two behind him and they'd just given away their positions.

'Your bridge?' Rudi raised an eyebrow. 'I suppose you have a title deed you can show me?' A small voice at the back of his mind marvelled at the fact that he was tacitly boasting of his newfound literacy at a time like this. The brigand's face darkened.

'Think you're smart, don't you? We don't like smartarses round here.' His eyes flickered past Rudi's shoulder, warning of the coming attack as effectively as if he'd shouted an order.

Without thinking, Rudi drew his sword with a reversed grip and thrust backwards under his own armpit, a trick he'd seen Theo practise during the time he and Hanna had travelled with the mercenary band. The blade met resistance and kept going, eliciting a startled grunt, and he withdrew it from the falling body of the footpad behind him in a single fluid movement, bringing it round to face the small knot of bandits on the bridge ahead of him.

A blur of motion in the corner of his eye was all the warning he needed to step out of the way of a descending club, and as he struck backwards with his elbow, something crunched under the impact and the second thug behind him pitched backwards, his larynx crushed. He thrashed on the ground for a moment, trying desperately to draw breath, and then went still.

Trying not to think about the fact that he'd just killed at least one man, probably both, Rudi strode forward confidently. There was no time for regret or recrimination now. His own life was still in danger.

'Don't just stand there! Get him!' The leader yelled, horror and indignation mingling on his features. He started forward, lunging with the knife he carried, one of his companions at his shoulder.

'You get him. I'm out of here,' another of the thugs said, turning away, clearly more afraid of Rudi than of anything his boss might do.

'Me too.' The third, a woman by the pitch of her voice, agreed, turning to follow.

'I won't forget this!' their erstwhile leader shouted, turning to look after them. 'You're both dead, you hear me?' The motion checked his rush just long enough for Rudi to block the clumsy swing of his remaining companion's club and kick him hard between the legs. The man fell, shrieking in a surprisingly high falsetto, then curled up moaning.

'You first,' Rudi said, backhanding the leader across the face with the hilt of his sword. The little man dropped his knife and reeled against the balustrade. Rudi put the tip of his sword to the man's throat.

'No, wait!' the fellow yelled, a damp patch appearing at the crotch of his britches with remarkable suddenness. 'We didn't mean no harm, honest. We were just having a bit of a joke, see?'

'Of course you were,' Rudi said. He lowered the blade a little. 'Am I right for Schwartzwasserstraat?'

'Yes, yes you are.' The man nodded vigorously. 'Just down that way, turn right, you can't miss it. Full of old houses, very smart, built in the old days.'

'Thank you.' Rudi punched him hard in the face, pitching him over the railing into the foetid depths below. Ignoring the glutinous splash and the faint, profanity-laden screams which followed, he resumed his journey. Word evidently travelled fast in the Dood-kanal. After that he had no more trouble and the streets were noticeably more empty.

SCHWARTZWASSERSTRAAT WAS EXACTLY where his would-be murderer had described it, wider and more open than the other streets he'd seen so far in this forgotten and blighted corner of the city. Clearly it had been prosperous at some time in the past, but like the rest of the Doodkanal those days were long gone. Commerce had trickled away decades ago, if not centuries, to the newer, larger facilities of the Suiddock, and the builders of the fine homes who'd prospered here when the city was little more than a town had followed it.

Some of their descendants, no doubt, had been content with the grander mansions of the Oudgeldwijk, their fortunes shrinking inexorably down the generations along with those of their neighbours, while the lucky ones had continued to prosper and crossed the river.

These days the once grand houses were little more than ruined shells, occupied for the most part by desperate, ragged tribes of people who swarmed over and around their residences with every sign of a determination to defend them from intruders, even though they were armed with nothing more deadly than shards of broken masonry. What allegiance they owed to one another Rudi couldn't tell, since whatever family resemblance he might have noticed was obscured by grime and the pinched expressions borne of the privations they endured.

Trusting again to his formidable appearance he started down the street, conscious of the pressure of innumerable eyes upon him.

Belatedly it began to occur to him that he had no way of identifying Magnus's house from any of the others, even if it was really here. The beggar could simply have been lying to him, as Gerrit had said. Now he'd seen the ravaged avenue for himself that possibility seemed all too likely.

'Excuse me.' He caught the eye of a woman slinking along the edge of the street in the lee of one of the walls. She looked about fifty to his eyes, but so did everyone else around here, even the children. 'Which of these houses belongs to Magnus von Blackenburg?'

Even allowing for the sullen reaction his presence had stirred up in the locals so far, her response startled him. Her eyes widened and she turned away, stooping, with a shriek of unmistakable terror. As she straightened up again, a lump of brick in her right hand, the woman made a curious gesture in his direction.

'Get away from me!' She flung the brick at him, missing by several feet, turned again and bolted. Too stunned to react, Rudi watched her disappear into the ruins of a nearby house. A moment later faces began to appear at the doors and windows.

Puzzled and not wanting to get sucked into another brawl, Rudi resumed his walk up the street. He'd already killed two men this morning, three if the bandit's leader hadn't managed to scramble out of the effluent before drowning, and he'd rather not take any more lives if he didn't have to. Part of him marvelled at the dispassionate way he was able to think about it. He'd expected more of the remorse and confusion he'd felt after slaying the bandits on the road, but those feelings refused to stir. The footpads had meant to kill him, he'd defended himself instinctively with none of the time to consider alternative strategies which Tilman's more cautious and methodical thugs had provided him with, and they'd died instead. That was all. He dismissed the matter from his mind and began to study the buildings around him for clues.

In the end he found the place more easily than he'd expected. Towards the far end of the street one of the houses stood a little apart from its neighbours, surrounded by the tumbled remains of a stone wall and the overgrown remnants of what might once have been a small garden. Although it seemed equally shabby, unlike the others there was no sign of unauthorised occupancy, stout shutters closing off most of the windows. His heart beginning to beat a little faster, Rudi picked up his pace.

As he neared the gap in the ruined wall where once a gate would have stood, his sense of cautious optimism gave way to one of elation. The family crest he remembered from Magnus's mansion back in Kohlstadt was painted on the tumbling stump of the gatepost in colours so faded and peeling they were almost illegible and had it not been for their familiarity they might just as well have been. But it was enough. Breaking into a run, he hurried towards the front door.

'Magnus!' He couldn't restrain himself from shouting. 'Magnus, it's Rudi!' But echoes were his only answer.

This wasn't good. He slowed his pace again and began moving with the caution of the woodsman he used to be. Approaching the door, he raised a hand to knock, then hesitated, chills of apprehension chasing themselves along his spine. The thick slab of wood was ajar.

'Magnus?' Rudi pushed the door open. It creaked loudly, the echoes resounding like a pistol shot. The door had been forced, the timber of the frame splintered and bent where the lock had burst away from it. He tried to imagine the strength that would require and shuddered. No one replied, so he stepped inside, drawing his sword again.

Having little idea of the layout of the place, Rudi explored the whole house methodically, finding room after room full of decaying furniture, the air heavy with must and damp. There were signs of recent occupancy too, though, footprints in the dust and food in the kitchen, already days old and beginning to rot. Reminded abruptly of the fact that he hadn't eaten properly since the previous evening, he looked for something still edible, but common sense reasserted itself just as he was on the point of picking up some mould-encrusted cheese. A faint sense of disappointment rippled through his head as he pushed it away and he resolved to eat again as soon as he had the opportunity.

From the kitchen it was a short step to the trapdoor leading down to the cellar. As he lifted it, the sweet, pungent scent of decay wafted up to him, so strong as to seem almost pleasant. Lighting a stub of candle he found on a nearby shelf with the tinderbox from his belt pouch he ventured down the rickety wooden steps.

The cellar was larger than he'd expected, vaulted brick forming a ceiling high enough to stand with no difficulty. He was even able to raise the candle over his head to widen the circle of illumination without touching it. He glanced around, trying to orientate himself.

The smell of putrefaction was even stronger here, emanating from a pile of rotting refuse in the corner, which was the first thing to attract his attention. Fascinated and repelled at the same time, Rudi walked towards it. All kinds of organic waste seemed mixed up in it, including what looked like faeces. Curiously there was a sense of symmetry about it, as if the filth had been carefully arranged in some way. Symbols he didn't recognise had been daubed on the walls around it, apparently in the same substances as constituted the heap itself, and despite their strangeness he felt a curious sense of recognition stir in the depths of his mind as he stared at them, as if with a little more concentration they would fall into place and make sense.

Turning away after contemplating the enigmatic sigils for another moment or two, he began to explore the rest of the chamber carefully. In the far corner the flame of his candle stub flickered, indicating a draft from somewhere, and a few moments of trial and error led him to another trapdoor set in the floor of the cellar. Seizing the ring, he pulled on it with all his strength, but it refused to budge.

That was curious. The slab of timber was free of dust, indicating that it had been opened very recently. Rudi bent down, placing an ear to it. Listening hard he thought he could hear the faint sounds of running water. Some kind of sewer, perhaps, or one of the minor waterways built over and forgotten in the early years of the city. Probing round the edge with the

blade of his belt knife was enough to show that it had
been firmly bolted from underneath. Finding nothing
else of interest, the young watchman returned to the
ground floor in a state of some confusion, mingled
with a growing sense of frustration. Surely the house
must contain some clue as to Magnus's whereabouts?

After another desultory sweep of the ground floor
rooms he returned to the entrance hall. The morning
was well advanced and the sunlight streaming in
through the half-open door was bright enough to
pick out something he'd missed when he entered.
The flagstones flooring the chamber were darkened
in one spot, charred as if a fire had been kindled on
them. Rudi felt the hairs on the back of his neck stir.
Was he too late? Had Gerhard been here ahead of
him?

A moment's thought was enough to dismiss the
notion. Given what he'd seen of the witch hunter's
methods he would undoubtedly have burned the
whole building down, not just scorched the hall floor.

The idea which displaced it was even more disturbing. The horned sorceress used fire as a weapon, he'd
seen that several times, and she and Magnus were evidently mortal enemies. Had she tracked him here and
slain him with her pyromancy?

Sick with apprehension, Rudi bent to examine the
burned patch. Whatever had caused this had been far
from natural, producing enough heat to make the hard
stone brittle. But there were no traces of bone or ash
that he could see. He glanced up, relying on his
hunter's instincts, taking in the relative positions of
the doors around him. He was almost exactly on a line
between the front door and the entrance to the kitchen

and close to the foot of the stairs. If Magnus had been descending them when the door was forced…

He let the scene play out in his mind's eye. The merchant would have been about here, there was no doubt about that, but so stout a door would certainly have resisted assault for a moment or two. Long enough for him to have turned and run for the kitchen, the magical bolt meant to incinerate him expending itself where he'd been standing an instant before.

It made sense, every instinct he possessed as a tracker told him that. He turned slowly and began to examine the kitchen door. After a moment he nodded in satisfaction. There were faint scratch marks around the handle, as if inhumanly large hands tipped with claws had fumbled with the latch. Hans Katzenjammer, without a doubt, which meant that the horned sorceress had indeed been here.

Despair threatened to overwhelm Rudi for a moment. If Magnus was really dead, then the answers he so desperately needed were lost to him forever. Then reason reasserted itself. The trapdoor in the cellar had been bolted from the other side. Magnus must have escaped, or it would still have been open.

His breath left him abruptly in a spontaneous sigh of relief. There was still hope. All he had to do was find the man before Gerhard or the horned witch did.

That would be no small task. The merchant must surely know that his enemies were on his trail and would be making strenuous efforts not to be found. Nevertheless he was determined to try. He was a member of the city watch, after all, there might be some avenues of inquiry open to him that his rivals wouldn't be able to use.

Feeling somewhat encouraged, Rudi ascended the stairs cautiously. As he'd hoped, one of the rooms on the upper floor was evidently Magnus's bedroom, although like everything else in the house it was neglected and derelict. Only the fact that stained sheets still lay on the bed under a rumpled eiderdown betrayed the fact that it was still in use. Clothes hung in a dust-encrusted wardrobe, but nothing indicated where their owner might be or whether he'd ever come back to claim them.

Moved by an impulse he couldn't quite account for he traced the tip of his index finger along the top of a chest, leaving a streak of clear wood. Laboriously he spelt out RUDI in the patina of dust, shaping the letters carefully as Artemus had taught him. Now if Magnus did return he would at least know his old friend from Kohlstadt was somewhere in the city and trying to make contact. He debated with himself for another moment, wondering whether to add any more information, and decided against it. If Magnus might come back here, so too could his enemies.

Finding nothing else to help him in the upper rooms, which Hans and the sorceress had evidently already searched judging by the way some of the furniture had been disarrayed, unless the mutant had simply been venting his frustration at the escape of their prey, Rudi began to descend the staircase. He was almost halfway down when he realised that someone else was standing in the hallway.

'Who's there?' He drew his sword as he spoke and continued to descend.

'Sam Warble.' The halfling he'd seen with Kris at the Dancing Pirate was glancing around with barely concealed distaste. 'I take it this is the maid's day off.'

'What are you doing here?' Rudi asked. 'Have you been following me?' Sam looked at the sword as though it were no more dangerous than a potato peeler and shrugged, apparently completely unconcerned.

'Why bother. I thought I might find you here.' His eyes were direct and stared at Rudi appraisingly. 'It's taken you long enough to find the place though.'

Feeling oddly embarrassed, Rudi put his weapon away. 'What do you want?' he asked. The halfling nodded, as though he'd just made some kind of point.

'Lunch,' he said. 'Then maybe we can talk a little business.'

'What kind of business?' Rudi asked warily.

Sam smiled, although the expression failed to reach his eyes. 'I think we might be able to help one another,' he said.

CHAPTER NINETEEN

'THAT'S BETTER.' SAM nodded at the plate full of eel pie in front of him with evident satisfaction and began to ply his cutlery with enthusiasm. 'It's been a long walk.'

'Long enough,' Rudi agreed, breaking the crust on his own portion with almost as much gusto. He was ravenous and the scent of the fresh food was almost intoxicating. Sam had led the way out of the Doodkanal with the air of a man who knew the tangled streets well, doubling back several times and passing through derelict buildings on a couple of occasions. When Rudi had asked why, the halfling had simply shrugged.

'We probably weren't being followed – but now we definitely aren't.' Rudi had half expected him to lead the way into the Kleinmoot, but Sam had avoided that part of the city completely and they'd ended up at the Blind Eye, a tavern opposite the Winkelmarkt watch barracks popular with off-duty Black Caps. Rudi had been surprised at this and kept a wary eye out for Gerrit, as they'd been in there a few times together, but to his relief there was no sign of his friend. Sam had evidently noticed the motion of his head, because he chuckled around a mouthful of pie and mashed turnip.

'Safest place in the ward to discuss business,' he said, washing it down with a generous swallow of ale. He nodded at the crowd around the bar. 'Half the customers are Black Caps and most of the others are small-time crooks.' His mouth quirked with cynical amusement. 'That way they can keep an eye on each other without getting their feet wet.'

'So which are you?' Rudi asked. Sam stopped chewing for a moment to gaze levelly at him, and despite the difference in their relative sizes, Rudi found himself remembering Koos's description of the halfling as being someone you didn't want to cross. He seemed to think it was a fair question, because after a moment he nodded.

'I'm one of the exceptions,' he said, pushing his empty platter to one side.

'So I gather.' Rudi ate a little more of his own meal and waited while the halfling ordered a second portion. 'A lot of people seem to know you. Why?'

'Because of what I do. Thanks Milli, you're an angel.' Sam took his fresh plate of food and smiled at the serving girl, who blushed and returned to the bar.

'And what is that, exactly?' Rudi asked.

The halfling smiled sardonically. 'I solve people's problems. For the right price.'

'Which is how much?' Rudi took another spoonful of turnip.

'That depends on a few things.'

'Like what?' Rudi was beginning to get a feel for how the game was played. Sam was annoyingly laconic, especially for a halfling; the others he'd encountered since arriving in the city tended to be garrulous in the extreme. He assumed it was something to do with maintaining his reputation, whatever that was.

'How desperate they are. How much they can afford. How likely I am to get killed. That kind of thing.' Rudi nodded and was about to speak when Sam went on. 'I normally start at thirty a day, plus expenses.'

'Thirty shillings a day? That's a lot of money,' Rudi said, trying to mask his surprise.

The halfling grinned, the first genuine smile Rudi had seen on his face since they met. 'That's guilders, country boy. I play in the big leagues.'

'Well I don't,' Rudi said. 'Not at that price.'

'I know. And unless you start taking bribes like most of the other fine upstanding agents of the law around here, you never will.' A flicker of amusement crossed his features. 'Don't pretend you haven't noticed.' Rudi flushed. He'd realised early on that most of his colleagues would take a shilling here or there to look the other way when some act of petty theft forced itself on their attention, or levied more fines than they declared back at the watch house. He had decided from the outset that such a course was not for him. That was something else he had in common with Gerrit, and he suspected it was one of the reasons Rijgen paired them off so often, although whether that was to keep them both from picking up bad habits from older, more cynical watchmen or to prevent them from rocking the boat he still hadn't made up his mind.

'It happens.' He shrugged. 'It's not for me, that's all.'

'I heard you had principles,' Sam said, although Rudi couldn't tell from his tone whether he thought that a good or a bad thing. Maybe it was something else which depended on the context. He plied his cutlery again. 'You're looking for someone. Maybe I can help.'

'Not for thirty guilders,' Rudi said. He didn't bother asking how the halfling knew that. It was evident from his conversation with the destitute aristocrat the previous night that it was a piece of information which had travelled a long way.

'Not even for one. Like I said, we might be able to help one another,' Sam said.

'How, exactly?' Rudi asked, pushing his empty plate aside. The halfling drained his tankard and signalled to Milli for a refill. She bustled across with two tankards and Rudi accepted the second one dubiously.

'What do you know about an Imperial nobleman called von Eckstein?' Sam asked when she'd gone. Taken completely by surprise, Rudi took a mouthful of ale while he composed an answer.

'Not much,' he said at last, deciding he might as well be as truthful as possible. 'I've only met him once.'

'At Tilman's, I know.' Sam nodded. 'I saw you there. And your friends.'

'Then you know about as much as I do,' Rudi said. 'I haven't seen him since.'

'I know,' Sam repeated and nodded his head thoughtfully again. 'But one of your friends has.'

'Hanna saw him at the college a couple of weeks ago,' Rudi began, before the chain of reasoning completed itself. He nodded too. 'Oh. You mean Fritz.'

'That's right.' Sam leaned forwards across the table and Rudi felt an irrational impulse to withdraw. 'I'm sure he knows all about von Eckstein and his business in Marienburg.'

'Then why don't you ask him yourself?' Rudi asked. Sam's eyes locked on his for a moment, and despite himself Rudi shivered.

'That wouldn't be a very good idea,' he said. 'I'm sure the Imperial embassy has agents watching our friend the graf and anyone approaching his entourage. I'd stick out like an orc in the Moot.' The idea seemed to amuse him for some reason. 'An old friend of his bodyguard, on the other hand, going out for a quiet, sociable drink...'

'You want me to ask Fritz about von Eckstein,' Rudi said, and the halfling nodded.

'Discreetly, of course.'

'Of course.' Rudi took another mouthful of ale, his mind whirling. Trying to sound as cool as Sam he replaced the tankard carefully on the tabletop. 'I could do that. The question is, why should I?'

'For one thing, I've got more contacts in this city than anyone else I know, and believe me, I know an awful lot of people.' Sam paused, letting the idea sink in. 'If I can't find von Blackenburg for you, I can definitely point you in the right direction.'

'And you'd do that for nothing,' Rudi said, with heavy sarcasm. 'Just out of the goodness of your heart.'

'I don't have one,' Sam said. 'I hear they're bad for business. I'm talking about a straight exchange of information. Something you can get for me, for something I can get for you. Then we're square. Deal?'

'I don't know,' Rudi said. He looked at the halfling narrowly. 'You seem very keen to get me to help you. What's all this about?'

'What's anything about in Marienburg?' Sam asked rhetorically. 'Money, and lots of it.' He looked appraisingly at Rudi and appeared to come to a decision. 'OK, you seem solid enough. Do I have your word you won't repeat what I'm about to tell you to anyone else?'

'All right.' Rudi nodded. 'If I'm going to get involved in whatever you're up to, I want to know what the stakes are first.'

'Fair enough.' Sam nodded and lowered his voice a little. 'Basically, your life. If anyone else finds out you're stringing for me, it's guilders to fish guts you'll end up floating in a canal somewhere with a second mouth where your throat used to be. Clear?'

'Clear,.' Rudi replied, unable to believe that the halfling was threatening him so openly. Evidently sensing his doubts, Sam nodded grimly.

'I mean it. If the Imperials find out you've been sniffing around von Eckstein's business they'll go to any lengths to stop you from passing on what you've learned. And if the Fog Walkers even suspect you've betrayed my confidence you'll be shark bait by dawn.'

'The Fog Walkers?' Rudi echoed, surprised beyond measure. Like everyone else in Marienburg, he'd heard whispers of the ruthlessly efficient network of agents the city government allegedly kept looking out for their interests throughout the city and far beyond, but like most had dismissed them as fanciful gossip. 'You're working for them?'

'I never said that,' Sam replied flatly. Rudi nodded, taking his meaning. 'Let's just say I'm as patriotic as any other Marienburger and I'm willing to help out when the interests of the city may be under threat.'

'From von Eckstein?' Rudi asked, and Sam nodded again.

'There are others behind him, I'm sure, but he's the point man. He has a habit of turning up wherever the Empire's playing games behind the scenes. Bretonnia, Tilea, even Araby. He talks, people listen, money changes hands and things happen. Things favourable to them, not necessarily in anyone else's interests.'

'Who's he been talking to in Marienburg?' Rudi asked.

'We don't know. He's been having meetings somewhere in the Elfsgemeente, but who with is anyone's guess. He's covering his tracks very carefully.'

'He didn't seem to be keeping such a low profile when I saw him,' Rudi said. 'Playing cards in a back-street gambling den.'

'He's being a lot more careful now. Not from personal inclination, if I know my mark, but someone's got nervous and started holding his leash more tightly. Which is why we haven't had another chance to set him up, and why we're desperate enough to come to you.'

'Set him up?' Rudi echoed, then the full realisation hit. 'You mean the card game.'

'It should have worked. Take him for a small fortune over several nights and threaten to expose him to his bosses unless he told us what he's here for.' He sighed and shook his head ruefully. 'And after all the trouble we went to, finding an honest establishment, getting a mage to gimmick the deck, giving our catspaws amulets that let them see the marks on the cards, you have to come barging in with someone gifted with witchsight on the first night.'

'We nearly lost everything we had,' Rudi riposted, beginning to raise his voice.

'Couldn't be helped,' he said. 'We needed some genuine players in the game too, or it would have been too obvious a set-up. Most of them had the sense to quit when they saw they were on a losing streak.'

'But not Artemus,' Rudi said.

'It takes some people like that,' he said. He leaned back in his seat again. 'So, do we have a deal or not?'

'I suppose we do,' Rudi said, trying to ignore the sense of foreboding which settled across him as he spoke. This was going to lead to trouble, he could feel it, but he didn't seem to have any other choice. Finding Magnus was the only possible way to answer the questions which continued to plague him, and making use of Sam's network of contacts was by far the best way of doing that.

'Good,' he said, hopping down from his chair. 'I'll be in touch.'

Rudi watched him weave his way through the clientele towards the door with mixed feelings. On the one hand his chances of finding the missing merchant had just improved immeasurably. On the other, he'd just been pitched into a bewildering new world of secrets and covert diplomacy, where, it seemed, his life was in grave danger. Well, that at least was hardly new. Draining the rest of his tankard, he stood to follow Sam towards the street, feeling in sudden need of his bed and a few hours' rest.

'Sam.' Hearing someone call his erstwhile companion's name, Rudi checked his pace, not wanting to catch up with the halfling and reinforce the idea that they'd been together if anyone had noticed them talking. Sam had been hailed by Captain Marcus, who was turning away from the bar. 'Haven't seen you in here for a while. Something going on I should know about?'

'I don't think so, Gil,' Sam replied. Rudi noted that he was on first name terms with the captain without much surprise. 'But if you buy me a drink we can swap unattributable rumours.' He moved to join Marcus and Rudi hurried on by towards the street. He needed to think about things and he needed to sleep, although he strongly suspected that the two impulses would turn out to be mutually incompatible.

CHAPTER TWENTY

DESPITE HIS DOUBTS, Rudi slept soundly for most of the day. The lingering fatigue left by the events of the night shift and his subsequent expedition into the depths of the Doodkanal combined with the effects of a full stomach and the ale he'd drunk with Sam to send him off to sleep almost as soon as he stretched out on his bed. He didn't stir until the insistent knocking on his door finally penetrated the fog of exhaustion which had wrapped itself around his mind.

'Who is it?' He forced himself to sit upright, yawning loudly.

'Who do you think?' Gerrit's face appeared round the door, grinning broadly. 'Manann's little dolphins, you look like dreck.'

'What do you want?' Rudi asked, in no mood to exchange banter with his friend. Though sound, his sleep had been far from restful, invaded by dreams he couldn't quite recall but whose shadows had left him with a vague impression of grim foreboding. Perhaps his bargain with the halfling had been a mistake, but there was no way of changing that now.

'Nothing much,' Gerrit said, still grinning. 'Just wanted to know if you still wanted a job in the morning.'

'What?' Rudi swung his legs over the side of the bed, suddenly aware of the angle of the sunlight creeping in around the shutters. The afternoon was already well advanced. 'Is it time for the shift change already?'

'Not quite,' Gerrit said cheerfully. 'But if you want to grab something to eat and poison yourself with more of that Lustrian muck before it starts you'd better get a move on.'

'Thanks,' Rudi responded, with as much grace as he could muster, and started looking for his clothes.

'No problem. See you in the mess.' Gerrit vanished again, closing the door behind him, and Rudi winced at the cheerful whistling which receded down the corridor in the young Cap's wake.

By dusk, however, he felt much better, restored by a meal which made up for its lack of flavour with its warmth and copiousness, and two mugs of kaffee, which drove the fog from his brain with ruthless efficiency.

'You'll be paying for that later,' Gerrit admonished him as they approached the watch house. 'That stuff might wake you up, but it leaves you feeling worse than ever when it wears off.'

'Maybe.' Rudi shrugged. 'But by that time we'll probably have been in at least two fights. I'll be wide awake then, won't I?'

'Good point,' Gerrit conceded, trying to slip into the briefing unnoticed. Sergeant Rijgen looked up as the two young watchmen entered the room, narrowed his eyes slightly in a fashion which made it clear that their tardiness was a topic to be deferred until later, and resumed his preliminary remarks.

'Item two. Cutpurses are getting more active in the vegetable market. Keep an eye out for any known faces spending more money than usual in the taverns around there and pull in a few if you get the chance. Let's shake the tree and see what falls out.' Having heard enough on the way in to know that item one had just been a routine round-up of the day's arrests, Rudi relaxed and let part of his mind assimilate the rest of the briefing while the back of it mulled over the events of the morning.

Whether or not he could trust Sam, he was committed to helping him now, and he'd have to find some excuse to catch Fritz on his own. That might be difficult. The Paleisbuurt was on the other side of the river, where he had no reason to go in the normal course of events, so contriving a casual encounter wasn't going to be easy.

'Item twelve,' Rijgen said, grabbing Rudi's full attention so suddenly that he had to fight the impulse to twitch like a startled rabbit. 'The witch hunter we heard about last night has been petitioning the watch commanders in the Paleisbuurt. He wants bodies for a raid on the Doodkanal.' He paused ironically. 'Any volunteers?' After the chorus of derisive laughter and catcalls had died down, he nodded and continued. 'Thought not.'

Rudi shuddered, feeling a chill of apprehension. Had Gerhard been able to track Magnus down that quickly? He supposed it was possible. There must have been someone in Kohlstadt who knew the merchant's address in the city. Pushing his fears to the back of his mind, he tried to listen to Rijgen as calmly as he could, hoping to pick up some more information about his enemy and what he might be planning.

'Maybe he'll have better luck with the River Watch,' Rijgen went on. 'It's on their patch after all.' More derisive laughter followed. There was little love lost between the Black Caps and their opposite numbers charged with maintaining maritime law. In theory the River Watch's jurisdiction was city-wide rather than being organised ward by ward, and although it was strictly restricted to the docks and waterways, they used the wider mandate they'd been given to interfere in other matters to an extent most Black Caps found irksome in the extreme. With no City Watch post in the Doodkanal the responsibility for maintaining law and order theoretically fell to the Winkelmarkt Caps, as the nearest barracks, but they could reasonably argue that, for once, their despised colleagues had a better claim. An argument, Rudi was certain, that Captain Marcus would pursue energetically.

'I'm glad you're all so well disposed to our colleagues in the excise service,' Rijgen said. 'Because that brings me on to item thirteen. A joint operation between ourselves and the River Watch.' He held up a hand to quieten the chorus of groans and protest. 'I know, but they've promised it won't be another fiasco like last time.' He turned aside, making room for Captain Marcus at the front of the room. 'For one thing Sergeant Flaaken was tragically drowned trying to board a suspect vessel last month, so that's one less thing to worry about.'

'Thanks Jaak.' Captain Marcus took over the briefing smoothly, and a sense of suppressed urgency settled over the room. Rudi could feel the tension beginning to build. Marcus looked around with an air of mild interest. 'I'm sure you're all eager to volunteer, but let me put your minds at rest. The assignments have already been made. Sergeant Rijgen will be leading the operation. Loos, Anders, Kuyper, Gerrit, Walder, Maartens and Strijker, you're assisting. The rest of you, bugger off and find a lowlife to happen to.' He waited until the majority of the watchmen had left the room, most of them palpably gloating at their good fortune, and turned to the little knot of Black Caps remaining. None of them, apart from Gerrit, seemed particularly enthusiastic to have been chosen for the assignment so far as Rudi could see.

'Right.' Rijgen nodded in agreement. 'For one thing, the waterboys haven't got jurisdiction on this one, or even a claim of it. We've got complete operational control.'

'That's what we thought last time,' one of the Black Caps said sourly. 'Until a bunch of them turned up and tried to claim the arrest.'

'Sorry, sergeant, I don't understand.' Rudi hesitated, feeling everyone's eyes on him, then went on. 'I thought everything on dry land was ours and everything wet was theirs.'

'Oh right, you're new in town.' Rijgen nodded and looked questioningly at Marcus. 'Captain?'

'Better fill him in,' Marcus said. 'We've got time.'

Rijgen nodded and turned back to Rudi. 'You're more or less right. But like most things in Marienburg, it's open to interpretation. By the strict letter of the law, their remit on land is limited to within a hundred yards of a waterway. Which seems clear enough.'

'I see.' Rudi nodded. 'So this raid was within a hundred yards of the water and they butted in.'

The Black Cap who'd spoken before, Maartens he thought, snorted in disgust. 'Nowhere near it,' he said. 'Two hundred and fifty at least, if it was an inch.'

Rijgen nodded in agreement. 'That's about right,' he said. 'It was our collar, no question about it. Warehouse full of Tilean cheeses someone had evaded the excise on.'

'Stank to high heaven,' Loos put in.

'Then how could they justify interfering?' Rudi said.

'Sewers,' Rijgen said in disgust. 'There was a sewer running underneath the place, right? And the smart bugger just grins at me and says, "That's a waterway." So while we were busy arguing the toss about it, the smugglers legged it. Bloody embarrassing. For weeks afterwards every time we felt a collar we got "hang on, I've just pissed myself, shouldn't you hand me over to the river watch?"'

'Well that's not going to happen on this one,' Captain Marcus said shortly. 'We're well away from the water, there's nothing underneath the place, and I've politely informed my opposite number in the waterboys that if any of his mob happens to wander into the vicinity he'll be looking for a new career with the cathedral choir.' The little knot of watchmen sniggered appreciatively and most of them began to relax. 'How it's going to work is very simple. We find the smugglers, we bust the smugglers, we bring them back here and we send a runner to let the waterboys know they're in custody.'

'But he doesn't have to run very fast,' Sergeant Rijgen put in. 'Some of the villains we pull in might have information we can use too.'

'Quite. By the time our esteemed colleagues turn up to collect them, I want them wrung dry.'

'Any questions so far? No? Good.' Rijgen paused for a moment and resumed his briefing. 'The target's a boarding house in the Kleinmoot. The owner's an old friend of ours, Rollo Meadowsweet.' Most of the watchmen present nodded in recognition of the name. 'He also owns a flash tavern in the Elfsgemeente, which backs on to a waterway, with a small landing stage at the rear. Our information is that leakage from the docks finds its way there, and then back out to riverboats on their way up the Reik. The waterboys are busting it tonight.'

'But if the contraband's being stashed on the other side of the city, why are we turning over a halfling flophouse?' Gerrit asked, frowning in puzzlement. Rudi nodded, feeling equally baffled.

'Because Meadowsweet's too smart to do business like that,' Captain Marcus explained. 'The money changes hands here, in the Winkelmarkt, where there's no direct connection. Our job is to grab the paperwork before he hears about the raid over the water and destroys the evidence.'

'Any more questions?' Rijgen asked.

RUDI HAD BEEN in the Kleinmoot several times since his arrival in Marienburg, so he knew roughly what to expect. The first time he'd been there he'd been vaguely surprised to find that most of the buildings were normal sized ones, left over from earlier occupants, although the newer structures which crowded every vacant or semi-vacant space in typical Marienburg fashion had waist-high doorways perfectly sized for the halfling physique.

Perhaps Meadowsweet, whoever he was, had been pretty smart basing his operation down here, where human-sized watchmen would find their usual tactic of kicking down doors and charging into suspect premises difficult at best.

Having less need for space than their human neighbours many of the local residents had erected homes or businesses in the middle of the wider thoroughfares, narrowing them to choke points barely wide enough for the party of watchmen to slip through in single file. By the time they neared their objective Rudi was getting heartily sick of small, curly-haired heads barging past at a pace and height which made him even more grateful than usual for the armoured codpiece which, on the advice of his more experienced colleagues, had accounted for most of his first week's wages.

Halflings being halflings, which is to say outgoing, cheerful and curious, by the time the purposeful little group of Black Caps had reached its destination it had acquired a comet tail of diminutive followers, chattering cheerfully and loudly about their probable destination and reason for being there, augmented by several enterprising street hawkers who had seen the need for snacks to go along with the evening's entertainment.

'I heard it's mutants in the sewers,' a young female said, tugging eagerly at Rudi's trouser leg. 'Is that right, mister, you're hunting mutants?'

'Witches,' her companion asserted, nodding his head with the complete assurance of total ignorance, spraying crumbs from the pastry he'd just purchased as he spoke. 'A whole coven of 'em. That's what I heard.'

'Piffle, young Shem. Ain't no witches in the Kleinmoot, not now, never have been.' An older halfling nodded sagely and drew on a pipe which directed a stream of choking smoke into Rudi's face. 'Mark my words, it be body snatchers they be after.'

'What about old mother Goosegreen?' Shem persisted. 'She got cursed, didn't she? Got turned into a lobster a fortnight ago last Festag. Who done that then if it weren't witches?'

'I saw old mother Goosegreen yesterday,' his girlfriend said scornfully, 'and she looked just the same as she always did.'

Shem nodded sagely and swallowed the rest of his pastry. 'I never said she didn't get better, though, did I?'

'Right!' Sergeant Rijgen's bellow cut through the bedlam of excited chatter. Scores of small faces turned expectantly in his direction. 'That's better. Now hands up everyone who wants to be run in here and now for obstructing the watch.' A ripple of agitation ran through the crowd, and a few halflings on the fringes began to slip quietly away. 'No takers? Good. Then bugger off!' He sighed in mingled exasperation and relief as the crowd began to disperse, then lunged at one of the diminutive inhabitants of the quarter. 'Not you, Drogo.' He hoisted the kicking, squealing halfling into the air by one arm. 'Give that lady her purse back.'

'All right, all right, no need to make such a song and dance about it.' The pickpocket glared resentfully at the sergeant as he was lowered back to the cobbles and handed a small bag of coins to a plump matronly halfling, who received it with an audible sniff. 'I'm entitled to make a living, aren't I?'

'What you're entitled to is six months on Rijker's Island.' Rijgen fixed the halfling thief with his best intimidating glare. 'Just think yourself lucky I've got better things to do tonight than run in some penny-ha'penny dip.'

'Did you see that?' Drogo expostulated as the watchmen turned away and resumed their march. 'That's just what I've been talking about. A whole city full of mutants and witches to arrest and they've got nothing better to do than pick on an innocent thief...'

'You should have taken him in, Sarge,' Gerrit said. 'He wouldn't have slowed us down much.' Rijgen laughed.

'Bring in my best informant? You must be joking. That little pantomime will have done him no end of good in keeping his cover solid.' Rudi sighed and shook his head. Everywhere he went in Marienburg, it seemed, he found nothing but deception and duplicity.

To his relief the boarding house turned out to be one of the older, human-sized buildings, although like many of its neighbours a halfling-sized doorway had been cut into the original one. According to the briefing the original ceilings were still in place too, so at least the raiding party wouldn't have to bend double once they were inside. Rijgen paused on the front step to glare at the remains of the audience which had continued to follow them at a safe distance, and redirected his attention to the watchmen.

'Anders, Loos, stay here. Grab anyone trying to make a run for it. Kuyper and Gerrit, round the back.' The four designated watchmen nodded and shifted away from the others. As he went, Gerrit flashed a grin at Rudi.

'Right then.' Rijgen watched Loos and Anders take up their positions by the door, waited a few moments for the others to reach the rear of the building, and gathered the rest of the party together. 'Let's get on with it.' Rudi half expected him to break the door down, but instead he knocked on the slab of wood almost gently.

After a moment the small door in the middle of it opened and a halfling girl dressed like a kitchen maid stuck her head out.

'Yes?' After a moment the size of the visitors dawned on her and she glanced up, the expression of polite enquiry freezing on her face. 'It's the Caps!' she shrieked and tried to duck back inside, but Rijgen was faster, yanking her out of the hole like a dog with a rabbit.

Seeing an opportunity, Rudi bent double and ducked through the tiny portal, straightening up again just in time to avoid a punch in the face from a halfling tall and muscular enough to have passed for a shaven dwarf in a bad light. Not that such a thing existed so far as Rudi knew, among the male ones at least. Instead the blow clanged harmlessly against his single piece of armour and his assailant danced around the hallway nursing his bruised knuckles.

'Ow! Ow! You broke my hand, you orc-snogging git!' While he was distracted Rudi tripped the latch on the main door and the remaining watchmen piled in.

'You're under arrest,' Rudi snapped, turning on the diminutive bouncer. 'Assaulting a watchman, abusive language and gross indecency.' Leaving the door party to scoop the fellow up, he followed Rijgen.

'Smart work, lad,' the sergeant said, acknowledging him with a nod. He gestured to the main staircase. 'We'll take upstairs. Maartens, Strijker, you've got the ground floor.'

'Right, Sarge.' Maartens nodded, and the two watchmen began systematically kicking down the doors leading off from the hallway. Rudi followed Rijgen up the stairs and found him contemplating a corridor lined with similar entrances, presumably leading to bedrooms. The nearest one seemed more elaborate, larger and panelled, no doubt marking what used to be the master bedroom when this was a more prosperous establishment.

'You take the left side, I'll take the ones on the right,' Rijgen said. Rudi nodded. The sergeant kicked out at the door in front of him; it burst open with a crack of splintering wood and Rijgen disappeared inside. Most of the room was invisible from where Rudi was standing, but he could clearly hear a squeal of feminine outrage. Rijgen raised his hat politely. 'Pardon the intrusion, ma'am. Rollo, get your breeches on, you're nicked.'

Rudi lost no time in following the sergeant's lead. The first room was empty, apart from the same utilitarian furniture he'd seen in taverns and boarding houses before, and the next two held nothing more sinister than sleeping halflings who seemed too confused or terrified at being confronted by a sword-wielding watchman to do anything more than stutter out their names and occupations before scuttling down the stairs to join the growing throng in the hall being penned in by the Caps guarding the door. When he entered the next room, though, he was the one taken by surprise.

'Don't move! City watch!' This time the occupant was awake, dressed, and sitting in a chair, the expression of bored anticipation on his face giving way to shock and surprise. He was human and familiar, dressed in a fading blue coat that didn't quite fit. As he looked up and saw Rudi's face his expression changed again, to one of astonishment.

The vague sense of recognition crystallised and Rudi felt as though he'd just been punched in the stomach. Shenk, the riverboat captain who'd tried to turn him and Hanna in for the bounty Gerhard had put on their heads.

'It's you! Rudi whatsisname.' The man's expression changed again as he took in the watchman's headgear, to one of almost comical bafflement. 'You're a Black Cap now?'

'Damn right,' Rudi said, wondering what on earth to do, but determined to retain the initiative. 'Feel like resisting arrest?' Shenk's face paled, clearly wondering if Rudi was capable of killing him to keep his secret. Now the idea had been planted, it was seductively simple. One quick sword thrust and the only man in Marienburg who could identify him as a fugitive from Imperial justice would never be able to testify against him.

'I won't say anything,' Shenk said hastily. 'Honest. I swear on my boat. I've never seen you before tonight, all right?'

'I can't take the chance,' Rudi said, and the riverboat captain's face paled even more. He pointed to the bed. 'Hide under there and wait till it goes quiet. Don't try to get out the back, there are men posted.'

'Thanks. Thanks, I owe you one.' Relief flooded Shenk's features. 'Really . The *Reikmaiden*'s berthed at

the candle wharf in Suiddock, halfway down the Luydenhoek Reach. Anything I can do for you…'

'You can start by shutting up before my sergeant
hears you,' Rudi said, backing out of the room. He
turned to call to Rijgen. 'Another empty one.'

'No problem.' The sergeant was carrying a set of
account books under one arm, an expression of
intense satisfaction on his face. 'I think we've got what
we came for.'

CHAPTER TWENTY-ONE

BY THE TIME the suspects had been assembled in a grumbling huddle in the street outside, ready to be taken to the watch house for interrogation, the first faint blush of dawn was beginning to appear over the rooftops. A surprising number of them were non-halflings: several human men and women, a couple of dwarfs and a well-dressed elf, who somehow managed to convey the impression that he was doing the watchmen a tremendous favour by condescending to be arrested by them, towered over the majority of the group.

Rudi didn't envy his colleagues the job of herding them through the constricted streets of the Kleinmoot, especially as the respectable inhabitants of the quarter were beginning to stir and go about their business. Rijgen nodded at the elf as the loudly-protesting prisoners shuffled past the doorway of the boarding house, surrounded by watchmen like sheep by dogs.

'That's a bonus,' he remarked. 'Pretty much confirms the Elfsgemeente connection.'

Overhearing, the suspect favoured him with a disdainful look. 'I'm here to discuss the delivery of a consignment of Lustrian spices to Esmeralda's Apron with Mineer Meadowsweet. And my lawyers will be speaking to you shortly, you can be sure of that.'

'Course you are. Course they will.' Rijgen didn't sound terribly convinced of either statement. 'But we'll be having a nice little chat ourselves before then.'

'Savages,' he said, turning away. 'Shave an ape and find a human, as they say in Uluthan.'

'Who are you calling a monkey?' one of the human prisoners demanded, clearly feeling that if he was to be denied the satisfaction of punching the watchman who had interrupted his evening's assignation, an elf would be an acceptable alternative, and Gerrit waded into the ensuing fracas with a short club and his habitual expression of cheerful goodwill.

'What about these other people?' Rudi asked, ignoring the noise.

'We'll find out. There's a lot more going on in there than just smuggling, you can bet on that.' He nodded at one of the human women, who smiled and nodded back as though in response to a friendly greeting. 'Kamilla there's the second biggest fence in the Winkelmarkt, for a start. And some of those rooms rent by the hour, if you get my drift.'

Rudi, who had been in the city long enough to do so, nodded, and regarded a few of the female suspects with renewed and slightly guilty interest. Not that he had, or would, of course, but sometimes he couldn't help wondering.

'Well that about wraps it up,' Rijgen concluded. He yawned loudly. 'All we need to do now is send a note to the waterboys over in the Paleisbuurt telling them to come and collect their presents.'

'I can take it for you,' Rudi said, blessing whichever of the gods had handed him the chance of crossing the city without arousing suspicion. If he had legitimate business in the Paleisbuurt, what could be more natural than taking the opportunity for a social call on Fritz while he was there?

Rijgen looked at him with a hint of surprise. 'Bucking for promotion already, Walder? Didn't think you were the type.'

'I'm not,' Rudi said without thinking. 'I mean, I want to get on of course, but...' That sounded even worse, and he trailed off, embarrassed. 'A friend of mine works over there and I haven't seen him in a while. I just thought if someone had to go over the bridge today I might as well do it and see if he's free for a drink.'

'I see.' Rijgen nodded again and began to follow the rest of his command back towards the Winkelmarkt. Rudi glanced back, just in time to see a furtive figure in a blue coat dart out of the building behind them and disappear down a nearby alleyway, and breathed a faint sigh of relief. At least Shenk had got away clean and wouldn't be compromising him. Not for a while, anyway. Forcing down the suspicion that he had merely postponed a problem he'd hoped to avoid, Rudi returned his attention to the sergeant. 'Well, since you've volunteered, you might as well go. But don't think I'm authorising overtime. If you want to get ratted with your mates you can do it in your off hours.'

'No, sergeant,' Rudi said, trying to hide his elation. It seemed his covert commission would turn out to be easier than he'd anticipated, and fulfilling that would bring him closer to the answers he needed.

'No hurry, though,' Rijgen said. 'Grab some breakfast before you go.'

RUDI FOLLOWED THE sergeant's advice, booking out at the end of the shift and heading for the Blind Eye with Gerrit and a couple of the other Caps who had accompanied them on the raid. They were all in high spirits, reliving the highlights of the night's events for their own amusement and that of their colleagues who had, as Gerrit put it, 'missed all the fun.'

'So Kuyper and me are waiting by the back door,' he said, piling into a plateful of sausage, 'when it bursts open and this shorty runs out like someone's just shouted "free cake!" So Kuyper grabs him and chucks him back inside and there's a whole bunch of them there, jammed up in the doorway, and he just says "skittles. Don't you love it?"'

'I thought the best bit,' Rudi said, as the laughter around the table died down, 'was when Maarten brought that elf out. You know, when he looked at sergeant Rijgen all down his nose and said "Have you any idea who I am?"' He took a bite of sausage and bread, blessing the foresight that had made him warn Shenk to stay hidden instead of trying to get out of the back of the building.

Gerrit nodded enthusiastically. 'Oh yeah. The old man just looks back at him for a moment, then shouts, "Does anyone here know who this gentleman is? He appears to have forgotten!"'

'That's right,' Maarten confirmed. 'I never knew they could go that colour.' Despite their cynicism about the previous evening, most of the night shift present looked a little envious of their colleagues who had made such a successful foray, and the men from the noon shift were clearly feeling that they'd missed out too.

'You know the real cherry on the cake?' one of the listening watchmen cut in.

Rudi shook his head. 'What?' he asked, his voice muffled slightly by another mouthful of food.

'The waterboys cocked up their end completely.' A chorus of delight and disbelief swept the taproom.

'How do you know?' he asked.

'Ran into Beren from the Suiddock post.' That sometimes happened, patrols from neighbouring wards meeting by chance at their mutual border and pausing for a while to exchange gossip and rumour. 'He'd just bought a snack from Granny Hetta, who heard it from a boatman who'd come across the water half an hour before. Seems they hit the Apron and it was perfectly clean. No contraband anywhere.' Gleeful hoots of derisive laughter followed the announcement. Rudi chewed his sausage thoughtfully. Artemus's experiences had put him off the idea of gambling for life, but he would cheerfully have bet the two guilders remaining in his purse that whatever had been in the back room of Esmeralda's Apron was now safely stowed in the hold of the *Reikmaiden*.

'I bet they were choked,' Gerrit said, with a cheerful lack of sympathy. The watchman nodded.

'It gets better. Apparently they forgot to clear it with the Mannikins first.' After a moment of bafflement,

Rudi recognised the common nickname for their elven counterparts. 'Seems that as it was a halfling tavern on a waterway it never occurred to them that the elves might claim jurisdiction, even if the landward side was on their patch. And the Mannikins aren't at all happy about it.' Rudi could understand that. The borders of the Elfsgemeente were rigidly defined and jealously guarded. The political ripples of such a fiasco were likely to run on for weeks, if not years. The elves had long memories.

'Sounds like someone's going to be looking for another job,' Maartens said, with some satisfaction.

'Which reminds me,' Rudi said, pushing his empty plate away and standing slowly. 'I've an errand to run. Catch you later.'

'Now?' Gerrit stared at him, astonished, and stifled a yawn. 'I swear, I don't know where you get the energy from.'

DESPITE HAVING BEEN in Marienburg for nearly two months, Rudi had never been north of the river before, so it was with a strange mixture of anticipation and apprehension that he began his journey. Captain Marcus had the letter for the commander of the River Watch ready and waiting and Rudi nodded attentively as he added some last minute verbal instructions.

'Make sure you give it directly to Commandant Vanderfalk,' he said. 'We've done our part. I don't want him trying to deflect attention from his people's failure by claiming he never got the message.'

'Yes, captain.' Rudi nodded again and glanced at the name scrawled on the folded sheet of paper, close to the seal. Sure enough he was able to read it,

Commandant Vanderfalk, just as Marcus had said. He felt a faint flush of pride in his newly acquired ability. Back in Kohlstadt he'd carried innumerable letters like this for Magnus, having to rely on memory tricks to ensure they reached the right recipient.

The stray thought sparked a storm of memories of his former life, which, if by comparison with his present one had been dull and circumscribed, had at least seemed secure. For the first time in weeks he missed his adoptive father, whose solid presence had been the cornerstone of his existence for as long as he could remember.

'Are you all right, Walder?' Marcus was looking at him doubtfully, and Rudi forced the memories away.

'Fine, captain,' he said hastily.

'I can always get someone else to take it if you'd rather turn in. You've had a long night.'

'I'll be fine,' Rudi repeated. Once he found Magnus and the answers the merchant held, perhaps things would start to make sense again. The merchant knew who his real family was, Gunther had said as much before he died. That was a secret worth taking a few risks to uncover.

'Better get going, then,' Marcus said, already turning to the next piece of paperwork.

Outside, the morning was crisp and chill, a keen wind rippling up the street from the direction of the river. Even over the all-pervading stench of the city, which by now he scarcely noticed, Rudi could smell the onset of winter in it. Before long the Sea of Claws would begin to live up to its name, and the only ships entering or leaving the harbour would be those of the elves, the occasional Norscan, or skippers whose debts or desperation had driven them to the brink of insanity.

For now, trade flourished, and as he left the familiar streets of the Winkelmarkt for the lesser-known byways of the Suiddock, the evidence of that was all around him. The bustle of activity was just as intense as he remembered it on the morning Kris had taken him and Hanna through the ward on their way to the college in the Templewijk. Several times he had to step out of the way of laden carts or straining stevedores moving the lifeblood of the city from river to warehouse or back again. Once, a coach passed him from the direction of the Westenpoort gate, although whether it had come from Altdorf or Gisoreux he had no idea. Something was written on the side, but it was so obscured with mud that it had gone before he had time to puzzle it out. That meant he was still moving in the right direction, though. The coaches entering the city by either gate terminated their journeys in the Beulsplaats, one of the few open spaces in the ward, on the island of Luydenhoek.

A ripple of apprehension disturbed the surface of his mind at that thought. *Reikmaiden* was berthed at the docks and he'd rather not run into Shenk again. Not for a while, anyway, until he'd had time to assimilate the implications of their unexpected encounter the previous night. He had no option, though; the only route to the Hoogbrug bridge was across the largest island of the small chain making up the Suiddock ward.

Getting to Luydenhoek in the first place meant crossing the Bruynwater, the main canal used by ocean-going vessels, and as he neared it the breeze flowing through the streets began to take on a sharper edge. The thoroughfares began to seem more crowded too, pedestrians, carts and carriages mingling in confusion as they were funnelled into the approaches of the only bridge across the shipping channel. Thanks to his distinctive headgear, Rudi was able to make better progress than most, the authority it lent him and his purposeful stride nudging people out of his way as effectively as his elbows would have done.

As he neared the bridge itself, he was surprised to find the traffic continuing to flow unimpeded by anything other than the eddies induced into the current of pedestrians by its own mass. Unlike any of the other bridges he'd seen in Marienburg, the Draainbrug which spanned the Bruynwater was free of obstructing houses or market stalls. Faintly puzzled by this at first, Rudi was soon to discover why.

He had almost reached the bridge himself when a horn blew, louder than any he'd ever heard before. Startled, he glanced across at the single, massive stone archway which towered over the roadway in the centre of the bridge. A dwarf stood on a small balcony there, blowing energetically into a brass instrument almost as large as he was.

In response to the clarion call the foot traffic around him slowed and a couple of riders spurred their horses to a canter, hurrying across the span in almost indecent haste. Rudi was about to take a step after them when a solid oak pole, which looked as though it had once been the mast of a riverboat, descended abruptly on a counterweighted pivot to bar his way.

'Sorry mate,' the Black Cap manning it said, clearly not meaning it, then realised she was talking to another member of the watch. Her voice changed, acquiring a more friendly tone. 'Not in a hurry, are you?'

'No.' Rudi shook his head, faintly surprised. There were only a couple of female Caps in the Winkelmarkt watch, and the shift patterns meant that he'd never been on duty with either of them . 'Just taking a message over the water.'

'Good.' The Cap motioned to him to duck under the barrier and Rudi did so, relieved to be out of the growing press of bodies behind him. 'You might just make it over if you run for it.'

'It'll wait,' Rudi said, mindful of his instructions not to hurry. The longer he took, the longer Marcus and Rijgen would have to interrogate the suspects before the River Watch got their hands on them. 'We've done enough for the waterboys for one night.'

'Thought you were from the Winkelmarkt ward,' the Cap said. She glanced at the bow and quiver of arrows slung over his back. 'You must be Walder, am I right?'

'You are,' Rudi said, surprised.

The Black Cap smiled. 'Thought so. Not too many Caps in Marienburg carrying those things around.' Rudi smiled politely, trying to conceal the alarm he felt. It seemed his reputation had already spread beyond the Winkelmarkt, and that was disturbing. If Gerhard heard any gossip about a young watchman named Walder he'd undoubtedly waste no time in following it up. 'I'm Rauke, by the way. Rauke van Stolke.'

'Rudi.' He shook the proffered hand. 'I had no idea I was so famous.'

'Not famous, exactly.' Rauke laughed. As she tilted her head back, Rudi caught a glimpse of brown hair, brown eyes and freckles under the floppy hat she wore. 'Just a bit unusual. You know how these things get about.'

That idea was a bit worrying too, but before Rudi had time to reflect on it or frame a reply his attention was diverted by a loud grating sound. A few yards away, the cobbles of the street appeared to be moving, and a momentary surge of vertigo made him sway on his feet.

'I bet you never saw anything like that in the Empire.' No point in asking how she knew where he came from, his accent betrayed his origins to native Marienburgers every time he opened his mouth. Another detail for Gerhard to absorb and draw conclusions from if he heard the gossip about him. Then the full magnitude of what he was seeing finally sunk in, and he felt his jaw slackening with surprise.

'You'd bet right,' he admitted. The entire bridge was rotating around the massive stone pillar beneath the archway, smoke belching from a chimney and wisps of steam escaping from vents in the carriageway. A metallic clatter and screech echoed across the water, louder than anything of the kind he'd ever heard. The spectacle was breathtaking, although Rauke seemed completely unimpressed by it.

'Now that's a sight I never get tired of,' she said after a moment. Following the direction of her gaze, Rudi saw an ocean going carrack, its sails cracking in the wind, tacking cautiously around the bridge, which now lay parallel to the flow of the Bruynwater. A wall of wood seemed to glide majestically past the two Caps, bigger than Rudi had ever thought possible. The only vessel he'd ever seen close up was the *Reikmaiden*, and the sturdy little riverboat would have been dwarfed by the mighty vessel in front of them now. 'One of these days...'

'You'll leave?' Rudi guessed.

Rauke nodded. 'I'm nearly twenty. I don't want to be stuck here rousting drunks and busting heads all my life. There's a whole world out there to explore. Araby, Lustria, even Cathay.' She shrugged. 'We're a seafaring nation. I don't think there's anyone in the Wasteland who doesn't feel the urge to go wandering to some extent.'

'It's not all it's cracked up to be,' Rudi said, without thinking.

'Maybe you just haven't gone far enough,' she suggested.

DESPITE HIS APPREHENSION, Rudi passed through the streets of Luydenhoek without encountering Shenk again, or any of his crew, although that was hardly surprising once he'd got a good look at the place. If anything it was even more bustling than the precincts south of the canal, which was all he'd seen of the Suiddock so far. The sketchy knowledge of the city beyond the Winkelmarkt which he'd absorbed since his arrival, mainly from conversations with Artemus and Gerrit, included the fact that the so-called east end of the island was where the most modern and efficient facilities were, but seeing it for himself was entirely different. Houses, taverns, shops and all manner of other enterprises were jammed together between warehouses and docks, all crammed with vessels like the one he'd seen sailing down the Bruynwater. The riverboats were mainly confined to the side canals, over which the streets ran on bridges just sufficiently high to let them glide past with inches to spare between the tops of the masts and the keystones supporting the arches above, docking at smaller wharves abutting the warehouses. The first time he saw this arrangement, Rudi was troubled by a faint, nagging sense of familiarity, until he realised that this echoed the layout of the warehouse in the Doodkanal where he'd seen Magnus and the horned sorceress.

Absorbed in these reflections, he reached the north side of the island before he was expecting to and found himself striding out across the Neiderbrug, the wide bridge connecting Luydenhoek to Hightower Island where the mighty Hoogbrug terminated. Like the swing bridge, the Neiderbrug was completely clear of the obstructions which he'd grown accustomed to seeing on all the others he'd crossed, although this time the reason was different. It and the Hoogbrug were kept clear by law. The Directors of the city would tolerate no hindrance to the free flow of commerce across the river, and anyone attempting to do so would quickly find new lodgings at their expense on the fortress prison of Rijker's Isle, the lonely outcrop which guarded the mouth of the harbour.

The main result of this was that Rudi got his first unobstructed view of the Hoogbrug and the huge tower leading up to it, which cast its shadow across the whole ward like the gnomon of a gigantic sundial. As Kris had boasted, the roadway wound its way around it in a vast spiral, wide enough for the traffic to flow unobstructed in both directions, and had he not been caught up in the remorseless motion of people and animals he might well have stopped dead in stupefaction at the awe-inspiring sight. As it was, he merely checked his pace a moment and went on, ignoring the oaths of a sedan chair bearer plodding grimly up the steepening ramp behind him. How the fellow and his compatriot at the other end of the contraption were able to keep up the pace was a mystery to him. Fit as he was, his calves were aching by the time he passed beneath the massive arch which carried the span of the bridge and felt the ground begin to level off.

As he stepped out onto the Hoogbrug itself he felt the urge to check his pace again and simply stare. Absorbed in the long climb up the ramp and buffeted by the other traffic he hadn't had much attention to spare for the view beyond the balustrade, but now the entire city seemed spread out below him.

His first impression was one of water, the broad sweep of the Reik to the east, receding into the far distance beyond the walls, scything through the greens and browns of the Wasteland until it merged with the horizon, and the deep, infinite blue of the open sea in the other direction.

Mighty ships, shrunk by perspective to the size of children's toys, crowded the water, surrounded by the scudding sails of skiffs and water coaches. On the far side gleaming white spires marked the elven quarter, while closer at hand, almost at the foot of the northern tower, a building larger and more ornate than any of its neighbours was undoubtedly the official residence of the staadholder, the chairman of the council of ten who ran the city and all its affairs.

Rudi glanced at it and then to the street behind, wondering which of the buildings was the Imperial embassy. There was no time to wonder how he was going to contact Fritz. Now, though, even loitering as much as he dared, he was almost halfway across the titanic span of the bridge.

Glancing back, Rudi took in the prospect of the southern bank, trying to identify the landmarks in the part of the city he knew. From up here it dawned on him just how little that really was.

Far in the distance the sun struck gold from the dome of the temple of Manann in the Templewijk, and from that starting point he was easily able to pick out the college. He wondered what Hanna was doing now and narrowed his eyes as he had in the wilderness to try to make out distant details, but even if she'd been standing on the roof waving at him he would never have been able to see her from this distance.

Still moving as slowly as he could, and trusting in his watchman's hat to deflect the wrath of other road users, he tried to pick out some more familiar landmarks. He found the Scrivener's guildhall easily enough, where he was due to visit Artemus again the following day, then turned his attention to the Winkelmarkt. The watch barracks was easy enough to find, along with the watch house he was assigned to, but he couldn't make out the location of the Dancing Pirate.

The Westernpoort gate was easy enough to see, however and beyond that he was able to trace the ribbon of the coach road back to the point where it diverged, heading westwards to Gisoreux and Bretonnia and south-eastwards towards Altdorf, roughly parallel to the broad blue highway of the Reik. Somewhere out there, beyond the horizon and the vaguely defined

border of the Empire, was Kohlstadt and the life he'd
left forever.

Between the city and the strip of mud flats enclosed
by the thick, broad line of the Vloedmuur, the Doodkanal struck highlights from the rippling water. From
up here it looked little different from any of the other
waterways, the thick, oily tide of mud and effluent
indistinguishable from the more wholesome fluid surrounding it. The blight which had struck the
neighbourhood was less obvious too, although even
from this distance the buildings showed signs of struc-
tural weakness, sagging rooflines and haphazard
patches of tumbled masonry pointing up their poor
state of repair. A thin thread of smoke was rising from
somewhere in the quarter, which at first Rudi put
down to someone seeking refuge from the autumnal
chill, then a shock of recognition made his heart race.
That broad avenue, so different from most of its neighbours, had to be the Schwartzwasserstraat.

A quick glance at the surrounding topography confirmed it. There was the bridge over the open sewer
where he'd fought off the footpads. Even before he
looked again, his suspicions were hardening into cer-
tainty. There could be no doubt about it, the thread of
smoke marked the site of the von Blackenburg mansion. There was only one conclusion he could draw.

'Gerhard!' The name escaped him involuntarily,
drawing a couple of curious glances from passers-by
who met his eyes and hurried on, turning away as they
did so. It seemed the witch hunter had found allies in
the city after all.

Rudi picked up his pace, conscious that now he had
even more reason to talk to Fritz. If he was right, their

lives, and Hanna's too, hung in the balance just as much as they ever had.

CHAPTER TWENTY-TWO

THE HEADQUARTERS OF the River Watch were easy
enough to find, Captain Marcus's directions having
been clear and concise, and Rudi located it with little
difficulty. The Paleisbuurt was the least congested part
of the city he'd seen so far, the streets broad, and many
of the houses even had modest gardens around them.
That had seemed impressive enough at first sight, but
even this profligate use of the city's limited space was
eclipsed by the largest open area he'd seen since his
arrival in Marienburg. The square in front of the staadholder's palace was wide enough for a company of
soldiers to have drilled in without difficulty, unless
they got tangled up in the large, ornate fountain in the
centre of it encrusted with dolphins and other sea life.

Unable to resist the impulse, Rudi slowed his pace,
taking in the magnificent frontage of the palace. It towered over the buildings surrounding it, and everything

apart from the windows seemed decorated with carvings.

'Impressive, isn't it?' Rudi turned in response to the voice at his elbow, which sounded vaguely familiar. Mathilde was grinning at him, clearly enjoying his expression of surprise. 'Screaming bad taste, of course, but that's Wastelanders for you. If you've got it, flaunt it. Come to that, they like to flaunt it even if they haven't got it.' She looked at him speculatively. 'What are you doing here? Decided the Black Caps can manage without you after all?'

'I'm taking a message to the River Watch,' Rudi said. Now his mind was working again, the coincidence of meeting the woman was too fortuitous not to follow up. 'I thought it might be a chance to catch up with Fritz, see how he's doing.'

'He's doing all right,' Mathilde said, smiling at something Rudi didn't quite get. She shrugged. 'I'll tell him I've seen you. You know the Gull and Trident?'

'I've never been this side of the river before,' Rudi said.

'Not a problem, it's hard to miss.' Mathilde gave him directions to the tavern. 'Bit poncey for my taste, but Fritz likes it. I'll send him over there when I get back to the embassy.' She started to turn away, then glanced back at him, her eyes holding a hint of mischief. 'Better take your hat off before you go in, though.'

'I'll do that.' Rudi wasn't entirely sure what she meant by that, but he'd got into the habit of doing so before entering taverns on anything other than official business in any case. Most landlords felt a visible watchman on the premises was bad for trade even if they had nothing to hide, and he was beginning to suspect that there were precious few people in Marienburg who did.

He watched Mathilde disappear in the direction of Embassy Row, behind the palace, and resumed his leisurely walk towards the headquarters of the River Watch. Like most of the buildings connected with the administration of the city's affairs, it was adjacent to the palace, down a narrow side street ending in a dock. Several skiffs and other small craft were moored there, most of them flying the distinctive pennant of the Watch, which depicted a protective hand wrapped around the crest of the city.

Rudi made his way to the landward entrance, an imposing wooden door giving way to a wide lobby floored with a mosaic of frolicking fish. It was a far cry from the austere facilities the Winkelmarkt watch had to make do with and he tried to stifle a grimace of disapproval as he walked in.

'Can I help you?' A waterboy barred his way, with a disdainful glance at his City watchman's hat.

'Message for Commandant Vanderfalk.' He held up the missive.

The River watchman nodded, making no attempt to get out of his way. 'I'll see that he gets it.'

'I'm supposed to give it to him in person,' Rudi said. He smiled ingenuously. 'In case there's an answer.'

'Fine.' The waterboy stood aside with ill grace. 'Wait here. I'll see if he's available.' He disappeared through a polished wooden door at the other end of the entrance hall, leaving Rudi to sit on one of the chairs lining it. They were upholstered in leather and overly padded, and he squirmed uncomfortably for a moment before standing again and helping himself to a mug of kaffee from an urn on a nearby table.

After a moment, the watchman returned and regarded Rudi with a jaundiced eye.

'Make yourself at home. Have a drink.' He went back to watching the door with every sign of complete indifference.

'Hard luck about last night,' Rudi volunteered after a moment, unable to resist responding to the man's churlishness with a little teasing.

The watchman's jaw tensed a little. 'Luck had nothing to do with it,' he said shortly. 'They must have been tipped off. One of your mob taking a backhander, probably.'

'Maybe,' Rudi replied cheerfully. 'But then you'd have expected them to warn our local villains too, wouldn't you? And we bagged the lot.' He smiled, trying not to think about the single exception. 'Maybe your leak was a bit closer to home.'

'And maybe we just got a bad tip-off. It happens.'

A portly man in early middle age entered the hallway and held out a hand impatiently. 'You've got a letter for me, I hear.'

'Yes sir.' Rudi saluted smartly, to the commandant's visible surprise, and handed him the note. Vanderfalk took it, slit the seal with his thumbnail, and skimmed the contents.

'At least your end of the operation seems to have gone well.' He sighed. 'That's something I suppose. It says here you've got hold of the account books.'

'That's right.' Rudi nodded.

'Maybe that'll tell us something.' The commandant shrugged. 'Unless those were the books we were supposed to find, of course.'

'I wouldn't know about that, sir,' Rudi said. 'I just kicked a few doors in.'

'No doubt.' Vanderfalk thought for a moment. 'Thank you for waiting, but there won't be a reply. We'll send a barge over to pick up the suspects.' He turned back on the verge of leaving, to add an afterthought. 'You're welcome to hitch a ride on it if you like.'

'No thank you, sir.' Rudi took his hat off and tucked it inside his shirt. 'I'm off duty now. I'm meeting a friend for a drink.' There was no real reason to mention that, but it wouldn't hurt to make his cover a little more solid. He was beginning to suspect he had a gift for duplicity, and the thought wasn't altogether comforting.

To HIS RELIEF Fritz was alone when he arrived at the Gull and Trident, which turned out to be far larger and more prosperous than the simple tavern he was expecting. Most of the patrons were well dressed and he felt uncomfortably conspicuous in his simple attire. The bow and arrows he carried attracted a fair amount of attention too, and he was sure he overheard a couple of whispered comments about them.

'Rudi! Over here!' Fritz stood and waved at him from a table in the corner of the taproom, next to a large glazed window with a view across the river. With a wave in return, he wove his way between the tables to join the hulking youth. 'I've ordered already. I hope you don't mind.'

'Not at all,' Rudi said, feeling a little bemused. Fritz seemed more confident than he remembered, less sullen and far less defensive. He was wearing a dark blue doublet, with matching britches, and a cloak of the same material was draped over the back of his chair. His hair had been neatly trimmed and a small, perfectly symmetrical beard adorned his chin. No one from Kohlstadt would have recognised him as the awkward bully he used to be.

'Good.' Fritz poured some wine from a flagon on the table into a waiting goblet and handed it to him. 'Is wine all right? I can get you some ale if you prefer.'

'This is fine,' Rudi said, taking his seat. He sipped at the drink cautiously; he'd never tried wine before. It was richer than he expected, with a sharp aftertaste which cleansed his palate and left his tongue tingling pleasantly.

'I'm glad you like it. They've got a pretty good cellar here.' He sipped from his own goblet and looked at Rudi over the top of it. 'I was surprised when Mathilde gave me your message though.'

'Well, you know how it is.' Rudi shrugged. 'I had to come over the bridge this morning and it wouldn't have felt right going back without asking how you were.'

'Pretty good, actually.' Fritz paused, while a serving girl set plates in front of them. 'I ordered the turbot, I hope that's all right.'

'It's fine,' Rudi said again, staring in some perplexity at the cutlery in front of him. The knife and spoon he recognised, but there was another implement there too, three short prongs fixed to a handle. Fritz picked it up and speared a morsel of fish with it, transferring it to his mouth with practiced ease.

'You flake it off the bones with the fork,' he explained. Rudi nodded and followed suit. Evidently von Eckstein had arranged some instruction in formal etiquette for his new bodyguard.

'Working for the nobility obviously suits you,' he said. 'New clothes, new...' he choked himself off before adding 'table manners,' and nodded at the rapier Fritz now carried at his belt in place of the cudgel he'd seen before. 'Sword,' he finished instead.

'Mathilde's been giving me fencing lessons,' Fritz said, and to Rudi's astonishment blushed a little. 'She says I'm very physical.'

'I suppose that's an asset in a bodyguard,' Rudi said, trying to nudge the conversation around to the information Sam wanted.

'We've had a couple of scrapes. Nothing too serious though.'

'Really?' Rudi took another mouthful of the fish. It had been poached to perfection, dissolving on his tongue, and the rich, creamy sauce offset it perfectly. 'Where was that?'

'Not on your patch,' Fritz assured him. 'We had a run-in with a gang of footpads in the Guilderveld a couple of nights ago.'

'The Guilderveld?' Rudi repeated. 'I didn't think there was anything much there in the way of entertainment.'

'You'd be surprised,' Fritz said. 'Those bankers really know how to throw a party. But we were on our way back from Elftown at the time.'

'Really?' Rudi feigned only the mildest of interest, although his pulse began to race. Sam had mentioned that von Eckstein was meeting someone in the Elfsgemeente and was particularly interested in finding out who. 'What were you doing over there?'

'Eating, mostly,' Fritz said. 'They've got some of the best restaurants in the city.' He shrugged. 'Of course most of the chefs are halflings, but the elves try not to mention that. Most of them are so stuck up you'd think their farts didn't smell.' Evidently his earlier fascination with the race hadn't survived much close contact with them.

'I'm sure there are some who are all right,' Rudi said, topping up his companion's drink.

'Oh yes, there's this friend of the boss's who's all right. Lamiel Silvershine. They hang out a lot together.' He took the refilled goblet and drank. 'They've got similar interests.'

'Losing money at cards?' Rudi asked, refilling his own cup. The turbot had vanished and he pushed his empty plate aside.

'That too. I think the main thing is they're doing some kind of business together. Silvershine's involved in one of the merchant houses.' Rudi nodded, not wanting to push the simpleton too hard. Sam, or his paymasters, would know which one, or could find out easily enough now they knew the identity of von Eckstein's contact. His mission completed, he began to nudge the conversation onto safer ground.

'I saw Hanna the other day,' he said. 'She asked after you.' Fritz waited while the serving girl cleared the plates before replying.

'Was she well?' His face took on an unexpected expression of concern. 'I saw her a few weeks back and things sounded really rough for her.'

'Not much improvement,' Rudi said, unwilling to discuss the details in public. A new suit and a haircut might have made Fritz look like a gentleman, but he was still an idiot and he didn't trust his discretion at all. Especially given the ease with which he'd just been able to worm the information he wanted out of him. Fortunately, it seemed, even Fritz wasn't that stupid. He just nodded.

'I was afraid of that,' he said. 'But it was nice seeing her again. Even made what happened afterwards seem worth it.'

'What happened afterwards?' Rudi asked, leaning to one side to let the serving girl put a bowl of something on the table in front of him. To his unspoken relief Fritz picked up a spoon and attacked his portion with evident enthusiasm, so he wouldn't have to juggle with unfamiliar cutlery this time. He followed suit cautiously, finding something hot, creamy and tasting of apples under a thick, brittle crust.

'We got into a fight,' Fritz said. He shrugged. 'Shouldn't complain, I suppose – it's what I'm paid for. But I never killed anyone before.' He turned his eyes on Rudi for a moment and the two of them shared a moment of silent understanding. 'It's a big thing to come to terms with.'

'It is,' Rudi confirmed. 'What happened?'

'We were just getting back in the boat when they jumped us,' Fritz said. 'Mathilde and I fought them off, but one of them fell in the water after I hit him and went down like a stone.'

'It wasn't your fault,' Rudi assured him.

Fritz took another drink of wine and nodded. 'The stupid thing is, they were after the boss's bag, and there wasn't anything valuable in it anyway. Just some old papers he picked up from the college.' Something else seemed to strike him and he laughed out loud,

without humour. 'It's just struck me, that's all the
footpads in the Guilderveld would have got too.
Hardly worth dying for, is it?'

'I suppose it would depend on what the papers were,'
Rudi said, privately certain who had sent the luckless
desperados to their deaths.

'No idea. Just old maps. I suppose they must just
have seen a rich man and assumed he was carrying
something valuable.'

'Sounds right to me,' Rudi said. He poured the last of
the wine into Fritz's goblet. 'What did von Eckstein
have to say about them?'

'Nothing much,' Fritz said. 'He did say something
funny to Silvershine though. Something about someone being desperate to keep Riemaan from being
vindicated.' He shrugged. 'Does that mean anything to
you?'

'Nothing at all,' Rudi said. The rest of the meal
passed in small talk, and it wasn't until after they'd left
the tavern, Fritz insisting on paying the bill which
would have swallowed a week's wages for Rudi, that he
got the opportunity to warn him about Gerhard's
arrival in the city. Fearful of being overheard, he waited
until they were passing through the square in front of
the palace before broaching the subject, and glanced
around cautiously to make sure no one else was in
earshot.

'Are you sure it's him?' Fritz asked, pausing to throw
a copper coin into the fountain. It was apparently a
custom of the place, to ensure good luck, and Rudi followed suit. Right now he felt he needed all the luck he
could get. Privately, though, he suspected that the only
good fortune the fountain provided was reserved for

the beggar's guild. 'There are plenty of other witch hunters in the Empire.' Rudi nodded and looked around to make sure none of the other passers-by had wandered close enough to overhear their conversation.

'Pretty certain,' he said. 'He knew Magnus had a house in Marienburg. I found it myself a couple of days ago.'

'Was he there?' Fritz asked.

Rudi shook his head. 'No. I think Hans and the witch he works for frightened him off.'

'Hans is here?' Fritz asked, looking really concerned for the first time. 'If Gerhard's around he's in real danger!'

'We all are,' Rudi said. Unbelievably, it seemed, Fritz was still incapable of grasping the full extent of his brother's transformation.

The half-wit nodded. 'True. But you're in the watch, Hanna's a registered student of magic now and I've got the boss to hide behind. Hans doesn't have any protection at all.'

'I don't think any of us will if Gerhard starts throwing accusations of Chaos worship around again,' Rudi said. Fritz nodded.

'Good point.' Fritz lowered his voice a little, with a furtive glance around them to make sure no one else had drifted into earshot. 'Someone should warn Hans, though. Where can I find him?'

'I haven't a clue,' Rudi said. 'The only time I've seen him, he found me.' Reluctant to go into details he added, 'he seems quite capable of looking after himself.'

'That's true,' Fritz said. He shrugged. 'Well, it's a big city. Gerhard ought to be easy enough to avoid. It's not as though he's got any definite proof that we're here, is it?'

'I suppose not,' Rudi said, trying not to think of his name scrawled in the dust of the von Blackenburg mansion.

CHAPTER TWENTY-THREE

BY THE TIME he returned to the Winkelmarkt, hiring a boat to take him to his destination in order to save time and avoid the possibility of meeting Shenk on his way back through the Suiddock, Rudi was exhausted. The trip across the river had been unexpectedly relaxing despite the non-stop monologue of the water-coachman, who had an apparently inexhaustible fund of stories about the notable citizens of Marienburg, most of whom appeared to have been in the front of his boat at some time or other.

'So I says "I don't care if you're Manann himself, I'm not going south of the river at this time of night," and he says…'

'Thanks, this'll do.' Rudi interrupted the torrent of words and gestured at a landing stage which looked vaguely familiar. Lulled by the rocking of the tiny craft, he yawned widely.

'Suit yourself, governor.' The boatman pulled in smartly to the dock and watched Rudi disembark with the weary amusement of the water-dweller at the unsteady gait of the landlubber. 'Fourpence to you and cheap at half the price.'

'Keep the change.' Rudi dredged a sixpenny piece out of his purse, and the boatman smiled with the first show of genuine warmth since the young watchman had hailed the little craft.

'Very decent of you, squire. Mind how you go.' He pushed off and Rudi climbed the steps slowly. At the top he glanced around, orientating himself, and realised with faint surprise that he'd disembarked at the landing stage Artemus had told him to make for if he got lost on his first day in Marienburg. The barracks weren't far and his bed seemed almost infinitely attractive. It was well past noon already and he was due back on duty in a few hours. Nevertheless, moved by an impulse he couldn't quite explain, he turned the other way, towards the Dancing Pirate.

'Rudi.' Nikolaas looked up as he entered, a broad smile on his face. 'I was beginning to think you'd forgotten us.'

'How could I forget Marta's cooking?' Rudi asked, feeling immediately comfortable in the familiar surroundings. 'We don't eat half so well in the barracks, I can tell you that.'

'Well sit down and get some proper food inside you,' Marta said, bustling over to welcome him. Despite the meal he'd eaten with Fritz a couple of hours before, Rudi found the suggestion appealing. The cuisine in the Gull and Trident had been tasty enough, but hardly filling, and the substantial breakfast he'd enjoyed at the Blind Eye seemed a long time ago. He nodded gratefully. An early supper here and he would sleep all the more soundly until his shift started again, a disturbingly low number of hours from now.

'I'll do that.' With a thrill of quiet pride he realised he could now read the menu chalked up at the side of the bar, albeit slowly. 'Lentil broth, please.'

'The reading's coming on then,' the landlady commented, turning to enter the kitchen.

Rudi flushed. 'I didn't know anyone else knew about that.'

'Hanna told me,' Marta said. 'She still comes in with Kris once or twice a week.' Rudi frowned, stilling a faint flutter of jealousy. He knew the wizard had rooms over a baker's shop in the next street, but hadn't realised Hanna was visiting him quite so often. It was hardly surprising, though, when he came to think about it. Apart from whoever she knew at the college, himself and Fritz, she had no other friends in Marienburg. The landlady shook her head dubiously. 'I can't help wishing you'd found yourself a more respectable teacher, though.'

'Artemus is all right,' Rudi said. 'Once you get to know him.'

'I know him a lot better than you, laddie.' She put a steaming bowl of broth on the table in front of him and sighed. 'Granted, there's no malice in him. But don't take his word for too much, and don't lend him money.'

'On my pay?' Rudi asked, savouring the food. It was warming, wholesome and, if he was honest, far more to his taste than the gourmet meal he'd shared with Fritz. Marta laughed and went back to the kitchen.

'Mind if I join you?' Sam hauled himself up onto the human-sized chair opposite and waved to Nikolaas. 'Fish pie, carrots, turnips and a bowl of what he's having on the side.'

'Be my guest,' Rudi said.

The halfling smiled sardonically. 'I was about to say the same.' He raised his voice again. 'Put his meal on my slate, will you?'

'That's very kind of you,' Rudi said. He caught Nikolaas's eye as the landlord was about to turn away. 'I'll have an ale to wash it down then, too.'

'I'm hoping you're worth it,' Sam said. He glanced up as his meal arrived, along with the ale Rudi had ordered. After Koos had gone and he'd taken a mouthful of pie, he nodded thoughtfully. 'After your trip across the bridge this morning.'

'Word gets around,' Rudi said.

'It has a habit of doing that.' He plied his spoon energetically for a moment. 'The question is, has it got around to you?'

'Von Eckstein's been meeting an elf called Lamiel Silvershine,' Rudi said, coming straight to the point. 'He's a merchant of some kind, I don't know what.'

'He's a smuggler,' Sam said. 'And the River Watch would very much like to prove it. But that's their problem.' He shrugged. 'Good luck to them. The connections he's got with the Lianllach clan, he's pretty much fireproof.'

'With who?' Rudi asked.

'The second-biggest trading cartel in the Elfsgemeente. They'd very much like to be the biggest, and if they weren't split into so many competing factions they'd be well on the way. Silvershine's the mouthpiece for one that's not too particular how they manage it. Which doesn't explain why von Eckstein's playing footsie with him, or why he's been looking at old navigational charts down at the college.'

'Maybe he's doing it for Riemaan,' Rudi suggested.

The halfling stopped chewing and stared at him. 'Who did you say?'

'Riemaan.' Rudi took a gulp at his ale. Something in the intensity of the halfling's gaze was subtly unnerving. 'Any idea who that might be?'

'I might. Why did you bring up the name?'

'I didn't,' Rudi said. 'It was just that Fritz mentioned he'd heard it during one of the meetings with Silvershine.'

'That makes sense,' Sam said, nodding thoughtfully. He must have noticed Rudi's perplexity, because he smiled then. 'Riemaan was an Imperial speculator, about fifty years ago, who thought it would be a good idea to bypass Marienburg and trade directly with Lustria and Cathay. He persuaded a lot of wealthy people to develop a couple of ports in Ostland and Nordland.'

'What happened?' Rudi asked. Marienburg was still the gateway to the Empire, so presumably the scheme had failed.

'We outspent him,' Sam said. 'Offered the traders better deals than he could match, even though every single one of them made a loss. Marienburg's pockets are deep. He went bust, the ports he built are now derelict and life here went back to normal.'

'So von Eckstein's planning to revive them,' Rudi said.

Sam nodded. 'Maybe. What really sunk Riemaan was that the elves stayed with us, and they've got the Lustrian trade pretty much sewn up. Even now, the humans just get the leftovers the clans can't be bothered with. If he can persuade one of the Lianllach factions to start dealing directly with the Empire, things could work out very differently next time.'

'I'm sure you'll find a way to deal with it,' Rudi said. 'I hear you're very resourceful.'

'You hear right,' Sam acknowledged, pushing his plate aside. 'Which is how come I can help with your problem too.'

'I'm glad to hear it.' Rudi drank again, afraid to get his hopes up too much. Good as Sam's contacts were supposed to be, he doubted that the halfling would have been able to track Magnus down this quickly. Sam nodded, accepting the implied compliment.

'Cornelius van Crackenmeer. He's a lawyer, represents von Blackenburg's interests while he's out of town. If anyone knows where your boy is, it'll be him.'

'I see.' Rudi nodded his thanks. 'Where do I find him?'

Sam grinned. 'About this time of day? With a streetwalker, probably. Your best bet's his office. Halfway along the Deedsalee in the Tempelwijk. Know it?'

'Yes.' Rudi nodded. The narrow thoroughfare was only a couple of streets away from the Scrivener's guildhall and he'd passed it several times on his way to visit Artemus. Sam nodded.

'Good.' He slipped to the floor, his head just visible beyond the table. 'See you around.'

'Maybe,' Rudi said, his head spinning with fatigue and confusion. He couldn't deny though that the halfling had given him the best lead he'd had so far. He stood abruptly, on the verge of heading over to the Tempelwijk on the spot, then paused, common sense reasserting itself. He was in no condition to go after the lawyer now, and even if he was he would never make it over to the far side of the city and back before his shift began. He shoved the fly-cloud of buzzing questions resolutely to the back of his mind, waved goodbye to the landlord and his wife and headed out into the street.

The way back to the barracks took him past the bakery where Kris lived, and as he turned the corner of the street he caught a glimpse of blonde hair in the distance. Though he dismissed it as a coincidence, he couldn't help increasing his pace a little, and as he neared the shop the milling crowd parted enough for him to realise he'd been right after all. It was Hanna, the blue scarf over her forehead as usual, her arm linked through Kris's. He was still too far away to call out a greeting by the time they reached the side door leading to the wizard's apartment and Kris turned aside for a moment to unlock it.

As the mage turned back Hanna moved to face him and they kissed, with an easy intimacy which made it clear it was far from the first time. Rudi stopped moving, a hammer blow of mixed emotions stilling him dead in his tracks.

'Mind out the way,' someone said irritably, barging into his back and starting him moving again. Snapping out of his momentary stupor, Rudi looked at the bakery again, but the door was already closing. Unsure what to think, afraid of what he might feel, he hurried back to the barracks without a backward glance and sought the refuge of his bed. Exhausted as he was, though, he still took a long time to get to sleep.

THE NIGHT SHIFT was uncharacteristically quiet, which Rudi was grateful for. Word of the previous night's raid in the Kleinmoot had evidently got around and most of the petty criminals in the ward were keeping a low profile. He and Gerrit had little more to do than round up their usual quota of drunks, and he wasn't too inconvenienced by the lack of sleep, which he would otherwise have felt far more keenly.

'Thank Verena for small mercies,' Gerrit said, as they booked out at the end of the shift. He glanced curiously at Rudi. 'Planning to get any sleep today, or are you hoping to keep going entirely on that Lustrian muck?'

'Sleep,' Rudi replied, yawning loudly.

Gerrit grinned. 'Me too. But breakfast first.' He turned the corner of the street leading back to the watch barracks. 'I'm not sorry to be rotating today, I can tell you.' Rudi nodded. They were switching to the morning shift the next day, which meant for the next couple of weeks the nights would be just for sleeping again. This afternoon he was due to meet Artemus and, with a tingle of excitement at the thought, he realised he could swing by the Deedsalee on the way and talk to van Crackenmeer. By this evening, with any luck, he would have found Magnus.

Lost in thought, it took him a moment to realise that someone was calling his name.

'Rudi!' Hanna was waving to him across the street, her other arm linked with Kris's again. He forced a smile to his face and waved back.

'You're up early.' It was a long walk here from the Tempelwijk. She must have set out before dawn.

Hanna flushed slightly. 'I could say the same.'

'I've been on duty.' Despite himself, a yawn escaped him and the girl nodded sympathetically.

'You must be all in.' She glanced at Kris for confirmation before continuing. 'We're just on our way to the Pirate for some breakfast. Care to join us?' Something in her manner seemed oddly defensive and he couldn't help noticing a faint flicker of relief in her eyes as he shook his head.

'Thanks, but I'm dead on my feet. I'm just heading back to the barracks for some sleep.'

'See you later, then,' Kris said, seeming oddly relieved as well.

'We'll be at the college all day. This is your afternoon for visiting Artemus, isn't it?'

'Yes.' Rudi nodded in response, then hesitated. 'I've got something else to do as well though. I'm not sure when I'll be free.'

'Well, suit yourself,' Kris said, and after a few more reflexive pleasantries he and Hanna moved away in the direction of the inn.

'Are you all right?' Gerrit asked, gazing at Rudi curiously. Rudi nodded and resumed his march back to the barracks.

'Of course I am,' he replied shortly, although part of him wondered if that was entirely true.

CHAPTER TWENTY-FOUR

RUDI SLEPT UNTIL shortly after noon, then breakfasted in the mess hall feeling fully restored. To his relief, Gerrit had already woken and left the premises, so he was able to eat without having to deflect any well-meaning questions about his errand that afternoon, or about his relationship with Hanna. The latter topic was something he didn't want to think about too much. The feelings stirred up in him by her apparent closeness to the young mage were too raw and confusing to contemplate, and he took refuge in anticipation of finally coming within reach of getting the answers he so desperately wanted to the questions which continued to torment him. Assuming the lawyer really knew where Magnus was, of course, and could be persuaded to tell him. In a fever of impatience he pushed his empty plate away and stood abruptly – there was only one way to find out.

The streets outside were as crowded as ever and the wind from the Manannspoort sea even keener than before. He shivered, resolving to buy some warmer clothing before the autumn advanced much further. As a compromise, he stopped at a market stall for a woollen cap, which kept his head warmer than his uniform hat. The Black Cap of his calling disappeared once again inside his shirt.

Impelled partly by his impatience to get the answers he sought, and partly by the need to stay warm, Rudi kept up a brisk pace, passing through the shabby gentility of the Oudgeldwijk almost without noticing. As he entered the precincts of the Tempelwijk, the great bell in the temple of Manann tolled the hour and he slowed down, becoming fully aware of his surroundings again for the first time since leaving the barracks. He was far too early for his appointment with Artemus. So much the better. He turned aside from his usual course and wandered down the Deedsalee, a diffuse sense of anticipation fluttering in the pit of his stomach.

The narrow passageway was lined with lawyers' offices and an air of self-importance hung about most of the passers-by. Many wore black gowns and almost all of them carried document cases. Rudi stared at the plethora of signs lining the narrow alleyway, all depicting symbols of Verena, and wondered for a moment how he could possibly find the right one. Once again, his new-found literacy came to his rescue, and he discovered on closer inspection that the names of the lawyers appeared to be written by the doors of their premises. A few of the more prosperous ones had theirs engraved on brass plates screwed to the walls, while the majority were simply painted there in ornate, flowing script which he found hard to puzzle out. Nevertheless he persevered, despite the curious glances he attracted as he laboriously decoded the more lavish renderings, eventually discovering the name he sought about halfway along as Sam had promised. *Cornelius van Crackenmeer, Attorney at Law*.

He paused in front of the offices, suddenly unsure of what he was going to say, then dismissed his doubts with a surge of resolve. He had no doubt that Magnus would be delighted to see him and that he could convince the lawyer of that without too much difficulty.

He approached the door, on which the paint was flaking and tried the handle. It resisted. Despite the flecks of rust on it, the lock was evidently still sound. He stepped back a pace and knocked, in the manner he'd learned in the watch, loud, resonant and peremptory. Echoes were his only answer.

This was a setback he hadn't been expecting, although he supposed Sam's comment about the lawyer's irregular habits ought to have prepared him for the possibility. Frustration boiled up in him and he clenched his fists. Reluctant to accept defeat so close to finding an answer, he examined the building carefully.

It seemed a little shabbier than its neighbours, but other than that there was nothing to distinguish it. He assumed that van Crackenmeer was somewhat less successful in his chosen profession than the lawyers surrounding him. A small side passage separated the building from the one adjacent, and after a moment's consideration he followed it, finding, as he suspected, that it led to a small landing stage on one of the innumerable back canals which threaded the city.

Presumably the local lawyers used it to hail a water-coach, or be dropped off by one, when they couldn't be bothered to walk wherever they happened to be going.

Rudi walked out onto the narrow platform, the timbers creaking under his weight, and looked around. The thin ribbon of water was deserted, save for the usual coating of flotsam and scum, and lapped against the pilings languidly. The rear of van Crackenmeer's offices backed on to the waterway, an open window looking out over the canal too far away to reach. Rudi was about to turn back, disappointed, and try again after he'd seen Artemus, when he noticed the drainpipe clinging to the wall between the window and the corner of the house.

Telling himself he was insane, Rudi clambered up onto the handrail edging the dock and leaned out, trying to reach the pipe. It was just too far, wavering tantalisingly less than an inch beyond his grasp.

Muttering prayers under his breath to whichever deities might have happened to be listening, he inched his fingertips outwards, right to the limit of his balance. And beyond. For a moment he toppled sideways, bracing himself for the shock of cold water, then his scrabbling hands found chill metal and clung grimly.

The downpipe creaked and shifted under his weight, then took it. Muscles burning with the strain, Rudi brought his legs over, balancing his left foot precariously on the spout.

Heart hammering, he reached out for the windowsill, hoping that he'd judged the distance right. If not, he faced an unenviable choice between an ignominious plunge into the murky water below, or hanging there until somebody noticed him, probably followed by a long and uncomfortable conversation with his colleagues from the Tempelwijk watch. After a moment, his groping hands found some purchase, and with a sigh of relief he was able to hitch himself over to the window.

After that, pushing the aperture slightly wider was the work of a moment, and he was able to worm his way through. The hilt of his sword caught on the sill. He had to free it before he was able to get inside, and he blessed the foresight which had made him leave his bow back at the barracks.

He regained his feet and looked around, finding himself in a musty room stuffed with papers. Shelves of them lined the walls, broken up into pigeonholes, each of which bore a faded paper label. Squinting in the feeble sunlight which somehow managed to elbow its way into the room through the coating of grime on the window glass, Rudi glanced at the nearest one and found a name printed in neat, fussy letters. *Molenwijk*. He looked at another. *Strossel*. After a moment the notion that they'd been filed in alphabetical order occurred to him. That meant that somewhere around here should be…

'Magnus.' Sure enough, one of the wooden compartments bore the name *von Blackenburg*. He bent to examine it, his elation evaporating as he realised the box was empty. 'That can't be right.'

But it was. As he turned away disappointed, something else caught his attention. Deep, recent scratches in the wood of the shelf. They seemed familiar, and after a moment he recognised the same scoring which had marred the door in Magnus's house. His scalp prickled. There was only one obvious conclusion to draw from that: Hans had been here ahead of him, and probably the sorceress too. Apprehension began to displace his disappointment. Could his old adversary still be on the premises?

He dismissed the thought almost at once. Hans was hardly the stealthiest of individuals, even after his transformation, and he'd made enough noise getting in here to have attracted the attention of anyone still in the offices. He was alone, he was certain of that.

Turning to leave, he froze suddenly and bent to examine the floor. Something white was just visible under the lowest shelf of the filing racks, jammed into the narrow crack between the piece of furniture and the floor. If one of the papers had fallen unnoticed as Hans removed them and been kicked by a careless foot, it would have ended up about there...

Hardly daring to hope, he squatted down, as though he were examining tracks in the forest, and pulled it out carefully. It was indeed a sheet of paper, folded, with a faint discoloration across the join where a seal had once been. With a mounting sense of excitement he unfolded it.

'Yes!' The involuntary exclamation escaped him before he could suppress it, and he strained his ears, fearful of discovery once more. If he was wrong about being alone, he'd just betrayed his presence in no uncertain terms. After a moment, hearing no raised voices or hurrying footsteps, he relaxed again and examined the letter he held.

It was short, and unquestionably from Magnus. Rudi perused it slowly, sounding out some of the longer words under his breath, quietly elated at being able to decipher so complex a document without prompting or assistance. After a date less than a year ago, the missive continued:

My dear Cornelius,

Your fears are well founded. As the time approaches, we can expect further attempts to prevent the von Karien heir from coming into his inheritance. As yet our enemies remain unaware of his identity, although the Reifenstahl woman undoubtedly suspects. So far, however, I believe I have successfully hidden my own part in the affair from her.

I will discuss all this in detail with you and the rest of the grandchildren on my next visit to Marienburg.

Warmest regards,

Magnus.

His mind reeling, Rudi read the brief note again, taking inordinate care over every word. They still came out the same, so his inexperience with letters didn't seem to have betrayed him.

Their meaning continued to elude him, however. He'd never heard of the von Kariens, and so far as he knew neither had anyone else in Kohlstadt. Apart from Magnus, of course, and perhaps if the merchant's suspicions were true, Greta Riefenstahl. The healer was dead, though, burned by Gerhard along with her cottage, so there was no way to find out for sure. Unless she'd mentioned it to her daughter, of course. He resolved to ask Hanna the next time he saw her.

Perhaps he could visit her at the college after he'd been to see Artemus. It wouldn't be that much of an imposition, as she'd intimated that she was half expecting to see him today when they'd met that morning. Besides, she needed to know that Gerhard was in town. He could hardly have told her that while Gerrit was standing right next to him. For some reason, the image of her kissing Kris the previous night rose up in his mind at that point and he forced it away angrily. It was none of his business. He had no right to feel resentful, and anyway this was much more important.

Tucking the letter away carefully inside his belt pouch he approached the door to the narrow room and opened it cautiously. As he'd expected, the lock had been broken, the wood splintered and the surface scored by the mutant's talons.

He paused then and almost choked. The room beyond stank of blood and recent death. Dropping his hand to the hilt of his sword, he advanced into the centre of it and looked around. It was obviously van Crackenmeer's private office. The large wooden desk and the bookshelves lined with leather-bound books made that abundantly clear.

Rudi examined the door, finding that once again it had been forced by inhuman strength. The lawyer had evidently fled in here and tried to bar it, but the effort had been futile. He was sprawled on the floor behind his desk, his throat ripped out, glued to the threadbare carpet by most of the blood his body had once contained. In life he had evidently been corpulent, the flesh of his face and belly sagging sadly, like a badly-stuffed sack.

Rudi had seen enough violent death, and caused enough of it himself to be all but inured to the sight, and felt little more than irritation and disappointment that once again his attempts to contact Magnus had been blocked.

Sighing, he turned away. No doubt Hans and the horned sorceress had searched both room and corpse thoroughly and removed any clues to Magnus's whereabouts. That meant they were closer to finding him than Rudi was. Cold sweat prickled his back at the thought. If they got to the merchant first they would undoubtedly kill him, and the answers he sought would be lost for ever. All he had to show for coming here was even more confusion.

Nevertheless, he supposed, his adversaries might have missed something. They'd left the enigmatic letter behind, after all. Encouraged by the thought, he turned back to the lawyer's corpse.

As he'd expected, the man had nothing on his person which might help, although his purse contained seventeen guilders, a scattering of silver and a handful of pennies. After a brief struggle with his conscience, which pragmatism won, Rudi transferred the money to his own. Van Crackenmeer didn't need it any more, and with Gerhard in town anything might happen. One thing he'd learned from his sojourn in the city was that in Marienburg money could solve a lot of problems.

The desk contained nothing of any help either. One drawer was locked, which raised his hopes, but when he forced it he found the only thing it contained was a collection of crudely-printed woodcuts which made him blush and return them hastily to where he'd found them. Reluctant to give up, he turned his attention to the bookshelves. Most of the volumes had titles like *Van Meegren's Compendium of Statutes on the*

Importation of Antiquities or *Case Law of the Admiralty Assizes*, which he skipped over, his slow reading speed taxed to the limit by the density of the text on their spines.

On the verge of giving up, he stepped back and examined the shelf from a distance. He hadn't needed to be able to read to deduce meaning from the traces invisible to others in the wilderness; perhaps it was time to start thinking like a tracker again. Sure enough, when he came to look at the pattern of volumes as a whole, something seemed subtly wrong about them. One book stood a little proud of the others, as though it had been recently removed and replaced. Unlike the rest of them, it had no lettering on the spine.

Hardly daring to hope or expect anything, Rudi reached out and plucked it from the shelf. The pages inside it were hand written in a language he didn't know, but as he turned the leaves he felt the same sense of rightness he'd experienced that night in the woods outside Kohlstadt, when he'd been drawn to the gathering in the clearing.

Something stirred in the depths of his mind, and he paused. The page he was looking at was a sketch map, and after a moment's thought he recognised a couple of the landmarks. That was the Doodkanal, a cross on its banks marking the location of the warehouse where he'd first seen Magnus and confronted Hans. The second was on the Schwartzwasserstraat and obviously pinpointed the von Blackenburg mansion. A memory stirred, of the triangle of landmarks on the map he and Hanna had found in the hut he'd shared with his father, and he scanned the page eagerly, hoping to complete a similar pattern.

'There!' Buoyed up by elation he was barely aware of having spoken aloud. A third mark, deep within the derelict area of the Doodkanal, caught his eye. Memorising its location was the work of a moment and he closed the book – considering his options. Taking it with him was pointless, he couldn't read the language it was written in, but leaving it here would be dangerous too. Hans and the sorceress might return and find it after a more thorough search.

There was only one safe thing to do. Hurrying into the back room he pitched it out of the window and into the canal. It floated away, becoming steadily more waterlogged, and after a moment it vanished from sight. With a sigh of relief, Rudi returned to the outer office. Leaving by the front door would be a risk, he knew, but he doubted that anyone would notice him and he wasn't about to take his chances with the drainpipe again if he could avoid it.

He reached the hallway, finding it unexceptional in every respect. Beside him, next to the door of the office, a narrow staircase led upwards, presumably to the living quarters above, and another door at the end of the hall stood open, revealing a small kitchen next to the records room. Sure there would be nothing there to detain him, Rudi hurried to the front door and stopped, perplexed. The door was locked, he knew that, but there was no sign of a key. Hans or the sorceress must have taken it with them, hoping the barred door would delay the discovery of the lawyer's body.

There was nothing else for it, he would just have to look for a spare. If he couldn't find one, perhaps he could trip the lock with the point of his knife somehow.

He jumped, startled, jolted out of his reverie by a loud hammering on the door. As the initial surge of adrenalin kicked in, he forced himself to breathe slowly and calmly. There were no windows here, no one could tell he was inside and if whoever was standing beyond the door had a key they wouldn't have bothered with knocking. He strained his ears, hearing a murmur of conversation outside in the street, but the speakers were keeping their voices low and none of the actual words were distinguishable. It sounded as though there were two of them though, a man and a woman.

Abruptly, without warning, the lock clicked. Taken completely by surprise as the door swung open, revealing a couple of cloak-swathed figures and a sliver of the street outside, he had no time to do anything other than bring his sword up into a defensive position.

'Locks? No problem.' The woman who spoke had half-turned to address her unseen companion and Rudi had a moment of formless familiarity before she turned to face him. 'Sigmar's hammer, it's you!' She began to draw her own blade.

'Alwyn?' The last time he'd seen the mercenary sorceress she'd been sprawled out unconscious along with the rest of her companions, the night he, Hanna and Fritz had escaped from Krieger's band of bounty hunters.

'Damn right.' An expression of anger curdled her features and she moved into the attack. 'Surprised to see me?'

'Wait.' Her companion stepped over the threshold and Rudi's blood turned to ice. Gerhard smiled thinly. 'I told you, I want him alive.'

CHAPTER TWENTY-FIVE

'DON'T WORRY.' ALWYN hesitated, on the point of lunging at Rudi. 'I'm not about to throw thirty crowns away. But you didn't say anything about bringing them in unharmed.' Rudi tensed. He'd seen enough of the mage's swordsmanship not to underestimate her abilities, although she was far from the most formidable fighter in the group. He'd learned a lot since the last time they had met and he ought to be able to hold his own against her. Unless she employed magic against him, of course, but he'd picked up enough knowledge from Hanna and Kris to be sure she wouldn't resort to spellcasting unless she had to. Even the routine use of magic had its dangers and in the rough and tumble of combat when she wouldn't be able to concentrate undisturbed, the chances of something going wrong were far greater. All in all he would be safer engaging her straight away and taking his chances with her fighting abilities. While she hesitated, he cut at her torso, making her jump back reflexively, blocking the blow with her blade.

'Just back off. I don't want to hurt you.'

'What you want doesn't come into it, Chaos-lover.' Alwyn rallied and seemed on the point of renewing her attack when Gerhard put a restraining hand on her shoulder.

'Go and fetch the others. I'll deal with this.'

'Whatever you say.' Alwyn stepped away, breaking contact with Rudi and re-sheathing her sword. 'You've got the money.' Then her outline shimmered, in the manner Rudi remembered from the time they'd spent travelling together, and she vanished.

Rudi breathed a little more easily and stepped in to challenge the witch hunter. If he could finish this quickly, Gerhard's over-confident air might work to his advantage. One opponent would always be easier to defeat than two, and if he could take him down fast enough he should be able to get away before the rest of the mercenary band returned. No telling how soon that might be, though.

'So I'm worth thirty crowns, am I? I suppose I ought to be flattered.' He aimed a cut at Gerhard's head. To his surprise the witch hunter stepped back and evaded the blow without drawing his own weapon.

'You and the girl as well.' Gerhard stood poised, ready to evade again, keeping his hands well away from the sword at his belt. Remembering the knife concealed up his sleeve, Rudi remained wary, alert for any movement which might betray an intention to throw it. 'Put your sword away. We need to talk.'

'I've heard everything I care to from you,' Rudi said. 'And I've seen what you're capable of. Back off, or I'll split you where you stand.'

'I don't think so.' Gerhard's voice was as calm as ever. 'You might have killed a couple of bandits on the Altdorf road, but you're not a murderer. Killing in cold blood is very different to doing it in the heat of self-defence.'

'You'd know more about that than I do,' Rudi said. As he'd feared, it seemed his journey to Marienburg had left traces the witch hunter had been able to follow.

'I don't enjoy killing, whatever you may think. But sometimes it's necessary.'

'Of course it is. Frau Katzenjammer was a real menace to civilisation.' Conscious of every moment that passed, Rudi edged forward, the tip of his blade pointed unerringly at the witch hunter's throat. Gerhard sighed, but showed no sign of giving ground.

'You saw what her son had become. There was no telling how far the taint in that house had spread.'

'Fritz is still normal.' Rudi spoke angrily, without thinking, and a flicker of interest appeared in Gerhard's eyes.

'So he's here too.' He shrugged. 'Never mind, he'll keep. You and the girl are the main problem.'

It was now or never. If he delayed any longer Alwyn would be certain to return with the rest of the bounty hunters before he could escape. Gerhard's whole attitude was that of a man who was playing for time, knowing he wouldn't have to do so for long. Rudi lunged forward, thrusting for the man's torso with the point of his blade.

Fast as he was, Gerhard was quicker. Evading the young watchman's rush, he stepped to one side and drew his own sword. Steel clashed against steel as he deflected the strike, his expression as neutral as ever.

'I'm surprised,' he admitted. 'And disappointed. I didn't think you'd try to kill an unarmed man.'

'Why not? You don't seem to have a problem with it.' Rudi closed again, undeterred. He hadn't really expected the blow to connect, but it had disconcerted his opponent and made him react in haste. He launched a flurry of blows at the witch hunter, driving him back, heedless of the risk of leaving himself open to a counterattack. Gerhard had told Alwyn he wanted to take him alive, which would force him onto the defensive, and Rudi could exploit that.

'Believe me, I've no intention of killing you.' Gerhard parried with exceptional skill, countering every blow Rudi aimed at him, giving ground gradually. By now he was almost at the door. 'There's far more at stake here than you realise. Put the sword down and let's talk like civilised men.'

'I wouldn't believe you if you told me the sun goes down at night,' Rudi said.

'That's unfortunate. What I have to tell you is complicated. But this is bigger than either of us. Thousands of lives are at stake. You must listen...' For the first time in their acquaintance Rudi heard an edge of desperation enter the witch hunter's voice. Carried away by his own words, Gerhard's concentration faltered for a moment. It was just an instant's opening, but Rudi took full advantage of it. Pivoting on the ball of his forward foot he drove his elbow into the witch hunter's midriff and as the man folded he struck down with the hilt of his sword to deliver a stunning blow to the back of his neck.

Gerhard collapsed, unconscious before he hit the floor. Rudi resheathed his sword, breathing heavily, and took a moment to compose himself before he left the building. He needed to blend into the crowd and to do that he had to look calm and unconcerned. He closed the front door of the lawyer's office carefully behind him as he made his way out onto the street.

The narrow thoroughfare was as crowded as ever and he slipped easily into the stream of pedestrians, keeping his eyes open for a familiar face. No sounds of pursuit seemed to follow him, but he remained tense, glancing around as he reached the junction of the alleyway with the main thoroughfare.

It was as well that he did. Bodun the dwarf was hurrying through the crowds, surprisingly fast for such stocky legs, complaining loudly about the size and slowness of the passers-by impeding him.

'And another thing,' Rudi heard above the chorus of complaint provoked by the dwarf's progress, 'that was the first half-decent mug of ale I've been able to find since we arrived in this gods-forsaken cess pit and...' Ignoring the rest of the tirade Rudi scanned the street, making out the tall figure of Conrad, Alwyn's husband, jogging along at the dwarf's side.

Sinking back into the mouth of the Deedsalee, Rudi glanced back. If he was quick, he might just be able to slip back past the lawyer's office and out the other end. He only had time for a single pace in that direction, however, before Alwyn appeared through the front door and glanced up and down the passageway. Catching sight of him, she drew her sword and began to run too, heedless of the startled lawyers scattering around her like suddenly disturbed chickens.

'Damn it!' Rudi began to run too, along the street, heedless of the stares of the passers-by, leaving a trail of bruised shins and mumbled apologies in his wake.

'There!' Conrad shouted, spotting him at last, just as Alwyn appeared at the mouth of the Deedsalee. The sorceress joined her husband and the dwarf, but the crowds continued to impede them, blocking a party of three much more effectively than they did Rudi's solitary progress.

'Mind where you're going!' somebody said angrily, and Rudi dodged around a figure wearing a well-cut student's gown and a belligerent expression. He knew the type, a minor aristocrat packed off to the college for the social connections it would provide rather than any intellectual ability. Hanna had pointed some out scornfully on an earlier visit to the Tempelwijk. There was a whole crowd of them spilling out of a crowded tavern, which he vaguely remembered the girl telling him was a favourite haunt of one of the exclusive drinking clubs such parasites tended to join. An idea began to form in his head. 'You nearly spilled my drink!'

'Did I?' Rudi turned back and jogged the youth's arm. Ale slopped out of the tankard he was holding and splashed the expensive fabric. 'Sorry, I hate to leave a job half done.'

'You're going to regret that,' the young aristocrat threatened. The rest of the well-dressed students hanging around outside the tavern began to close in, muttering among themselves.

'Think so? Me and my mates there can take a bunch of pansies like you with one hand tied behind our backs.' Rudi shoved the student hard in the chest, pitching him back among his friends.

It was like throwing a brand into a barrel of pitch. The students surged towards him just as the pursuing bounty hunters caught up.

'One side, manlings!' Bodun hurled one of the obstructing students out of his way and most of them turned on the mercenaries with whoops and yells. 'Grungi's beard, are they all insane?'

'This is Marienburg,' Conrad reminded him, punching out an aristocrat who seemed to be trying to part his hair with a heavy pewter tankard. 'Of course they are!'

'Much obliged.' Rudi decked the young man who'd challenged him and began running again. He doubted that the drunken students would slow the bounty hunters down for long, but he should be able to open up an impressive lead on them before they fought their way free of the brawl he'd created. 'Oh, for Sigmar's sake!'

Theo and Bruno appeared at the other end of the street, spotting him almost at the same instant. Clearly trusting in their comrades' ability to take care of themselves, they ignored the street fight and began to run too, heading straight for him. Rudi swerved, taking a narrow side passage he'd never been down before. It was completely empty of foot traffic, which struck him as unusual, and with a grim sinking feeling his intellect told him the reason an instant before his eyes confirmed it. It led to another landing stage, on the same back canal he'd seen before.

'Dreck!' The planks of the narrow platform clattered under his boot soles and he glanced around frantically. Echoing shouts from the mouth of the passageway told him that Theo and Bruno, the two most dangerous swordsmen in the entire band, had spotted him and were in hot pursuit. There was no escape back the way he'd come. So far as he could see he had two options, fight or swim.

Or maybe not. A flicker of motion in the corner of his eye offered him the faint possibility of a third alternative. Without thinking, before his conscious mind could intervene to dissuade him, he increased his pace as much as he could and leapt out over the water.

Time stretched, as it sometimes seemed to in combat, and he had all the leisure he needed to take in the startled expression on the face of the bargee piloting the lighter he'd just had time to register was passing before he jumped. For a moment he thought he wasn't going to make it after all, but at least one of the gods must have been with him, because his boots sank into the springy surface of the taut sheet of canvas covering the hold.

'Hey!' the riverman just had time to shout before Rudi leapt again, the coarse fabric snapping straight beneath his feet and bouncing him out across the waterway. Another ramshackle landing stage loomed larger and larger in front of him and a dispassionate voice at the back of his mind wondered if he could possibly make it.

Desperately, he lunged forward, falling across the planks with an impact which jarred the breath from his body, his legs dangling over the waters of the canal. He began to slide, his hands groping frantically for something to arrest his progress. Just as it seemed he was doomed to plunge into the water, his scrabbling fingertips found a gap in the planking. Slowly, agonisingly, he pulled himself up onto the hard wooden surface.

'Come on!' Theo's voice echoed across the water. 'There's a bridge over there. We can still catch him!' Rudi struggled to his feet and turned, just in time to see the two bounty hunters running back up the side passage leading to the landing stage on the other side of the water. He knew the bridge the mercenary captain had meant. He took it every time he came to see Artemus, and if they ran as hard as he expected his pursuers to they'd be across it in a matter of minutes. He had to get out of here. Despite the pain in his ribs he forced himself into an unsteady jog.

The side passage leading to the landing stage gave way onto a narrow alley, almost identical to the one where he'd found the dead lawyer and the enigmatic notebook with its tantalising clue to Magnus's possible whereabouts, except that most of the businesses here seemed to be selling incense for supplicants to burn in the numerous temples which gave the ward its name. He didn't recognise it, but he knew the district well enough to surmise that if he turned away from the bridge it would bring him out on another thoroughfare he was familiar with, and to his relief this guess turned out to be correct. He was barely a hundred yards from the Scrivener's guildhall.

Every step of the way he expected to hear sounds of pursuit, but luck or the gods appeared to be with him and he reached his goal with no further sign of the mercenaries.

'ARE YOU SURE you're all right?' Artemus asked, looking at Rudi with an expression of mild concern. 'You do seem a trifle incommoded, I have to say.'

'I'm fine,' he said, still a little short of breath. The scribe nodded and looked at him sceptically, taking in his dishevelled appearance.

'I'm delighted to hear it.' He nodded thoughtfully. 'Even if you do seem a trifle breathless, and those contusions on your hands look most uncomfortable.'

Now that he'd mentioned it, Rudi suddenly found the grazes where he'd scrabbled for purchase on the landing stage were itching like mad. Looking back on the incident, he could hardly believe he'd acted so recklessly. He shrugged, trying to ignore the discomfort.

'I've had worse.'

'The rigours of life as a Black Cap, no doubt.' The scribe nodded again. 'You do seem to find yourself in harm's way an inordinate amount of the time, my young friend, even for a watchman.'

'It's what I'm paid for,' Rudi said, happy to reinforce the conclusion Artemus had just drawn without actually lying about it. He shrugged again. 'Besides, I'm seeing Hanna later. I'm sure she can do something to help.'

'So long as the healers' guild doesn't get to hear about it,' Artemus said, leaving Rudi to wonder if he was joking or not. He began to rearrange the writing materials on his desk. 'I thought today we might consider the place of the comma, a humble mark of punctuation to be sure, but vital in conveying the full nuances of meaning. You think I exaggerate? Let me enlighten you. A single misplaced comma can alter the entire meaning of a sentence, and by extension the whole document of which it forms a part. Court cases have hung on just such ambiguities, lives and fortunes made forfeit or unexpectedly reprieved by a simple curl of ink. If you wish to be clearly understood, then let me assure you that mastery of the comma is an essential step towards that aim.'

'I see,' said Rudi, lost as usual in the torrent of words. The scribe's enthusiasm for his craft was undiminished, even after years of toil, and the subtleties of language was a subject which never ceased to fascinate him. Much of what he said went over the young watchman's head, but he usually listened attentively and tried to remember as much as he could. Today, though, another topic was uppermost in his mind.

'You travelled a lot in the Empire, didn't you?' he asked abruptly. If Artemus was surprised at the sudden change of subject he didn't show it, just nodding in response.

'A fair amount, even if I do say so myself. Why do you ask?'

'I came across a name recently, looking for that friend I told you about.' He'd mentioned a little of his search for Magnus to the scribe, without going into too many details. 'He might have been trading with them or something and I thought if anyone I know might have heard it before it would most likely be you.'

'And the name would be?' Artemus enquired.

'Von Karien. Does that mean anything to you?' The question was all but redundant; the moment he'd spoken the name the scribe's eyes had darkened.

'I've heard it before,' he admitted. 'They're minor aristocracy from somewhere near Altdorf. But if your friend has really had dealings with them, then perhaps it's best for all concerned that he remains lost.'

'How do you mean?' Rudi asked, masking the shiver of apprehension which gripped him as well as he could.

'There was a scandal some years ago,' Artemus said at last. 'I don't remember the details, but there were accusations of heresy. The old graf was supposed to have made some kind of pact with the Dark Powers.' He made the sign of the trident. 'Of course these stories grow in the telling, but even today the family is shunned by most of its neighbours.'

'Did he leave an heir?' Rudi asked, feeling a tingle of unease as he recalled the lines of the mysterious letter.

'That was the odd thing,' he said, 'now you come to mention it. His son disappeared without trace. When the old graf was executed, his cousin inherited the estate.'

'And the son,' Rudi persisted, trying to ignore the idea which was growing in his mind despite his rational self insisting that it was utterly absurd. 'How old was he?'

'Just a toddler. If he was still alive these days, though, he'd be about sixteen or seventeen, I suppose. Why do you ask?'

'No reason,' Rudi said, his mind reeling with the enormity of the thought. About his own age. And he'd been adopted, no one having any idea who his parents were. Except Magnus, who had written the letter to Cornelius van Crackenmeer, mentioning the von Karien heir...

It was ridiculous, of course, but the idea was curiously seductive. Masking his excitement as best he could, he turned the conversation to more neutral subjects and tried to lose himself in the mysteries of the comma.

CHAPTER TWENTY-SIX

'YOU REALLY THINK you could be an aristocrat?' Hanna
asked, her face twisting with amusement at the idea.
She dropped an exaggerated curtsy and stifled a giggle.
'My lord.'

Rudi sighed. Now he'd spoken his suspicions out
loud, he had to admit they did sound pretty absurd.

'I just thought your mother might have said something to you about the von Kariens, that's all.' He
looked around the cluttered workroom in the bowels
of the college, where the porter at the gate had
directed him to. Dishes of herbs and other substances
he couldn't identify lay on a couple of stout wooden
workbenches, where several pots bubbled away on
spirit burners, and the walls were lined with shelves
crammed with pots and storage jars. Hanna looked
very much at home, preparing materials for the students and putting together a few remedies for her

own use as well. No one seemed to mind, and as she said the college had plenty of resources at its disposal.

'I'm afraid not.' Hanna took one of her preparations from a nearby shelf and daubed it on his outstretched hands. The itching eased at once and Rudi sighed gratefully.

'That's much better, thank you.'

The girl smiled at him, all trace of mockery gone. 'Don't mention it. I was waiting for a chance to try it out anyway.' She dropped the little pot into her satchel, which was hanging on a hook by the door. It chinked gently, betraying the presence of several others already inside. The task completed, she sniffed suspiciously at one of the bubbling concoctions and removed it from the heat. 'Are you sure my mother knew something about all this?'

'That's what the letter said.' Rudi drew it out of his pouch and handed it to her. Hanna scanned it, an expression of puzzlement growing on her face.

'He only says he thinks she might suspect,' she pointed out, but the expression remained. She glanced up at him again. 'But I can see why you might think he's talking about you.' A grin spread slowly across her features, erasing the marks of care and stress which the last few weeks had placed there. Despite her manner, she still seemed frailer than usual, the talisman on her forehead continuing to do its malevolent work, and Rudi felt a pang of concern for her. 'It's like one of the melodramas the travelling players perform. A long-lost heir, a peasant lad with a destiny…'

'You're right, it is pretty stupid,' Rudi agreed, feeling oddly deflated. 'It must have been some other business

Magnus was involved in.' He shrugged. 'I mean, how's a two-year-old supposed to get all the way to Kohlstadt from Altdorf on his own? It's ridiculous.'

'Well, yes.' Hanna nodded, then grinned again. 'But suppose it was true. Wouldn't that be exciting?'

'I suppose. If I can't find Magnus in Marienburg I'll have to go to Altdorf and talk to the von Kariens anyway. Maybe they know how to get in touch with him.'

'With Gerhard in town that might be the safest thing to do,' Hanna said, all trace of merriment suddenly leaving her face. 'He won't give up on either of us, you know.'

'The college should be able to protect you,' Rudi pointed out. 'Now you're a licensed student of magic he's got no grounds to come after you. Especially under Marienburg law.'

'I don't think the letter of the law concerns him all that much,' Hanna said. She shook her head dejectedly. 'And being licensed isn't going to help much if he cries Chaos on us again.'

'He'll have to prove it,' Rudi said stoutly, 'in the temple courts.' Sergeant Rijgen had been called on to give evidence in the trial of a mage accused of necromancy a few weeks before and had held forth on the legal arguments involved at great length in the taproom of the Blind Eye afterwards. 'If he tries that they'll throw the case straight out again for lack of evidence.'

'If I can't get this thing off soon, it's all academic anyway,' Hanna said. Gerhard's talisman continued to defy every attempt to remove or nullify it, and the faculty of the college was beginning to run out of ideas.

She shrugged. 'So I can't run anyway. Besides, how would we get out of town?'

'I've an idea about that,' Rudi said.

FINDING SHENK AGAIN wasn't the most difficult thing to do. After leaving Hanna, with a few brief words of encouragement which completely failed to hide the concern he was feeling for her welfare, Rudi headed back to the barracks the long way round, through the Suiddock. This time the Draainbrug was open to traffic, so he was able to make his way north to Luydenhoek without hindrance.

Once there, it had simply been a matter of asking a few passers-by for directions to the Candle Wharf, where the *Reikmaiden* was still tied to the dock, surrounded by other riverboats which looked almost identical to Rudi. The boat he sought was easy enough to pick out, though – having left her in midstream, she would be hard to forget. And if he'd needed any further prompting, her name was emblazoned on her prow in neat, white letters.

Only one man was on the deck as Rudi approached, lounging against the rail with the unmistakable air of bored resentment peculiar to those left on watch while their friends enjoyed themselves ashore. He squinted through the gathering dusk as the young watchman approached the gangplank and sauntered across the deck to meet him.

'Rudi.' He nodded affably enough and stood aside to let him board, clearly unsurprised to see him. After a moment Rudi recalled the man's name.

'Evening, Pieter.' The deckhand had been welcoming enough the last time he'd been on the boat, showing him the duties he'd been assigned in return for passage, until Shenk's treachery had forced him and Hanna into fleeing again. Pieter brushed his brown fringe out of his eyes.

'Thought you might turn up before too long.' He shrugged. 'You'll be looking for the skipper, then.'

'That's right,' Rudi confirmed.

'Try the Mermaid. I don't know how pleased he'll be to see you, but a lot happier than the last time, I'm sure.' Evidently the whole crew knew something of the circumstances of their captain's foray into the Kleinmoot and his encounter there with Rudi. The deckhand looked at him sharply. 'Unless you're putting your hat back on, I suppose.'

'Wrong ward,' Rudi assured him. 'Whatever he's up to in Suiddock is no concern of mine.'

'Glad to hear it.' Pieter smiled, his reserve melting a little. 'And I'm glad you didn't drown. I hope your friend made it too.'

'She did,' Rudi said, and the deckhand nodded.

'Good. I liked her.'

'Pleased to hear it.' Rudi exchanged a few more pleasantries and set out in search of the Mermaid.

THE TAVERN WAS identical to innumerable others around the city, being noisy, cramped and full of people. Most of them appeared to be riverboat crew, the sailors of ocean-going craft preferring to frequent the bars fronting the deep water docks, and most of the exceptions seemed to be there to part them from their money. Shenk was seated towards the back of the room, talking earnestly to a well-dressed halfling, who nodded in satisfaction at something the captain said and turned to go. As Shenk's gaze followed his erst-while companion towards the door, it fell on Rudi and he gave a small start of recognition.

Rudi smiled in return, bought two tankards of ale and made his way over to the table.

'Very kind of you,' Shenk said, a wary edge to his voice as he took the drink. 'I must admit I hadn't expected to see you again quite so soon.'

'Nor I, you,' Rudi said, sipping from his own mug. It was thin, sour stuff, but at least it was cheap. The gods alone knew what Bodun would have made of it. 'But something's come up. I might need that favour before long.'

'I see.' Shenk looked a little concerned. 'This wouldn't have anything to do with whatever your problem was when we met on the river, would it?'

'Not really,' Rudi assured him. 'I may need to see some people in Altdorf before long, that's all.'

'Well, you can always rely on the *Reikmaiden* to get you there,' Shenk assured him. 'We'll be back here in about a month, if you'll be ready to go by then.'

'I see.' Rudi nodded, slowly. 'And if my business turns out to be a little more urgent than that?'

'You could always go by coach,' Shenk suggested, with a tone which made it clear which alternative he'd prefer Rudi to take. 'The roads should still be passable for another few weeks. Even longer if the rains hold off.'

'So you're leaving soon?' Rudi asked casually.

'Dawn tomorrow.' He shot Rudi a narrow look. 'I don't suppose you'll be ready to leave by then?'

'I doubt it.' Hanna certainly wouldn't. Right now, it seemed, her life depended on remaining in the city and the hope that the mages at the college would somehow find a way to remove the talisman. Rudi sipped his ale, trying to mask his disappointment. The escape route he'd hoped to find here appeared to be closed after all, or at least unavailable for the time being. On the other hand, he supposed, the delay would give him another month to try and find Magnus. He couldn't leave Marienburg now, not while some hope remained of finding his friend here, especially since the horned sorceress and Hans would undoubtedly kill the merchant if they discovered him first. He rose to his feet. 'See you in a month, then. Maybe.'

'Maybe.' Shenk's tone made it clear he hoped he wouldn't. After a moment, curiosity won out over his reticence. 'That night on the river. What were you running from, anyway?'

'A misunderstanding,' Rudi said shortly. He'd taken it for granted that the riverboat captain had been unaware of Gerhard's accusations of heresy, otherwise he would have been a great deal more reluctant to deal with him. Shenk nodded wisely.

'Had a few of those myself,' he said.

'I don't doubt it,' Rudi replied. Pieter had told him the first time they met that the captain would do whatever it took to keep his boat in work, and judging by his apparent involvement in a smuggling ring the deckhand hadn't been exaggerating. Despite the disappointment he felt, he grinned. 'Like taking a room in the wrong boarding house.'

'It seemed like a good idea at the time,' Shenk said. 'Thanks for the drink.'

Lost in thought, Rudi began the long walk back to the Winkelmarkt. The sun was going down now, the first torches beginning to flare and the street traders starting to dismantle their stalls. As he left the warmth of the tavern, he shivered in the sudden cold. The air was bitter tonight and the scent of frost hovered in it.

His options were beginning to look limited. He had one further clue to Magnus's whereabouts, the mysterious address in the Doodkanal, and if that turned out to be a dead end too he was out of leads. He doubted that Sam would help him again. He'd already provided the halfling with the information he needed and he had nothing else to trade. And the longer he remained in the city, the more likely it was that Gerhard and the mercenaries would find some way of tracking him down.

He adjusted his new woollen hat with fingers beginning to tingle from the cold. Had it not been for the sudden impulse which had made him purchase it that afternoon, his watchman's cap would have betrayed his new profession in an instant and the witch hunter would have been able to find him easily.

As it was, he still had the advantage of anonymity, and at least Gerhard and his cronies would now be concentrating their efforts in the Tempelwijk, on the far side of the city.

Hanna! He'd all but led the witch hunter to her door. Well there was nothing he could do about that now, he'd just have to hope that the college protected her. They should do. Once again he reminded himself that the law was on their side and that anyone claiming to act in the name of Sigmar would be less than popular in Marienburg. No doubt that was why Gerhard had continued to employ the bounty hunters; as any official help he could expect would be grudging at best.

'Walder.' A hand fell on his shoulder. Without thinking, he reached for his sword and turned, already grasping the hilt. Rauke took a step back, reaching for her own weapon, a flicker of concern visible in the brown eyes below the floppy brim of her uniform cap. 'Woah, steady boy.' She grinned as he relaxed. 'Good reflexes, I'll give you that.'

'Sorry.' Rudi smiled sheepishly. 'I was miles away.'

'Bad idea around here,' the Cap said, smiling. 'Unless you want to lose your purse.' She glared at a couple of locals, who slunk into the shadows under her scrutiny. 'Not that they'd get anywhere with you,' she added.

'I hope not.' Rudi nodded. 'I lost it once before, on my first night in town.' Rauke lifted an eyebrow in polite enquiry, her expression disbelieving. 'Long story. I got it back, got in a fight, got a job in the watch.'

'I'd like to hear it,' Rauke said. She smiled at him. 'If you've got time, there's a place round the corner I like. The owner's Cathayan, does these little white tube things. Bit like Tilean spaghetti, but spicier.' Rudi had never heard of spaghetti, but the mention of food reminded him it had been a long time since he last ate.

'Sounds interesting,' he said. 'When do you book out?'

'Just did,' Rauke said cheerfully, removing her hat. A cascade of glossy brown curls descended around her shoulders. 'I was just on my way home when I saw you.' A quizzical expression crossed her face. 'So what are you doing on my patch, anyway?'

'Just having a *bon voyage* drink with someone I know who works on a riverboat,' Rudi said.

'Bet he's got some stories. Some of them go right up the river as far as Kislev, you know.'

'I'll ask him the next time I see him,' Rudi said, following the young woman through the congested streets.

THE CATHAYAN FOOD, although strange, was plentiful, and accompanied by small bowls of some herbal infusion similar to the ones Hanna made, which Rauke called tea. To his surprise, he found that in spite of the turmoil of questions which continued to seethe in the back of his mind, and the apprehension induced by the knowledge that Gerhard was scouring the city for him, he felt relaxed in her company in a way he'd never experienced before. It was some time before they parted, with a promise to meet again later in the week, and despite the other matters which continued to weigh on his mind, Rudi returned to the Winkelmarkt with a smile on his face. That lasted until he reached the gate of the barracks.

'Walder.' Sam Warble detached himself from the surrounding shadows and shivered. 'You're lucky, kid. I was only going to give it another few minutes before I gave up on you.'

'What do you want?' Rudi asked.

'Same as everyone, I guess. A warm fire, six decent meals a day and the love of a good woman. Failing that, money. How about you?'

'A straight answer,' Rudi shot back. 'What are you doing here?'

'Waiting for you.' Sam paused just long enough to make the point that his answer had been straight, though singularly uninformative, before continuing.

'I've got a message from Kris. His girlfriend's in trouble.'

'What kind of trouble?' After a moment Rudi realised the halfling was talking about Hanna. The sudden rush of concern was so strong it displaced all other emotions, even the pang of hearing her referred to like that.

'She's been arrested. The watch are holding her for attempted murder.' He turned and melted into the shadows again. 'Just thought you'd like to know.'

CHAPTER TWENTY-SEVEN

As SOON AS the halfling had disappeared, Rudi hurried back to his room. Events were moving too fast for his liking and it seemed they might have to take passage on the *Reikmaiden* sooner than he'd expected. He put his meagre possessions into his pack with a twinge of regret: he was beginning to enjoy the life he'd made for himself and would happily have remained in Marienburg indefinitely had things turned out differently.

Well, perhaps it wouldn't come to that, but after having fled from Kohlstadt with virtually nothing, he wasn't going to take any chances. He could always put the stuff back later if things worked out for the best. Last of all, he slung the bow and the quiver of arrows across his back.

'Rudi?' Gerrit stared at him curiously as he stepped out into the corridor. 'Where are you going?'

'To see a friend,' Rudi replied, as casually as he could.

'Anyone I know?' Gerrit asked, clearly unconvinced. Rudi forced his features into a conspiratorial smile.

'One of the Caps from Suiddock. Rauke van Stolke. I met her the other day when I took that message across the water for the captain and I promised her an archery lesson.' He flushed, certain his friend would detect the lie, but Gerrit merely grinned at him, obviously mistaking his unease for embarrassment.

'The brunette with the freckles?' Gerrit nudged him in the ribs. 'You're a dark horse, aren't you? I thought you were keen on that Anna whatsername.'

'I might be gone for some time,' Rudi said, deflecting the conversation as best he could.

Gerrit's grin widened. 'I should hope so,' he said.

Rudi left the barracks as quickly as he could, then hesitated, wondering which way to turn. He didn't even know which ward Hanna had been arrested in, and cursed himself for not asking Sam for more details while he'd had the chance.

He couldn't act without more information, and there was only one place he was likely to get it. Hurrying as best he could without attracting unwelcome attention, his breath misting visibly around his head, he made for the bakery and Kris's rooms above it.

'Damn.' The apartment was dark when he got there, the windows shuttered, but he knocked anyway, feeling a curious sense of déjà vu. It was only as the echoes faded that the association fell into place and he recalled knocking on the door of van Crackenmeer's office that afternoon. So much seemed to have happened in the interim that it seemed like an eternity ago, rather than a few short hours. He turned away, wondering where else the mage might have gone, and the answer came to him almost at once: the Dancing Pirate.

HIS GUESS TURNED out to be right. Kris was sitting at a table near the door and looked up as he entered, an expression of relief passing across his chubby features as he registered Rudi's presence.

'Thank Shallya you're here,' he said. Rudi nodded, joining him at the table. The inn was relatively empty at this hour of the evening, but he kept his voice low in any case.

'I got your message,' he replied, and then another thought struck him. 'I didn't think Sam was in the business of doing people favours.'

'Not as a rule,' Kris said. 'But he has his soft spots. One of them's for young women in trouble.' He shrugged. 'Besides, I've done some work for him from time to time and he might want me to do some more. Why spend money when a sense of obligation's so much cheaper?'

'Work like gimmicking the cards at Tilman's, for instance?' Rudi asked.

'That sort of thing,' he agreed. 'But right now we need to think about Hanna.'

'Right.' Rudi nodded his agreement. 'What happened, exactly? Who did she try to kill?'

'Me,' Marta said heavily, dropping into a seat between them. 'At least that's what they're saying.' Her voice was strained, her face redder than usual, and Rudi suspected she'd been crying. 'It's not fair! She was only trying to help!'

'What happened, exactly?' Rudi asked. The landlady sniffed, wiped her eyes on her apron, and took a gulp of her nephew's drink to steady her nerves. Kris didn't seem to object.

'I just told her about my back. It's not been right for years now, you know…' Kris nodded sympathetically, clearly having heard the details many times before. 'All that heavy lifting I suppose. Anyway, she gave me some ointment for it.'

'That's not a crime, is it?' Kris asked hotly.

Rudi felt his stomach sink. 'Technically it is,' he said. 'She's not a member of the healers' or physicians' guilds. Who did you tell?'

'No one.' Marta stared at him indignantly. 'Well, hardly anyone. Mrs Angsteen over at the laundry's been a martyr to haemorrhoids for years now and her niece, lovely young thing, always so cheerful, she's had this rash on and off for ages. The apothecaries are all so expensive and Hanna said she'd be happy to help…' She trailed off, taking in Rudi's expression of horrified understanding.

'In other words she's been prescribing remedies without a licence,' he said heavily.

'It's not as if she took any money for it,' he said. 'You know what she's like, she just wanted to help people.'

'And the remedies worked,' Marta added. 'Everyone who took something got better!'

'That doesn't make any difference,' Rudi explained gently. 'The law classifies unlicensed prescribing as attempted murder. It's stupid and unfair, but it's what the statute says.' He shook his head. Originally it had been intended to protect the citizens from mountebanks peddling patent medicines which could have been actively harmful, at least in theory, but in practice the law seemed to exist purely to protect the lucrative monopoly of the physicians' and healers' guilds. 'If it comes to court there's no doubt she'll be convicted.'

'Oh the poor lamb!' Marta dabbed at her eyes again. 'Whatever will become of her?'

'Depending on the judge, between five and twenty years on Rijker's,' Rudi said bleakly.

Kris's face went white. 'Then she's dead,' he said flatly. 'The college won't lift a finger to help a convicted felon.'

'She's not dead yet,' Rudi said. Grim determination made his jaw stiffen, so much so that he had to force the words out. 'I know a riverboat heading for Altdorf tomorrow morning and the captain owes me a favour. Whatever happens, I swear she'll be on it.'

'But the talisman will kill her if she leaves!' Kris almost shouted the words, keeping his voice low with an obvious effort.

'You said yourself if she stays the college will disown her. Maybe one of the ones in Altdorf can help. She'll live long enough to get there, won't she?'

'You're right.' Kris nodded bleakly. Marta looked from one young man to the other, her face a mask of incomprehension.

'What do you mean she'll die?' she asked.

'It's complicated,' he said, standing abruptly. 'Kris will explain.'

'And what are you going to do?' the mage asked.

'Rescue her.' He pulled his watchman's cap out from inside his shirt, removed his new hat and placed the black floppy one firmly on his head. 'Where's she being held?'

To HIS GREAT relief, it turned out that Hanna had been arrested just outside the Pirate after a meal with Kris, and was being held by the Winkelmarkt Caps at the ward's main watch house. That was going to make things a great deal easier. He entered the familiar building briskly, as though he was on an important errand, and stifled a twinge of regret at the thought that this was probably the last time he'd ever cross the threshold. A couple of watchmen looked up, nodded a greeting, and resumed their conversation over a game of cards.

'Walder.' Sergeant Rijgen greeted him with an expression of puzzlement. 'I thought you were finished with nights for a while.'

'So did I.' Rudi injected what he hoped was just the right tone of resigned irritation into his voice. 'Captain Marcus sent me over. Something's come up.' The sergeant looked no more than mildly curious, but it wouldn't hurt to reinforce the impression that he was on official business. He smiled wryly. 'I hope you're going to authorise the overtime on this one.'

'That depends,' Rijgen said. 'What do you want?'

'Hanna Riefenstahl,' Rudi replied at once. 'Young woman, arrested this afternoon. Is she still here?'

'Yes.' Rijgen looked at him again, no hint of suspicion in his eyes yet. 'You know the procedure. She'll be here until the assizes open in the morning.' For the first time he looked mildly regretful. 'It's a pity. She's young, good-looking. She's going to have a hard time on Rijker's.'

'That's if she's lucky,' Rudi said. The sergeant looked at him sharply. 'The temple court's claimed jurisdiction in the case.'

'Are you sure?' Rijgen asked.

'The captain's drawing up the transfer order now. It seems she's the one that Imperial witch hunter's been after.'

'Hendryk's purse.' Rijgen shook his head. 'That's hard to believe.'

'We'll soon know for sure. If she is I'm supposed to take her back to the barracks, to wait for the templars. Gerrit's gone over to the Tempelwijk to get them.'

'How can you tell if she is the right one?' To Rudi's relief Rijgen was picking up the heavy ring of keys to the cell doors as he spoke.

'I'll show you.' He followed the sergeant down the corridor, past the row of barred doors from behind which a steady drone of weeping, cursing, or snoring seeped, depending on the occupant's temperament and degree of inebriation. Rijgen stopped at one of them, from which no sound at all could be distinguished, and turned the key in the lock.

As he pulled it open, Rudi stepped into the cell through the widening gap, blocking the sergeant's view for a second or two. Hanna was sitting on the narrow cot, the sole item of furniture apart from a foul smelling bucket, and glanced up, her eyes widening with shock as she realised who it was.

'Trust me,' Rudi mouthed, hoping she would pick it up and have the presence of mind to respond. Evidently she did: she inclined her head a fraction and launched into a typical tirade.

'This is absolutely outrageous! I demand that you send a message to Professor Aaldbrugh at the college at once! You have absolutely no right to keep me here...' Her voice stopped abruptly, with a strangulated shriek, as Rudi reached out a hand, grabbed her headscarf and yanked it from her head. Her hands snapped up reflexively, trying to cover the wax seal seared into the middle of her forehead.

'Manann's bloody trident!' Rijgen said, staring at it. 'You were right.'

'I'm afraid so,' Rudi said. He held out a peremptory hand. 'Come with me, please.'

'Where?' The note of panic in her voice sounded as though it was not entirely counterfeit. She grabbed the headscarf and retied it, glaring at him angrily.

'I'm escorting you back to the main watch barracks,' Rudi said. He rested his hand on the hilt of his sword. 'If you try to run, I'll kill you. Do you understand?'

'Yes.' Hanna nodded, her face white.

'Good.' Rudi took hold of her upper arm and urged her into motion. As they passed Rijgen he favoured the sergeant with the most disgusted look he could contrive. 'Witches,' he said vehemently. 'I'm not being paid enough for this.'

'None of us are, lad,' Rijgen agreed. 'But we keep right on doing it.'

RUDI KEPT UP the pose of escorting a prisoner until they were well out of sight of the watch house, then steered them down a narrow alleyway he knew well from his night patrols. Very little light ever penetrated down there and they would be able to converse unobserved.

'What the hell do you think you're doing?' Hanna snapped, wrenching her arm free of his grip. 'Are you out of your mind, showing him that?' Words failed her for once.

'I had no choice,' Rudi snapped back, in no mood for a debate. 'If I'd left you there you'd be on your way to Rijker's by noon.'

'What are you talking about?' Her voice was a little quieter, but no less vehement. 'It was just a misunder-standing, that's all. I could have sorted it out.'

'Trust me, you couldn't,' Rudi replied. 'Under Marien-burg law you didn't have a leg to stand on. The college couldn't help you either, not in a criminal case. And in case you were wondering, they'll be after me too as soon as they realise I helped you escape.'

'I see.' Her voice was brittle. 'I assume you have some kind of plan? Or are you just making it up as you go along again?'

'Shenk's sailing for Altdorf at dawn,' Rudi said. 'We're going with him. Kris thinks the colleges there might be able to help you, even if Baron Hendryk's can't.'

'I see,' Hanna said again. 'And is anyone going to ask what I think?' She sneezed, suddenly. 'Gods, it's cold!'

'Come on.' Rudi urged her into motion. 'We're meet-ing Kris back at his place. The sooner you're back in the warm the better.'

'Are you mad?' Hanna asked, stopping to stare at him. 'That's the first place they'll look!' Abruptly she started walking again. 'Still, at least I won't die of cold I suppose.'

'You're not going to die at all,' Rudi said, trotting a few paces to catch up with her. 'Not if I can help it.'

'Me neither,' Hanna said.

* * *

IN DEFERENCE TO Hanna's concern that Kris's rooms would be an obvious place to start looking for them, Rudi stayed out in the street to keep watch while she went inside to take her farewell. At least that's what he told himself. In truth, he felt that things were being said that neither of them would want him to overhear, and he didn't want to make their parting any more awkward or painful than it would otherwise have been. At length she reappeared, swathed in the travelling cloak and carrying her satchel. It seemed quite bulky and Rudi gazed at it as she slipped it over her shoulder.

'We won't be able to get any of your stuff from the Tempelwijk,' he said. 'I'm sorry.'

'It can't be helped,' she said. 'Besides, most of it was here.' She sniffed and wiped her eyes with the back of her hand.

'Right,' Rudi said, feeling awkward again. A shadow in the upstairs window gazed down at them and he raised a hand in farewell. 'We'd better get moving. There ought to be a patrol along here fairly soon.'

'Right,' Hanna said, the familiar decisive tone entering her voice again. It faltered slightly as she waved too and the shadowy figure echoed the gesture, its shoulders slumping forlornly. 'Where to, then?'

'There's an address in the Doodkanal I found,' Rudi began hesitantly as they slipped away down a convenient alley. 'If Magnus is still in Marienburg, I'm sure that's where he'll be. I can't leave here without checking it out. I can tell you how to get to the boat...'

'Forget it,' Hanna said. 'I'm coming too.' She shrugged. 'I'm on borrowed time as it is. I might as well start living dangerously.'

CHAPTER TWENTY-EIGHT

THE DOODKANAL WAS as unprepossessing as ever, and although Rudi was beginning to become familiar enough with the derelict surroundings to feel less uncertain about venturing into them for a third time, Hanna was clearly nervous, glancing at the dark shadows surrounding them with every sign of apprehension.

They'd already passed through the marginally habitable area fringing the Winkelmarkt, the degraded and degenerate inhabitants of the quarter staring at them resentfully from the safety of their lairs, or scuttling out of their way as they moved through the streets. None of them had plucked up enough courage to offer a challenge, though. Even the gangs who had clustered in the deeper patches of darkness as they passed, and the two fugitives were now picking their way cautiously through an area of dereliction worse than any

Rudi had yet seen in this blighted and forgotten part of the city. Hardly a roof remained on the buildings surrounding them and tumbled brick marked the memory of walls almost as often as the reality. Firelight gleamed in a few places, where souls even less fortunate than the rest of the inhabitants gathered together in whatever makeshift shelters they could contrive from the detritus surrounding them, but for the most part Rudi and Hanna were forced to rely on the uncertain moonlight to see by.

For this, at least, Rudi thanked Taal. The frosty night was clear for the most part, with only a few scattered clouds to diffuse the silver glow of Mannslieb and the necrotic light cast by the pale green disk of its ill-favoured cousin. Even so, little enough of it penetrated to street level, so down here there were still too many patches of impenetrable darkness to leave him feeling entirely at ease.

'Don't worry about it,' Rudi assured her as a couple of furtive silhouettes slipped away into the murk. 'They're more afraid of us than we are of them.'

'Speak for yourself,' Hanna said, but with just enough of a hint of humour to make it clear that her resolve was undiminished. Although Rudi had spoken more to reassure her than anything else, it seemed that there was more truth to his words than he realised. The impression he'd made on his last visit, when he'd casually dispatched the footpads who'd dared to waylay him, seemed fresh in the minds of the local denizens and none of them was willing to force a confrontation.

'It must be down here somewhere,' Rudi said. The location he'd memorised was clear in his mind and he hurried through the tumbledown streets towards his goal with as much assurance as if he'd been there before. Just as he had on the night when he found the warehouse, he felt absolutely certain that he was on the right road and that if he simply relaxed and followed his instincts he would be drawn to his destination as surely as a leaf would follow the current of a stream. And, as on that occasion and the night in the forest when he'd found the strange celebration in the dying and blighted clearing, a small part of his mind wondered at that.

'What I wouldn't give for a light,' Hanna said, with heavy irony. The reminder of her lost powers must have stirred something within her, because she stumbled and clutched at her temples with a faint cry of pain. Rudi stopped, despite the nameless urge pulling him onwards, and tried to support her. It was a shock. She felt frailer than ever, light in his arms, as though the power coursing through her was leaching away her substance as well as her vitality.

'Here, let me...' Rudi began, but Hanna shrugged him off.

'I'm all right,' she insisted, despite every indication to the contrary. Rudi would have demurred, but he knew the girl well enough by now to realise how futile the attempt would be, so he simply nodded.

'Better keep moving,' he said instead.

'Right.' Hanna took a few more paces, then an expression of puzzlement crossed her face. 'That's odd.' She reached inside the cloak which swathed her, blurring her outline against the surrounding dark.

'What is?' Rudi asked. A moment later Hanna's hand emerged, with the small leather pouch she'd taken from the skaven clenched in it. As it did so, Rudi realised that he could see her face more clearly. Hanna loosened the drawstring and tipped the piece of stone into her hand.

'It's never done that before,' she said. Rudi drew in his breath. The stone was glowing faintly, with some strange internal radiance. As they watched, it faded and died and became nothing more than an inert chip of rock again.

'What do you think it means?' he asked.

'I have no idea whatsoever.' She replaced the enigmatic stone in the pouch and slipped the thong over her head again. 'Better keep moving, like you said.'

'Right,' Rudi agreed, the sense of urgency he'd felt ever since he'd found the mysterious map, growing stronger than ever. If Magnus really was waiting for him at the point they were moving towards, then the answers he craved would be within his grasp at last.

Despite the cold, he felt feverish with anticipation. Heedless of the treacherous footing afforded by the frosty ground beneath his feet, he hurried on as fast as he could without taxing Hanna too much.

'Is it much further?' she asked after a while. Struck by renewed concern, Rudi slowed his pace. The girl seemed weaker than ever, stumbling from more than just the uneven ground.

'Almost there,' he assured her, although how he could be so certain continued to elude him. He scanned the panorama of dereliction ahead of them and trusted to whatever instinct or power had guided him this far.

The prospect was far from encouraging. A shanty town of roughly constructed hovels stood on the shore of a rank and scummy inlet, ill-shaped shacks thrown together from whatever scraps of wood and canvas their owners had been able to scavenge from the water and the tumbled detritus surrounding them. Hanna frowned.

'Are you sure?' she asked dubiously.

'Yes.' With growing assurance. Rudi walked into the cluster of stinking huts, grateful for the chill night air which deadened the worst of it. Oddly, as he began to get used to it, the stench became less offensive, so that after a while it became more tolerable, even pleasant in some peculiar way. Piles of filth lay between the ramshackle dwellings, which he strode through unconcerned. Hanna lifted her skirts with a grimace of distaste and picked her way around the worst of it as best she could.

'Here.' Without pausing to wonder how he could be so positive, Rudi lifted his hand and rapped loudly on the door of a hut which seemed a little more sturdy than the others. The timbers which formed most of it appeared to have been salvaged from a boat. After a short pause he heard the rattle of a latch and the door creaked open.

'Grandfather's buboes, is it really you?' Magnus stepped back a pace, his face a mask of astonishment. Then he rallied, a broad smile spreading across his thin features and embraced the young man for a moment.

'I could ask you the same thing,' Rudi said. The merchant seemed more cadaverous than ever, his skin taut and glossy with unhealed burns, from which thin, clear fluid wept continuously, and his hair all but gone. His clothes were charred rags, damp patches betraying where they adhered to the seared flesh beneath them. His injuries should have left him in agony, barely able to move, but to Rudi's astonishment he seemed almost well.

'I'VE CHANGED A bit,' Magnus agreed, standing aside to motion his unexpected guests inside the hut. 'But for the better, I like to think.'

Hanna stared at him in horror. 'I've some ointment here that might help,' she said, reaching for her satchel. Magnus shook his head and gestured to a small table in the centre of the hut. Four rickety chairs were placed around it, and a bundle of stained rags in the corner evidently did duty as a bed. Hanna gagged as she crossed the threshold and lifted a fold of the cloak across her face. Rudi looked at her in some puzzlement. The air inside the hut was warm and close, but that felt welcome after the chill night air, and the thick, cloying odour reminded him more of incense than anything else.

'That's very kind,' Magnus said, the skin of his face tearing slightly under the pressure of his smile to release a thin dribble of yellow pus, 'but I can assure you I've never felt better in my life.'

'Then you've lost all feeling in your skin?' Hanna asked, professional curiosity overcoming her revulsion. 'I've heard of cases like that, where the damage was severe, but…'

'I can assure you I feel no discomfort,' Magnus said. He lifted the lid off a shallow dish, with a faint echo of the courteous host Rudi remembered from Kohlstadt. 'Can I offer you some refreshment? It's not much, but we do the best we can down here.'

Hanna gasped and recoiled from the contents. In spite of himself, Rudi felt his mouth begin to water at the sight and smell of the putrescent mess, but gestured a refusal.

'We've already eaten, thank you.'

'As you wish,' Magnus said, slobbering up something squishy and slick with mould. Hanna made a faint choking sound in the base of her throat.

'I think I'll wait outside,' she said, leaving with almost indecent haste. As the door banged to behind her, Rudi thought he heard the sound of retching.

'So, my young friend, what brings you here?' Magnus asked, as though they were still sitting in the cosy parlour of his home in Kohlstadt. Now he'd finally found the man he'd been searching for all this time, he wasn't quite sure where to begin.

'You do,' he began. 'After that night in the woods...'

'Ah yes.' Magnus nodded gravely. 'A great disappointment to us all. The beastmen could hardly have chosen a less opportune time to intervene. Which was, no doubt, the point. We have enemies, Rudi, powerful ones, who would stop at nothing to cheat you of your destiny.'

'You mentioned that,' Rudi said. 'Just before they attacked, you said my destiny was foretold. What were you talking about?' The merchant reached across the table to grip Rudi's arm with astonishing strength, his eyes sparkling in his ruined face with an intensity which made the young watchman flinch.

'You are the vessel of all our hopes, Rudi. The one whose way we prepared for years. But, as I say, we have powerful enemies and they chose their time to strike well.'

'You mean the sorceress,' Rudi said. In so far as it was possible for him to register an expression at all now, Magnus looked surprised.

'You know about her?' he asked, glancing towards the door. 'Then you're playing a very dangerous game, it seems to me.'

'I know she's been trying to kill you,' Rudi said. 'But I don't understand. Who is she? And why does she hate you so much?'

'We serve different masters,' Magnus said. 'I suspected her true allegiance for some time and she made it clear that she suspected mine, but neither of us really knew for sure until that night in the Blessed Grove. They were her creatures that attacked us, you can be sure of that.'

'I know,' Rudi said. 'I saw her with them. And Hans Katzenjammer. What he became, I mean.'

'A remarkable transformation,' Magnus said. 'They came to my house a few nights ago and I barely escaped with my life. Again.' He chuckled throatily, hawking up a gobbet of phlegm. 'I'm harder to kill than she bargained for, it seems.' He shrugged. 'Fortunately I had this refuge already prepared, against just such a contingency.'

'I know. I found a map in van Crackenmeer's office,' Rudi said. He paused, unsure quite how to break the news. 'They'd already been there, but they missed it.'

'Then Cornelius is dead,' Magnus concluded, and Rudi nodded soberly. 'And the map?'

'I destroyed it,' Rudi said. 'Just in time, too. Gerhard found the office just after I did.'

'The witch hunter?' Magnus shook his head, apparently amused. 'He's certainly persistent, isn't he?'

'He's dangerous,' Rudi insisted, surprised by the merchant's levity. 'He killed Greta Reifenstahl, and Sigmar knows how many others. He's been on our trail ever since we left Kohlstadt, and since he reached Marienburg he's been after you as well.'

'Then we must work fast,' Magnus said. 'Our preparations here have been far more hurried than in Kohlstadt, and on a much smaller scale, but they should prove adequate.' He stood, fast and decisive. 'Morrsleib is full tonight. There's no time to lose.'

'Wait,' Rudi said. Things were beginning to make sense now, but there was still so much he didn't understand. 'My father...' The words caught in his throat for a moment and he felt as if he was choking. The image of the last sight he'd had of the man who'd raised him, blood pouring from the terrible wounds inflicted by the leader of the beastmen, gasping out his last words, rose up in his mind, blotting out everything else. 'He said you knew my family. Where I came from.' His voice rose, his desperation for answers palpable in the tone of it. 'I have to know! Am I von Karien?'

'You are the heir,' Magnus said slowly, 'and the vessel. Your father and I...' He hesitated. 'Gunther Walder and I were charged with your protection. Even now there are those who would stop at nothing to prevent you from coming into your legacy.' He strode decisively towards the door of the ramshackle hut. 'And if we are to frustrate them we have to act tonight.'

His head spinning, Rudi tried to make sense of everything he'd heard. The answers he'd sought so desperately were in his hand at last, but he was as confused as ever. It seemed he really was the missing

heir to the von Karien estates, and that shadowy enemies were stalking him to prevent him from claiming
his birthright. But if Hans and the horned sorceress
were working for them, why had they intervened to
save him from harm so many times before? Was there
someone else out there he needed to be wary of,
whose existence he'd never even suspected? He turned
back to Magnus, determined not to move until everything had been laid out before him.

'Rudi!' Before he could speak again Hanna's voice
echoed through the tiny hovel, shrill with panic. 'Rudi,
help!'

'Hanna!' He leapt for the door, his hand reaching for
the sword at his belt, but before he could grasp it Magnus was there, barring his way.

'Leaving already?' the merchant asked, moving with
the speed of a striking serpent.

'Get out of the way!' Rudi cried, trying to dodge past
him.

'I don't think so.' The pose of affability was shrugged
off like a garment, and an inhumanly strong hand
reached out to grab the young watchman by the throat.
Choking and kicking, Rudi found himself being lifted
clear of the foetid floor. He tried to draw his sword, but
Magnus clamped his other hand around his wrist, stilling it easily. 'We've wasted enough time as it is.'

CHAPTER TWENTY-NINE

GASPING AND CHOKING, Rudi was hauled outside. The whole shanty town seemed to be in an uproar, although how much of that was due to the pounding of his own blood in his ears he couldn't be sure. Voices were raised, harsh guttural tones barely recognisable as human, echoing the chant he'd heard in the warehouse the first time he'd seen Magnus.

'*Barhum yu! Barhum yu!*' There was a terrible power in that sound and Rudi felt his bones vibrate with it.

'Hanna!' he choked out, trying to twist his head to look for her, but the fingers holding his neck were like bands of iron and he was unable to catch more than a glimpse of her out of the corner of his eye. She was still fighting, but it was a losing battle, he could tell. 'Run!'

'I'm trying to!' she snapped back, a trace of her old asperity beginning to assert itself. She punched one hunched figure hard in the face and it fell back. No sooner was it down than another stepped in to take its place, and then another. In moments she would be overwhelmed by the sheer force of numbers.

Before that could be put to the test, however, the girl was wracked by another seizure, the worst he'd seen so far. She fell to the ground and lay there, spasming, foam dribbling though her tightly clenched teeth. Blood began to trickle from her nose. Clearly, once again, the dammed power within her had burst its bounds under the impetus of anger and fear.

'Help her!' Rudi croaked, and Magnus laughed, a harsh sound devoid of any trace of fellowship or good-will.

'And why would I do that?' He half-dragged, half-carried Rudi away from the prostrate girl, who by now was lying almost inert, the only signs of life remaining an occasional moan or twitch. 'Meat's hard to come by in the Doodkanal.'

In the moonlight, Rudi caught fleeting glimpses of the faces of the people surrounding them, although perhaps calling them people was no longer entirely accurate, and a mounting sense of horror swept over him. Beneath the bundles of rags which swathed them all he could make out features as ravaged as those of the man he'd once thought of as a friend; diseased, necrotic, rotting away, yet somehow imbued with a vitality which went beyond mere health. Their bodies too, what little he could discern of them, were equally twisted and misshapen, as though they'd been made of wax and been left too close to the fire.

'Hail the vessel!' Magnus cried, just as he had that fateful night in the forest outside the village they'd both called home, and the diseased congregation echoed his call.

'What the hell do you think you're doing?' Rudi demanded, trying to pry the merchant's fingers away from his throat, but the effort was completely futile. Magnus laughed again, and with a shiver Rudi recognised the edge of insanity in it.

'Fulfilling your destiny! Hail the vessel!'

'Hail the vessel!' the damned things surrounding him echoed, and several more hands took hold of him. Completely immobilised, Rudi struggled in their grasp, and Magnus finally let go of his throat.

'The wards!' The charred figure gestured peremptorily and a couple of the misshapen acolytes began to scratch strange symbols in the mud of the ground. They seemed to be making hard work of it, the harsh frost having solidified it to the consistency of brick, but they kept at it grimly, heedless of the traces of blood and other substances their ripped and tattered hands left on the rime hardened surface.

Rudi craned his neck, trying to see what they were doing, but the details of the strange designs eluded him. Nevertheless they seemed hauntingly familiar, like the time he'd walked the pattern of furrows in Altman's field and felt his very sense of his own identity shifting, slipping away.

He had to stay focussed. He forced the sensation down, feeling something stir in the depths of his mind, and a strange kaleidoscope of emotions washed over him. Resentment, anticipation and a gloating sense of impending triumph. A faint voice whispered in the back of his mind, urging him to relax, let go…

The breath was driven abruptly from his body as the twisted monstrosities holding him threw him to the ground, the impact snapping him back to himself and the wood of his bow digging deeply and uncomfortably into his back. He struggled desperately against the hands immobilising him, trying to reach his sword, or the knife concealed in his boot, but the effort was futile.

'Hail the vessel! Hail the vessel!' Magnus was chanting the meaningless phrase over and over again, looming over him, blotting out the cool, silver light of Mannsleib. The diseased light of the Chaos moon shone fully on his face, however, turning it into something less than human. Sickly green light flashed from the blade of a rusted knife as his former friend raised it high above his head and gripped it with both hands. 'In our Grandfather's name…' Rudi flinched, anticipating the downward plunge of the filthy blade and powerless to prevent it.

Thwip! An arrow appeared suddenly in Magnus's throat. An almost comical expression of surprise followed the impact, then the light went out of his eyes and he toppled slowly to the ground. The grips restraining him slackened, misshapen heads turning to react to the threat, and Rudi surged to his feet, drawing his sword. Moonlight flashed on the blade, silver and green, and he lashed out at the nearest mutant. It fell back, shrieking, blood fountaining black in the colourless light.

'Remember, he must be taken alive!' Rudi whirled, the familiar voice already betraying the identity of its speaker. Gerhard was standing a few yards away, his own weapon drawn, something dark and rectangular in his other hand. He tucked it inside his cloak as he moved forwards and Rudi belatedly recognised the warped remains of the notebook he'd thrown into the canal. It must have floated near enough to the landing stage for Gerhard or one of his mercenaries to have noticed it and fished it out, leading him straight to Magnus's last hiding place.

'You're welcome to try,' Rudi said grimly.

Gerhard took up a guard position, advancing cautiously towards him.

'It should be obvious even to you by now that I'm not your enemy,' the witch hunter said, his voice as matter-of fact as ever. As if to emphasise the point, one of the diseased monstrosities charged in between them, flinging itself at Gerhard with a shriek no human throat should have been able to produce. The man in black parried its attack easily, opening up a wound which left its entrails spilling out onto the ground.

The distraction was all that Rudi needed. While Gerhard dealt with the mutant, he turned and ran, trying to orientate himself. A scene of pure pandemonium met his eyes.

Gerhard was not alone, as he'd already surmised, the band of mercenaries fanning out to engage the warped inhabitants of the festering slum. The once-human creatures were everywhere, swarming from their hovels with whatever makeshift weapons they could lay their hands on, their sheer weight of numbers going at least part of the way to counterbalance the superior fighting ability of the bounty hunters.

As he'd expected, Conrad was hovering on the fringes of the battle, dropping one mutant after another with well-placed arrows, relieving the pressure on the others as best he could. Alwyn had her sword out, but appeared to be relying on her mystical abilities rather than her fencing skills. A nimbus of deeper darkness seemed to surround her, coalescing around her hand, and wherever she pointed it would flow, enveloping one mutant at a time. As the shadows surrounded their victim they seemed to thicken and the unfortunate monstrosity would collapse as though borne to the ground by their weight. None rose again, at least where Rudi could see.

'Khazahai!' A gleeful battle-cry attracted his attention for a moment, to where Bodun's battleaxe was cleaving its way through the densest group of the degenerate creatures the dwarf had been able to find. Theo stood close to him, almost back to back, fending off any incautious enough to try flanking them and cursing monotonously under his breath.

'Sometimes I wonder why you don't just become a trollslayer and have done with it,' the mercenary captain grumbled. 'If you've got a bloody deathwish anyway…'

'Oh come on,' Bodun riposted, neatly bisecting a cudgel wielding mutant. 'Where's the fun in picking on the easy ones?'

Rudi had taken in all this in a matter of seconds and moved to defend himself from another pair of mutants even as he did so. His sword deflected a cut from what looked like the rusted remains of a kitchen knife, snapping it in two, and plunged into the torso of the creature next to the one wielding it. As it went down, he kicked out at the first one, breaking its kneecap, and it sprawled on the ground, shrieking. He watched it thrashing around for a moment, savouring its agony, then finished it off with a thrust through the heart.

A berserker rage had him in its grip, a fury of disappointment and anger boiling up from somewhere deep within his mind. Magnus had betrayed him and now he couldn't even trust the memory of his father any more. Had Gunther been a part of whatever strange and twisted agenda the merchant had been pursuing, or had he been another innocent dupe like himself? The only way to find out was to go to Altdorf and confront the von Kariens, but before then he could at least vent his frustration in bloodletting.

Gerhard was engaging a whole swarm of the things, hacking away grimly as he tried to force his way through to get to Rudi, and the young watchman started cutting his way back towards the witch hunter. With him dead, at least he could continue his quest without the fear of pursuit and discovery which had dogged him throughout his sojourn in Marienburg.

'Not so fast.' Rudi turned, just in time to parry a stroke aimed at his head. 'He might want you alive, but I don't.' Blades clashed, the stroke was deflected, and he found himself staring at Bruno. The youth glared back at him, hatred in his eyes, and renewed the attack. That was fine with Rudi. He'd never liked the young adventurer anyway and he'd kill him just as easily as one of the mutants.

'You won't be popular,' Rudi sneered. 'Cheating your friends out of thirty crowns.'

'It'll be worth it.' Bruno thrust at his chest. Rudi stepped aside, turning, and tried to take him down with a kick to the back of the knee. Bruno was too quick and spun to face him, deflecting the attack with the flat of his blade. 'That one was old when Sigmar was in swaddling. Is that the best you can do?'

'You tell me.' Rudi countered, letting the momentum of the blow keep him moving, and struck out with his sword again. Bruno jumped back just in time to avoid being disembowelled. 'I'm the one who moves like a ruptured duck, remember? Surely no match for an expert like you.'

'Sneer while you can, Chaos-lover.' Bruno drove in furiously, forcing Rudi to give ground, and would probably have killed him if a mutant hadn't leapt on his back at the crucial moment. Rudi laughed, spun round behind his opponent, and slashed the creature's throat.

'Get off him, he's mine.' He laughed exultantly, high on the rush of combat. Around him, the melee continued, but the bounty hunters were getting the upper hand by now. Pretty soon there would be no more mutants standing between them. No matter, he could kill them all and Gerhard too.

'Don't laugh at me!' Bruno howled, returning to the attack like a madman. 'That's all you were doing, wasn't it, you and your slut. Pretending she was your sister, letting me feel... And all the time you were laughing at me!'

So that was it. His pride had been hurt by the ruse Rudi and Hanna had used to conceal their identities while they were on the run. Evading the clumsy rush, Rudi rammed his elbow into the young mercenary's chest, driving the breath out of him. Bruno folded and Rudi raised his sword for the killing stroke. He'd known the youth had been smitten with the girl, but he hadn't realised...

'Hanna.' The thought of her snapped him back to himself abruptly and he stilled the blow just on the point of delivering it. She was in danger, possibly dying. He had to help her. The killing rage drained out of him as though it had never been.

Leaving Bruno gasping and retching on the frozen ground, heedless of the skirmish raging about him, Rudi ran back towards Magnus's hut.

Hanna was still lying where he'd left her, stirring feebly. Her eyes were open at least, and she seemed to be trying to speak. Rudi ran as hard as he could, shoulder charging a mutant out of the way, driving the hilt of his sword into its throat with a crunch of breaking cartilage, and hurdling its falling body as he did so. A grim foreboding took hold of him. He was going to be too late, he just knew it.

'No!' he howled, as a cloaked and hooded figure stepped out of the shadows and walked unhurriedly towards the supine girl. 'Leave her alone!' Another group of degenerate acolytes got between them and he hacked and slashed frantically with his sword, desperate to break through. The figure knelt next to Hanna, who stirred feebly.

Stepping over the corpses of the cultists who'd dared to challenge him, Rudi sprinted towards the girl and her assailant. The cloaked figure pulled back its hood, and Rudi gasped as moonlight gleamed from a small pair of gently curving horns. The sorceress! She was obviously too late to claim Magnus, but there was no telling what mischief she might still be capable of wreaking. An expression of shock passed across Hanna's face and her lips moved, but whatever she said he was too far away to hear it.

Before Rudi could prevent her, or even realise what she intended, the horned sorceress reached out with surprising delicacy and brushed her fingertips against the sigil fused to Hanna's forehead.

The girl cried out and lapsed into another seizure, spasming as the wax flowed and melted under the sorceress's touch, the foul thing seeming to sublime into vapour as Rudi watched. Within arm's reach at last, he seized the sorceress by the shoulder, trying to drag her hand away, but he might as well have been trying to bend the arm of a marble statue.

'What are you doing to her?' he shouted.

'Helping her,' the woman replied, in a surprisingly warm and gentle tone. There was something familiar about the voice and the blonde hair through which the horns protruded, and Rudi felt the same sense of formless recognition that he'd had when he'd seen the woman back in the soldiers' camp. 'She'll need to rest for a while, but by the time you reach Altdorf she'll be fine.'

Rudi stared, as the sorceress drew back her hand at last. The talisman had vanished and the skin of Hanna's forehead was completely unblemished, as though the vile thing had never been there. His head reeled.

'Who are you?' he demanded. 'How do you know we're going to Altdorf?'

'The Changer sees all the paths we walk, long before we do,' the woman said, with a trace of amusement. She turned her head slightly, bringing her profile into the mingled light of the twin moons, and Rudi gasped with astonishment. No wonder she'd seemed familiar... But before he could speak, Hanna opened her eyes, staring at the face of the woman who had just saved her life with an expression of wonderment.

'Mother?' she asked, scarcely daring to believe her own words as she struggled to rise. 'Is it really you?'

'Yes, my dear.' Greta Reifenstahl smiled and helped her daughter to her feet, a protective arm around her shoulders. Hanna hugged her fiercely, tears starting visibly in her eyes, almost choking on the words as she spoke them.

'I thought you were dead!'

'So did I.' Gerhard loomed out of the shadows, his sword at the ready. The witch hunter smiled bleakly, without humour. 'But that's a mistake which can easily be corrected.'

CHAPTER THIRTY

'You.' HANNA TURNED her head slowly towards the witch hunter, an expression of loathing on her face. A new strength seemed to flow into her as Rudi watched: her body straightened, no longer debilitated, and she stood firmly on her feet, shrugging her mother's supporting arm away. The air in front of her began to ripple, shimmering with heat, and the dull, red flames Rudi had seen before when she'd killed the skaven flared into existence. Hanna smiled, with a level of malice which froze Rudi's blood. 'Your turn to burn, I think.'

'No, child.' Greta stepped between them. 'This one has a long path still to walk.'

'I don't need your protection, witch.' Gerhard raised his hand, in which something silver reflected the light of the moons. 'I have the blessing of Sigmar and that's more than enough.' If he was surprised by Greta's words he gave no sign of it. With a shiver, Rudi recognised the amulet, or whatever it was, which had robbed Hanna of her powers back on the moorland. In a moment, he had no doubt, it would wreak its baleful influence once more. Without thinking, he charged forward, raising his sword.

'No!' he bellowed. 'I won't let you hurt her again!'

Taken by surprise, Gerhard turned to defend himself, steel clashing in the moonlight, and the object in his other hand fell to the ground. Rudi caught a brief glimpse of the twin comet tail symbol of Sigmar lying in the mud, then drove in hard against his enemy.

'There's more at stake here than the life of a worthless hedge witch!' Gerhard responded, parrying Rudi's attacks, but making no attempt to press home any countermoves. 'If you'd just listen to me for a moment...'

'I've heard all I'm going to from you!' Rudi yelled, incensed at the man's casual dismissal of the girl. He thrust at the witch hunter's heart, only to find his blade turned away at the last moment by a skilful parry. He braced himself for the counter-attack he knew must be coming, but again, inexplicably, the witch hunter let the opportunity go, allowing him to get back on balance. This was like the fight in the lawyer's office, when, for whatever reason, he'd been reluctant to move in for the kill. Rudi smiled. He had no such scruples...

'Rudi!' Hanna shouted. 'Get out of the way! I can't hold it!' There was an edge of panic in her voice now, and despite himself Rudi turned to glance in her direction. The ball of fire was bigger than anything he'd ever seen her conjure up before, the heat of it beating against his back, the dull red flames illuminating the squalid shanty town in hues of flickering blood. The girl's body was shaking with the effort of restraining it, but to no avail. Even as he took the information in, in a single horrified glance, the sphere of flame began to move.

'Get down!' Gerhard tackled him, taking advantage of his momentary distraction to dive at his knees. Rudi crashed to the frozen ground, the breath driven from his lungs. Searing heat blistered the air above his back and there was a crack like thunder as the fireball streaked through the space he'd occupied an instant before. Gasping, he rolled over, just in time to see it burst against a mob of club-wielding mutants, consuming them utterly. Writhing in agony, a couple of them stumbled into their squalid dwellings, which began to burn in turn.

'Hanna!' The girl's name emerged from his mouth as a barely audible wheeze, but even if he'd shouted it she'd never have heard him. She was sprawled out on the ground again, her face white, while Greta bent over her solicitously.

'Get up.' Gerhard had regained his feet easily and bent to grip the front of Rudi's jerkin. He yanked hard, hauling the young watchman upright. 'You see what happens when you put your trust in witches?'

'Hail the vessel!' Magnus, his voice gurgling around the arrow still embedded in his throat, shoulder charged the witch hunter, knocking him to the ground again. The light of madness was in his eyes, which reflected the hellish glow of the burning huts. Fanned by the onshore breeze, the inferno was spreading even as Rudi watched, leaping from one to the other almost at the speed of thought. Another flashed into flame in front of his eyes and he turned, looking for an avenue of escape. He wasn't the only one.

'Fall back!' Theo yelled to his confederates. 'Get out while we still can!' The mercenaries began to retreat, disengaging from the little groups of mutants still surviving, racing the flames back to the safety of the open mudflats. They barely made it, disappearing through the curtain of flames and smoke just as the last of the huts surrounding the open space whooshed into incandescence. As they went, Rudi noticed with a certain amount of satisfaction that Bodun was half-carrying Bruno. Despite the danger they were in, he smiled to himself. The cocky youth would be far more cautious about challenging him if they ever met again, of that he was certain.

He inhaled a lungful of foetid smoke and coughed. The chances of that were looking increasingly remote, he suspected. Retrieving his sword from where it had fallen, he glanced around for a way out.

Gerhard and Magnus were still fighting, a vicious, hand-to-hand duel. The deranged former merchant was unarmed, but apparently possessed of an inhuman strength and resilience. His ravaged body bore the marks of several wounds which should have killed him, but he fought on, clearly determined to force his way past the witch hunter or die trying.

'Hail the vessel!' he howled, catching sight of Rudi and redoubling his efforts. Gerhard thrust his sword deep into Magnus's chest, twisting the blade as he withdrew it to prevent the wound from closing, and kicked out hard as he did so, forcing the insane cultist back a pace.

'Hanna!' Content to leave them to it, Rudi turned, taking in the wider scene. The few remaining mutants surrounding them seemed to have forgotten their existence, running to and fro with shrill screams of panic as the flames grew ever closer. The air was growing too hot to breathe and as he watched, the rags swathing a couple of the grotesque parodies of the human form smouldered into flame, the shrieking redoubling in volume.

'In the name of the holy church of Sigmar, I find you guilty of heresy!' Gerhard shouted, closing in on the reeling figure of the cult leader. As his voice rose, Rudi found himself thinking that the witch hunter sounded barely more sane than Magnus had done. 'And I sentence you to burn!' He kicked the stumbling wreck of a man again, square in the chest, propelling him back into the middle of a blazing hut. After a moment, the roof collapsed, burying the flailing silhouette. If his former friend ever screamed, Rudi couldn't hear it, his ears full of the roaring of the surrounding flames.

He glanced down. The fabric of his shirt was beginning to smoulder, thin wisps of smoke rising from the linen. Every square inch of skin felt raw, presaging the agony which could only be seconds away by now. Despite the knowledge of an immanent and painful death, the sense of exultation and impending triumph rose up in him again.

'This way.' Greta beckoned and he walked over to her: as he got closer the heat seemed to diminish, until the surrounding air seemed no more than pleasantly warm. He glanced down at Hanna, who was still lying on the ground, her eyes wide with shock.

'I couldn't control it,' she whispered. 'Once that thing was gone, it just flooded back into me. It was so strong. I couldn't…' Her eyes rolled up in her head and she fainted.

Rudi glanced at Greta in consternation. 'We have to help her!' he said.

'She'll recover,' Greta reassured him. 'Just as I told you before.' She gestured to her daughter. 'Would you mind carrying her please? I need to concentrate.'

Completely bemused, Rudi sheathed his sword and bent to pick up the unconscious girl. Once again, he found her disturbingly light in his arms, but didn't comment. He wasn't sure what Greta was trying to do, but it was clear their only hope of survival lay in her magical powers.

'What about him?' he asked. Gerhard was stumbling towards them, his sword raised, the skin on his face beginning to blister, choking in the smoke which billowed about them all. Noticing the way it twisted in the air currents, Rudi realised for the first time that it was flowing around him and the sorceresses, as though they were enclosed in a small bubble of cool, fresh air. So that was how Greta had survived the burning of her cottage, he thought.

'His path will open for him,' Greta said, apparently unconcerned. 'The Changer will see to that.' She nodded in satisfaction as a swirl of smoke next to the witch hunter solidified into a human figure.

'Hold on!' Alwyn grabbed Gerhard by the arm and the two of them vanished as abruptly as she'd appeared. As she went, she locked eyes momentarily with Rudi and he shuddered. If they ever met again, he had no doubt that the mercenaries would prove to be as implacable enemies as the witch hunter had been.

'You'll meet again,' Greta assured him, as though she could read his thoughts.

'When?' Rudi asked.

'When it's time.' The sorceress glanced disdainfully at the blazing hut where Magnus had been left to burn. 'The fool was right about one thing anyway. You do have a destiny.'

'What?' Stunned at her words, Rudi almost forgot the weight of the girl in his arms. 'What am I supposed to do?'

'Right now?' Greta looked amused. 'Carry Hanna and try not to trip over anything. Do you think you can manage that?' Without waiting for a reply, she began walking out of the furnace surrounding them and Rudi followed, too stunned to protest or argue. As the little group approached the flames, they twisted aside, just as the smoke had done, and within minutes the reassuringly familiar stench of Marienburg surrounded them. Rudi gasped, and inhaled the cool air gratefully.

'Hanna.' He laid the girl gently on a crumbling quayside and turned to look back at the shanty town. It was a sheet of flame from end to end, whatever secrets it held gone forever, and a good thing too probably. Hanna stirred fitfully and opened her eyes.

'Mother?' she asked. After a moment she tried to sit up. 'Rudi, where's she gone?'

'I don't know.' Rudi glanced around them, confused and perplexed. 'She was right here!' The familiar sensation of angry frustration welled up in him. The answers he thought he wanted so badly had been nothing of the kind, and the one person who sounded

as though she might be able to help him to understand had apparently vanished into thin air. He glared
at the crumbling desolation of the Doodkanal as
though it were somehow responsible.

'Then she'll be back,' Hanna said calmly. 'When we
need her help again.' Despite the confusion in her
eyes, she smiled happily. 'She's alive! I can't believe it!'

Rudi tried not to think about the woman's horns, or
the time he'd seen her in the forest with the beastmen
and the mutated form of Hans Katzenjammer, or the
casual way she'd slaughtered the soldiers threatening
them at the camp on the moors. He was by no means
sure that Greta Reifenstahl would be a comfortable
ally to have. But he kept his doubts to himself and
nodded.

'Can you walk?'

Hanna nodded too, and climbed gingerly to her feet.
'Of course I can walk,' she said, a little testily. Rudi pretended not to notice her swaying gently as she did so.

'Good. It's a long way to the Suiddock and Shenk
won't wait for us.'

'I don't suppose he will.' Hanna took a slightly
unsteady step forward. 'Better get moving, then.'

'Right.' Rudi fell into step beside her. As they left the
blazing ruins of his hopes behind them, the first
snowflakes of winter began to fall.

ABOUT THE AUTHOR

Sandy Mitchell is a pseudonym of Alex Stewart, who has been working as a freelance writer for the last couple of decades. He has written science fiction and fantasy in both personae, as well as television scripts, magazine articles, comics, and gaming material. His television credits include the high tech espionage series *Bugs*, for which, as Sandy, he also wrote one of the novelisations.

Apart from both miniatures and roleplaying gaming his hobbies include the martial arts of Aikido and Iaido, rifle shooting, and playing the guitar badly.

He lives in a quiet village in North Essex with a very tolerant wife, their first child, and a small mountain of unpainted figures.

WARHAMMER

THE BROKEN LANCE

The second explosive Blackhearts novel by
Nathan Long

Coming soon from the Black Library

BROKEN LANCE

A Warhammer novel
by Nathan Long

THE HAMMER BRANDS were gone. The shameful scars
that had been burnt into their flesh had been removed
at last by a sorcery so painful it made the original
branding a pleasant memory by comparison. The skin
of their hands was clean, unblemished, as if the red
iron had never touched it. But the blood beneath that
skin, that was another story.

Reiner Hetsau and his convict companions; the
pikemen Hals Kiir and Pavel Voss, the Tilean cross-
bowman Giano Ostini, and Franka Shoentag, the
dark-haired archer who only Reiner knew was not the
boy she pretended to be, had been given the deserter's
brand by Baron Albrecht Valdenheim as a way to force
them to help him betray his brother, Count Manfred
Valdenheim. He had promised them that when their
service to him was done, he would remove the brands.
But after they learned that he intended to betray them

as well as his brother, they had helped Manfred instead, in hopes that he would make good on Albrecht's promise.

And he had. Manfred had been so impressed by the unorthodox ways in which Reiner and his companions had escaped their predicaments, by their ability to adapt and survive in any situation, and by their utter disregard for what respectable men might call right and wrong, that he had decided to make them agents of the Empire whether they wished it or not. The country, he said, had need of blackhearts who would not flinch at dishonourable duty. So he had ordered his personal sorcerer to remove the brands – which marked them deserters who could be shot on sight, and therefore useless as spies – and instead bound them to him with a much more subtle leash.

He had poisoned their blood.

It was a latent poison, which would lie dormant within them unless they attempted to leave Manfred's service or betray him. Then a spell could be read that would wake the poison and kill them wherever they might run, within the Empire or beyond.

There might be some, Reiner thought, as he folded his compact frame into the bay of a mullioned dormer window and looked out over the moonlit rooftops of Altdorf, who would be happy with the arrangement. Manfred had installed them in his townhouse and given them the run of the place, allowing them to read in the library and practise at swords in the garden, and had provided them with warm beds, fine food and obsequious servants – a soft life in these days of hardship and war, when many in the Empire were maimed and starving and hadn't a roof over their heads to call their own – but Reiner hated it.

The townhouse might be the epitome of comfort, but it was still a prison. Manfred wanted their existence kept a secret, so they were not allowed beyond its walls. It tortured Reiner that Altdorf was just outside and he couldn't reach it. The brothels and gambling halls, the dog-pits and theatres he called home, were within walking distance – on some nights he could hear singing and laughing and perhaps even the rattle of dice. But he couldn't get to them. They might as well have been in Lustria. It was agony.

Not that the others didn't suffer as well. When Manfred had recruited them, he had promised the Blackhearts action – secret missions, assassinations, kidnappings – but for the last two months they had done nothing but sit, waiting for orders that never came, and it was driving them stir crazy. It wasn't that Reiner relished the thought of risking life and limb for the Empire that had falsely branded him sorcerer and traitor, but endlessly waiting to be sent to one's death was a misery all its own – an edgy, endless boredom which set him and his companions at each other's throats. Casual conversations suddenly erupted into shouting matches, or broke off into sullen silences. Though he liked them all, Reiner's companions' tics and mannerisms, which he had once found amusing, now grated like brick on flesh: Hals's incessant barbs and jokes, Pavel's little clearing of the throat before he asked a question, Giano's moaning about how everything was better in Tilea, Franka's…

Well, it was Franka that was the real problem, wasn't it? Reiner had made a terrible mistake falling for the girl. He hadn't thought it would happen. After he had gotten over the shock of learning her true sex he hadn't given her a second thought. She wasn't really his sort – a wiry hoyden with hair shorter than his own – nothing like the laughing, lusty harlots he usually favoured, with painted lips and voluptuous hips. But that day on the crag above Nordbergbusche, when together they had killed Albrecht, they had exchanged a look that had awakened a flame of desire in him he knew could only be quenched in her arms. The trouble was, though she had admitted to him that she shared his passion, had in fact kissed him once with a fervour that had nearly carried them both away, she refused to consummate their lust. She…

The latch in the door behind him clicked. Reiner turned from the window as Franka entered the room, candle in hand. He held his breath. She closed the door, set the candle on a dresser, and began unlacing her jerkin.

'Slowly, beloved,' said Reiner, twirling his moustaches like a stage villain. ''Tis too nice a job to rush.'

Franka gasped, covering herself, then let out an annoyed breath when she realized who was sitting in the window seat. 'Reiner. How did you get in here?'

'Klaus was asleep again, as usual.'

'And so should you be.'

Reiner grinned. 'An excellent idea. Turn down the covers and let's to bed.'

Franka sighed and sat on a divan. 'Must you continue to persist?'

'Must you continue to resist?'

'The year of my vow is not yet up. I still mourn for Yarl.'

Reiner groaned. 'Is it still two months?'

'Three.'

'Three!'

'Only two days have passed since you last asked.'

'It feels like two years.' He stood and began to pace. 'Beloved, we could be dead in three months! Sigmar knows what madness Manfred has in store for us. He could send us to Ulthuan for all we know.'

'A man of honour would not press me on this,' said Franka, tight-lipped.

'Have I ever said I was a man of honour?' He sat on the divan beside her. 'Franka. There is a reason for a soldier's loose morals. He knows every day that he might die tomorrow, and therefore lives each night as if it were his last. You are a soldier now. You know this. You must seize what stands before you before Morr snatches it from your grasp forever.'

Franka rolled her eyes as he opened his arms in invitation. 'You make a compelling argument, captain, but unfortunately I have honour – or at least stubborn pride – enough for the both of us, and so…'

Reiner dropped his arms. 'Very well, very well. I will retire. But could you not at least grant me a kiss to dream on?'

Franka chuckled. 'And have you take advantage as always?'

'On my honour, beloved…'

'Did you not just say you had no honour?'

'I… er, yes, I suppose I did.' Reiner sighed and stood. 'Once again you defeat me, lady. But one day…' He shrugged and stepped to the door.

'Reiner.'

Reiner turned. Franka was beside him. She stretched up on her tiptoes and kissed him lightly on the lips. 'Now go to bed.'

'Torturer,' he said, then turned the latch and left.

UNSURPRISINGLY, REINER FOUND it difficult to sleep, which was unfortunate, for he was woken much too early the next morning. He had been dreaming of Franka unlacing her jerkin and pulling off her shirt, and it was a rude shock to open his eyes to the ugly face of dear old Klaus, the guard in charge of watching over him and his companions, glaring down at him.

'Get yer boots on, y'lazy slug,' Klaus barked, kicking Reiner's four-poster.

'Piss off.' Reiner pulled the covers over his head. 'I was with a lady.'

'None of your sauce!' Klaus kicked the bed again. 'His lordship requests yer presence in the yard, on the double.'

Reiner poked an eye above the blanket. 'Manfred's back?' He yawned and sat up, rubbing the sleep from his eyes. 'Thought he'd forgotten about us.'

'Manfred never forgets nothing,' said Klaus. 'You'd do well to remember it.'

'WHAT HAPPENINGS?' ASKED Giano as the Blackhearts shuffled sleepily down the curving mahogany staircase behind Reiner and Klaus to the townhouse's marble-floored entryway. The curly haired Tilean was still doing up his breeches.

'No idea,' said Reiner. Klaus motioned them through a service door and they entered the kitchen.

'It's something different, though,' said Pavel. He stole a pastry from a tray and stuffed it in his mouth. 'Makes a change,' he said, spitting crumbs.

Reiner chuckled at the sight. The pikeman was as ugly as a wet rat, and utterly unconcerned about it: long necked and scrawny, with a patch over his lost left eye and a scarred mouth that was missing three front teeth.

'Probably just sword drills again,' said Hals, Pavel's bald, burly, red bearded brother-in-arms. 'Or worse, horsemanship.'

Klaus opened the kitchen door and they stepped into the gravelled stable yard. 'Maybe not,' said Franka. 'Look at that.'

Reiner and the others looked ahead. A coach with louvred windows sat just inside the back gate. Two guards stood before it. The Blackhearts groaned.

'Not the coach again,' said Hals.

'We'd all kill each other before we got where we were going,' agreed Pavel.

Klaus stopped in the centre of the yard and called them to attention. They straightened, but only half-heartedly. Months of enforced familiarity with him had bred contempt for his authority. They waited. The morning fog hid the world beyond the stone walls in a pearly embrace, and though it was summer, the sun was not yet high enough in the sky to chase the night's chill away. Reiner shivered and wished he had thought to don his cloak. His stomach growled. He had become used to a regular breakfast.

After a quarter of an hour, the gate to the garden opened and Count Manfred stepped into the yard. Tall and broad, with silver in his hair and beard, the count looked the part of a kind, wise king out of legend, but Reiner knew better. Manfred might be wise, but he was hard as flint. A bright-eyed young corporal in the uniform of a lancer followed in his wake.

Manfred nodded curtly to the Blackhearts. 'Klaus, open the coach, then retire to the gate with Moegen and Valch.'

'M'lord?' said Klaus. 'I wouldn't trust these villains near yer lordship…'

'Obey my orders, Klaus. I am perfectly safe.'

Klaus saluted reluctantly and crossed to the coach. He took a key from one of the guards and unlocked it. Reiner expected Manfred to order them into it, but when Klaus opened the door, four men ducked out and stepped down to the gravel. The Blackhearts exchanged uneasy glances. The men were filthy, unshaved, and half starved, and wore the remains of military uniforms.

'Fall in,' said Manfred.

The four men shambled over and lined up next to the Blackhearts, squaring their shoulders reflexively.

Manfred faced the Blackhearts. 'We have work for you at last,' he said, then sighed. 'There have actually been many jobs on which we would have liked to have used you. There is much turmoil in Altdorf at the moment. Much finger pointing over our losses in the recent conflict, and much clamouring for changes at the top – particularly among the younger barons. It would have been nice to have used you to "calm" some of the more strident voices, but we were hesitant to try an untested tool so close to home where it might fly back into our faces.' He clasped his hands behind his back. 'Now a perfect test has presented itself. Of utmost importance to the well-being of the Empire, but far enough away that you will not embarrass us if you fail.'

'Your confidence in us is inspiring, m'lord,' said Reiner wryly.

'Be thankful I have any at all after your insubordination at Groffholt.'

'Did you not recruit us particularly for our penchant for insubordination, m'lord?' asked Reiner.

'Enough,' said Manfred, and though he didn't raise his voice, Reiner did not feel inclined to push his insolence any further.

'Listen well,' said Manfred. 'For I will not repeat these orders and they will not be written down.' He cleared his throat and looked them all in the eye, then began. 'Deep in the Black Mountains is an Empire fort which guards an isolated pass and protects a nearby gold mine. The mine helps the Empire pay for reconstruction and defence in these troubled times, but in the last few months the mine's output has slowed to a trickle, and we have not received from the fort satisfactory answers to our queries. I sent a courier two months ago. He has not returned. I do not know what has befallen him.' Manfred frowned. 'All that is certain is that the fort is still in Imperial hands, for an agent of mine saw recruitment notices for the fort's regiment going up in Averheim not a week ago.' He looked at Reiner. 'This recruitment is your opportunity. You are to sign on, install yourselves in the fort, discover what is occurring, and if it is treasonous, stop it.'

'You have reason to suspect treason?'

'It is possible,' said Manfred. 'The fort's commander, General Broder Gutzmann, is rumoured to be angry that he was kept in the south when the fate of the Empire was being decided in the north. He may have become angry enough to do something rash.'

'And if he has?'

Manfred hesitated, then spoke. 'If there is a traitor in the fort, he must be "removed", no matter who he is. But know that Gutzmann is an excellent general and loved by his men. They are fiercely loyal. If it is he you must remove, it should look like an accident. If his men discovered that he was the victim of foul play, they would revolt, and the Empire is stretched too thin now to lose an entire garrison.'

'Pardon, m'lord,' said Reiner, 'but I don't understand. If Gutzmann is such an excellent general, why not bring him north and let him hunt Kurgan like he wants? Would that not stop his grumbling?'

Manfred sighed. 'I cannot. There are some in Altdorf who feel that Gutzmann is too good a general, that if he won great victories in the north, he might begin to have ambitions – that, er, he might seek to be more than a leader of soldiers.'

'Ah,' said Reiner. 'So he was kept in the south on purpose. He has reason to be angry.'

Manfred scowled. 'No "reason" can excuse stealing from the Emperor. If he is guilty, he must be stopped. Do you all understand your orders?'

The Blackhearts nodded, as did the newcomers.

Manfred glanced at the new men, then back to the Blackhearts. 'This will be a difficult mission, and it was felt you should be returned to full strength. Therefore we have found you some new recruits. These four men will be under your command, Hetsau. Corporal Karelinus Eberhart,' he indicated the young junior officer who stood to his left, 'will also obey your orders, but is answerable only to me. He is my eyes and ears, and will report to me at the end of this venture on…' He paused, then smirked. 'On how true and useful a tool you and your Blackhearts are. His report will determine whether we will be able to employ you in the future, and consequently, whether we will suffer you to live henceforth. Do you understand me?'

Reiner nodded. 'Yes my lord. Perfectly.' He shot a look at Corporal Eberhart, who was gaping at Manfred with wide blue eyes. Reiner chuckled. The poor lad didn't expect Manfred to be so open about his role in the enterprise. He was unused to the count's bluntness. Reiner was not. Manfred was not accustomed to hiding his cannon behind roses.

'Are these men subject to the same constraints as we, m'lord?' asked Reiner, indicating the four new recruits. 'Have they been…'

'Yes, captain,' said Manfred. 'They have agreed to the same conditions. Their blood bears the same taint as your own.' He laughed. 'They are now your brothers. Blackhearts one and all!'

WARHAMMER

FANTASY ROLEPLAY

GAME MASTER'S P.

ASHES OF MIDDENHEIM

A GRIM WORLD OF

PERILOUS ADVENTURE

The Warhammer world is a dangerous place. It bears a vague resemblance to history; but it is a dark and twisted reflection of our past. The civilized nations cluster together, forever perched upon the brink of apocalypse, and but a knife thrust from anarchy. To play *Warhammer Fantasy Roleplay* is to step into this land of peril and intrigue.

Step forth brave adventurer,
death or glory awaits...

www.blackindustries.com

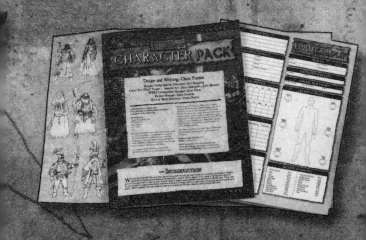

READ TILL YOU BLEED
DO YOU HAVE THEM ALL?

1 Trollslayer – William King
2 First & Only – Dan Abnett
3 Skavenslayer – William King
4 Into the Maelstrom – Ed. Marc Gascoigne & Andy Jones
5 Daemonslayer – William King
6 Eye of Terror – Barrington J Bayley
7 Space Wolf – William King
8 Realm of Chaos – Ed. Marc Gas-coigne & Andy Jones
9 Ghostmaker – Dan Abnett
10 Hammers of Ulric – Dan Abnett, Nik Vincent & James Wallis
11 Ragnar's Claw – William King
12 Status: Deadzone – Ed. Marc Gascoigne & Andy Jones
13 Dragonslayer – William King
14 The Wine of Dreams – Brian Craig
15 Necropolis – Dan Abnett
16 13th Legion – Gav Thorpe
17 Dark Imperium – Ed. Marc Gascoigne & Andy Jones
18 Beastslayer – William King
19 Gilead's Blood – Abnett & Vincent
20 Pawns of Chaos – Brian Craig
21 Xenos – Dan Abnett
22 Lords of Valour – Ed. Marc Gascoigne & Christian Dunn
23 Execution Hour – Gordon Rennie
24 Honour Guard – Dan Abnett
25 Vampireslayer – William King
26 Kill Team – Gav Thorpe
27 Drachenfels – Jack Yeovil
28 Deathwing – Ed. David Pringle & Neil Jones
29 Zavant – Gordon Rennie
30 Malleus – Dan Abnett
31 Konrad – David Ferring
32 Nightbringer – Graham McNeill
33 Genevieve Undead – Jack Yeovil
34 Grey Hunter – William King
35 Shadowbreed – David Ferring
36 Words of Blood – Ed. Marc Gascoigne & Christian Dunn
37 Zaragoz – Brian Craig
38 The Guns of Tanith – Dan Abnett
39 Warblade – David Ferring
40 Farseer – William King
41 Beasts in Velvet – Jack Yeovil
42 Hereticus – Dan Abnett
43 The Laughter of Dark Gods – Ed. David Pringle
44 Plague Daemon – Brian Craig
45 Storm of Iron – Graham McNeill
46 The Claws of Chaos – Gav Thorpe
47 Draco – Ian Watson
48 Silver Nails – Jack Yeovil
49 Soul Drinker – Ben Counter
50 Harlequin – Ian Watson
51 Storm Warriors – Brian Craig
52 Straight Silver – Dan Abnett
53 Star of Erengrad – Neil McIntosh
54 Chaos Child – Ian Watson
55 The Dead & the Damned – Jonathan Green
56 Shadow Point – Gordon Rennie
57 Blood Money – C L Werner
58 Angels of Darkness – Gav Thorpe
59 Mark of Damnation – James Wallis
60 Warriors of Ultramar – Graham McNeill
61 Riders of the Dead – Dan Abnett
62 Daemon World – Ben Counter
63 Giantslayer – William King
64 Crucible of War – Ed. Marc Gascoigne & Christian Dunn
65 Honour of the Grave – Robin D Laws
66 Crossfire – Matthew Farrer
67 Blood & Steel – C L Werner